PRAISE FOR LANA WITT
and
The Heart of a Thirsty Woman

"Two particular delights in this novel are Witt's impeccable ear for speech and her depiction of small-town life in eastern Kentucky, of the people and the mores. Her characters throughout have a sharpness and realness to them."

—*San Diego Union-Tribune*

"Sage, Arizona, turns out to be populated by the most colorful characters this side of consciousness, including twin sisters Venus Lily and Lily Venus, who own and operate the local watering hole, catering alternately to a migrant mining population and a local artist's colony."

—*Library Journal*

"Rooted in a starkly realistic American landscape, Josie's tales get all caught up in the fashion of a Shakespearean comedy of errors before being restored to order by one lean, long, cool cowboy."

—*Entertainment Weekly*

"A journey to self via eastern Kentucky. . . . Witt creates a world that is distinctly southern, refreshingly intelligent, and evidently eastern Kentucky . . . the reader always feels connected to her characters' souls. . . . Witt takes her time in her storytelling, pacing herself according to her characters' travels and discoveries. . . . In revisiting the 1970s with Witt, one catches a glimpse of America as the Age of Aquarius gave way to disco. We discover polyester leisure suits, the satellite dish . . . not as clichéd relics of an era gone by, but rather as evidence that times are changing and that the options of the future are vast. Witt writes with a sense of humor that does not poke fun but rather serves to lighten the load of her characters' pains and regrets."

—*Leo* (Louisville, KY)

PRAISE FOR
Slow Dancing on Dinosaur Bones

"Rich characterization and black humor with a thick Southern accent distinguish this irresistible debut novel. . . . Witt's talent, big and pleasingly quirky, marks her as a fresh new voice."

—*Publishers Weekly*

"An impressive literary debut, with characters not soon forgotten."

—*Booklist*

"Readers who enjoy the regional flavor of Fannie Flagg, Lee Smith, and John Dufresne will heartily embrace Lana Witt's irresistible debut novel."

—Barnes & Noble Discover Great New Writers Program

Also by Lana Witt
Slow Dancing on Dinosaur Bones

The Heart of a Thirsty Woman

LANA WITT

WSP

WASHINGTON SQUARE PRESS
PUBLISHED BY POCKET BOOKS

New York   London   Toronto   Sydney   Singapore

For my children, Darren and Andrea
And for Kenneth, who got away

WSP

A Washington Square Press Publication of
POCKET BOOKS, a division of Simon & Schuster Inc.
1230 Avenue of the Americas, New York, NY 10020

ISBN: 0-671-01146-4

First Washington Square Press trade paperback printing June 2000

10 9 8 7 6 5 4 3 2 1

WASHINGTON SQUARE PRESS and colophon are registered trademarks
of Simon & Schuster Inc.

Cover design by Brigid Pearson; front cover illustration by Marc Burckhardt

Printed in the U.S.A.

Acknowledgments

A special thanks to Frank Parker, owner of the real Don Juan's Cocktails in Oracle, Arizona, for allowing me to use the name of his bar, for telling me about copper mines, and for being so hospitable during my visits. I loved meeting the people who frequent the place, especially Don McLeod, who answered all my questions about miners and small-town desert bars.

Further thanks to:

- My father, Ernest Dixon, for telling me about the war.
- Dosha Witt, who has always inspired me.
- The Flower Hill Writers: Bonnie ZoBell, Rhonda Johnson, Patty Santana, John Dacapias, Tom Larson, and Cory Meacham. I don't know what I'd do without them.
- Michael Carlisle and Jane Rosenman. Without them, I might be writing to myself.
- My son, Darren Witt, who was the first to read the beginning chapters and encourage me.
- My daughter, Andrea Witt, who read a later draft and provided fresh criticism when I really needed it.
- Kenneth Witt, a great friend, who takes everything in stride.
- Crystal Goodman and Marc Bradley, who read all or part of my manuscript and gave encouragement.
- The Virginia Center for Creative Arts for providing a place to write uninterrupted. I did a lot of work in the short time I was there.

Lastly, it is with the highest regard that I salute the happy inmates of 5201.

I to the world am like a drop of water,
That in the ocean seeks another drop. . . .
—William Shakespeare, *The Comedy of Errors*

Contents

PART ONE

Inner State West

1

Clarence and Josie lie bowed together in the dark bed after a slow session of lovemaking. Outside silence has descended on the mountain, and all is quiet except the soft rustle of leaves. Clarence's arm is draped around his wife's shoulder, his hand resting on her collarbone as she talks. Josie has been talking nonstop for weeks, telling every story she can dredge up from her childhood, talking about weird topics too, at least Clarence thinks they're weird. Although she turned twenty-seven last month, Clarence figures she acts more like a twelve year old than anything else. He's beginning to worry she'll never grow up.

Lately she's been going on and on about separate realities—saying a tree isn't necessarily a tree just because it looks like one, that there's a good chance it's an ancient spirit of some kind—and she claims to have seen things, dark shadowy things, out of the corners of her eyes. The other night she told him she'd had an out-of-body experience, that she'd come out of herself somehow. Josie is a bookworm. Lying on top of her bookshelf is an annotated Shakespeare that she's read over and over again. Half the time she'll pretend to be some crazy person from one of the plays. Just last night she was prancing around, shouting, "O heat, dry up my brains! tears seven times salt/Burn out the sense and virtue of mine eye!"

"Why the hell do you do that? What good is it, Josie?" Clarence asked.

"I'm not Josie," she responded. "I'm Laertes."

For months she's been studying the *I Ching*, a little green book that has Clarence mystified. She's also been reading books by Carlos Castaneda, who writes about an old Yaqui Indian named don Juan. Don Juan has some pretty strange notions that she has sunk her teeth into hard and fast. Among them is the one about the separate realities. Clarence believes something is going more and more wrong with Josie, but still he tries to listen as she talks.

"It was when we was in Arizona back in '58, '59," she's saying, "when Daddy had got that job in a copper mine." Josie sounds as though she's giving a report to a class at school, as if she has to include all the facts and get them straight. "We just stayed out there a year. At first we lived in the town of Rustle, but when school got out that summer we moved up to the mountains to this little place called Sage. Cheyenne was still alive then. She was fourteen years old, and I was ten. I don't remember nothing being in Sage but two or three houses, a post office, church, and store. And, of course, that big old Mexican mansion made out of adobe. I guess you'd call it a hacienda, I don't know. They'd turned it into a apartment building for the miners, and we lived on the bottom floor. It had walls a foot thick and French doors. God, I love French doors."

"A hacienda?" Clarence asks, wondering where this story is leading. He sighs, hoping Josie doesn't branch off on more weird tales from don Juan and his Yaqui way of knowledge. Wasn't that where don Juan was from? Arizona?

"Anyway when Daddy got laid off at the copper mine, we had to move back here to Kentucky," Josie says. "The day we packed up to leave, me and Cheyenne was so excited we kept running from one room to the other. Just the sight of that U-Haul trailer hitched to the back of our '56 Ford was too much to take, I reckon. Besides we'd been holed up for months in the apartment—Cheyenne laying in bed with her bad heart most of the summer—and it was too hot to go outside anyway."

"I remember that Ford," Clarence mutters, trying to latch onto something good and solid and American.

"Daddy was out front checking under the hood, and he was yelling at the same time,'Come on. Let's get out of here before it gets dark!' Mommy didn't make a move, though, just stood there at the front door staring out. It was evening and the sun was setting. All at once she turned to me and Cheyenne and said, 'Settle down, you fellers, and look at this. It may be the last Arizona sunset you'll ever see.' But we wouldn't pay attention, kept trying to get past her to the outside, jumping up and down and yelling like fools, even though Mommy had already warned us that Cheyenne was goin to have another heart attack if she didn't keep still."

As Josie talks, Clarence runs a hand over the contours of her body, runs his fingers through her hair, now tangled and spilling over the pillow. Her wild chestnut hair was the thing that attracted him in the first place, that and her pale gray eyes. He tries to remember how she looked when she was a child, but he can't get a clear picture. All he remembers is that she couldn't play marbles worth a shit. Josie's sister, Cheyenne, was in the same grade as Clarence when they were in school—he remembers her as a bold streak shooting down hallways, shouting out her latest plans to skip class. Clarence brings himself back to the present, back to the sound of Josie's voice. Her voice is soft as feathers.

"Mommy put her hands on her hips and glared at us, mad as a wet hornet," Josie tells Clarence. "We stopped dead in our tracks because we knew that look in her eye. When Mommy was riled, she wouldn't no one to fool around with. She said, 'You fellers ought to never leave a place, just throw it aside, without stopping to think about it for a minute. I know you don't realize this now, but you really *may* never see a Arizona sunset again. Right now you prob'ly think you can just move back here any time you want to, but that's not the way it is. Sometimes you turn a corner and can never get back to where you were before.'

"Cheyenne got on one side of her and me on the other, and we all stood at the door looking out. I've never seen anything like it since— it was so pretty it made you sad. The sky right around the horizon was this beautiful red-orange, tinged with blue, green, purple, and gold. We leaned there against the door-facing quiet as mice and let all that color sink inside us. Mommy could always do that—make you see every side of a thing, the sadness right along with the excitement.

And there was this little hill . . . I guess you'd call it a hill. Anyway all at once this cowboy came riding along it. He was completely silhouetted in the sunset, and there was two or three cactuses there, growing along the top. You know, the saguaros? And they was silhouetted too. I'm telling you, Clarence, it took my breath, it was so beautiful. It was a gift, a parting gift from Arizona. And if it wasn't for my mother making me and Cheyenne settle down, we'd have lost out on the whole thing."

Josie stops talking for a minute and stares out the window at the moonlight, tears shining in her eyes. "Cheyenne got missing a few months after we come back here. She's dead, I reckon, or may as well be. Anyway we never found her, and Mommy died that same year."

Josie waits for Clarence to say something, but he doesn't.

"Well, I'm still here, at least I think I am. You're here, and Daddy is too. I want us to move out West. I don't want that Arizona sunset back in 1959 to be the last one I'll ever see. I want to prove my mother wrong, at least where I'm concerned."

Clarence doesn't comment.

"Clarence?"

He's breathing deeply, his hand lying heavy in her hair.

"Are you asleep?"

Clarence still doesn't answer, but he begins to tick. When Clarence Tolliver sleeps, he doesn't snore, he ticks. Josie has never been able to figure out if he's tapping his tongue on the roof of his mouth or if the sound comes from a vibrating membrane in his nose or if his tonsils keep detaching and reattaching themselves to small mysterious growths at the back of his throat.

"Well, goddamned, son of a bitch!" she shouts and, jumping out of bed, runs out of the house, her stomach aching as if it's weighted down with lead balls.

Their house is a small two-bedroom at the head of a hollow, deeded to them by Clarence's father on their wedding day seven years ago. Josie runs down the porch steps, heads for a grove of beech trees, then stumbles into a briar patch and falls, thorns tearing the skin on her arms and legs. Rolling out of the briars, she picks them out of her skin and lies face up on the cool damp ground. The moon is so bright it leaves an opaque band of light that shafts down toward her and disappears into the folds of her gown. She imagines it seeping inside her, flooding her body with old truths, seducing her spirit with the mystery of night. "Go ahead and get me, you big, white-faced screwball. Take me away!" she yells. Then out of nowhere fog rolls around the mountain and envelopes her until she's wrapped like a caterpillar in a cocoon. Josie Tolliver lies dead still, waiting to be born.

2

It's 1976, and TV satellite dishes are sprouting up like mushrooms after a long hard rain. Clarence Tolliver, who always keeps abreast of the latest trends in electronics, figures this is the most exciting thing to happen since transistors replaced tubes. At present he owns and operates a TV repair shop, where he sells and repairs TVs, radios, stereos, and cassette players. Business is flourishing since his is the only TV repair shop in Burr County. Even so, Clarence has greater dreams. He envisions himself as having the first satellite dish business in eastern Kentucky and figures he'll call his new enterprise CLARENCE, THE SATELLITE MAN.

His acquaintances tell him he's crazy, that such an outfit will never catch on in Burr County, that satellite dishes are too expensive for the local people to buy. Clarence claims the naysayers are wrong and that people from all over the eastern part of the state will soon be coming to him for their satellite dish needs.

Clarence is tall and lanky with clear blue eyes, a straight nose, and paper thin lips, and when he starts talking about the future of the satellite dish, his lips get even thinner. "These satellites are changing the world," he often informs Bernard Boggs, who works for him in his TV repair shop. "I don't even know if anyone can control it. They pick up everything, Bernard. Every little signal floating in the air. You can see news shows before they *officially* go on the air. You can watch newsmen getting ready to go on, see them drinking coffee and straightening their ties, hear them belch and fart."

Deep down inside, though, Clarence worries that somebody will figure a way to ruin things, and he frequently mutters under his breath, "You know if you can get something free right out of the air, it ain't goin to last. I bet you right now they's a roomful of long-toothed men, sitting around a table somewhere in Washington or New York, trying to figure out what to do about free air. Do you think CBS likes the fact that dish users catch their newsmen off guard? They don't want people to see Walter Cronkite picking his nose."

Still Clarence Tolliver dreams of the day when he'll become CLARENCE, THE SATELLITE MAN and figures that if the dish business ever dwindles he'll go into cable, reasoning that cable will last forever because you can charge people for it once a month. Either way he figures his future is solid and that his whole life will be set if only Josie stays on track. I'd blame her troubles on Carlos Castaneda, Clarence thinks, but Josie was off-center way before she started reading his books.

The thing is, there's no one Clarence can talk to about his worries. Josie may have lost it, but he doesn't want to be the one to spread the news. He looks around at Bernard. They've been in the repair shop all day, busy as beavers with three radios, five TVs, and four cassette players. "Bernard," Clarence says, casually, "what would you say if I told you someone I personally know had a out-of-body experience?"

"A out of what?"

"Body experience," Clarence says.

"Who had one?" Bernard asks. "Josie?"

Clarence turns red. He squeezes the trigger of his soldering gun and drips solder all over his bench. "What makes you think I'm talking about Josie?"

"Well, you are, ain't you? What *is* a out-of-body experience anyway?"

Clarence looks at Bernard and constricts his eyes into slits. "Bernard, what I'm about to tell you ain't to leave this room. Do you hear me? It's for your ears only."

Bernard Boggs is an emotional man. He'll cry over almost anything. People always say he's the best-hearted man they know. Even now tears start to well up in his eyes. He feels sorry for Clarence, who works at his business twelve hours a day and reads electronics books in his spare time, trying to keep up with the latest technology. For Clarence to have a wife like Josie, who won't even let him build her a new house, is a dirty shame in Bernard's mind. What kind of woman wouldn't give her eye teeth to have a new house? "I won't say a word, buddy," Bernard says, his voice quivering.

Clarence braces himself and begins his tale. "Josie said she was laying on the bed the other day and that all at once she rose right up out of herself and started spinning like a ball in the air, spun right down the hill and started hovering over the creek, and that she liked to never got herself back up the hill and into her own body. Said it was the most exciting thing that had ever happened to her but that she was scared to death at the same time."

Bernard shudders. "Reckon you ought to take her to a doctor?"

Clarence bristles. "You think she's off her rocker, don't you? I'd of thought so too, if it was just her that went around talking about things like that, but Bernard, they's other people claims it happens to them too. I just don't know . . ."

"I don't either," Bernard says, but he does know. He knows that Josie Tolliver has always stood on shaky ground, but he won't say it because he can't bring himself to worry Clarence even more.

"She wants to leave here," Clarence says. "She wants us to move out West."

A look of horror sweeps over Bernard's face. He sees himself without a job, having to leave Burr County too, because he can't find work. "Well, you're not goin, are you?"

"No," Clarence says. "I'm staying right here."

Bernard sighs with relief.

After the men close shop for the night, Bernard heads for home with more to think about than usual, and Clarence gets into his car, a 1969 Chevy Nova, and drives out of town as if his is the lead vehicle in a funeral parade. Clarence never goes more than thirty-five miles an hour. The teenagers of Burr County hate him, swearing to each other that his slow driving is done with mean-spirited intent, that he gets a kick out of holding people up. Clarence has caused three accidents that people know of. When Burr County's more high-strung drivers get behind him on the road out of town, that narrow curvy road with its double yellow line, they gnash their teeth in rage. Occasionally their impatience gets the best of them, and they chance passing him around a blind curve. Most of the time they make it—sometimes they don't.

When Josie points out to Clarence that people resent his driving habits, that he'd probably realize a 20 percent increase in business profits if he'd speed up a little, he smiles and turns away, causing Josie herself to think that Clarence has a mean streak she's never fully explored.

Clarence gets home that night and finds Josie sitting in the middle of the living room floor with a United States map spread before her.

"Right there's where I want to go," she says. "See? Sage. It's not very far from Tucson."

Clarence plops down on the couch and pulls off his shoes. "And just how do you think I'd make a living in Sage? Get a job in a copper mine like your daddy? I bet that copper mine ain't even around no more. I wouldn't work in it even if it was."

"You could start you a TV repair business. People out there have TVs too."

"What with?" Clarence reaches for the fingernail clips lying on the end table, and in order to get to them he has to pass his hand over that book, *The Teachings of Don Juan: A Yaqui Way of Knowledge.* Grabbing the clips hurriedly, he starts nervously pruning his nails.

"Don't tell me you don't have any money," Josie says. "You wanted to build us a house, claimed you had the money for that."

"I ain't wasting my money on Sage. Them people out there prob'ly already have a TV repair shop. Ever think of that?"

"Well, maybe they need two. Besides, you don't have to work on TVs. Don Juan says . . ."

Clarence stands up and shouts, "I don't want to hear any more about don Juan or his YUCKY way of knowledge!" Then he stomps out of the house and pees on the ground in the front yard. Nothing works better to ease Clarence's worries than peeing on his own property. Josie tells him she thinks he likes to do this because somewhere deep down in his primordial mind he's marking his territory just like male animals have done throughout the centuries.

Shit, Clarence thinks. I'm married to a woman that's full of shit.

3

By '76 the hippie phenomenon is as blurred as the rained-on pages of a *Whole Earth Catalog.* Flowers have crumbled and fallen from young women's hair; their frayed headbands have been tossed in the trash. Psychedelic Volkswagens have been repainted in solid blues and yellows and greens, and as if to add insult to injury, disco is alive and kicking.

Josie Tolliver refuses to believe this.

She thinks that if she can just get to Arizona or California—someplace out west—she'll find people on every corner divulging the secrets of strange Eastern philosophies, spouting radical political points of view. She laments the fact that in Pick, Kentucky, the sixties didn't happen in a big way. It's true that a variation on the times—mountain-style—finally caught a small foothold in Burr County with the assistance of pot and music and all-night jam sessions in the backs of vans; but by then Josie was married to Clarence, and she missed out on the whole thing.

How can I get Clarence to change his mind about going west? she wonders, never entertaining the idea of leaving him, of going by herself. Josie can't imagine traveling anywhere without Clarence Tolliver at her side—he's been with her since she was a child. Not long after her mother died, Josie's father, Brewster Clay, began running a filling station at the edge of Pick and hired Clarence to help him pump gas. Josie was eleven years old at the time, and Clarence fifteen. Since Brewster and Josie had moved into the apartment upstairs from the station, she was around Clarence most of the time and developed a crush on him even then. With his blue eyes and black hair, he looked like a mix between Ricky Nelson and Elvis. Her young heart fluttered like a bird's wing every time he walked near her, but he acted as if he didn't know she was alive.

She often had long, involved daydreams in which she imagined that she and Clarence spent their days roaming the English moors—Cathy and Heathcliff reborn—but her daydreams were a far cry from reality. Clarence paid little attention to her until the next year when her body started developing. Although she had high hopes, nothing resulted from her new physique but a small mutual flirtation that lasted several years.

It wasn't until she graduated from high school that they went out on a date of sorts. Josie had got it into her head that she wanted to go to the senior prom, but no one had asked her for a date. This was no surprise because, although she was attractive, she was an abnormally shy girl, unfriendly and downright sullen. It was her father, Brewster, who talked Clarence into taking her. Clarence showed up that evening in his freshly waxed pickup and tied an orchid corsage around her wrist. They passed the entire evening glued to the wall of the Pick High School gymnasium, too shy to dance.

Then a few months before Clarence was drafted into the army, his lackadaisical attitude changed. Later he would admit to Josie that it was the prospect of going to war, of perhaps dying in a strange country, that caused him to see what was important in his life. They began to date in earnest, snuggling on his parents' living room sofa and nearly going all the way in the back of his father's car at the local drive-in theatre. Occasionally they had conversations in which they asked each other important philosophical questions such as: If your house were on fire and you could only save one thing, what would it be? Josie said she'd take her guitar even though she'd feel guilty about not taking her books, but after all a person could go to the library for books, whereas a guitar of your own was hard to come by. Clarence, who had just finished a two-year stint at an electronics school, said he'd take his ohm meter. Another question was the one everyone was asking: What do you think about the war in Vietnam? Josie said she thought it sucked, but Clarence said he didn't think the president would be sending so many people over there if they didn't need to go.

These talks unveiled the first hints that perhaps their views didn't always coincide.

When Clarence returned from Vietnam in 1969, he breezed up to the service station driving his new Chevy Nova and asked Josie to marry him. She said yes immediately, but she couldn't help remembering how she had once pretended they were Heathcliff and Cathy. She hoped she hadn't agreed to the marriage merely to create a happy ending for one of her favorite novels. Ignoring the germ of uncertainty that kept sneaking into her thoughts, she focused on the fact that Clarence was the boy she had dreamed of marrying every night of her pubescent life. Now, here he was, obviously wanting her as much as she had ever wanted him. It had to be right. Besides, didn't her heart still race when he stepped near her? Wasn't she still charmed by his quiet nature that seemed to hold secrets she wanted to unravel? More importantly, didn't she know instinctively that he would always be there? That he wouldn't die prematurely like her mother? Or disappear from the face of the earth like Cheyenne? Didn't she know that he would never leave her unless she wanted him to go?

Josie walks outside the house and sits down on the porch. It's already past noon and as usual she's alone on the mountain. Clarence left for Pick early this morning to work on his TVs. I don't know if I'm in love with him anymore, she thinks, but he's like family, as close to me as blood kin, like part of my body—another arm or leg. You can't run away from your leg.

Inside the house, Bob Dylan is playing on the stereo. As his sad, angry, sarcastic voice drifts out the open door, she is filled with longing and nostalgia for something she doesn't have the words to describe. Josie often feels that way. Yesterday she spent the entire day playing one song on the guitar—"High Flying Bird"—started singing it as soon as Clarence left for work and sang it until he came home that evening. Today her voice is hoarse and her fingers bruised from the steel strings of her Gibson guitar.

Josie has always felt there should be a higher purpose in life, something mysterious and intriguing that takes the boredom out of ordinary existence, but lately she's begun to suspect that there may be no such purpose, that nothing in this world really matters, that people fool themselves into thinking they feel love for others when in reality they only love the reflection of themselves in other people's eyes.

She doesn't want her suspicions to be true, but since she can't prove otherwise, she wants to not care one way or the other. In *A Separate Reality*, don Juan says ". . . *it doesn't matter to me that nothing matters* . . ." Josie is dying to reach that state of mind, not simply to repeat those words but to mean them with all her heart. It's why she's so fascinated with Castaneda's books. Why can't I be like don Juan? she wonders. If only I could live by those eight little words, I'd be happy as a lark.

"Have children," her mother-in-law, Ida, used to tell her. "You won't be bored if you have young'uns." But Josie can't have them. Her fallopian tubes are too narrow, her womb too small. She doesn't have room inside her for a child. She isn't sure she wants one anyway.

"Well, then, why don't you help out Clarence down at his shop?" Ida often persists.

"You know I don't like wires and little diodes and stuff."

That usually shuts her mother-in-law up, since Ida knows there are no more jobs to be had, that there are slim pickings in Pick.

When Clarence offers his opinion on Josie's boredom it usually involves her going to college. "If you had a degree, you could teach down at the high school. Don't that sound like fun?"

"I don't want to go to college," Josie tells him, "and I sure don't want to teach high school. What would I teach anybody? I don't know nothing."

Clarence sighs. "Well, that's what the college is for, Josie. They'd learn you what to teach."

"I don't think they'd learn me the right things. They might show me some techniques, ways of doing, but it wouldn't be what I want to know. It wouldn't be real. The questions I'd ask my teachers are the ones no one knows the answers to. If I ever became a teacher myself, I wouldn't want to show high school children how to dissect a frog or diagram a sentence. I'd want to give them the answers to the unanswerable questions, but you see I don't know them and no one else knows them either."

"What unanswerable questions? Name me one."

"Okay, how about, 'What does it all mean?' "

Now as Josie looks around at the empty house, she keeps running those conversations through her mind. Then unable to be alone a minute longer, she grabs her purse and keys, thinking she'll drive down to her father's house and visit him for a while.

Brewster Clay, who was in his forties when Josie was born, is now seventy years old and in poor health. He has arthritis that is sometimes so painful he can hardly think. When Brewster was young, he was quite a looker, muscular as a prizefighter, and his smattering of Indian blood had given him bronze skin and a shock of black hair that women ached to run their fingers through. Now, gray hair slouches over his ears in skimpy wisps, his complexion is pale, and frail arms and legs dangle from his body like dishrags. The only feature that has retained its youthful brilliance is his black eyes, still clear, still flashing with contrariness.

No longer able to work, he closed down his service station and turned it into his own private living quarters so he doesn't have to walk upstairs to his apartment. He put a stove, refrigerator, sink, and bathroom in one end of the garage and a bed, TV, couch, and chair in the other. He left the grease rack, the hydraulic hoist that allowed him to do car tune-ups, standing in the middle of the room. He has it hoisted midair and uses it for a dining table and all-round counter on which to lay odds and ends. All day Brewster does very little except watch TV, drink beer, and fix himself something to eat. His only other daily duty is to go to his next door neighbor's house at twelve o'clock to take their Pomeranian dogs out for a walk, to let them sniff the ground and pee on a rosebush in the front yard.

Brewster is drinking beer and watching TV when the telephone rings. At first he thinks it's Josie—she's usually the only one who calls—but it's a man's voice who greets him.

"Hello, is this Brewster Clay?"

"Yeah, it is," Brewster says, almost in a groan, his knees throbbing with pain.

"Mr. Clay, this is Dr. Matthew Fierros, calling from San Diego, California."

"Who?" Brewster asks.

"I'm trying to track down an ex-patient . . . a friend of mine. I've performed surgery on her a couple of times. Her name is Ramona Clay. She told me she was from Appalachia, a little town called Pick. Do you realize how many Picks there are in Appalachia? There's one in Tennessee, Virginia, West Virginia—there's one in every state. Do you realize how many Clays there are in each of those towns? Do you have a daughter named Ramona?"

"Who?" The man is talking so fast Brewster can hardly understand a word he's saying.

"Ramona. I usually don't get this involved with . . . Do you have a daughter named Ramona who lives out West? It's imperative that I find her."

"No."

"Do you have any daughters?"

"Yeah, I've got Josie. She lives right here in Pick. My other daughter is dead."

"Well, thank you for your time, Mr. Clay," the man says and hangs up.

What was that all about? Brewster wonders. Somewhere in the back of his mind, an image of Cheyenne rises up, but he quickly douses it. He always ignores images of Cheyenne—if he didn't, he'd go crazy with grief. Brewster looks up at the TV, where Channel 10's News at Noon is just beginning. He hates to see the noontime news come on because that means it's dog time, time to feed the little dogs next door.

My mind is gone, Brewster thinks. I'm senile or I'd of been able to answer that man with some sense. But he said her name was Ramona. I don't know a Ramona. Brewster looks down at his watch as the newsmen with their smug little faces and matching gold jackets tell the news in their broadcasting-school drone. Yep, it's ten past twelve, he thinks. No doubt about that. He especially dreads letting the dogs out for their walk today. They've been mad at him for the past week. It all started when Brewster told his neighbors about how the dogs get so excited when they're let out that they usually start fighting. The fat one jumps on the skinny one and starts nipping at her legs. The concerned pet owners told Brewster to swat the fat one on his nose to let him know who was boss.

Brewster did just that, but he must have swatted too hard because now both Pomeranians are mad at him. He goes over there and they don't even want to walk outside with him. When they do finally relent, they won't pee, choosing to wait until they get back inside to let it rip.

And the *looks* they give me, Brewster thinks.

He's sure he didn't swat the dog's nose too hard. "Why, I just barely touched it," he grumbles out loud. "All I done was take the soft straw-end of a broom and swipe at its face."

Still the fact remains that deep down there is cause for him to doubt himself. All of his life he's had an unnatural desire to pester dogs. There's just something about them that makes him want to clamp their nozzles shut for a minute and listen to that squeaky little sound they make. He wants to pull their tails and flick their ears, but he's been fairly successful at controlling these impulses ever since he was a child and his father whipped him for catching their bird dog asleep and tying his hind legs together with a string. Eight-year-old Brewster had thought it was funny when old General woke, tried to walk, and fell, but Brewster's father hadn't thought it was a bit funny.

Brewster gets up, walks to his neighbor's house, and opens the front door. The Pomeranians are waiting—they stand just inside the foyer glaring at him angrily.

By the time Josie arrives at her father's, the dogs have already been let out and back in, and Brewster is sitting on the couch, watching a rerun of *The Virginian*, downing his third beer of the afternoon when she walks in the door.

Josie sits down in the wing-back chair, turns to him and sighs. The

TV is so loud she can hardly think. "Daddy, can we turn it down a little? I've got a headache."

"Go ahead."

She gets up and turns down the volume. "How's your arthritis?"

"All right." Although he's glad Josie is here, he wishes she'd just sit there and watch TV with him. He isn't in the mood to talk. In addition to his irritation at the dogs, the phone call won't leave his mind. I ought to of listened closer, he thinks, but it all happened so fast. Come right out of the blue. I didn't have time to . . .

"How's them little dogs doing?" Josie asks.

"They're all right, too," Brewster snaps defensively. "What makes you think anything's wrong with 'em?"

"Nothing . . . I just . . ." Josie looks at her father and shakes her head. Something seems to be wrong with him, and she can't imagine what it is.

"Daddy, do you ever think about Sage?"

"No."

"Well, I do. Sometimes that's all I think about. It reminds me of Mommy and Cheyenne."

Startled by the sound of Cheyenne's name, Brewster wheels around and looks at Josie. Why did I tell that man she was dead? he asks himself. Why didn't I say she got missing a long time ago? Which is what she did. Where did he say he was from? If them goddamned people wouldn't talk so fast, a body could understand them. I can't remember hardly a word he said. I can't remember nothing no more. "She ain't alive, Josie," Brewster suddenly blurts out. "The whole state of Kentucky was out looking for her. Every police department in the United States had her on their lists. Her heart was bad, remember? Even if she wouldn't kidnapped, even if she run away and somehow didn't get killed by somebody, there's her heart to think about. She was all slated to go to the hospital to have that operation. She needed to have it." That man said something about a operation, said he was her doctor, Brewster thinks.

What has come over him? Josie wonders as she sits there with her mouth open in the wake of her father's outburst. "I know that,

Daddy. I know that," she says. "Anyway I've been thinking about Sage. Wasn't much there as I recall, but I'd like to see it again. Did you like it out there?" She hasn't seen Brewster this agitated in a long time.

"It was all right. Yeah, I liked it. I liked both of them little places— Rustle and Sage." Brewster remembers the copper mine that was located halfway between the two small towns. His job was basically to sit there and watch the ore go down the conveyor. The Mexican workers would bring marijuana and share it with him on their lunch breaks. It was the first and only period in his life that he ever smoked it. Back then, he and Josie's mother, Dora, were at the peak of an up-cycle in their marriage. Even the children were getting along, and that was unusual since Josie and Cheyenne were always at each other, picking, hitting, and name-calling. But there in Sage they sat around most of the summer playing records and singing songs, huddled together like they were plotting something, cracking jokes and laughing like regular people. Brewster considers that maybe their truce had something to do with Cheyenne's bad heart. Anyway, it was a pretty good time.

"Do you ever think you'd want to go out there again?" Josie asks.

Brewster can't help smiling. It's amazing to him that Josie can't see he's over the hill. Don't she know I'm too old to go places anymore? he wonders. She must not know it, or she wouldn't ask me a question like that. "Do you figure I ought to pull up stakes and leave?" he asks her. "Are you forgetting about my arthritis? I can't hardly drive."

"What if I moved out there?" she asks. "Would you go with me?"

"Are you figuring on leaving Clarence?" he asks her.

"No, I'm planning on him goin too."

"He'll never do it."

"Maybe, but would you go with us?"

Brewster pictures himself standing by a saguaro cactus in 110-degree weather, eating a watermelon. He pictures the land of horned toads, gila monsters, and rattlers—a land where Pomeranians don't dare to tread.

"If I was able," he says, "I might."

"You're able, Daddy," Josie says. "You're as able as anyone else."

After Josie leaves, Brewster gets up and paces the floor, and all the while he's trying to remember the particulars of the phone call—where the man was from, what he said about that person, Ramona. All he remembers is that he was a doctor, said something about surgery, and asked if Brewster had a daughter living in the West. Brewster walks outside, forgetting to watch his favorite afternoon soap, *Another World*. He props an old dinette chair against the side of the house and watches the cars go by instead.

Josie drives through Pick and passes Clarence's TV repair shop, a wooden structure that looks more like a house than a business. A small sign above the front door says:

Clarence TolliVer's REPAIR

How can he stand to be in that place every day of his life? she wonders. How can he be satisfied to fiddle around with transistors and shit all the time? There has to be more going on inside him. Somehow I've got to wake him up, to make him want to go places and do things. I've got to break through all that technical crap and get to the meat of Clarence Tolliver.

Josie drives past the bank, the IGA, the dime store, and the dollar store, drives past the high school, where she discovered she could actually make good grades in history and English. To her right stands the Palace Bowl-a-Rama, which is located in the same building that was once the Palace Theatre. Every Saturday night Brewster and Dora used to take their young daughters to the Palace, where Josie and Cheyenne became well-versed in the lore of the West, Hollywood-style. Although the Palace showed a variety of movies, Westerns were its mainstay, and Brewster made sure his family saw them all. He loved stories about cowboys, but—perhaps because of his one-sixteenth of Cherokee blood—he was especially in awe of Indians, was so taken with them that he'd named his oldest daughter after a tribe.

Josie drives on down the winding river road. Today the river is muddy and high on the banks, and she likes gazing at it through the branches of trees that line the road. The river's velvet, coiling presence is just as alive as any person she's ever known. I'm as much a part of this place as the mountains and trees, she thinks. It made me who I am, but it doesn't tell the whole story, least I don't think it does.

4

If a person is prone to strange thoughts, she'll often find that they build gradually through the night, peak at three o'clock in the morning, remain in an eerie kind of limbo until about four, then fade with the appearance of dawn.

Josie hasn't slept a wink this cool September night, and it's now two-thirty in the morning. Clothed in nothing but a thin gown, she sits on the hill behind her house. She came out here expecting to do battle with her foe, her spiritual arch enemy, whoever that is. Josie is sure she has one. Since she was a child, there have been times when she's caught a glimpse of the being lurking at the edge of her peripheral vision, a dark shadow that she knows is there.

Occasionally, she manages to convince herself that this phantom was born out of the anguish she went through when she lost both her sister and mother in the space of one year. Josie didn't begin to think otherwise until she interpreted the Castaneda books to say that the phantom is real, that everybody has one. Tonight she has been staring at the branch of an oak tree that is silhouetted in the moonlight, focusing on the branch and nothing else, hoping the concentration will cause her foe to materialize right in front of her. Even if he doesn't come, she hopes something unnatural will happen, that at the very least a door will open to another reality.

If only don Juan were here to lead me in the right direction, Josie thinks. I can't do it alone. You have to abandon your family to do this right. Naturally I'm goin about it half-assed. That's the way I always do things. But how can a person truly and for all time abandon her family? Is that what Cheyenne did? Did she leave us without giving it a second thought? Was she really kidnapped and murdered? Or did she run off, free as the wind, without ever needing to look back?

If my foe made an appearance tonight, he'd kill me, Josie reasons. I'd be such a easy target, and obviously I'm not concentrating hard enough or these doubts wouldn't be taking over. Not to mention that I don't have any drugs, ain't never took a single one in my life, and I'm prob'ly so weak-spirited I need drugs to get myself into the right frame of mind. Why do I think I oughta be staring at this tree branch? Was I instructed to do so by some all-knowing spiritual guide? No, I just made it up, decided on my own that I needed to be doing this in particular. I'm prob'ly staring at the wrong thing. No doubt I'm supposed to be staring at the sky or a rock or a . . .

She forces these thoughts from her mind and concentrates on the tree branch. Silhouetted, its dark leaves dance in a light breeze, but determined to see more, Josie finds they're beginning to mutate into different forms. She sees small figures square dancing and playing fiddles, discovers the shapes of dogs and cats, the face of a human being. The human face holds a blank babylike expression that hints at a barely contained horror lying just beneath its surface. On the same branch, but closer to the trunk of the tree, she notices a shadow that she hasn't seen before. A large clump of gnarled twigs? A hornet's nest? She quickly looks away from it, back to the fiddlers and dancers and the pale baby-face with the suspect smile, but Josie knows the shadow is moving, sees it out of the corner of her eye. Wind shifting a hornet's nest, she thinks.

There's something familiar about the shadow, though. Why didn't I see it before? Josie wonders. Maybe if I just pretend it isn't there, it'll disappear. None of this is real anyway.

The shadow floats off the tree branch and glides steadily toward her, and the baby-face, having attached itself to the dark form, is coming along for the ride. Josie looks more closely and sees that the thing floating toward her is really her lost sister, that it was Cheyenne all along, her dead face demanding recognition. Like a feather

Cheyenne falls, gently wafting through the air until she touches lightly on the ground and comes to rest a few feet away, her face turned toward Josie, her eyes wide open.

Josie tries to get up and run, but she can't move.

Cheyenne points at Josie with her spectral finger. "Yon'ta climb a tree, Josie? Let's me and you climb that tree." Her voice is as clear as a mountain stream.

Josie tries to say something, but her mouth won't open.

Cheyenne begins to laugh her same old taunting laugh. Then she starts to dissipate, thins like smoke until not a trace is left.

Josie jumps up and runs down the hill, her heart beating so wildly it hurts. What have I done? she screams silently to herself. What have I started now? She opens the door and slips quietly inside her house, hoping not to wake Clarence, but there's no danger of that. Clarence is ticking like a clock, snoozing like a passed-out drunk. Climbing into bed, she scoots up close behind him, puts her arm around his waist and squeezes hard, trying to block the image of her dead sister from her mind, but the closeness of Clarence's body is no comfort to her. He doesn't know anything about me, Josie thinks. She imagines the look he'd give her if she were to tell him what just happened—the no-nonsense smirk he'd have. In a voice that would sting like a kick to the stomach, he'd bellow, "What the hell are you talking about?" And he'd think he was doing her a favor by shouting, that he was jarring her back to reality.

She can still see the look in Cheyenne's eyes as she floated from the tree to the ground and lay there staring at her. It was the same look that had sent Josie running and screaming from the room when they were children. It was true that Cheyenne sometimes gave her reason to be afraid, but Josie's awe of her sister was and still is more complicated than that. Most of the time Cheyenne didn't seem to care about anything or anyone, and her attitude amazed Josie. It still does.

The sun is rising when she drifts off to sleep. In her dreams she hears wind blowing like a child's scream, sees a sunset burning a blue Arizona sky, beholds Cheyenne standing in the doorway of the adobe mansion in Sage, beckoning. When Josie wakes midday, she barely remembers the dreams from the night before. One particular dream she doesn't remember at all. It was one of those true dreams, a noteworthy event that really happened a long time ago.

They didn't look at all alike. With fair skin and chestnut hair, seven-year-old Josie favored their mother, while eleven-year-old Cheyenne had a dark complexion like their father. A hot summer sun beat down on the sisters as they played cowgirl and Indian near the creek behind their house in Pick. They'd been running through the mountains all day—Josie, wearing her brand-new Dale Evans cowgirl outfit, and Cheyenne, sporting a face painted red with clay. Cheyenne always played the Indian role, due in part to her high cheekbones, flashing black eyes, dark hair, and Indian name, but also she was the brave one, the one with stealth, the warrior with a bone to pick—while Josie remained the hapless cowgirl, the frail, gray-eyed target of Cheyenne's wrath.

Most of the time Cheyenne preferred to play alone, but Josie followed her relentlessly, knowing that excitement lay wherever her sister went. In an attempt to get away from her, Cheyenne would throw rocks at Josie and call her names: "Get away from me, you little weasel," she'd yell. "You're driving me crazy." But nothing worked—Josie couldn't stop herself from tagging behind. Sometimes Cheyenne's resolve would weaken, she'd agree to play with her, and the girls would get lost in their own world where anything was possible. Cheyenne chased Josie up and down creeks and trees, swung after her on grapevines, and searched for her in the darkest corners of caves. With her fiery imagination and power to execute, she was the engineer of all their feats: "Josie, look out! I'm goin to jump off this cliff and see if I can land on you," or, "Let's run inside that cave. I bet it's got bats in it!" or, "Why don't we climb that tree and have a fight right in the top of it?" It was as if all the world's danger and excitement had gathered inside one person, and that person was Cheyenne Clay.

Across the creek behind their house stood the mountain that

served as their backyard. It was a mountain filled with ferns, pines, the smell of mint, and the cry of birds. Through the fully leafed trees, sun spangled the earth with patterns of magic, and the two girls were caught in its shiny spell. On rare days Cheyenne would allow Josie to be the hero. She'd yell, "Come on, Josie. You can do it. All you have to do is swim across that bottomless hole of water, tear your way through them honeysuckle vines swarming with bees, and climb that sheer, bald-faced cliff. That's all you have to do." Shaking, Josie would shut her eyes and wade through the perils to capture Cheyenne, who would pretend she was cowering in fear. Later Cheyenne would say, "See? You didn't think you could do that, but you did. You can do anything, Josie. Anything in the world." And as she spoke, Josie would beam with pride. Many of their days were spent in high adventure, but then a mood would descend that changed everything.

Today Cheyenne was playing her usual role of Indian hero, and she'd captured her sister after Josie had slipped and fallen on a slick rock in the creek. "Let's pretend I'm goin to burn you at the stake," Cheyenne said. "I'll tie you to that poplar tree."

"What with?" Josie asked.

"Twine. I'll run to the house and get some. You stand right there and don't move."

As usual Josie did as she was told, and a few minutes later her arms and legs were being bound tightly to the tree. "That's too tight," she told Cheyenne.

"You want this to be real, don't you?"

"Yeah, but why can't we just make believe it's tight?"

"Cause it's better this way," Cheyenne said. "And you can't do nothing about it now cause you're tied up."

"But it's hurting my arms."

Standing back to admire her work, Cheyenne said, "There's just one more thing it needs." And she began to gather weeds, small tree branches, and twigs to lay around Josie's feet.

"What're you doing?" Josie shouted, beginning to get scared. She could tell that the situation had changed, that a new agenda was at hand.

Cheyenne dragged a book of matches out of her pocket. "What if I struck one of these and let it fall in them dry weeds?" Her eyes dug into Josie like small burrowing animals.

Josie began to cry. "We was just making believe. You ain't supposed to really do it."

Cheyenne laughed, and it reminded Josie of a witch's laughter as she stood over a big tub, boiling someone for supper.

"You're just pretending," Josie said.

"Is that what you think? Well, I hate you, Josie. How about that? I hate your guts. All you do is cry and whine and follow me around. Maybe this'll teach you to stay away from me." Cheyenne lit a match and waved it in front her, and Josie was crying in earnest now, tears streaming down her face, mucus running out of her nose. The match went out and Cheyenne lit another as she stood there for what seemed to Josie like hours. The look in her sister's eyes was one of victory mixed with shame.

Finally Cheyenne leaned close to Josie and said, "All right, I'll let you go, but you'll have to pay for it. Do you hear me? From now on you'll do everything I say. Tell me you will or I'll drop this match. And no one'll come to save you either. Daddy's at work and Mommy's way over there in the garden hoeing corn. No one'll know you're on fire."

"OK," Josie sputtered. There was something in her sister's eyes that said she was capable of anything.

Cheyenne untied the rope and Josie dropped to the ground, exhausted. Cheyenne sat down beside her. "I'm goin to hit you on the shoulder, and I'm goin to keep on hitting—not real hard but hard enough so it hurts. You ain't to tell Mommy. If you tell her, you'll be sorry. You ain't to cry, either. I don't want to even see you blink."

Josie held her breath as Cheyenne began pounding her shoulder. Her face was still—nothing on it moved with a sign of life. She was like a statue. I'm a statue, Josie said to herself over and over again.

"We're goin to do this every day. Just wait and see how strong it'll make you," Cheyenne whispered. "You'll be the strongest person on earth."

Josie barely heard her sister. She was freezing solid, clicking and clacking, becoming a stone, and stones can't hear a word.

5

Brewster Clay keeps waiting to get another call; so far it hasn't happened. Occasionally he thinks he remembers the man saying something about California, but he isn't sure. California is a big state, he thinks. He's thought of telling Josie about the call, but he figures there's no use getting her all riled up over nothing. If only I hadn't screwed up by not getting the facts straight, he thinks, and he feels like banging his head against the wall to shake up his mind.

It's twelve o'clock, time to walk the dogs, but he's not in the mood to do it. "Fuck 'em," he snarls as he walks to the sink. He turns on the faucet, cups some water in his hands, and slicks back his hair, thinking he'll go down to the Pick Clinic and pick up a prescription for some Solganal for his arthritis. He hates going to the clinic because the doctors and nurses there, most of whom are from out of state, are condescending, nearly always behaving like the benevolent saviors of the ignorant, impoverished people of eastern Kentucky. Still, he needs the medicine and promises himself that he'll try to hold his tongue when they say things that grate on his nerves. Opening the door, he steps out into the cool crisp air. I ought to get out more, he thinks. I stay cooped up way too much.

At the clinic, it is one of the younger doctors who sees him, an eager-looking boy who has just returned from a vacation in Vermont, and it is all he talks about as he pokes into Brewster's ears, listens to his heart, and takes his blood pressure. "The foliage in Vermont is out of this world this time of year," he's saying. "The trees around here are pretty, but they're nothing when compared to . . . If you ever get a chance, you should vacation in New England."

Yeah, Brewster thinks, as soon as I make my next million I'll make Vermont my first stop.

The doctor steps out of the examining room, leaving the door ajar. A few minutes later Brewster overhears another doctor admonish the younger one. "You shouldn't be talking about your vacations to that old man. I doubt if he's been out of this town in his entire life. You have to be careful not to insult these people. They're proud." He lowers his voice. "Though what they're so proud about is a mystery to me." Chuckling, the two doctors' voices fade as they walk out of hearing range.

Idiots, Brewster thinks to himself. As soon as he gets his prescription, he stomps out of the clinic. He's beginning to think the medicine isn't worth it. Marching down the sidewalk, he notices Ed Gibbs sitting on the courthouse steps. The courthouse, a two-story structure built of stone, stands in the middle of town, and a small grassy lawn completely shaded by a huge mulberry tree extends in front of the building, making it one of the prettiest locations in Pick. Brewster stares at Ed. In all these years he's never said more to him than howdy, but today he's itching for a conversation. Before he speculates any further, he finds himself walking toward the man, grinning.

"Howdy, Ed," Brewster says. "How're ye faring?"

"Pretty good," Ed says. "How about you?"

Brewster shakes his head. "I just got out of that clinic. Don't know why I bother, though. Every time I go, I get so mad I'm sicker than I was before I went."

"How's that?" Ed asks, seemingly glad to have company.

"Ah, it's them damned little doctors. I reckon they think everyone around here is dumb. Act like we ain't never been nowhere before."

Ed nods knowingly.

"Not that they's anything wrong with staying put," Brewster continues. "They ain't a thing wrong with sitting in the same spot all your life." He adds this last part because—now that he thinks of it—he doesn't ever remember seeing Ed Gibbs any other place than on the courthouse steps.

"Ijits," Ed gripes, as he spits a cud of tobacco on the cement walk. "Ain't got a lick of sense."

"I bet I've been more places in my life than they could count if they tried," Brewster says.

Ed looks around at him and narrows his eyes. "Where all ye been?"

"Why, I was in the war, Ed. World War Two. Didn't you go?"

Ed looks down at his shoe. "Shot myself in the foot to get out of it."

Brewster looks at Ed with disgust, thinking he picked the wrong man to talk to, that this whole conversation is a waste of time. He'd forgotten for the moment that there were three men in Burr County who got drunk and shot bullets through their feet to keep from fighting in World War II and that Ed Gibbs was one of them. Years ago it was the talk of the town, and the talk still follows the three shirkers, will follow them till the day they die.

"Well, I went," Brewster says, forging ahead. "I was older than most others—in my late thirties. But I was bound to go. I seen the world, Ed. No doubt about that. Been all over France, Germany, England, you name it, but I didn't see them places the fancy way. Didn't check into a expensive hotel and claim I'd been to a foreign country. I seen almost every inch of France and Germany, crawling on my belly, trailing behind Sherman tanks, hoofing it through snow, hunkering in foxholes until my feet and legs was frostbit black all the way up to my knees. And them two little dumb-ass doctors think I ain't been nowhere. Think I'm a fool, I reckon."

"It's a wonder you didn't lose your legs if they was frosbit that bad."

"I know it," Brewster says. "A buddy of mine—name of George Wells—did lose his'n. We was in a foxhole all night, and it was way below zero. Next morning both of us had legs that was froze black. Except mine got better, and his had to be amputated. Poor old George," Brewster says, thinking about the injustice of it all. "He acted like he was mad at me afterwards. Wonder what ever happened to him."

Ed Gibbs shakes his head and looks down the street as a Jeep screeches by, carting a bunch of high school kids who are screaming and hollering as if to let the whole world know they're ditching school. "It wouldn't that I was a coward," he says. "That ain't the reason I didn't want to go to the war. I just don't like killing things. Never did like it—never would butcher a hog or wring a chicken's neck, wouldn't hunt. Never held a gun till the day I shot my own foot."

Brewster sighs. "Well, everybody's got their beliefs, I reckon. If you ain't got your beliefs, what have you got?"

Ed looks relieved. He puts a fresh plug of tobacco in his mouth and starts chewing. "You've lived a lot of places right here in this country, ain't you? Where was that you and Dora moved that time? Arizona?"

"Not just Arizona, Ed. Me and Dora moved around a lot when we was first married. Lived in California, got married there. Lived in Montana, Ohio, New Mexico, and Idaho before we decided to come back home and settle down here. We didn't go to Arizona until later."

"I never did marry," Ed said. "Never run up against the right womern."

"They ain't many right ones. I just found one. When she was gone, they wouldn't no more."

The two men talk until evening and the katydids have started to chirp in the mulberry tree on the courthouse lawn. Brewster is beginning to think about heading home when the two doctors step out of the clinic.

"There they come," Ed says. "Anybody ought to give them a piece of their mind."

Brewster looks around at Ed. "You got a point there," and bolstered by the encouragement, he stands up and yells at the older doctor, "Hey, Dr. Brodie, come here a minute."

The two doctors walk toward them. "What can I do for you, Mr. Clay?" the younger doctor asks. "Did you get your prescription from the nurse?"

"Yeah, I got it. I also heard what you fellers was saying. Heard Dr. Brodie there say that I'd prob'ly never been out of this town in my whole life. Bet I've been more places than both of y'uns put together. I've been all over the world almost. If you fellers love to travel so much, I hope you can get over to Germany sometime and get lost in the Hürtgen Forest. That's a real treat, especially when it's late at night and people're shooting at you. I know it's something I'll never forget."

Dr. Brodie's face turns red with embarrassment. "I didn't mean to . . . ah . . . You were in the war, I bet."

The younger doctor stares down at the ground.

"You're damned right," Brewster says.

"I should have realized . . ." Dr. Brodie folds his arms tightly as if getting a grip on himself. "Well, take care of yourself, Brewster." He walks away with the younger doctor trailing behind him.

"Guess you told them," Ed says, grinning.

"Guess I did," Brewster says.

The two men keep sitting there until almost dark, talking about a multitude of subjects, including war, politics, love, and philosophy. Brewster keeps waiting around, hoping Ed gets up to leave first so he can find out what direction he goes. After seeing Ed at the courthouse all his life, Brewster still doesn't know exactly where the man lives. Is it up the river or down? The road toward Harlan, the road toward Manchester, or the one to Hazard? He starts to just ask him, but somehow it seems too private a matter to inquire about. Finally, he gives up waiting and takes off down the street, but before he gets out of viewing distance, he turns and glances toward the courthouse. Ed is still sitting there, looking this way and that.

Brewster stops by his neighbors' house and tells the nice young couple that he doesn't like their Pomeranians any more than their Pomeranians like him, says he can't be a dog sitter any longer. Then back in his apartment, he rehashes how he told off the doctors. Holding himself erect, he struts back and forth like a banty rooster, pausing only occasionally to reach down and readjust his balls. He feels better than he's felt in a long time, feels so good that he figures if Josie goes to Arizona, he might tag along after all. Yes, sir. Even his arthritis pain has gone away.

6

"Arizona is a hellhole!" Clarence shouts, sitting at the supper table, his thin lips white with anger. "It was put here to show people what it's like to be in hell. Old dry ground, no rain. No water, either, if they didn't pump it in. Black widows, tarantulas, poison snakes everywhere you step."

"So when are we goin?" Josie asks.

"I hate the fuckin place. I don't want to hear another word about it."

"You're not goin then?" Josie stands by the sink, defiantly running dishwater.

"You're damn right I'm not!" he yells.

They've been arguing since he came home from work, and neither of them has won a point. Josie's long chestnut hair is uncombed and hanging everywhere, and her furious eyes are almost glowing as she stares around the room at the same old kitchen cabinets, at the scarred Mediterranean dinette table with its wrought-iron stand. She glances out the window at wires running down from the giant TV antenna Clarence constructed himself and then nailed to the top of a spruce pine after he'd sheared off all the tree branches, an antenna that looks as if it were brought to earth centuries ago by creatures from strange worlds. My surroundings are surreal, Josie thinks, but they're surreal in an uninteresting way. I hate it all. I wish everything on this hill would disintegrate into a big pile of mulch.

"You hate me, don't you?" she asks, her voice rising louder with every word. "I know you do, you little weasel, you day-old slimy puke, you scum that crawled out from under a rock. You must hate me or you'd take me to Sage, knowing how much I want to go."

"If you want to go so much, GOOOOOO! They ain't no one stopping you. God, I wish you would. I wish you'd go right now and leave me the hell alone."

Josie turns and runs outside. There's no use wasting my breath, she thinks. He's a wire, a diode, a 19-inch-wide TV screen. I bet if anyone cut him open transistors would fall out. She runs up the hill behind her house and stares at the branch on the oak tree, almost hoping the ghost of Cheyenne returns. Josie sits there alone for hours, thoughts racing through her mind so fast she can't catch onto one. Finally she begins to think more clearly and comes to the reluctant conclusion that it's at least possible Clarence is blameless in this whole affair. He's just a man, she thinks. A normal man. He wants a wife and a house, children and a dog—maybe a cat. He didn't get what he bargained for when he got me. Then again, maybe it *is* his fault. Maybe people who don't want nothing from life but a job and a house are evil. Maybe they oughta be blamed for all the atrocities in the world. After all Clarence does get a charge out of holding people up, making them wait, slowing them down.

Why can't I forget him and go by myself? Why do I want to drag someone with me who doesn't want to go? Why am I so afraid to do anything on my own? Josie remembers how it used to be when she lived in that big adobe house. In spite of Cheyenne's heart attack, it was one of the happiest times of her life. Everything seemed to click. It was as if all of them, the whole family, were caught up in the same rhythm, were dancing to a beat that only existed for them in Sage, Arizona.

She imagines herself taking off in the car and driving until she gets to Sage. She walks up to the adobe mansion and, as luck would have it, the very apartment she lived in when she was a child is available for rent. Josie moves in and becomes a waitress at a local café, and on her days off she takes long walks in the desert. On one of these walks she happens upon don Juan and Carlos Castaneda, newly arrived from Mexico. As might be expected, they're playing strange games in the middle of a cactus forest—running around like wild men up to their eyeballs in dreams. Eventually Josie makes in with the grouchy old sorcerer and his prize apprentice, and they teach her how to fly.

Josie plays this fantasy again and again with slight variations on each new run. Finally noticing that dawn is breaking, she returns to the house to fix breakfast for Clarence. She perks coffee, fries bacon, and makes pancakes. "I'm sorry about what I called you last night," she tells him. "I don't really think you're scum or puke or anything like that. I was just mad. People say things they don't mean when they're mad."

Clarence doesn't look up. He drinks his coffee, eats his pancakes in silence. Finally he says, "Well, I'll see you tonight," and walks out the door.

I'll prob'ly leave pretty soon, Josie thinks when he's gone. I'll just get in the car and go. I'm free to do it any time. But a week passes and she's still on the mountain—she can't articulate the reason why—and Clarence is still giving her the silent treatment, playing her guilt like a steel guitar. It's now the end of October, and the air around Pick is tinged with a growing chill. Josie figures she might hang around a little while longer, that she may as well wait till spring.

Noticing the fierce beep of a horn, Clarence looks into the rearview mirror and sees a car riding his tail. Why do they always want to go so fast? he wonders as he drops in speed from thirty-five to thirty. There, let 'em deal with that. Let 'em have a heart attack. Clarence's mother lives at the head of a rugged hollow. Six years a widow, she's sixty-two with no intentions of remarrying. It's Sunday, and Clarence figures she'll be piddling around in the yard. She always works in her yard on Sundays after church. Earlier Clarence told Josie that he was going to Pick to catch up on a pile of work, but there is no pile. He intends to talk to his mother about his problems today, and he doesn't want Josie to have the slightest notion of his intentions. Clarence hasn't talked to his mother about his problems since he was in elementary school, and he doesn't know how to go about it. He's embarrassed by the whole idea.

When he pulls into her drive, he gets out of the car and stands for a moment staring at the house where he grew up. It used to be so huge when he was a child, but with each passing year it seems to grow smaller. It's even begun to look shabby—the latticework under the front porch is broken in places and needs a coat of paint. I ought to do some work around here, he thinks as he walks up the long row of stairs and into the house.

"Look at my bird feeder," his mother, Ida, says to him a few minutes later. "Ain't it pretty?" They're standing in the backyard near an elaborate structure that looks like a small castle. Birds fly in and out of rectangular openings in the castle's walls and dive-bomb the towers that are stuffed with seed.

"Yeah, that's something," Clarence says. He wishes Josie had interests like this. Why can't she get into bird feeders?

Ida steps closer to the structure. Already having changed out of her church clothes, she's wearing brown pants and an orange sweater that fit snugly on her petite body. She has kept in remarkably good shape from years of outdoor gardening, from scaling mountains and trees without giving them a second thought. Only her pepper-gray hair and weathered face betray her age.

"I ordered it out of a catalogue," she says. "Reckon they put it on sale because it's so late in the year. Next spring the price'll shoot right back up. I love my little birds. If you ask me, they ain't nothing comes close to a bird. I might order me another one of these." Ida stands back and squints at Clarence as if she thinks he's against the idea. "But they're on *saaale*," she protests, scrunching her small round face into a dramatic pout.

"Well, you ought to get anothern then," Clarence says.

Ida goes inside the house and brings out some coffee for the two of them to drink while they sit on the porch and watch the bird feeder. As the birds fly in and out, she makes a gurgling sound in her throat that causes Clarence to wonder if she's bubbling over with sheer joy.

"You won't believe who come up here, trying to court me," Ida says, turning a minute from the birds. As if wanting Clarence to guess, she leans close to his face. "Well?"

"I don't know," Clarence says.

"Old Lindsay Burns, that sorry old thing." Ida opens her mouth until her lips are in the shape of an egg, a look of disdain gleaming in her eyes. "Can you believe that? Him grinning at me with them big old green-looking buck teeth. Law' have mercy. I wouldn't have him on a Christmas tree, and he knows it or ought to." Her arms fly up in the air like wire springs.

"What did you do?" Clarence asks.

"I turned him down. What did you think I done?" She looks at Clarence as if he has just accused her of a heinous crime. The two of them sit in silence for a few moments, then Ida turns back to the birds. "Now, you tell me this ain't the sweetest sight you've ever seen," she says, as though she's challenging him to come up with something better. Then her expression changes to one of awe. "Look! A redbird—a little cardinal. Shhh! Don't talk. You'll scare him off."

"We've got a few around the house," Clarence says, casually. "Don't see 'em as much as I used to, but they're around."

"Well, you'd see 'em all the time if you had one of these bird feeders. You ought to get you one."

"Maybe I will," Clarence says. "Where'd you order it from?"

Ida goes inside and brings back the catalogue, and they zealously pore over its pages. Clarence and Ida always do this when he comes to visit—they go on and on about Ida's latest fascination, and she always has one. If it isn't bird feeders, it's American Beauty Roses, or wind chimes, or copper-plated cookware, or those new orange plastic-handled scissors that are so lightweight you can hardly tell you're holding them in your hand.

I ain't about to let Mom know about Josie wanting to move out West, Clarence decides, and I sure can't say anything about don Juan or out-of-body experiences. If I was to tell Mom that her only son's wife spends half her nights sitting outside on the hill, she'd worry herself to death. When Clarence leaves a few hours later, he drives slowly down the rugged hollow. He loves this place where he grew up, loves this mountain, where turning leaves can drive a person crazy with color. How could anyone want to move to a burnt-up desert? he wonders.

Before going home, he stops by his repair shop, fills out the order form for the bird feeder, and figures he'll drop it in the mail tomorrow.

7

Winter comes at the end of November, brings its baggage and settles in. Then with cold shoulders and icy feet, 1977 shows up too. Now it's the second week in January. The mountains have been brown and barren for two months, but so far there has been no snow, not one flake in the entire county. Some of the old-timers say it's too cold to snow, that it would have to warm up first.

All day yesterday, Josie played Springsteen, the songs making her want to run out of the house in a frenzied, neverending search for Saturday night. She saw herself riding in a convertible, top rolled down, younger than she is now, her hair blowing wildly in the breeze, music on the radio, other people in the car too, young men, young girls, maybe four or five of them. They were all drinking beer, open cans stuck between their knees, their fingers laced around cigarettes, and, like Josie, these fun-seeking maniacs were not trapped on this earth but were ever free to push the gas pedal a little bit harder, to keep whirling out of town, out of state, out of this world, always driving to a drum beat, to the hard-hitting strings of a rock-and-roll guitar. It was not a time remembered but a time never had.

Yet the vision was such a strong one, so mercilessly real, that Josie actually did run outside once—she ran to the top of the mountain and screamed as loud as she could scream, but no one heard except the ghostly dead hills that reach as far as one can see. Then the cold winter air sent her back inside, cowardly and defeated, her heart forever tangled in the dry, gnarled branches of a thousand dead trees.

Calmer today, she is watching TV, a rerun of *Perry Mason*. She figures watching *Perry Mason* puts a person in the same state as transcendental meditation except it doesn't require half the effort. For
one thing, you don't have to sit in the Buddha position on a hard floor
with your palms held open, being careful how you breathe. You can
just sprawl yourself on the couch any old way, knowing that Perry
always does a bang-up job representing the defendant, that the real
killer invariably breaks down on the stand, and that at the end Perry
always explains to his secretary, Della Street, how he arrived at his
brilliant conclusions—just in case she didn't get it. It's like a mantra
and *all is one*.

Josie hasn't mentioned Arizona to Clarence since their last big
argument, but more bored than ever, she still dreams of going there.
Last month she hauled herself over to Hazard and got a job as a waitress, but she quit after two weeks since she kept forgetting to supply
the customers with silverware, and they would just sit there, staring
helplessly from Josie to their porterhouse steaks. Lately she's even
started having sexual fantasies. She imagines tall dark men—several
of them—taking her in their arms, having their way with her while
she groans deliriously.

In spite of the cold weather, she's gone a few times to her spot
behind the house in hopes of seeing Cheyenne again, but the vision of
her sister has never returned. Josie shuts her eyes and tries to imagine
how Cheyenne would look at present if by some miracle she were still
alive, but all she sees is her sister as she appeared shortly before she
vanished—tall and lean with a sassy smile—back when the two of
them were finally getting along. Although Josie knows there is a good
possibility that her sister met with foul play at some point after her disappearance, she can't imagine that a person with a smile like
Cheyenne's was kidnapped. No one would have had the nerve. Nope,
they didn't steal her, Josie thinks. She ran. *But why didn't she tell me
what she was planning to do?* Josie hears Brewster's voice clear as a bell,
telling relatives how Cheyenne was born mad at the world, telling
them with pride, happy to have a character on his hands. Josie can

hear her mother's voice, too. "When Josie was born and I brought her home from the hospital that first day, Cheyenne took one look at her and said, 'Take her back.' "

Josie hopes that one day she'll somehow discover the truth about her sister's motives. In the meantime, she remains obsessed with the details of every memory she can find.

It was about a month after the shoulder-hitting began. Josie and Cheyenne had been picking blackberries with their mother. It was one of those warm, slow-moving days when the green hills shimmered with sunlight and the nearby creek purred like a fed cat. With their pails filled to the brim and their faces and hands stained purple, Josie and Cheyenne sat with Dora on a huge rock at the edge of the field, eating handfuls of ripe berries. They had been singing Irish folk songs all morning. Dora's mother's side of the family had an Irish last name, O'Neil, and lately she had been obsessed with her Irish ancestry, of which she knew nothing. Last week she had bought a record album of Irish folk songs in an attempt to get closer to her heritage. Dora loved all of the ballads, but "The Rising of the Moon" was Josie's favorite and "Paddy West" was Cheyenne's. Every time Josie and Dora would start singing one of the other songs on the album, Cheyenne would break in with "Paddy West."

It was a magical day, one where a person might expect a leprechaun to step out from behind a tree any minute, but that all changed when a bee crawled up Josie's blouse and stung her several times. As soon as she let out the first scream, Dora grabbed Josie and yanked off her blouse to let the bee fly away. And that's when the secret was exposed.

"What's wrong with your arm?" Dora shouted, staring in horror at the bruises on her seven-year-old daughter. They began just above the scar left by a smallpox vaccination and extended to the collarbone. The whole area was blue mixed with magenta, green, and yellow, where bruise upon bruise had been accumulating for weeks.

"I don't know," Josie muttered, still wincing from the bee stings.

Dora grabbed her arm to get a closer look. "You don't know? What do you mean you don't know?" Dora looked around at Cheyenne, who was still calmly eating blackberries. "If you fellers don't tell me what happened, I'll beat the living daylights out of both of you. Tell me what happened right now."

Standing at five foot eleven with sharp gray eyes and long curly brown hair, Dora Clay was an imposing woman to begin with, but when she allowed her temper to run free, she could strike fear into the bravest of souls. Josie sat there silently. The pain from the bee stings was overwhelming, and her mother's threats pounded down like rain. She watched as Dora grabbed Cheyenne and pulled her to her feet, shouting, "You did this, didn't you? I know you did. Admit it, or I swear you'll regret the day you were born."

Cheyenne didn't say a word.

Dora stared from one daughter to the other, trembling with rage. Josie had never seen her that angry. She looked as if she might take off down the road running and screaming and never come back. Suddenly Dora grabbed Cheyenne's face and drew it within an inch of Josie's bruised arm. "Look at what you've done to her. Look at it! What kind of person would do something like that? Lordy mercy, you're just eleven years old. What'll you be like when you're grown? How long have you been doing this?"

"A few weeks," Cheyenne said. Her voice was emotionless.

"What have you been hitting her with?"

"My fist." Cheyenne's head was slightly bowed, the flash gone from her black eyes.

"Tell me why you'd do something like this. Start talking."

Cheyenne looked straight at her mother. "She won't leave me alone. I don't want to play with her all the time. I want to be left alone."

"Well, you can forget that. You won't never be left alone again. I intend to watch every move you make from now on," Dora yelled, then she turned her attention to Josie. "Why have you been letting her do this to you? Why didn't you tell me? What's wrong with you?"

"Cheyenne said it was a game," Josie muttered. "She said it'd make me strong."

"Strong? Anyone that would let someone do this to them is a far cry from strong. You're sweet as pie, Josie, meek as a lamb. You're too good. You're so goddamned low-lifed you'd stand still as a mouse and let someone beat you to death." Dora sagged to the ground and held her head with both hands, then she looked up at Cheyenne. "And you're a devil, Cheyenne. I've known it all along. The day you were born, a devil came out of my womb. I nursed a devil, sent a devil to school." Tears began streaming from Dora's eyes, and she couldn't say another word.

From that moment on, Josie kissed innocence good-bye. A shroud of gloom fell over all of them, and even when good times broke through, the mistrust was always there. Days went by, then weeks and months, and the mother and daughters still skirted each other warily. The shroud remained snugly bound until several years later when the hot Arizona sun dried it out, burnt it to ashes, and let some light in. Brewster was never told about the flare-up in the blackberry patch. He was never told much of anything.

I've got to do something, Josie thinks, and picking up the *Pick Times*, she scans down the front page. The top story concerns the Burr County High School football team's losing season. The Burr County Copperheads always lose, but in the article the coach assures people that the Copperheads' day will come. "You know how copperheads are!" he yells from the print. "They hide in the grass and jump out at you when you least expect it!" Page two is filled with advertisements—Bea Patterson's Hair By Bea beauty shop ad says, *"The Best Hair in Town is always HAIR BY BEA."* Donny Dale's dime-store ad runs just below: *"If you can't find it at DONNY DALE'S, you don't want it."*

Maybe I ought to put a ad in the paper, Josie thinks. If I had anything to advertise, I would. She picks up her well-worn copy of Castaneda's *Journey to Ixtlan: The Lessons of Don Juan,* and that's when it hits her—it falls on her like a roof. I'll put a ad in the paper! she thinks. I'll put a ad in the paper that tells people about don Juan. There might be a few around here that would be interested. Maybe I could let them borrow Castaneda's books. Maybe we could all get together and read them out loud. Maybe we could try to do some of the things. Oh, God . . . !

Josie grabs a pen and paper and starts trying to come up with jingles. She writes and erases several: *Life Is But a Dream, call 749-1122; Sorcery Is the Way to Go, call 749-1122; Abandon Your Family, call 749-1122.* Finally she settles on:

Tired of housework? Can't stand to watch another soap? Sick of always being there? <u>COME LEARN WITH DON JUAN.</u> If interested, send your response to P. O. Box ___ and await further instructions.

P.S. You don't have to put your name on the envelope or any place in the letter. All you have to do is say YES and give me an address.

Josie jumps up to get ready, figuring on going to Pick as quickly as possible, but as she's taking a shower reality sets in. *I can't put a ad in the paper,* she realizes. *People would think I'm crazy, and Clarence would be plagued to death. What I prob'ly ought to do is call a few people up and find out if they'd be interested in the books. That way it wouldn't be broadcast all over town.* Josie gets out of the shower and plops on the couch by the phone. She's scanning the phone book, holding the receiver in her hand, when it comes to her that she's taking the cowardly way out. *I'm way too low-key in public,* she thinks, *as mild-mannered as Clark Kent. Who gives a fuck if they think I'm crazy? At least they'll know I'm alive.*

So without working through the particulars, she finishes dressing and drives to Pick, first stopping at the post office to rent a second P.O. box just for her new enterprise, warning Myrtle Reese, the postmaster, that she doesn't want Clarence to know about the box, that she's cooking up a surprise for him. Next she goes to the newspaper office, a small three-room affair located upstairs above the hardware store. As usual, Harold Jacobs is sitting beside his printing press in the dark, dingy back room, doing nothing. The *Pick Times* is a weekly paper that comes out every Friday, and there isn't enough work to keep Harold busy eight hours a day, so he often just sits around, grinning at the walls, wearing his suspenders and smoking a cigar. Josie figures he sees the cigar and suspenders as the crowning touches on his newspaperman image.

"Why, I ain't seen you in a month of Sundays," Harold says to Josie.

"I want to put a ad in this Friday's paper," Josie announces. "Actually I want it to run two Fridays in a row."

"Don't tell me you're trying to sell afghans too. Seems like every woman that's got fingers is crocheting afghans. They're hard to sell, though, cause every house in Pick already has them stacked to the ceiling."

"That ain't what I'm selling," Josie says. She takes the crumpled paper out of her purse, adds her new P.O. box number to the ad, and hands it to Harold.

He puts on his reading glasses and reads silently, muttering aloud just some of the words: "*Tired of . . . Can't stand . . . Sick of . . .*" Then he reads in its entirety the next sentence, poses it like a question. "COME LEARN WITH DON JUAN?" Harold pulls off his glasses and looks at Josie, a suspicious frown on his face. "What is this?"

"It's a ad."

"Does Clarence know about it?"

Josie sighs, thinking, I should have known he'd bring Clarence into this. "No, he doesn't know about it. What difference does that make? Does he have to know about it?"

Harold rolls his cigar from one side of his mouth to the other. "I just wondered. And you want it in this Friday's paper?"

"Yes, I do."

Harold rubs his nose and grimaces. "What does it mean, Josie? Who's this don Juan? Is he a Italian? Puerto Rican? He ain't a Cuban, is he?" Ever since Cuba and the U.S. fell out, Harold has had a serious problem with the island. His disenchantment is due in part to the difference in political views, but mostly it stems from the fact that he can no longer buy cigars from Havana. "What is someone like that doing around here? Don Juan. Ain't he some kind of . . ." Harold reaches back thirty-five years to his days at a small religious college. "Seems like I've heard . . . Was there a poem about a don Juan?"

"If you want to know more about it, write to the post office box. And I want to make it clear that this is confidential. I don't want no one to know right off that it's my ad—not even Clarence."

"I hope you ain't got yourself hooked up with no Cubans."

"There's not a Cuban anywhere around."

Harold looks at her mistrustfully. "I ain't so sure I want to accommodate you."

"This is a free paper, ain't it? There's nothing nasty or criminal in my ad. So looks like you'll have to run it."

"Well, actually I don't *have* to do anything, but I reckon I will." Harold was never one to turn down money when it was staring him in the face.

After Josie pays for the ad, she drives over to Brewster's house and visits him for a while. He tells her he wants to go with her when she takes off for Arizona.

"You're still goin, ain't you?" he asks her. The idea of going west again has been smoldering in Brewster's mind. He daydreams of sitting by a desert stream, panning for gold, while the hot Arizona sun kills the pain in his joints.

Josie sighs. "Yeah."

"When?" he asks.

"In the spring, Daddy. In the spring." The Arizona questions irritate her. For the time being, she's trying to block the entire southwest region from her mind since she knows she won't depart Pick until spring. The thought of leaving Clarence is bad enough, but leaving him alone in the dead of winter is too pitiful to think about. When Brewster keeps slinging questions at her, she cuts her visit short.

Driving through town, she decides impulsively to stop by Clarence's shop. Since Bernard was called out to pick up a stereo, Clarence is by himself and so busy with his work that he doesn't hear her come in. She tiptoes past numerous stereos and console TVs to the back room, where he's bent over his workbench. Reaching around him, she covers his eyes with her hands and says, "Guess who?"

Clarence jumps a foot in the air and wheels around as if he might kill her any minute. "Don't you ever sneak up on me. I thought you knew better than that."

"I'm sorry," Josie says. "I just wanted to surprise you." Sometimes she forgets that since Clarence came back from Vietnam he hasn't liked surprises, especially physical surprises. "What're you working on?" she asks.

"A TV," Clarence says.

"I mean what's wrong with it?" Because Clarence doesn't seem to be interested in very much other than his work, Josie occasionally tries to show an interest, but she usually fades out after about five minutes.

"Well, you see, it's this right here. Look at this schematic." He holds up a paper with a bunch of squiggly lines and points to one.

Josie feels herself drifting.

Noticing her glazed expression, Clarence says, "You wouldn't understand, I don't reckon."

"Why don't we go out to the truck stop and get a hamburger?" Josie offers. "I'm kinda hungry."

Clarence smiles at her. "What's the matter with you? You never wanta go anywhere around here. I figured you was ashamed to be seen with me."

"Yeah, right," Josie says, grinning. "You're so ugly and all. I don't know if I oughta risk it, but I guess I'll make a exception just this one time."

At a corner booth in the Pick Truck Stop a few minutes later, they eat French fries, scarf down hamburgers, and drink milkshakes. Located a mile outside of town, the Pick Truck Stop is a favorite hangout for teenagers and adults alike. Sometimes truck drivers actually stop at the place, too, but today only a few hangers-on are passing time.

"Seems like you're in a awful good mood today," Clarence says to her.

"I am," Josie says. She stares at the waitress, Suzy Jennings, who is bustling toward the corner booth, carrying two trays on one arm.

Even if there are only two or three customers in the place, Suzy always acts as if she's working a noontime rush. "I've got a whole new outlook on life."

"What do you mean?"

"Never mind. You'd prob'ly think I was talking foolish."

Clarence takes a long drink from his milkshake, then removes the straw and sucks at it from the other end. "Do you like bird feeders?" he asks.

Josie looks confused. "Bird feeders?"

"I ordered us one," Clarence says. "It was in today's mail. I figured I'd put it right next to the front porch where we can watch the birds this spring. It looks like a castle. Real pretty."

"Why didn't you show it to me?"

"It's still in the box. I'll have to assemble it."

"Well, I bet it's pretty. Sounds like it anyway."

When they finish with the burgers, Josie drops Clarence off at his shop and begins the drive home. That was kinda nice, she thinks. Maybe I ought not give up on Clarence yet. About a mile out of town it starts to snow, slowly at first, then it peppers down as though someone had grabbed hold of a big shaker and started dusting.

8

Although many of Pick's citizens subscribe to the local paper, very few read it carefully unless a county election is near or there has been a murder in the vicinity. Most scan through it quickly, looking mainly at the obituary column or for sales at local stores, relying on TV, the *Lexington Herald Reader,* or the *Louisville Courier Journal* for the bulk of the news. Still, some of the more inquisitive citizens read the *Pick Times* religiously. Sarah Reese, mother of the postmaster, Myrtle Reese, reads every word in each issue, and she was one of the first to notice the small ad located at the bottom of page 3 in Friday's paper. She called Myrtle about it right away.

"Yeah, all right, I'll check it out," Myrtle said grumpily on the phone. It had been snowing for two days, and this morning she couldn't get her car started and had to bum a ride to the post office from sorry old Lindsay Burns, who kept asking her for a date. Myrtle hung up the phone and dragged a copy of the paper from a shelf under the counter. Finding the ad on page 3, she read it, rubbed her eyes, and read it again. "What the hell is this?" she asked, still staring at the print. She read it several times before it dawned on her what to do. "P. O. Box 556?" she spoke, coyly. "Well, we'll just see about that." She went to her file cabinet and began searching through her records to see who the box belonged to. Myrtle had thought it would turn out to be a man for sure, some worthless man who had gone off the deep end. Maybe it was Lindsay Burns. He seemed like a good candidate. Or maybe it was that wild-assed Gilman Lee, who ran a machine shop outside of town—yeah, it was prob'ly him, Myrtle thought.

When she discovered the name of the true owner, that it was Josie Tolliver of all people, she was thrown for a loop. Josie had always seemed like such a nice person, and Clarence too. What were they doing up there on that hill? she wondered. She tried to imagine it, but the visuals were too disturbing. Were Josie and Clarence swingers? Myrtle had read about swingers, knew all about them. Was Josie trying to drum up some women for Clarence, using the name of Don Juan to lure them? Myrtle knew all about Don Juan, too. Everyone knew about the famous Latin lover. *Come Learn with Don Juan*, my ass, Myrtle thought.

Gossip about the ad would have spread more quickly if not for the debilitating snow that continued to fall steadily for a week. Due to downed lines, phone service was sporadic, power lines were down for days, and throughout the county people had a hard time navigating the icy roads. Still, word about the strange plea in the Friday paper caused a stir among Pick's more news-conscious citizens, and theories began to fly as to who exactly it was that paid for the thing to be run. Harold Jacobs received numerous inquiries, but for the time being he has remained silent, telling people the ad was mailed in anonymously. Harold prefers to wait and see what will happen, and he has an idea that something will.

At first Myrtle Reese was ready and willing to set people straight, but when the letters started piling in, addressed to Josie's P.O. box, she decided to hold off. By the second Friday of the ad's run, more than twenty letters had arrived for Josie—all of them with return addresses but missing the senders' names. Myrtle went through her records again to see who would respond to such an ad. It was amazing what she found—no one would have believed in a million years the identities of the women who answered.

Josie got the flu at the same time it started snowing, and she didn't feel like moving, let alone driving to town to check her P.O. box. She saw the advertisement, though, having asked Clarence to pick her up a copy of the paper the day it first appeared. When he brought it to her that Friday evening, she fumbled through the copy frantically until she saw her own words staring up at her; then a smile spread from ear to ear.

From the opposite side of the room, Clarence watched her uneasily. Bernard Boggs had told him about the Don Juan ad that morning, but he'd said it meant the lover, Don Juan. That's what everyone thought, and Clarence wanted so much to believe his wife wasn't involved, he'd convinced himself people were right, that the whole newspaper incident had nothing to do with Josie's don Juan— with don Juan, the weird Mexican sorcerer. But if that were true, why had she made him promise to bring her a copy of the *Pick Times*? Why was she sitting there right now wearing a shit-eating grin even though she had the flu so bad she could hardly breathe? Part of him wanted to know the truth and part of him didn't. He hadn't looked at the paper yet and had even zoned out when Bernard read the ad to him word for word that morning. Clarence saw it like this: most troubles were easy to face, others were a challenge, but there were some troubles so big and harsh and ugly that the best you could do was close your eyes and hope they went away. Even so, Clarence's eyes fluttered open, and he glanced in Josie's direction. Her smile was unsettling.

"What're you reading?" he asked her, casually.

"Oh, nothing."

He decided to push the envelope. "Is they a funny ad in there somewhere?"

Josie started coughing uncontrollably. "What do you mean?"

Clarence yawned. "I just heard some people at the truck stop talking about a weird ad in the paper."

"Did they say what it was?"

"I was in a hurry to get back to the shop. Didn't get the details."

Josie sighed with relief. "Well, I don't see nothing funny in here." She had been worried to death that Harold Jacobs at the newspaper would go blabbing all over town, or that Myrtle, the postmaster, would see the ad, recognize the P.O. box, and spill her guts, but obviously they had somehow managed to keep their mouths shut.

Clarence smiled at Josie and said, "Well, they prob'ly didn't know what they was talking about anyway." He got up and walked outside, unzipped his pants, and peed.

Today Josie is feeling better. She puts on her coat, scarf, and gloves and drives the icy road to town. A few minutes later she's standing in the post office staring at her open mail box crammed full of letters. Myrtle, the postmaster, walks from behind the counter and says, "Josie, is that you? I never seen so much mail come to one person."

"Yeah, it's something, ain't it?"

While Josie is piling her mail together, Myrtle shuffles her feet and looks down at the floor, trying to think of how diplomatically to broach the subject at hand. Then she throws caution to the wind, puts her hands on her hips, and says, "I seen the ad, Josie. What're you trying to pull?"

Josie stares straight into her eyes. "I ain't trying to pull nothing. It's just a experiment. You ain't goin to tell, are you?"

"I've had to bite my tongue for more than a week to keep from it."

Josie keeps staring at Myrtle, trying to think of a story the woman will believe. Finally she comes up with: "You didn't know I was taking a class, did you, Myrtle? Yeah, I'm goin over there to Hazard to that community college. The ad in the paper? Well, it's goin to count as my final grade. I'm majoring in sociology. I was assigned to do that ad. It's to find out how normal people react to a odd situation, and then I'm supposed to write a report on it. Nobody is goin to get hurt. All that's goin to happen is I'll get a good grade. My dream is to become a teacher, Myrtle. I want to mold young minds."

"Sounds like you're pulling a trick on people if you ask me," Myrtle says, frowning. "What kind of class would ask someone to do that? When did you start goin to school? How come I didn't know nothing about it?"

"No one knows about it, not even Clarence. I want to surprise him someday real soon with my diploma." Oh, God, this is working out perfectly, Josie thinks. "You remember the other day when I said not to tell Clarence about the box because I wanted to surprise him? Well, this is what I meant. You've got to believe me. I'm just following my teacher's instructions."

Myrtle squints her eyes. "Well, I reckon it's all right, but what're you goin to do with all them letters?"

Josie smiles. "I'm goin to answer them. I'm goin to instruct everyone to meet me somewhere, you know, without telling them who I am, and then I'm goin to show up there and invite everyone up to my house for Cokes and cookies. They'll prob'ly be surprised to death."

Myrtle grins, thinking of the various women who might show up. "I bet they will," she says.

"You're not goin to let out my secret, are you?"

"I reckon not."

As Myrtle walks away, Josie stares at the letters, amazed and proud that so many people have written her back. Unable to wait another minute, she opens the top one. All it says is, yes. When she arrives home a little later, she opens every one of them, and they all say the same thing. "Yes," they say. "Yes, yes, yes."

It's February 15, the hour of reckoning. Several days ago, Josie wrote everyone and told them they could meet their instructor at ten o'clock in the morning near the double-trunked poplar tree a mile down the river at the wide spot in the road. She chose that particular location because of its close proximity to her house, which is just across the road and up the mountain. "You know the place," she said in her letters. And she was right—people knew. That particular site was where almost everyone in Burr County, at one time or another, had parked their cars late at night to make out with their love interests of the moment. Many a young boy had driven away from that wide spot a man, and many a young girl had driven away pregnant.

The minute Clarence leaves for work this morning, Josie begins making arrangements for the guests she'll be receiving later. On the coffee table she arranges all the Castaneda books she's acquired to date: *The Teachings of Don Juan: A Yaqui Way of Knowledge; A Separate Reality: Further Conversations with Don Juan; Journey to Ixtlan: The Lessons of Don Juan;* and *Tales of Power.* She doesn't have enough chairs to seat her guests if all who responded actually come, so she figures she'll just ask them to look around the room, find a spot on the floor that suits them, and sit. It'll be their first introduction to the ways of a warrior.

Josie will be serving hot Lipton tea. It's the most exotic drink she could find at the grocery store in Pick. She also picked up a large jar of olives, a couple boxes of Ritz crackers, a jar of Cheez Whiz, several cans of sardines, two packages of Oreo cookies, and Cokes for those who might not like tea. She bought a whole box of candles and borrowed a couple of kerosene lamps from her mother-in-law, Ida, to give the living room an eerie glow. "What on earth do ye want these old lamps for?" Ida had asked. "For reading," Josie had answered. "I want to know how Abraham Lincoln felt as a child when he read a book."

By nine-thirty, Josie figures she's as prepared as she'll ever be and walks down the mountain to wait by the poplar tree in case some of the guests arrive early. When she gets to the location, she decides to climb the tree and hide herself behind one of the larger branches, figuring she'll wait until several guests show up before she makes herself known. No one arrives early, and it is ten-fifteen when a car finally drives past her, goes up the road a piece, then drives slowly back.

Josie cranes her neck to see the identity of the driver, but the woman is wearing a scarf and a dark pair of glasses. Josie isn't positive she recognizes the car, either, although it is a new rust-colored Camaro very similar to the one Darrell and Cathy Fieldstone just bought. The Camaro hesitantly pulls to the side of the road, and the driver gets out, walks up to the tree, and leans against it. Josie looks down through the tree branches at the woman. "Cathy?" Josie whispers down at her. "Is that you?"

Cathy Fieldstone looks up at Josie and screams, then runs down the bank, disappearing along the edge of the river just as a Ford pickup slows down and stops. Louise Partridge, one of Burr County's best cheerleaders back in 1965, gets out of the truck, walks over to the Camaro, and peeps inside it. That's when Josie decides to come down out of the tree. She walks up behind Louise and taps her on the shoulder. Louise wheels around in an instant. "Josie? What're you doing here?"

"I . . . ah . . . ," Josie manages to grunt.

Louise laughs. "You don't have to say another word. I know why you're here. It's because of that ad, right?"

"Yeah, but . . ."

"Well, I'm just here to find out what it's about," Louise says. "I mean . . . I ain't here because I'm interested in it. It's just that . . ." She looks back at the Camaro. "This is Cathy Fieldstone's new car, ain't it?"

"Looks like it," Josie says. "She took off running when she seen me."

Just then three more cars pull up, and in her take-charge manner, Louise greets the newcomers who say they came out of curiosity too. Within half an hour, four more cars have arrived, and the latest ones are having a hard time finding a place to park. Even Harold Jacobs from the newspaper shows up, and Myrtle Reese from the post office.

Milling around, eyeing her guests, who—with the exception of Harold and Myrtle—don't know she's their host, Josie decides that she's never seen so much makeup and coiffed hair in her life. Why are they so dressed up? she wonders. Some of the more socially active women in Pick are here: Bea Patterson from the beauty shop, Delia Turner from the flower shop, and Marcy Little from the bank, and they're all saying they just came to see who made a fool out of themselves by putting that ad in the paper. When the women get bored of talking about that, they begin sharing recipes, griping about the cost of gasoline, talking about how they keep having to buy school clothes for their growing children. It's as if they've all been invited to a big PTA meeting. These people would never be interested in don Juan, Josie thinks. How could I ever have thought that they would be?

Harold Jacobs sidles up to her. "Ain't you goin to tell them you're the one who asked them to come out here?"

"I was just waiting to see if anyone else would show up," Josie says nervously. She's pretty sure now that this wasn't a good idea.

"Well, they's prob'ly about ten or eleven here, and it's been quite awhile since the last one come. This is prob'ly all they'll be," Harold says.

"I guess you're right," Josie mutters. She walks up to the poplar tree, positions her fingers on her lips, and lets out a screaming whistle. Everyone stops talking and turns around to look at her.

"Hello," Josie says loudly. "I'm the one who asked you fellers to come out here."

Gasps and wild mutterings run through the group. People turn to each other with expressions of disbelief, then they look at Josie and shake their heads. Myrtle Reese turns to Bea Patterson from the beauty shop and says, "She's just taking a class at the college in Hazard and this is goin to count as her final grade. That's all this is. She's majoring in sociology."

"Class?" Bea says. "She ain't taking no class. My Carol is goin over there. She'd have told me if Josie was goin. Besides, the semester got over in December. They won't be another final till June."

Myrtle harrumphs and looks off to the side. She hates it when to all appearances Bea is right about something and she's wrong.

"Are you Don Juan?" Bea yells out.

Everyone cackles.

"No," Josie answers. "But I wanted to share with you what I've learned from him."

Louise Partridge emits a thundering laugh as she looks around at the others. "What did he teach you?"

"Well, I'm afraid I've not learned much, but I thought if we could all learn together we might get somewhere."

Myrtle Reese turns to Bea Patterson. "Reckon she's trying to get us to join a orgy? I got a idy her and Clarence are swingers."

"I doubt that," Bea says. "She ain't got enough gumption to be a swinger."

Suzy Jennings, the waitress from the Pick Truck Stop, shouts, "What Don Juan're you talking about? They's a lot of Don Juans around here, least they think they are."

Everyone breaks up.

A look of confusion sweeps over Josie's face as she looks out at the heavily made-up faces of her audience. It finally hits her that they think she's talking about Don Juan, the lover. "The don Juan I'm talking about is a philosopher of sorts," she says. "He's in Mexico right now, I reckon. But that's all right because Carlos Castaneda wrote a lot of books about him, and that's what I want to talk to you about. I'd like any of you who are interested to come to my house so we can read the books together."

"A Mexican?" Myrtle Reese asks. "What does he do?"

Josie looks up the hill toward her house, wishing she was there right now. "He teaches people how to dream, how to fly," she says.

"I already know how to dream," Bea retorts.

Suzy, the waitress asks, "You mean he's a pilot?"

"Yeah," Josie says. "He's a kind of pilot. He's a pilot of the mind, I guess you'd say."

Louise Partridge says, "Shee-it," and walks to her pickup and drives off. Bea Patterson leaves too, but the others just stand there looking at Josie. The expressions on their faces reveal a variety of emotions, including anger and betrayal mixed with a whiff of fear.

Josie glances down the river bank and sees Cathy Fieldstone standing there. Her sunglasses are off now, and she has a big smile on her face. Josie starts walking across the road, and says, "If anyone wants to come, they can." She never looks back as she climbs the hill toward her house.

It is a group of eight who finally gather in Josie Tolliver's small but cozy living room, with its hardwood floors and early American furniture. Harold Jacobs and Myrtle Reese are among them, and Suzy Jennings and Cathy Fieldstone showed up too. Myrtle Reese spreads a Ritz cracker with Cheez Whiz and says, "Now what's this all about?"

"You fellers can sit down if you want to," Josie says.

"I'd just as soon stand," Myrtle replies.

"It might be more fun if you sat," Josie continues. "Don Juan says everyone has a spot that is just right for them, a spot they can draw power from. It'll prob'ly be on the floor somewhere. I don't have enough chairs anyway. The first thing let's do is find our spots. Look around and sit wherever it *feels* right to sit."

Harold Jacobs, who has kept pretty quiet until now, says, "Josie, they ain't none of us about to look around on the floor for no spot. You've got to tell us what this is about first."

Josie smiles. "I ain't goin to tell nobody nothing until everyone here has found their spot, so if I was you I'd start looking."

Millie Baker stares suspiciously at the books on the coffee table. Then she puts her hands on her hips and says, "That's it. I'm goin home. I got too much work to do to hang around here acting foolish." She glares at Josie. "You've lost a marble or two if you ask me." Then she walks out the door, leaving the group at seven.

Myrtle Reese, whose curiosity is as peaked as it ever was, sighs and casts her eyes to the floor, then hunkers down and sits. "This right here feels fine to me," she says. Soon the others follow suit, except for Harold, who defiantly plops down on the couch. Josie draws the drapes and lights the candles and kerosene lamps. She moves to her favorite spot in the corner of the room and sits down.

"Okay," Myrtle says. "Wade right into it, Josie. Tell us about this don Juan."

"Don Juan is a Yaqui Indian from Mexico," Josie begins. "He can make the most ordinary things seem like the most exciting things in the world. Don Juan teaches us how to control dreams, how to go inside our dreams and stay there till they become real."

"Wait a minute," Suzy Jennings says. "Are you talking about dreams, you know, like the dreams you have of doing something someday? Or do you mean the dreams you have when you go to sleep?"

Josie smiles. "Both, I guess, except mostly it's the dreams you have when you sleep. Did you ever have a dream that felt so real you thought it had really happened even after you woke up?"

"Yeah," Myrtle Reese says. One hot night last summer she dreamed that Leonard Burns crawled into her bedroom window and made love to her, and that she—Oh, God—that she enjoyed it. When she woke she felt all flushed and rested until she remembered that it was Leonard who'd made her feel that way. She checked the window beside her bed and it was open. What if it really happened? she thought. He lived next door to her so she saw him all the time out in his yard. How would she ever be able to speak to Leonard again? For months she couldn't look him in the eye.

"Well, that's what I'm talking about," Josie said. "The dream world is just as important as this world, maybe more important. That's kind of what don Juan says. Now, does this sound like something you fellers would be interested in learning?"

Harold nods an affirmative, although he isn't really interested except to see how far Josie will go. Betty James and Cindy Halpern, both of whom went to high school with Josie, get up and leave. Myrtle Reese, Suzy Jennings, Cathy Fieldstone, and a woman named Velma Wallace, who has been quiet as a mouse all day, decide to tough it out along with Harold.

"All right," Josie says. "I guess I ought to just start reading. Reckon I'll start with *A Separate Reality: Further Conversations with Don Juan*. I don't think it matters which one you begin with. Separate realities are what I'm interested in the most." She starts reading, and it goes pretty well—her group takes the strangeness in stride—until she gets to the first mention of peyote. Then everything breaks down in a hurry.

Harold jumps to his feet. "I knew it. I knew that somewhere down the line we'd find out this had to do with drugs. Josie, you're stupid for getting yourself into something like this. What was you goin to do? Give us drugs? Maybe you already have. What was in that tea? I bet you a dollar something was in it."

Myrtle Reese starts gargling as if she's trying to get something to come up. Suzy Jennings stands and grabs her purse. "Josie, you ought not to be messing with that stuff. My first cousin took it once, and now all he does is sit in a chair and rock back and forth. I have to go. Oughta be at home by now anyway. Gotta work the second shift."

"I can't believe you'd do me this a way," Myrtle says. "I've always been good to you, always been friendly."

Josie sighs. "This is not about drugs. Don Juan gave Carlos drugs because at the time Carlos couldn't get himself into the right mood without them. I didn't give anyone drugs. I don't have a drug on this place except some aspirin."

"That's what you say," Harold shouts, and he storms out of the house with Myrtle and Suzy right behind him.

Josie turns to Cathy and Velma. "I guess you fellers want to go, too."

"Not really," Cathy says. "I'd kinda like to know more about it."

"Me too," Velma agrees.

"Well, all right then." Josie sits down and continues reading. Cathy and Velma seem enthralled as Josie reads chapter after chapter, but finally her voice starts to crack, and she says, "I reckon we ought to take this up a little later. It won't be long before Clarence gets home. Do you fellers want to do this again? You could come tomorrow at the same time, ten o'clock, if you want."

"I would," Cathy says.

"Me too," Velma agrees.

Later, Josie watches them walk down the hill. Two out of the whole bunch, she thinks, only two people brave enough to sink inside their dreams.

9

By five o'clock in the evening the news is all over town. Bea Patterson and Louise Partridge were the first to spread the rumors. Then when Harold Jacobs and Myrtle Reese left Josie's house, they gave an update, and it wasn't a pretty addition. What the stories amount to are that Josie is mixed up in some pretty strange doings, involving witchcraft, drugs, and Mexicans. Since a few gossips have been unable to abandon their original belief that *Don Juan* refers to the famous Latin lover, a mysterious womanizer remains in some of the versions.

Brewster found out about it from Ed Gibbs, who from his perch on the courthouse steps always hears everything. Brewster sits on the couch, staring at the telephone, knowing he should simply call Josie and find out the true story. Not once has she ever given him trouble, not even in her teenage years. Now, if it had been Cheyenne they were talking about, if it was Cheyenne . . . But Josie? No, she wouldn't mess around with something like witchcraft.

"Hello, Josie," he says, after finally dialing her number.

"Is that you, Daddy?" Josie is walking toward the kitchen, carrying the phone, hoping the cord doesn't become disconnected this time. She's frying pork chops, cooking green beans and mashed potatoes. Clarence will be home from work any minute.

"Yeah." Brewster doesn't say anything else. He can't.

"How're you doing?" Josie asks, noticing a strange quality to his voice. "You ain't sick, are you?"

"No."

Josie flips her pork chops, listening to the silence on the other end of the line. "Something wrong, Daddy?" She's becoming alarmed.

"You don't believe in witchcraft, do you? Have you been taking drugs?"

Uh-oh, Josie thinks. "No."

"People're saying you have."

"People don't know what they're talking about." Josie sighs and tells him the whole story. "I don't have any peyote. I don't even know what it looks like. I've heard it looks like buttons."

Brewster laughs. "When're we goin to Arizona?" he asks.

"In the spring, Daddy. I've told you and told you."

When they hang up, Brewster stretches out on the couch and props his feet on the arm. I should have told her about that call from the California doctor, he thinks. God, I wish he'd call again. I'd get the facts straight this time. I wouldn't be so absentminded.

Josie walks back to the living room and hangs up the phone. It's all over town, she thinks. No telling what they're saying. Clarence has no doubt heard about it, too. She looks out the window and sees him driving his Nova up the steep hill. "Lord," she says out loud. "I dread what's coming." She returns to the kitchen and sets the table, takes her pork chops and vegetables off the stove, plops down in a dinette chair, and waits.

Clarence comes in and goes to the bathroom. She hears him flush the commode and wash his hands, hears his footsteps coming through the living room. He doesn't look at her when he enters the kitchen. He just sits down, cuts up a pork chop, and begins to chew.

"How did your day go?" Josie asks, figuring she may as well get the argument going.

"All right," Clarence says.

"That's good," Josie comments.

Clarence continues to eat, and he still isn't looking at her.

"I had a pretty good day, too," Josie says.

"Is that so?"

"Yeah, I invited some people up here. We had a little reading session."

"Well, how about that," Clarence says.

"We read about don Juan," Josie says.

"Really?"

"Yeah, it went pretty good."

"That's nice," Clarence says.

He finishes eating, gets up, and leaves the room. Josie hears him go outside to pee then come back in, hears him go into their bedroom and close the door. A few minutes later she opens the bedroom door a crack and finds him in bed, lying flat on his back pretending to be asleep. That's it then, she thinks. He's pulling his martyr act. Well, I'm not goin to let him get away with it. She walks over and shakes his shoulder until he finally opens his eyes. "People are saying some pretty bad things about me," Josie says. "I guess they misunderstood the books."

Veins pop out on Clarence's face. "I don't want to talk about it," he yells. "I don't want to hear another word. Now get outta here and leave me alone." He pulls the cover up to his chin and rolls over on his stomach.

"We ought to talk about this," Josie says.

"Shut up!" Clarence shouts.

Josie decides to let him stew. She goes into the living room and tries to read but finds she can't concentrate. Finally she gives up and goes to sleep herself.

The next morning things aren't any better. Clarence takes off for work without uttering a word. I wonder how long he'll hold out, Josie thinks. She's washing the breakfast dishes when she gets the first phone call. It's from Cathy Fieldstone, who says she won't be able to make the reading after all. Something came up that she'd rather not talk about. A few minutes later Josie gets a call from Velma Wallace, who says she has the stomach flu so bad she can't do anything but stand by the commode turning around and around, first puking and then the other. It's a good story, but Josie doesn't believe her.

She's running the vacuum when Silas Horn, a Pentecostal preacher, dials in to say that she will burn in the everlasting fires of hell for eternity. "It's these drugs," he shouts. "All of our young people are ruining their minds with marijuana. That's to be expected. Young'uns always ruin their minds with something. If it ain't liquor or drugs, it's something else, but to have someone like you, a grown woman with a husband that runs a business right in town, to not only be taking drugs but to be teaching the word of the devil, too, is . . . it's a abomination to the Lord."

"Yeah?" Josie says. "Well, I went to school with Sally Peters, and she told me that you used to take out your pecker and make her hold it. How about that, Mr. High-and-Mighty?"

"Sally Peters is a liar, and she'll rot in Hell," Silas shouts.

Josie hangs up.

The next person to call is Ida. "Josie, honey, what is goin on?"

Josie explains to Ida about the books, tells about the ad in the paper, says she put it there because she was so bored she couldn't go another day and have it be the same as the day before—she goes through the whole thing with Ida.

"I'm real worried about Clarence," Ida says. "He won't say a word about it. He gets that way sometimes, you know. I'm worried about how this'll be for his business."

Josie hasn't considered that, yet. It hasn't entered her mind that Clarence's business might suffer. His business is his whole life, she thinks. People wouldn't blame him for something I did, would they?

When Ida hangs up, Josie calls Brewster and says, "Daddy, what am I goin to do?"

"They ain't nothing you can do," he says. "You'll just have to wait till it blows over."

"But what did I do wrong?" she shouts at him. "All I did was try to get people to read."

"People don't like to read," Brewster says.

After that last phone call, Josie goes into her bedroom and lies down. She tries to imagine what Cheyenne would have done in a case like this. Cheyenne wouldn't have let this worry her a bit. She'd have laughed about it. She'd have loved the fact that everyone was talking about her, thinking she'd done the worst thing in the world.

She'd have thought the whole thing was a big joke. Josie lies there, remembering how both she and Cheyenne distinguished themselves at the school they attended when they lived in Arizona.

Before they moved to Sage that summer, the Clays lived in a small trailer in the Oasis Mobile Home Park in Rustle, Arizona. The largest bedroom (Brewster and Dora's) was at one end of the trailer; and at the opposite end, a tiny second bedroom, just large enough for a cot and a chest-of-drawers, had been awarded to Cheyenne. Josie slept on the couch in the living room.

The girls spent as little time as possible in the trailer. When not in school, they could often be found playing in the dry bed of the nearby San Pedro River, or scouring the desert for the entrances to lost gold mines, or hanging out at the drugstore reading movie magazines.

Their school, which accommodated grades one through eight, was situated at the edge of the small desert town. White-faced cattle, their hides dotted with clumps of stickers from cholla cactuses, roamed the open range around the school. Sometimes they even wandered onto the playground, and it was unfortunate that Cheyenne was the playground monitor on one such occasion. The principal of the school always designated two eighth-graders along with one teacher to monitor the playground during the lunch hour. On the day in question, the appointed teacher was at one end of the playground, breaking up a fight, when a cow meandered around the building from the other direction. As usual Cheyenne was in the wrong place at the right time, and the temptation was too great. The cafeteria was filled with grades four through six when she swung open the double doors and prodded the cow inside. The children began to clamor and scream while the cow freaked and started running around the room, knocking over tables and chairs. The first thing Josie thought when she saw the cow was, *Cheyenne*. Then when she glanced out the double doors and saw her sister running like a chased thief, her suspicions were confirmed. It took four teachers to get the situation under control—two to herd the children to the far end of the room, and two to get the cow to settle down enough to be led outside. The questioning began immediately, and Cheyenne was found out. When Dora was informed about it, she came down swift and hard, telling Cheyenne she couldn't leave the house for two weeks except to go to school.

Shortly after that misadventure, all grades—first through eighth—were called to the end-of-the-year awards ceremony held in the battered and abused cafeteria. Josie couldn't believe it when they announced her name. "The Courtesy Award goes to Josie Clay," the principal said. "Josie, please step forward and receive your reward." She didn't move. A *courtesy* award, she thought. Why couldn't I have won an academic award, or a beauty award, or how about a sarcasm award? A courtesy award was the worst thing a person could win. Although Josie and Cheyenne were getting along better since the move to Arizona, Josie dreaded the teasing she was sure she'd get from her that evening. She could just hear Cheyenne saying, "Excuse me, Miss Courtesy, may I sock you in the eye?"

Josie figured Brewster would be happy about the award—he was happy about everything—but she didn't think her mother would appreciate it at all. Dora was always claiming that Josie was too nice for her own good, and now here it was written in black-and-white on a certificate. It was official now. Josie was still speculating on these things when her fifth-grade teacher pushed her up the steps and onto the stage. The whole rest of the day was a blur.

The twelve children who lived in the Oasis Mobile Home Park always walked to and from school together, but that afternoon Josie ran ahead of the whole bunch in an attempt to avoid her sister completely. Not that Cheyenne had ever kidded her in public, but Josie was afraid she might start something new. When she finally got to their trailer, Josie bolted inside, threw her books down, slipped back out the door, and headed for her favorite spot. Not far away, four mesquite trees had grown in a circle, providing a hideout for anyone lucky enough to find it. Often Josie would crawl underneath the trees and play for hours. She'd hidden some treasures there—several turquoise stones, some fool's gold, and a grapefruit-sized geode with a sparkling white-and-purple interior that looked good enough to eat. That evening Josie didn't move from the shade of the trees until she heard her mother calling her to supper.

At the supper table she sat quietly, staring down at her food, avoiding eye contact with Cheyenne. Josie was beginning to think her sister hadn't gone to the awards ceremony, that she'd ditched the entire event, when suddenly Cheyenne said, "Josie, why ain't you told Mommy and Daddy about your award?"

"What award?" Dora asked.

Cheyenne broke into a smile. "Josie won the Courtesy Award, Mommy. I wish you could have seen it. The whole school was there. Josie was picked out of all the grades for being the most courteous."

As Cheyenne talked, Josie listened closely for a hint of sarcasm, but there was none.

"Well, that's something, Josie. Why didn't you tell us?" Dora asked. A hesitant smile spread on her face, suggesting that she thought courtesy and meekness were the same thing.

"It don't surprise me she won the Courtesy Award," Brewster said, beaming. "I've got the most courteous children in the world."

"I couldn't believe it, Mommy," Cheyenne said, obviously impressed. "There she was, wearing that little blue dress, walking up to the stage in front of all them people. I liked to died."

Wondering if she would ever figure out Cheyenne, Josie finally showed her family the certificate. Dora stared at it wordlessly then put it in a picture frame and hung it on the living room wall. Later Cheyenne slipped back to her old attitude—sequestered herself in her small room bedroom and began playing Jerry Lee Lewis records nonstop. When Josie attempted to join her, she yelled, "Get out of here. This is my room!" Josie retreated, wondering why things had to be the way they were, not dreaming that everything was about to change very shortly.

10

It has been three weeks since the advertisement appeared in the paper, and Clarence and Bernard are sitting in the TV repair shop, twiddling their thumbs. Last week they caught up on their workload, and now there is hardly anything to do. They're still getting a few requests from young married couples and teenagers who need their stereos repaired, but the backbone of Clarence's enterprise—the local TV repair business—has come to a screeching halt.

"I ain't never seen nothing like it," Bernard says. "To think that people'd blame a man for something his wife done."

Clarence glares at Bernard. "What did she do?"

"Well, nothing, but they think she done something. It's the same thing."

"No it ain't the same thing." Clarence is pissed off. He has never been this pissed off in his life. He's irritated at Josie for starting the whole thing and at his customers for leaving him high and dry, but more than anything he's irritated at the new nickname he's been tagged with. People are calling him Don Juan. They haven't begun calling him the name to his face yet; they're making the reference when he's out of hearing range. They'll say, "I heard ol' Don Juan didn't get no business today," or "Traffic is slowing. Don Juan must be driving by." Bernard told Clarence all about it. Clarence figures that eventually, when the full force of the scandal is over, people will become more relaxed and start calling him Don Juan right to his face. He realizes that his customers will come back to him, that after a few months they'll get tired of driving the thirty miles to Hazard to get their TVs repaired. But the nickname? The nickname will be with him forever. It ain't fair, Clarence thinks. I hate them all—every one of them.

"We may as well go home," Clarence says to Bernard. "They ain't no point in sitting around here."

They close shop, and Clarence is driving toward home when he suddenly turns the car around and starts driving in the opposite direction. Clarence has never been much of a drinker, but today he feels like tying one on. About five miles out of town, he stops his car in front of Lee's Machine Shop and gets out. Gilman Lee is standing outside talking to some of his cronies. When he sees Clarence, a smile spreads over his face. "Well, hello, Don Juan . . . I mean, Clarence. What are you doing here?"

Clarence glares at Gilman. "I just thought I'd . . . You wouldn't happen to have an extra beer in your refrigerator, would you?"

"Why, sure, ol' buddy."

The men wander inside the apartment in the back of the machine shop, and the drinking and music start up. Clarence was never a person to be wild about music, but he has always known that if he had the need to hear it, Gilman's shop was the place to go. Clarence sits down in a corner, starts drinking, and doesn't stop for three days. He keeps sending passers-by on runs to Hazard for cases of beer. On the evening of the first day, he begins to laugh, wheezing and slapping his knees like a crazy man, and he doesn't stop laughing for three days either, except to pass out periodically. Everything in Gilman Lee's apartment appears funny to Clarence—chairs, musical instruments, walls. People look funny too, their heads seem all elongated, their bodies bowed out in the middle, and they sound as funny as they look—voices shrill and cracking, breath heaving. He wonders why he never realized how funny everything was.

Gilman Lee has been taking Clarence's laughter in stride. He feels sorry for the man, having heard the rumors about drugs and witch-craft and how Clarence's business is failing, but by the third day his generosity is beginning to wear thin. "Clarence, old feller, what's so funny?"

Clarence starts pointing around at everything in sight.

"Yeah," Gilman says. "I agree. It is pretty amusing, but you need to take another approach for a while. They's other ways to look at things, sadder ways."

Ten-Fifteen, a high school boy who comes to the shop every evening after school, could tell Clarence a thing or two about nicknames, having been labeled with his numerical name due to the time-clock position of his deformed arms. Ten-Fifteen doesn't mind his handle, though. After all, Gilman Lee calls him by his nickname, and Gilman told Ten-Fifteen that if he would graduate from high school, he'd hire him as a mechanic in the shop. "What's the matter with him, Gilman?" he asks.

"Your guess is as good as mine," Gilman says, "but I think it's high time I called Josie, don't you? I mean we gotta get this laughing fool out of here." Gilman gets on the phone. "Hello, Josie? In case you're wondering where Clarence is, he's up here at my shop, been here three days." Gilman looks around at Clarence and continues talking. "I believe he needs you. Could you come up here and get him?"

Josie arrives at the shop fifteen minutes later. "I knew he was here. Joe Carter told me. I guess I figured this was the best place for him right now."

Gilman smiles. "I heard about your problems. You fellers ought not to pay attention to what people say. I don't listen to a word people say about me."

"Well, good for you," Josie says.

Clarence is still laughing maniacally.

"Josie looks like she's been crying for three days," Ten-Fifteen whispers to Gilman. "One laughing and one crying."

Gilman shakes his head.

Frightened by Clarence's strange behavior, Josie hauls off and slaps his face. "Snap out of it," she yells.

He recoils, stops laughing, and sags deeper into his chair.

She grabs his arm and pulls him to his feet. "Come on! We're goin home."

"Good luck with everything," Gilman says.

Josie smiles as she turns back to look at Gilman. "Thank you for your trouble. I'll bring Clarence up here tomorrow to pick up his car."

Clarence doesn't say a word as they're driving home, and when they walk inside the house, he staggers to the bedroom and passes out.

Josie stands in the doorway, staring at her sleeping husband. The post-ad weeks have been an awful time for her in more ways than one. It's not that people have been harassing her relentlessly. Actually she's received some fan calls from a few high school students, who want to know what kind of drugs she's doing. They're afraid she isn't taking the best kind, and they'd like to clue her in.

Some people have called her to say they completely understand the boat she's in, that they've been in the same one. Barbara Shaffer, a former pianist for the Starling Creek Baptist Church, who got pregnant by a married man and has never lived it down, was one of those callers. Sadie Williams was another. Sadie has been living—minus the benefit of marriage—with Ben Perkins, who just go out of prison. Quite a few of Pick's citizens, however, have been shunning Josie. She goes to town and they glare at her, turning their heads when she tries to speak. She no longer tries.

Yesterday she was walking down the street when she glanced into the beauty shop window and saw Bea Patterson and Louise Partridge pointing at her and talking, their expressions revealing the utmost disgust. Josie stopped dead still. Assholes, she thought as she stood there staring back at them. Stomp idiots. Then suddenly she lost it and stepped inside the shop, waving her arms and chanting like a witch casting a spell, "May your little raisin brains shrivel into specks, but more important than that, MAY YOU NEVER AGAIN GET FUCKED."

I can't believe I did that, Josie thinks as she stands at the bedroom door, peeping in at Clarence. He looks like a little boy who's had all his toys snatched from him by heathens. I've ruined him, she realizes. I've single-handedly ruined his life. She sits down in a chair by the bed and begins rereading *Tales of Power*.

* * *

When Clarence wakes the next morning, he's a changed man. "We're leaving," he tells Josie. "We're goin to Arizona."

Josie's mouth drops open in disbelief.

"You heard me right," Clarence says.

"Arizona? You mean Sage?"

"Yeah, goddamn it. Sage."

"When?"

"As soon as I can get rid of my TV business. I'm figuring on selling it to Bernard."

"Can Bernard afford to buy it?"

"No, but I'm selling it to him anyway. He can pay me what he can, you know, pay me by the month whatever he can."

Josie looks closely at Clarence. "I guess you hate me, don't you? I guess you blame me for everything."

Clarence sighs. "I don't hate anyone. I just want to get out of here. I never wanted anything so much in my life."

They have breakfast, drink coffee, and talk about travel routes. After about an hour, Clarence is even beginning to act excited about going.

"I really think you'll like it, Clarence," Josie says. "It'll be different. The scenery is just so different."

"It'll prob'ly be all right," Clarence says.

Josie looks away from him. So far, in all of their arguments about Arizona, she hasn't brought up the fact that she wants Brewster to go with them. She figured it wasn't important since Clarence would never agree to go anyway, but now things have changed. "What would you say about Daddy goin with us?" Josie asks.

Clarence looks amazed. "What?"

"I can't leave Daddy here. He's not in very good shape. I just can't leave him."

Clarence sets down his coffee cup and speaks calmly: "How about we bring Mom along too? As a matter of fact, why don't we bring all our relatives? We could invite everyone in town. I've got it. Why don't we put a ad in the paper?"

Even though Clarence looks calm, Josie knows he isn't because she can see those little muscles or joints (or whatever they are) working in his jaw. "Ida is as healthy as a bear," Josie says. "Daddy's sick."

Clarence stands up. "All the more reason not to take him with us. We don't even know what to expect when we get there. I don't have a job, a place to live, nothing. We can't take Brewster with us under them circumstances. What's wrong with you?"

"But he wants to go," Josie says.

"You mean you've talked to him about it? Lordy mercy."

"I just asked him if he wanted to go."

"You asked him?" The little muscles in Clarence's jaw are having spasms. "Josie, you can only push a man so far, and I've been pushed as far as I'll go. Do you hear me? I'm not about to take poor old Brewster out into the hot desert without a tree for shade. I'm not doing it, and you can get that through your head right now. You've got to be sensible about this."

Sensible? It crosses Josie's mind that Clarence loves that word as much as she hates it, and that he isn't about to take Brewster with them. "What about when we get settled? Could we send for him?"

"First things first," Clarence says.

It is the last week of March, and the wind is blowing in jumps and starts. Josie puts on her jacket and drives to Brewster's, but he isn't home. Where is he? she wonders. She sits down on the couch and starts watching the soaps, thinking he'll be back home in a minute, but he doesn't come. Finally, she gets up and starts rummaging through some old picture albums. There's Dora and Brewster when they were young, standing by a sign that says "Welcome to Idaho." Josie has forgotten how much taller her mother was than her father—stately and slender, she towered over his dark, stocky frame. And there's Josie and Cheyenne sitting in front of a Christmas tree in their old house in Pick, Cheyenne frowning near a new bicycle, and Josie laughing hysterically by a checkerboard. It wasn't always that way, Josie thinks. Cheyenne wasn't always in a bad mood, but she was at her worst on national or religious holidays. She seemed to hate designated days when the country, sometimes the whole world, said you were supposed to have fun.

There's a picture of Brewster and Dora on their wedding day. They're standing in a photographer's studio somewhere in California looking scared to death. God, I hope she loved him, Josie thinks. I hope she loved him more than anything in the world.

Josie is still sitting there, going through the album, when Brewster walks in. "Where've you been, Daddy?" she asks.

"I was down at the courthouse sitting around with Ed Gibbs," Brewster says. "I seen you drive by. Waved and hollered and everything, but you didn't see me, I don't reckon."

"I've just been looking at some of these pictures," Josie says.

Brewster goes to the refrigerator and gets a couple of beers. He hands her one and plops down on the couch.

"What was Mommy like?" Josie asks. "I mean, I know some of what she was like. Remember when I was real little and got hurt or upset about something? How I'd start crying out of control? She used to get me up in her lap and brush my hair. She'd just sit there, hum a tune, and brush my hair till I got all right." Josie stops talking for a minute, trying to recall the touch of her mother's hands. "But you know, I was just eleven when she died. Sometimes I feel like I never knew her at all. What she was really like?" Although Josie has heard Brewster tell his Dora stories many times, she never tires of hearing them.

Brewster takes a drink and smiles. "She was a firecracker, your mommy. One time we was walking down the streets of Dayton, Ohio, goin to a movie. She was wearing a real pretty dress and had on a new pair of suede high heels she'd just bought that day. I didn't like her to wear high heels cause they made her look so much taller than me, but every now and then she'd wear 'em. Anyway all at once one of the heels broke off, and it almost caused her to trip. She reached down and picked up the heel and just stared at it. I said, 'That's all right, Dora. I can glue it back when we get home.' But she kicked both shoes off and throwed them as far as she could send them—and us standing right in the middle of Dayton, Ohio. I asked her if she wanted to go home, but she said no, and then marched straight into that movie theatre barefooted. That's what your mommy was like. She was a firecracker."

"Kind of like Cheyenne?"

"Kind of. They could both change their moods pretty fast, you know, happy one minute and yelling and screaming the next." I ought to tell her right now about that doctor calling, he realizes.

Josie looks at Brewster, dreading what she has to say. "Daddy, I was just thinking that if I really did go to Arizona, it might be a good idea if you didn't go at first. I mean, I prob'ly ought to get settled in first. I don't even know where I'll be staying yet, and . . ."

Brewster stares straight ahead. "Did Clarence finally decide to go?"

"Yeah."

Brewster doesn't say anything.

"I mean it would be a pretty long trip, and it's so hot out there and everything. As soon as we get settled in, I'll send for you. You can come out on one of them big 747s. How'd that be? You've never rode on a plane that big, have you?"

"No," he says.

"Well, it'll be something you've never done then."

"I guess so."

"I wish you could go right now, but it would prob'ly be better if we was more sensible about it," Josie says, her voice shaking. "God, I hate being sensible. I hate everything about it."

Brewster gets up and walks over to the chair where Josie is sitting. He puts his arm around her and says, "It's all right, Josie. Besides, what would old Ed Gibbs do if I just up and left real sudden? Me and Ed sit there on the courthouse steps and talk all day sometimes. He's not a bad feller when you get to know him."

"Are you sure it's all right?"

"You're damn right. I don't care a bit. I'll just hang around here, and when you fellers get things straightened out, I'll get on one of them planes."

"I'll call you every weekend. I swear I will."

"Well, that'll be good." I reckon it's too late to tell her about that doctor now, he thinks. She's got too many other things on her mind.

Josie goes to the stove and pops some popcorn, and they spend the rest of the afternoon bent over the picture album, looking at their lives.

Not long before they're to head out, Josie gets an unexpected visit from Cathy Fieldstone.

"Josie," Cathy says, as they're sitting in the living room. "I just wanted to tell you something. I called a book store in Lexington and ordered all the Castaneda books they had. I just finished reading *Tales of Power* last night. His books are really something. I'm glad you turned me on to them."

"Thank you, Cathy."

Cathy grins shyly and pulls a book out of a bag. "I noticed your copy of *Journey to Ixtlan* was getting pretty ragged. I got you a new one." She reaches in her bag and hands it to Josie. "I heard about you fellers moving. I'm sorry to see you go."

"I'm happy about it," Josie says. "I've always wanted to go back out West. Do you believe what's in the books, Cathy? The stuff about the dreaming?"

"I'd like to."

"I would too. Course I don't know nothing for sure. Thank you for bringing me this new copy," she says, staring at the desert scene on the cover.

"See you sometime, I guess," Cathy says, as she walks out the door.

A few days later Ida invites Clarence, Josie, and Brewster to her house for Sunday dinner, which is always served at three-thirty in the afternoon. Ida's two bird feeders are crawling with spring birds, but although she still loves them, the fascination has dimmed. Back in December she started crocheting afghans, and it's afghans that interest her now.

"There ain't nothing'll keep you as warm as an afghan," Ida says.

"On a bad winter night when you're sitting on the couch watching TV, your feet so cold you can't wiggle your toes, pull a afghan over you. Law', it feels so good. They ain't nothing like it."

She drags Clarence, Josie, and Brewster into her bedroom, where there are enough afghans to keep an army warm. "See how pretty they are? I don't like to brag, but I make the prettiest 'uns around here. Other people follow patterns, but I don't need no pattern. I just make up my designs as I go."

Brewster smiles. "That's something, Ida. I ain't never seen none as pretty as this."

Ida scrunches up her face and bats her eyes. Later she sits them down to a table of chicken and dumplings, green beans, mashed potatoes, and collard greens, and when they've filled up on that, she brings out a cherry pie and coffee. "People say I'm the best cook around," Ida says. "I guess they're right."

"They sure are," Brewster says, and Clarence and Josie agree.

Just then a huge woman walks into the house and marches through the living room and into the kitchen.

"Well, hello, Viola," Ida says. "I bet you come over for a piece of my pie, didn't you?"

The woman doesn't say a word as she gets herself a piece of pie and pours a cup of coffee.

"This is my neighbor, Viola Watson," Ida explains. "She just moved here from down on Racer Creek. Did you ever know her, Brewster?"

"No," he says. Glancing up at the woman, he finds her staring directly at him. Staring and chewing. Chewing and staring.

"Viola, do you like the pie?" Ida asks.

Viola doesn't even nod.

"She don't talk much," Ida explains.

When the meal is over, they go into the living room to drink more coffee and talk. "Brewster," Ida says, "did you fellers have to sleep on cornshuck mattresses when you was growing up?"

"Yeah," he says.

"Us too. Hateful old things, wouldn't they? Noisy. You couldn't roll over without making such a racket you'd wake the dead, but them was the good old days, wouldn't they?"

"Yeah, they was." Brewster is beginning to get irritated at that woman, Viola. Her big blue ogling eyes have been on him since she walked through the door.

Ida turns to Clarence and Josie. "You fellers don't understand what we're talking about, but now things has changed. Law', I can't believe how things has changed."

They keep talking about the old days until finally Ida tells Josie they ought to wash the dishes. Viola comes in and sits at the table while they stand by the sink, Ida washing and Josie drying.

"Josie, you fellers be careful out there in that old dry place," Ida says. "I'm worried about y'uns. You don't know what kind of place that is, what kind of quare people are out there. They's real bad people away from here. I see it on the television every day. You take care of Clarence. He's all I've got."

As they leave for home, Ida says, "Clarence, you come by and see me again before you go, and Brewster, it wouldn't hurt you none to come over some time."

"I'll try to do that," Brewster says.

"Well, you see to it."

As Clarence, Josie, and Brewster drive down the hollow, the mountains beside the road are alive with color. Redbuds and dogwoods are in bloom, and tiny green leaves are budding out everywhere. They ride in silence, until finally Josie says, "This sure is a pretty place up here, Clarence. You grew up in a pretty place."

"I know I did," he says. "It's the prettiest holler around."

She can tell by the sound of his voice how upset he is, and when they pass the narrow dirt road that leads to their house, Clarence pulls to the side of the road. "Josie," he says. "Could you drive Brewster on home? I've got the worst headache. Think I'll just get out here."

Josie studies his face closely. "Well, drive on up to the house then. No point in walking."

"No," he says. "Think I'll walk." He gets out of the car, and Josie takes the wheel.

As she drives toward Pick, Brewster says, "Clarence sure don't like this moving business much, does he?"

"No, but I've got a feeling something's out there waiting for Clarence that he needs. I've heard you say that sometimes you don't want to leave the house but that once you're out of doors you're glad about it. I bet Clarence will feel the same way when we get moved."

"I hope you're right," Brewster says. Then the story he's been meaning to tell Josie for months comes tumbling out. "I got the oddest phone call a while ago," he tells her.

"Who from?"

"It was this doctor. He was looking for a patient of his, said her name was Ramona Clay. She'd disappeared on him. He asked me if I had a daughter named Ramona."

"Disappeared?" Josie asks, the wheel of the car swerving in her hand.

"Yeah," Brewster says. "Sounds familiar, don't it? He was from someplace out West, I think. Asked me if I had a daughter living in the West."

Josie feels as if a ghost just sat down beside her in the car. "He didn't say what state, what city?"

"Yeah, but I couldn't understand him. He was talking a mile a minute. You know how them people are."

"What did you tell him?" I knew it, she thinks. I knew she was alive.

"I told him I had you, and that you lived right here. I told him my other daughter was dead. And he hung up . . . hung up, and that was that. Sometimes you get a phone call, and if you ain't right on the tip of your toes, if you ain't thinking clear, ain't ready with a quick answer, you lose out for all time."

Josie is so rattled she passes the service station and has to hit her brakes and back up. "And you ain't got any idea where he was from?"

"Sometimes I think he mentioned California, but that's all, Josie. I've been trying to remember it, but I can't. The only other thing he said was that he'd operated on her. That's all I've been able to remember. Do you think he could have been talking about Cheyenne?"

"How did he get your phone number? Did he say?" They're still sitting in the car, haven't thought to get out.

"I don't remember."

"Well, Daddy, it's got to be her," Josie says, her voice rising with elation. "How else would he have known to call you? I knew she was alive all along." So many thoughts are racing through Josie's mind that she can no longer sit still. She jumps out of the car, and they go inside Brewster's service station. She sits with him for an hour trying to get him to recall other details, but he doesn't come up with any. Finally she drives home, thinking, I'll find out about this as soon as we get moved. I'll call every hospital in California if I have to. The main thing is that Cheyenne is still alive.

They decided to leave Josie's Volkswagen with Ida and to leave their furniture in the house, which they had already rented to some newly-weds. Clarence hitched a U-Haul behind his Chevy Nova last night, and they filled it with the essentials—cookware, bedding, towels, their clothes, books, record albums, and Josie's Gibson guitar. After the car and trailer were loaded, they lay down and tried to go to sleep. Clarence finally managed to doze off, but Josie didn't sleep a wink all night.

This morning they rise early, eat toast and jelly, drink some coffee, and walk out the door. Passing the bird feeder that Clarence put near the front porch at the first hint of spring, Josie says, "Reckon we ought to take it with us?"

"They prob'ly ain't no birds worth feeding in Arizona. It'll be put to better use right here."

They are getting into the car when Josie says, "Wait a minute," and runs back inside the house, remembering what her mother had said about not leaving a place without stopping to think. She looks around at the living room where she played the guitar for hours at a time, where she watched *Perry Mason* until falling into a trance, where she read all manner of books, got hooked on Carlos Castaneda and thought of putting the ad in the paper, where she stood in front of the mirror day after day, pretending to be Shakespeare's tragic female characters. Josie stands there a moment looking around. Suddenly becoming Lady Macbeth, she says, "O, these flaws and starts/(Impostors to true fear) would well become/A woman's story at a winter's fire . . . ."

As they drive through Pick on their way to the great Southwest, Josie sees Myrtle Reese park her car in front of the post office, get out, and go inside. She sees Bea Patterson raise the shade at the front window of her Hair By Bea beauty shop, sees Ed Gibbs sitting on the courthouse steps, looking this way and that. Tears fill her eyes when they pass Brewster's old service station at the edge of town. There's a light on in the garage. He's prob'ly up making himself some coffee, Josie thinks. She turns around and glares at Clarence, hating him for a moment, hating him for being sensible.

Then their car goes around the curve, and Pick is out of sight. It's still back there, though, Josie thinks. It's still back there, and people are goin about their business—they're making coffee, frying eggs, opening up shops—and they'll keep goin about their business even when we're gone. About sixty miles down the road, the sadness begins to dissipate. Taking their road map out of the glove compartment, she looks at the gnarled mass of roads that lie ahead. Then she rolls down the window, sticks her arms out, and yells like Tarzan. "I feel good," she says to Clarence. "Suddenly I feel real good."

PART TWO

Don Juan's Cocktails

11

W hy don't you let me drive a while?" Josie says to Clarence as a car whizzes past them at full speed. The man sitting on the passenger side leans his body halfway out the window and yells, "If you can't drive, get off the fuckin freeway!"

"No, I'll just go on a while longer," Clarence says calmly, and Josie doesn't know if he's talking to her or the man in the other car.

They're on I-40, leaving the city limits of Nashville. It's evening rush hour and the crowded freeway is filled with people who seem angry and desperate to get home. When another car barrels around them, a little boy sitting in the back seat gives Clarence the finger.

"Honey, you're goin to have to go faster. These people are fighting mad," Josie says.

Clarence smiles.

The minute they had turned onto I-40, the whole atmosphere of the road changed. People were definitely not out sightseeing—they were on missions, acting as though they'd just remembered they'd forgotten to unplug their irons that morning.

"We're goin to get killed," Josie says, resigned. "Our young lives cut short. Our dreams unfulfilled. We'll never . . ."

"Shut up," Clarence says, as an eighteen-wheeler bears down on them.

"Maybe we ought to just stop here for the night," Josie says.

"I ain't stopping. I want to make it to Memphis before we stop."

"That's over two hundred miles away. The way you're driving we'll be gray-headed before we get to Memphis."

"Well, I ain't stopping here. We're goin on," Clarence says.

It's eight o'clock that night before Clarence finally gives in and exits the interstate near a small town called Only, Tennessee. "Looks like Only only has one hotel," Josie says as they pull into the parking lot of a small roadside inn.

Clarence grins. "Yeah, I guess only the lonely stays in Only."

Later, in the room, they take showers and get ready for bed with intentions of setting out again at four o'clock the next morning. Clarence crawls into bed first and lies there with his road atlas while Josie checks out the situation, looking into dresser drawers, turning light switches on and off. She's still traipsing around the room when she suddenly feels she's being stared at and wheels around. Clarence is lying there gazing at her with a strange look on his face. A definite bulge is sticking up under the sheet.

Josie stares at the bulge and smiles. "What you got there, Clarence?"

"Just ol' Johnson," he says. But Clarence also has that intense look, his eyes fixated on Josie's body. There isn't a smile on his face or a frown or any expression that is easy to describe, but Josie knows exactly what it means. It means Clarence Tolliver is ready for some.

"Well, I ain't seen that feller in ages," Josie says.

Recently, due to the fights about Arizona, the controversy over the newspaper ad, and the general boredom of having slept in the same bed for years, their lovemaking has lost its spark, but here in Only, Tennessee, everything seems strange and new. Josie pulls off her gown and stands nude, then she starts doing a little dance, gyrating her hips and prancing around. She glances over at the bulge. "Looks like ol' Johnson's fit to be tied," she says.

"Yep, he's about to bust out of the pen."

"Guess I'll have to give him a talking to," Josie coos.

Clarence's face is red with heat, and the little blue vein on his right temple pulses as Josie does a slow sexy dance toward the bed. She climbs in beside him and begins gently sliding the cover off.

"Let's have a look at the ol' boy," she says. "You know, me and him have been on the outs here lately. Maybe we ought to kiss and make up." Josie bends down and gives Johnson a kiss.

That does it. Clarence pounces on Josie like a bobcat. If there is one thing Clarence Tolliver does well besides work on electronic devices, it's make love. Knowing it drives her crazy with desire, he begins by kissing her breasts, first one and then the other, wiping his tongue around the nipple like a child licking a cake bowl. Then he moves on down her body, leaving a trail of wet kisses. Josie shudders and wraps her legs around him. Clarence enters her, and there is that moment of "Yep, this is it. This is the way it's supposed to be." But the moment doesn't last long because *more* is wanted—more, more, more and beyond that, more. They can't get enough. Josie straddles Clarence singing, *"I'm just a ol' cowhand from the Rio Grande . . ."* Finally they end up in their familiar position, and everything comes to a head. Clarence lies quietly on her, moving only slightly, because if he moves around too much, she'll come.

"Wait," he says. "Not yet." They begin to kiss, his tongue exploring the depths of her throat, then as if they've both received their cue, they let go—rising and falling, groaning their way to oblivion.

Knocked for a loop, Clarence lies there, his arms raised over his head, his eyes half open, and he's already beginning to tick. In a few minutes he's sound asleep. On the other hand, Josie is rejuvenated. Feeling like a plant that has just been watered, she glances at the clock radio they brought along. It's eleven o'clock. I guess that means we've been at it nearly three hours, she thinks. Well, I ain't a bit sleepy now.

She grabs the road atlas and looks at what lies ahead. Their plan is to go I-40 to Amarillo, Texas, drop diagonally to Roswell, New Mexico, cross over to Alamogordo, then go south to Las Cruces, eventually winding up on I-10 to Tucson. Josie figures if she can take the wheel away from Clarence tomorrow and go sixty-five miles an hour, they should at least make it to Oklahoma City by evening. That will be a good place to stop, she thinks.

True to Josie's speculations they make faster time during her turn at driving the next day. When they get past the eastern part of Oklahoma, the trees take on a lighter shade and the soil becomes reddish in color. "Just look at it, Clarence," Josie says. "I told you how different things were."

"I've seen this before," Clarence replies. "See it in movies all the time, and besides when I got back from Vietnam I spent about a week in L.A."

"Yeah, but this is different. We're goin out here to live now. That makes it a entirely different thing."

As Josie planned, their second night on the road is spent in Oklahoma City, but the following morning it's Clarence's turn at the wheel. Josie dreads the long, grueling road ahead. When they enter the panhandle of Texas, that flat region where trees constantly lean in one direction from neverending wind, she begins to nod, her head bouncing on the car window as Clarence drives along at a snail's pace, and she dreams she's galloping on a horse, a russet brown horse, out in Sage, Arizona.

When the school term finally ended, Brewster moved his family from Rustle to Sage. Both Josie and Cheyenne loved their new apartment in the huge adobe house—it was so much cooler and nicer than the hot dusty trailer in Rustle. Shortly after the move, the girls began helping their mother make lamps. Lately Dora had become obsessed with making table lamps out of cholla cactuses and postcards—an upside-down cholla cactus became the stand, and the jumbo-sized postcards became the shade. She would construct the shades by punching holes around the edges of the postcards and then stringing the cards together with leather strands. Her lamps were just as pretty as any you could buy at the roadside souvenir stands. Dora was planning to set up her own stand.

On this particular day, the girls were out in the desert trying to find a cactus that had the right shape for a lamp. They had finally spotted a good one and were in the process of digging it out of the ground when a man on a horse rode up. "What're you doing?" he asked.

Cheyenne looked up at him and grinned. "We're goin to take this home. Our mommy makes lamps out of them."

"Did you know this is private property? It belongs to the woman I work for. She'd be mad if she knew you were digging up her cactuses. If people keep turning them into lamps, there won't be any left." The cowboy was fairly young and kind of good-looking, Josie noticed.

Cheyenne sighed. "Well, we're just trying to help our mommy out."

The cowboy took a closer look at Cheyenne. She was fourteen years old but looked older. Her long black hair hung down to her waist, and she was wearing a pair of white short-shorts and a halter top. He got down off his horse and tied it to a manzanita shrub. "I guess if you're bound to do this, I can help you out." He took their shovel from them and had the cactus out of the ground in no time. Then he got back on his horse. "Well, maybe I'll see you again sometime."

"Wait," Cheyenne said. "Buddy, can I take a little ride on your horse?"

Josie wheeled around and looked at her. She happened to know that Cheyenne had never been on a horse in her life.

"Just a little ride," Cheyenne said. "I ain't been on one since we left Kentucky. I sure do miss riding."

"You're from Kentucky? Well, I guess you can ride then. That's horse heaven from what I hear."

In a few minutes Cheyenne was in the saddle, riding like the wind. It was if she'd grown up on a horse, as if she'd never set foot on the ground.

"My God, look at that," the cowboy said to Josie.

"Yeah, it's a sight in the world," Josie agreed.

Cheyenne was standing up in the stirrups, her black hair flying out behind her, when suddenly she grabbed hold of the horse's mane and began screaming. Spooked, the horse started to buck, and Cheyenne went sailing through the air.

They ran to her as fast as they could. She was lying on the ground, passed out and pale as a ghost. The cowboy put his ear close to her face, started pumping on her chest, and blowing into her mouth. Josie just stood there watching everything as if it were happening in a movie. All at once the cowboy stood up. "She's breathing again. I'm goin for my car," he said. "We've gotta get her to the doctor." He was gone in a flash, and Josie was left standing there, staring at Cheyenne's blue lips. "God, please don't let her die," she kept saying over and over again. It seemed as though an hour passed before the cowboy returned, but in reality it was only a few minutes. He put Cheyenne in the back seat of his car, Josie in the front, pushed the pedal to the floor, and in a half hour they were in a hospital in Tucson. When Cheyenne was safely surrounded by doctors, the cowboy, who had by now introduced himself as Dan Hawkins, led Josie to a pay phone.

"We have to call your mother," he said.

A few seconds later, Josie was talking to Dora. "I'm in Tucson, Mommy. Cheyenne's sick. We was out there getting your cactus and . . ."

When Josie finished her tale, Dora said, "You just stay right close to that feller that brought you there. I'll be down as soon as I can. I'll have to call your daddy home from work. Put that feller on the phone. I want to talk to him." While Dan explained the situation to Dora, Josie stood there in the hallway watching nurses, patients, and visitors glide up and down the hallway like phantoms in a dream.

It was a heart attack, the doctors told them later. They said Cheyenne might not have lived if it hadn't been for Dan Hawkins, who had been a medic during the Korean War. It was his training that had kept her alive at the crucial moment. Cheyenne remained in the hospital for two weeks, not only because of her ailing heart—she'd broken her ankle in the fall from the horse.

Brewster and Dora were advised by the doctors that down the line Cheyenne would have to have heart surgery, but that in the mean time they should let her get some exercise everyday. Dora just nodded and smiled, but later she told Brewster, "I ain't about to let her get up and run around in her weak condition." She decided that Cheyenne ought to stay in bed for at least a month, maybe longer.

The day Cheyenne came home from the hospital, Dora offered to make her a bed in the living room so she could lie there and watch TV. They'd just bought their first television a month earlier and would watch anything that was on—game shows, soaps, commercials, news, and if the reception went out, they'd even watch the snow. Cheyenne refused Dora's offer, said she'd rather stay in the bedroom.

"But don't you want to be out here with us?"

Cheyenne didn't answer.

Josie had never seen her sister that gloomy and still. It was as if the life had been taken out of her. All of that first day, Cheyenne stayed in her room alone, and when anyone would come in to talk to her, she'd run them off. On her second day home, Josie went into her bedroom and sat down in a chair, deciding to stay, no matter what she said. Cheyenne didn't say anything, just kept staring at the ceiling like a zombie.

Finally Josie stood up and began singing "Paddy West," taking on an Irish accent and dancing an Irish jig. For several minutes, Cheyenne acted as if she didn't notice, then she glanced around at Josie, who looked pretty ridiculous the way she was hopping around. Gradually a smile spread across Cheyenne's face. "I've never seen such a bad hand. You couldn't dance if someone had a gun pointed at you," she said. "Can't sing either."

Josie kept hopping around like a crazy person, singing to the top of her lungs in the worst rendition of an Irish accent possible.

Finally, Cheyenne started laughing out loud. "Stop, you're causing my heart to hurt. Stop it." She was losing her breath, laughing. Then Josie began laughing too, and that's how it began. They sang Irish ballads, told each other secrets, pored over maps of the world, and talked about all the places they'd go someday. Over the next few weeks, the two sisters became closer than they'd ever been before.

Dan Hawkins was a regular visitor that summer—he turned up for supper two or three times a week. Dora cooked him huge meals, Southern-style, and made him eat every bite. Then he and Brewster would sit in front of the television, drinking beer, rehashing their respective war days. Dan often came into the bedroom with Cheyenne and Josie, and the three of them would talk about Elvis Presley, James Dean, and Jerry Lee Lewis. He read to them too, even gave them reading lists, handwritten on yellow notebook paper. "Read Conrad," he'd say. "Read Melville and Thoreau." Josie decided that Dan was the smartest person alive, and to top it off, he was good-looking with his strong wiry build and quiet, dark eyes.

Josie could tell that Cheyenne liked him too, often noticing that she gave him shy blushing smiles, especially when he brought books of poetry and read impassioned verses from William Carlos Williams and Allen Ginsberg. With rock-and-roll in its heyday and the beat generation smoldering in the background, every little item of discussion seemed like the most interesting thing possible. It was as if the whole world was begging to be taken, and nothing could put a damper on their high expectations, not even a bad heart.

Over the years, Josie has thought of Dan Hawkins sporadically, but as she and Clarence drive out of Amarillo, Texas, toward New Mexico, she can't get him out of her mind. She remembers that when Cheyenne disappeared, Dora wrote to him several times, asking him to call her if Cheyenne turned up in Sage. He wrote back that he was sorry to hear about her daughter, that he hadn't seen her but would be on the lookout. Josie has always wondered if he was lying. It seems logical that a fifteen-year-old runaway might have stopped off at one familiar place during her journey to the unknown.

Dan must be in his forties by now, she thinks. Shit, he prob'ly left Sage years ago. It would be my luck to find out he's in New York City. He prob'ly lives somewhere in Greenwich Village with poets and artists and people who sit up all night talking about the mysteries of life. She imagines him with a beard, wearing his cowboy hat and boots, lying beside some artsy woman in an attic apartment in the Village, gazing up at the starry night through a skylight in the roof. Yeah, she speculates, Dan's prob'ly gone on to other things.

* * *

Clarence and Josie spend their third night on the road in Roswell, New Mexico, the site of the rumored alien spaceship invasion of 1947. The land around Roswell is fairly colorless, and Clarence is becoming increasingly leery of things to come.

"This is the ugliest place I've ever seen in my life," he says as they stare out the window of their motel room.

"But just think," Josie reassures him. "A alien spaceship might have landed here. For all we know they may have mated with some of these people. That motel desk clerk that handed you the key might be part creature-from-outer-space. You never know."

"Shee-it," Clarence says, then he dives into bed and goes to sleep as Josie sits by the window, watching darkness fall. She sees a star (or is it a star?) shoot down through the sky and disappear into the black western night.

The next morning Clarence refuses to give Josie her turn at the wheel, and they drive slowly out of Roswell. Around Alamogordo, they enter a patch of green mountains that reminds them of Kentucky, and they pass the White Sands National Monument, where the sand looks like drifts of windswept snow. They witness an Indian walking by the side of the road, wearing Levi's and long black hair. Shortly after the Indian, they see a sign that says TO THE INN OF THE MOUNTAIN GODS.

"Hold up, Clarence. Turn off on that little road there. I want to see it."

"See what?"

"The Inn of the Mountain Gods."

"Fuck the Inn of the Mountain Gods," Clarence says. "We ain't never goin to get to Las Cruces if we stop every minute."

Josie keeps pleading for Clarence to turn back, but he won't. How can a person do that? she wonders. How can anyone pass a road that leads to the Inn of the Mountain Gods and not turn off on it? This is the difference between us, she thinks. This is precisely the difference between me and Clarence Tolliver.

Early that afternoon they make it to Las Cruces and stop for a bite to eat. Then finally they turn onto I-10, which will lead them to Tucson. It is just east of the town of Deming, New Mexico, that they begin seeing the billboards advertising THE THING, a roadside attraction that soon captures Josie's imagination. She wonders what The Thing could possibly be and conjures up images of dinosaurs, giant snakes, and mutant flies.

Noticing the billboards too, Clarence says, "That's a money trap if I ever seen one. I went to a carnival one time and paid to go in a tent where there was supposed to be a two-headed girl. It was just twins—that's all it was. One of them had her head leaned on the other one's shoulder."

They spend their fourth night on the road in Lordsburg, New Mexico, just a few short miles from the Arizona border. When they get up that fifth and last morning of their trip, Josie snatches the keys and runs out to the car, making sure she's the driver of the day. She plans on stopping to see The Thing whether Clarence likes it or not.

"What're you doing?" Clarence asks later that morning when Josie pulls off at the famous watering hole, located between the towns of Wilcox and Benson, Arizona.

"I want to see The Thing," Josie says.

"Give me the wheel," he shouts as he glares at families unwinding from cars, shaking off travel dust, and sauntering into the touristy establishment. "If you think I'm goin to get suckered like the rest of these fools, you've got another think coming."

Right now, Josie hates everything about Clarence. She hates the way he's holding his mouth, the way his nostrils are flaring, the way his eyebrows are drawn into a frown, the way he's never interested in anything unless it's money-, job-, tax-, or insurance-oriented. She simply can't take it anymore. "I'm *goiiiing* to *seeeeeee* the *fuckiiiing Thiiiiiing!*" she screams at him.

Clarence drops his mouth open and doesn't say a word, while people in the parking lot crane their necks to see what's happening.

Josie turns off the ignition and stuffs the keys into the depths of her Levi's. "Clarence," she says with a frightening calm, "if you don't go in there with me, it's over. I'll leave you, honey, and go off on my own."

"You'd leave me because of The Thing?" Clarence asks, incredulously.

"That's right, sweetheart."

A blank expression sweeps over his face, the expression he always gets when he's struggling to keep his rage contained. "Gee, I didn't realize it was that important to you."

"Well, it is, Clarence," Josie says genially.

A few minutes later they are filing past the strange, overly advertised attraction. "This is real cute," Clarence grumbles. "You drug me in here to see this?"

Josie assumes a look of awe. "Ain't it worth it? I think it's a mummy, a Indian mummy."

"Horseshit. Looks like somebody took some old rags and starched 'em, then wadded 'em up and shook some hair on top at the last minute."

"It doesn't look like old rags to me."

"Well, it don't look like something anybody ought to pay to see, neither," Clarence says.

"You don't want to see anything," Josie shouts, causing other viewers of The Thing to turn and glare at them uneasily. "You don't want to see no*thing.* Anybody like you might as well crawl back into a hole somewhere and die."

"That's exactly what I'm goin to do. I'm goin to crawl back in my hole, but you can stay here all day if you want to. Get a good long look at it, Josie. I hope you're enjoying yourself."

"Oh, but I am," Josie shouts as Clarence heads out of the building to the car. "I'm having the best time I ever had in my life."

The other tourists look at each other with expressions of superiority, their eyes glinting with *I'm-glad-we-don't-act-like-that-in-public* satisfaction.

"Feeling smug?" Josie yells at them and heads out to the car, too.

* * *

Driving toward Tucson, they remain silent until the worst of the anger is over, and it is during this long lull that the full impact of the Arizona desert hits them—a one-hundred-degree temperature sizzles overhead, purple mountains rim their view, and saguaro cactuses are everywhere. Josie pulls to the side of the road, jumps out of the car, and hugs the first saguaro within walking distance.

"I guess I'd forgot just how hot it is out here," she says, wiping her forehead when she gets back on the road. Their old Nova doesn't have air-conditioning, and they're paying the price.

"There they are again," Clarence says, pointing to the car that just passed them. For the past thirty miles the car, a Lincoln Continental, has been passing them, falling behind, then passing them again. There are four men in the vehicle—three in the front seat and one sprawled in the back seat, his bare feet sticking out a rolled-down window. All of the men have long hair and are wearing fur coats.

"Reckon that's real mink?" Josie asks.

"Looks like it," Clarence replies, his eyes bulging to get a better look. "I know they ain't got air-conditioning or they wouldn't have their windows rolled down. What in the hell is wrong with them fellers?"

"Beats me," Josie says. "Since it never gets cold out here, maybe rich people with mink coats have to pick a day to suffer through or they'll never get a chance to wear them."

"That ain't it, Josie. They're just gumps."

Clarence looks across the median to the other side of the freeway and sees a man riding a motorcycle, except he isn't riding it the regular way. He's doing handsprings on the handlebars, his body sticking straight up in the air. "Look at that fool. What kind of place is this? So far everyone I've seen out here is fools."

When they get to Tucson that afternoon, they stop at a Jack-in-the-Box and order tacos. "God, these are good," Josie says, downing her third one. It's the first tacos Josie and Clarence have ever eaten. "Ain't they good, Clarence?"

"They're all right, I reckon." His mind is on other things. He's wondering if they can locate a place to live today, if he can find a job tomorrow. "Guess we'll drive on up to Sage and find a place, then I'll bring the U-Haul back down here tomorrow morning and turn it in." He looks out the window of the restaurant, his eyes darting back and forth as he takes in the blinding hot street. "Does this place look familiar to you?" he asks Josie.

"No, but we didn't go to Tucson much, except when Cheyenne was sick. Of course we came down here to buy our first TV, that old Sylvania. Remember it?"

"Yeah," Clarence says. A lot of people in Burr County knew about the Sylvania television Brewster Clay brought home to Pick, Kentucky, from Arizona in 1959. Not everyone in Burr County had televisions at the time, especially not blond-colored, 23-inch Sylvanias. Almost every night visitors would show up unannounced to watch it.

A few minutes later Clarence and Josie are driving out of Tucson on the road to Sage. "Look," Josie says excitedly. "There's the Catalina Mountains. Ain't they pretty?"

"They'd be a lot prettier if they had a few trees on them," Clarence scoffs.

The elevation is increasing steadily, and by the time they get to Sage Junction it's nearly five thousand feet. "Is this beginning to look like the place you used to live?" Clarence asks.

"Yeah," Josie says, her voice hushed amid a flood of memories. "The air seems different up here. It's cooler for one thing, but it's more than that. Do you feel it?"

"It's cooler. I feel that. Don't know what else you're talking about."

They turn a bend in the road, and there it is—Hudson's Grocery where Dora used to shop, the post office where they mailed their letters, the Chevron station where Brewster gassed up, the Baptist Church they never got around to attending, the same Baptist church that was once an old hotel, accommodating such guests as Buffalo Bill and one of the early Western actors, Tom Mix. All of the buildings are there and more—there's a new U-Totem convenience store and a bar called Pop-a-Top's. Still everything seems practically the same with one notable exception. The old adobe mansion is nowhere in sight.

12

I t's got to be somewhere close by," Josie says, as she parks in front of Hudson's Grocery. "It was the biggest house here."

Clarence gets out of the car and turns around and around. "I didn't think a town could be any smaller than Pick, but looks like this one's got it beat. We can't live here, Josie. They ain't no place for us to stay."

"Well, let me just go into this little grocery store and ask."

Josie gets out of the car and walks inside, spots an old man by the produce section, and taps him on the shoulder. "Excuse me, sir. Wonder if you can help me out. I used to live in Sage back in 1959. We lived in a big old adobe mansion that had been turned into apartments. Is it still here?"

"I don't know what you're talking about," the old man says, grumpily. "I've lived here since 1944 and there was never a mansion here—adobe or otherwise. Maybe you got the wrong town."

Josie sighs. "Well, it might not have been a mansion. Maybe it was just a real big house, but I know it existed because we lived in a apartment on the bottom floor. Everyone that lived there worked in the copper mines."

The old man scratches his beard. "You might be talking about Marie Calderon's old house out there behind the U-Totem. Used to be people with families rented it, but now it's just some drunks that stay there. You don't remember where you used to live? I remember every house I've ever lived in. How could you forget?"

"I don't know," Josie says, becoming irritated. "Must be something wrong with me. Are there many places for a person to rent around here?"

"Check down at the real estate office. Maybe they can tell you something I don't know. Good luck to you," the old man says and walks away.

Disappointed by the lack of information, Josie turns to leave. As she passes the check-out counter, the cashier, a young woman in her twenties, says, "My dad claims it used to be the prettiest house around here."

Josie glances back at her. "You mean the house behind the U-Totem?"

"That's the one. Are you looking for a place to rent?"

"Yes," Josie says.

"Well, that old house doesn't have a vacancy, but I do know of a place that's empty. It's a mobile home. Tarantula Garcia owns it. She told me just the other day she was thinking about renting it out. Said she didn't want to rent it to the miners though. Said it would be more of a headache than it was worth."

"Can you give me the directions to it? I'd like to check it out."

The young woman smiles shyly. "I'll be getting off work in about twenty minutes. I live in that direction. You can follow me out there if you want."

"That would be great," Josie says. "I'm goin to take a look at that old house behind the U-Totem, but I'll be back in a few minutes. I'll just wait in the car till you're ready."

With the good news on the tip of her tongue, Josie goes outside where Clarence has been patiently waiting. "I found us a place . . . to look at anyway. The checker said she'd take us out there. It belongs to this old woman named Tarantula Garcia. Can you get over that name? What about being called Tarantula?"

"What kind of place?"

"A trailer, you know, a mobile home."

"So it's come to that. We're goin to be living in a trailer. Looks like we're really coming up in the world."

Josie sighs. "What's wrong with a trailer? They're real convenient. Anyway, they said the old house I used to live in was out there behind the U-Totem. Said it never was a mansion in the first place, and that it's real run-down now. Let's go out there and see for ourselves. That checker won't get off work for twenty minutes."

They drive around the curve to the small convenience store, walk behind it, and find the house of Josie's dreams. It's covered in dirty white plaster that is chipping off, revealing large irregular patches of the original adobe underneath. A ramshackle stairway leading to a second-story balcony comes straight down the front of the two-story affair, and it's those steps that cause Josie to recognize the place as their old house. She used to play behind that stairway, hide there from imaginary enemies. Tears well up in her eyes. "Oh God, this is it. It used to be so pretty. We lived right there, Clarence, right there in that end apartment. See the door? That was our front door. It looks like shit now. Mommy had poppies growing by the front step, had ivy trailing around that window."

Josie peeps through the window and sees nothing but beer and Coke cans, empty Doritos bags, and frozen-food cartons all over the floor. "Must be some single boys lives here now," she says to Clarence. Then they walk around to the back, where the French doors used to be. They're still there, but some of the panes have been broken out and replaced with cardboard. Josie starts to cry in earnest now. "You prob'ly think I've been lying all these years, but it really was a pretty place back then, and bigger. Everything was bigger."

Clarence puts his arm around her shoulder. "Things go downhill after a while."

She brightens and says, "Let's go back around to the front. I want to see if the view is still there. You know the little hill . . . Remember how I said the sun was setting and that me and Mommy and Cheyenne saw a cowboy and some cactuses silhouetted?"

They walk around to the front of the U-Totem in order to see across the road, but all they find are some tall shrubs. "They're not there," Josie says, her voice trembling. "That little hill doesn't even look as big as it used to be, and the saguaros are flat gone."

"I ain't seen a saguaro since we've been in Sage," Clarence says. "Not a single one."

"Well, there used to be some right across that road there. I know I ain't that crazy."

Clarence sighs. "Let's go on back to the grocery store before that woman takes off without us."

"Wait a minute," Josie says, continuing to look across the road, trying to see the land she remembers, but the whole terrain looks different. She wonders if she just imagined everything, if that evening with the sunset never actually happened. "No, goddamn it," she suddenly blurts out. "I stood right back there with Mommy and Cheyenne. That hill was way bigger than it is now. There were some saguaro cactuses and a cowboy, and by hell that is the way it was."

Clarence and Josie are sitting in the car, staring at Tarantula Garcia's house, a gold-colored stucco with dark brown trim. Situated a few hundred yards behind it is a small green-and-white trailer.

"This place looks awful lonesome," Clarence says. "They ain't no other houses close by."

"Well, there wouldn't any houses close to where we lived in Pick either," Josie says.

Finally they get out of the car and walk up to the door. The woman who answers their knock appears to be in her sixties. Wrinkles crisscross her face in deep grooves, and she's wearing a stained T-shirt and dirty jeans. Hanging to the waist, her hair is a gray, tangled mess, but she has the prettiest green eyes Josie has ever seen.

"What're you selling?" the woman asks.

"Nothing," Clarence answers her. "We came to see if you're interested in renting that little trailer out there?"

"I don't like to rent to people I don't know," Tarantula says, suspiciously. She glares at Clarence. "Do you work in the mines?"

"No, I'm a TV repairman," Clarence says proudly.

Still squinting warily, Tarantula says, "Well, come on in and we'll talk about it."

Her living room looks like a spider's nest, a small dark burrow where a person can hide away, and there's only one tiny window near the front door. She leads them into her kitchen, which is quite the opposite. It is large and airy with a window covering almost one entire wall, although, just outside, a row of tall oleanders shields the room from the sun. The floors and walls are covered with pink tile bordered with maroon, and all the kitchen appliances are white. Tarantula takes a bottle of Cuervo Gold from a kitchen cabinet, pours herself a drink, and offers to pour Clarence and Josie drinks as they sit down at the kitchen table preparing to discuss the trailer.

"I'll have one," Josie says, nodding toward the bottle.

"Not me, but thank you anyway," Clarence mutters, glaring at Josie as she takes her first sip.

"Is it just the two of you? No children?"

"No children," Josie says.

"Any pets?"

"None of them either," Clarence says, "but I've always wanted a dog. Just ain't got around to getting one."

"Well, if you do, you'll have to keep him out of my trailer. Did you say you're a TV repairman?"

"That's right."

Tarantula grins. "Good, maybe you can fix my TV. I'll tell you what. If you can fix my TV right now, I'll rent you my place."

"I'm not renting it till I see the inside," Clarence says. "Might not want it."

She leads them behind her house and shows them their prospective new home. "I'd charge you seventy-five dollars a month, utilities not included. That's a good deal. I doubt if you'll find anything better. This little trailer is just the right size for the two of you. I used to let the man that worked for me live here, but he doesn't work for me anymore."

Josie looks around at the down-sized furniture and appliances. "It's cute, Clarence. I sort of like it."

"Yeah, well, I guess it'll have to do. We'll take it," he says to Tarantula. "We're tired and'll take anything."

"Fix my TV first," Tarantula says.

Clarence goes out to their car to get his tools, and Tarantula takes Josie back to the house. As they sit down at the kitchen table, Tarantula says, "That TV has become my best friend. I used to have about twenty horses and fifty head of cattle. Now, all I've got left are two cows and a donkey. That's what happens when you get old. You start losing everything you own. Do you want another drink?"

Just then Clarence steps into the kitchen with his tool box. "No, she don't. As soon as I fix your TV, we've got to start moving in."

"Actually, I'd like a drink," Josie says.

A smile spreading on her face, Tarantula looks from one of her guests to the other, then she pours Josie another drink.

Clarence frowns. "You don't need that. We've got work to do."

"Don't tell me what I need, Clarence. You don't know nothing about it," Josie says.

Clarence sighs. "Where's your TV, Tarantula?"

"In the living room."

"Do you and him fight a lot?" Tarantula asks Josie when Clarence is gone.

"All the time," Josie says before she realizes that this is probably something a prospective landlady doesn't want to hear.

"Like me and my husband used to do, I bet," Tarantula says, seemingly too laid-back or too buzzed from the tequila to care about Josie and Clarence's squabbles. "He died when we were both real young. I never remarried."

Josie downs her shot of tequila. "Thanks, I needed that. Can I have one more?"

"You can have as many as you want."

"I used to live here when I was a child," Josie says, the heat from the tequila making her more talkative. "We lived in that old house behind the U-Totem. There used to be two or three saguaros growing across the road from that house, but they ain't there anymore. Wonder what happened to them."

Tarantula smiles. "Saguaros don't grow up here. It's too high. Too cool. But this old man I know liked 'em so good he dug up three big ones from down there in Rustle and planted them on his property. They never did very well—always looked sick—but somehow they survived. Then years later his son graded off that property to build a house on it. Graded down the cactuses in the process. The boy never got around to actually building the house, but those three sick-looking cactuses were gone for good. That's probably the saguaros you remember."

Josie sighs. "Prob'ly so."

Several minutes later, Clarence comes into the kitchen and tells Tarantula her TV is working fine.

"I can see that you're going to be handy to have around," Tarantula says when she checks it out. "If you'll write me a check for seventy-five dollars, you can move in."

The sun is setting as they unload the last of their belongings from the U-Haul and pile it inside the small living room of their new home. As soon as Josie pulls a set of sheets out of a box and makes the bed, Clarence jumps in. "I'm bone-tired," he says, "and I've got a big day ahead of me tomorrow. I don't even know where to look for a job. If I do find one, it won't be in Sage. There ain't nothing here."

"Maybe you could try Rustle. I bet they've got some TV repair shops."

"Guess I'll worry about that tomorrow." Clarence looks off to the side. "Do you think Tarantula is a Mexican? I mean, her name is Mexican, but she don't look like one."

"Maybe she married a Mexican. What difference does it make?" Josie asks.

"None . . . I just meant . . ."

"Well, gee, Clarence, I hope this place ain't too much for you to handle," Josie snaps, "because there's prob'ly a lot of Mexicans around here." It's the kind of argument they've had before when Clarence has shown discomfort around people with a different heritage than his own.

Clarence rolls his eyes. "Just shut up, Josie. I'm goin to sleep."

Josie steps outside and sits on the front steps. The yard around the trailer is covered with desert grass that appears to be barely surviving. A horned toad hunches in the thick of it, and a lizard scuttles past her feet. She looks west toward the horizon at a deep red-orange sunset, the prettiest one she's seen in eighteen years.

13

The next morning Josie drives down to Hudson's Grocery and picks up some essentials. When she returns, she prepares a hurried breakfast, and Clarence leaves, telling her that as soon as he deposits the U-Haul, he intends to drive down to Rustle, looking for work. After he has gone, she looks around for the switch to the swamp cooler. In the low eighties, the weather isn't uncomfortably hot, but Josie wants to turn on the contraption for old-time's sake, not having seen one since she was a child. At the far end of the trailer, she finds the switch, and the cool dank air begins filtering into the rooms.

She starts cleaning the place from one end to the other. It's a small two-bedroom with a tiny apartment-sized stove, miniature sink, and a washer and dryer that stack on top of each other. Josie has never seen such efficiency. The kitchen cabinets are equally compact, and in them she finds five or six pieces of toffee candy, a box of crackers, a jar of jalapeños—traces left by the previous occupant. The kitchen runs together with the living room, where the dinette set is efficiently positioned against the wall near the window, and where a sofa bed and recliner are gathered around a particleboard coffee table.

Tarantula Garcia had obviously cleaned the place sometime in the recent past. There isn't a lot to do. Josie packs away their belongings, pours herself a cup of coffee, and walks outside. The sun is already high in the sky, and Clarence won't be home until late that evening. Feeling like a ten-year-old with time on her hands, she puts on her walking shoes and sets out. The air is clear, the sky blue, and everything looks better today than it did the night before.

It is a thirty-minute walk from Tarantula's backyard to the main street of town. As Josie treks along in the moderate heat, she can't help noticing how different the surrounding landscape looks than she remembered. In addition to a few cholla cactuses, the hilly earth is covered with low-lying shrubs and a few trees that are unfamiliar to her. She realizes now that in her memories she might have blended the geography of Sage and Rustle, given Sage some of Rustle's purple mountains and saguaros, but one thing remains exactly as she thought: the atmosphere. Around Sage, the air is spirited with a distant past—chants from sacred ceremonies seem to dance from gully to wash, and old mysteries loiter over the land.

She walks past the grocery store and service station, keeps walking down the road that leads to Rustle, and that's when she sees the sign on a hill above the road. "Don Juan's Cocktails," the sign says. Josie stares at the sign in amazement. Was it here back in '59? No, it couldn't have been, she decides. This is an omen, an omen to beat all omens.

She climbs the narrow dirt road that leads up the hill, and there it is—Don Juan's—a small structure, painted white with blue trim. Cars are parked all the way around it. There are no windows, and a door is all that decorates the front. Moving closer, she hears country music and men's voices, loud and raucous. She stands there a minute listening to the laughter and feels a cool air-conditioned draft emanating from the door, which is slightly ajar.

I've got to go in there, she thinks. Don Juan led me here to this little town—he must have. For all I know he's sitting at the bar. Even though Carlos Castaneda describes him differently, Josie has always pictured don Juan as a shadowy form existing in a fragile mist, ethereal, with tiny sparkling stars shimmering all around him, but the sound coming from the bar is all too earthly—the men inside are really whooping it up. She figures if she were ever lucky enough to run into don Juan, she'd probably find a short little feller who was drunk as a skunk, red-eyed and belching, someone who would laugh at every word she said. No need to worry, Josie thinks. He ain't really in there, but even if he's not there in the flesh, some part of him is floating in the air, hanging from rafters, fizzing out of beer bottles, else why would this little hole-in-the-wall, standing in the middle of nowhere, in Sage, Arizona, for Christ's sake, a place I needed to come back to for unclear reasons—why would this bar be named Don Juan's Cocktails?

She becomes aware that the noise inside Don Juan's has taken on a different tone—an argument seems to be in process. Then a voice even more gruff than the others yells, "Knock that off or I'll throw you out on your ass." The argument stops and the general mayhem continues. I can't go in there, they'll probably rape and kill me, she thinks, and she longs to hear a female voice but can't make one out. She imagines stringy-haired, bearded, satan-eyed cowboys, hardened to steel from riding months-on-end in the blazing desert sun without the touch of a woman, men with hearts like dried leather who violently hate women because they think women are weak since they've been known to lie spread-eagle and give a man what he wants, especially when they've been clobbered over the head with the butt of a gun. Josie conjures images that only the most embittered feminist could ever think to muster and places those images behind the door that stands in front of her. I can't do it, she thinks, and starts to walk away. Then she realizes how ridiculous she's being and wheels back around, opens the door, and steps inside.

Silence strikes the crowded bar like a Louisville Slugger—controversies stop mid-sentence, laughter is caught in throats, drinks raised to mouths are not swallowed. The bar is lined three-deep with men, and the scene reminds Josie of a *Twilight Zone* episode where the primary victim is momentarily blessed with the ability to stop time. She scoots up to the bar, finds a tiny spot to squeeze into, and with a shaky voice orders a Bud. Josie is amazed to find that the bartender is a woman, a skinny-as-a-rail, pale-faced woman in her mid-fifties who appears fragile except for the set of her jaw and the feisty glint in her eyes. She produces a bottle and hands it to Josie without hesitation. Josie takes a long drink, hoping the other customers soon go back to their conversations, but they don't. Out of the corners of her eyes she scans the length of the counter and sees only two men who, because of the Stetsons they wear, could be construed as cowboys. The rest are dressed in jeans and T-shirts and appear to be entrenched in a long hard day of drinking.

The bar is dark and cool, heavy with the smell of beer, and the floors and walls are stained dark walnut. Taped to a mirror behind the counter is a photograph of a beautiful young woman standing in front of a giant clam shell, and she's almost naked except for a few strategically placed ostrich feathers. Right beside that photograph is another of an old man dressed in a Santa Claus suit with about twenty children gathered around him. Must be someone's grandpa, Josie thinks. Then she looks over her shoulder and sees a second room lined with booths and furnished with several small round tables. A large fireplace is situated at the center of the back wall, and two men stand by a pool table staring at her. One of them winks, shrugs, and racks the balls.

She turns back to the bar, trying to be as inconspicuous as possible. Suddenly the silence is interrupted when a tall man, wearing a cowboy hat, clamors out of the bathroom and yells, "What happened? Did somebody die?" The man swaggers up to the counter and finding no room to stand, taps Josie on the shoulder and shouts in a loud boisterous voice, "That's all right you took my place. Just stand there and beauty up the bar."

Josie grins. "Thanks, mister."

"Hell, I ain't a mister. I'm Johnny Walker, like the scotch, except for the Y. Pleased to meet you, Miss . . . ?"

"Josie Tolliver," Josie says. "I just moved here yesterday with my husband, Clarence."

"Husband? Why, you're too young and pretty for one of them."

Josie smiles at Johnny, who has a full head of black hair and pretty blue-green eyes. Noticing that the other men in the room have resumed talking, she begins to relax.

"What kind of accent you got?" Johnny asks. "Sounds familiar."

"Kentucky."

He looks surprised. "Lord, it's a small world. I'm from West Virginia myself, a little town called Red Jacket. Moved to Tucson about ten years ago. Then I come up here to work in the mines and beat the heat. I'm not like most of these fellers. They're what you call tramp miners. Come here to sink that big mine shaft. I don't work in the mines anymore—got a little ranch."

Happy to be in a conversation with a person from the mountains, Josie asks, "What's a tramp miner?"

Johnny laughs. "They go from one mine to the other, to wherever there's mine shafts to sink. This one's almost sunk, and their jobs'll be piddlin' out pretty soon." He turns to the men who line the bar. "How about giving a man some room?" Forcing himself into a small space, he yells to the bartender, "Uh, Venus Lily, anothern on the rocks."

"I used to live here when I was a kid," Josie says to him. "My dad worked in the mines."

"It's a fine place, ain't it?" He turns away from her and shouts, "Uh, Venus Lily, where's my scotch? And another beer for the little lady from Kentucky."

Some of the men stop talking and stare at Josie again.

"Venus Lily," Josie mutters. "That's a real pretty name."

Johnny grins. "Her full name is Venus Lily Stamper. Course I'm not a hundred percent sure she is Venus Lily. She's got a identical twin named Lily Venus. None of us can tell them apart. They've got the same shape, same face, wear the same clothes, have the same voice. The only difference is, one works the second shift and the other works the third."

Josie looks confused. "But this is the first shift, ain't it?"

"Well, usually there's another girl works this shift, but she ain't been here in a week, and Venus Lily's having to work two shifts." Johnny chuckles and points to the picture of the naked woman by the clam shell. "Right there is one of them. Could be Venus Lily or it could be Lily Venus. Whichever one it is, she was real pretty when she was young, wouldn't you say?"

"She sure was," Josie agrees, looking again at the photograph depicting one of the twins' delicate frame. "Why don't you just ask them who it is?"

Johnny rolls his eyes. "We *have* asked a thousand times."

Josie meets Johnny's eyes, and they both start laughing uncontrollably. "What kind of place have I stumbled into?" she sputters.

"Why, the finest place on earth."

Josie points to the other picture on the wall, "Who's that old man dressed like Santa Claus?"

Johnny chuckles. "Buffalo Bill. A long time ago, he played Santa Claus to the miners' children out there in the Catalinas."

She shakes her head, thinking Sage has a lot of history for such a small town.

Venus Lily brings the drinks and stares at Josie head on. "So what's the deal?" she asks, her thin brown hair hanging in wisps around her face. "You just moved here?" Her voice is as raspy and hoarse as an old man's. Now Josie realizes it is the same voice she heard earlier, that it was Venus Lily who threatened to throw someone out on his ass if he didn't behave.

"Just got here yesterday. We're living in the trailer that Tarantula Garcia owns," Josie says, looking around. "Is this place always so busy?"

"That mine out there works three shifts, and we get customers from all three. Most of the men you see now have been here since they got off the third shift this morning."

"I'm kinda looking for work. It wouldn't have to be full-time. Just whatever you've got. You wouldn't happen to need any help, would you?"

Venus Lily narrows her pale blue eyes and studies Josie more closely. "Maybe."

"Really? That'd be great. You don't know how I'd . . . I've just got to work here."

Venus looks askance at Johnny Walker, who points to his head and twirls his finger.

"Believe me, it's not that exciting," Venus says. "I'm not exactly sure I'll have an opening. It's according to whether Lori comes back from Tucson this week. Lori's got man problems. Her ex-husband lives down in Tucson, and she lives up here. They've been fighting and making up for the past year. If she isn't back by Thursday, you've got a job if you want it. Have you ever tended bar?"

"No, but I've been a waitress."

"That's good enough. You can call me Thursday and see what's up."

Someone yells for a beer, and Venus scoots down to the far end of the bar.

Josie finishes her second beer and says, "Well, I reckon I'd better go. It was nice to meet you, Johnny. Thanks for the beer. Maybe I'll be the one that's serving your drinks pretty soon."

Johnny winks. "That'd be good. I hope Lori doesn't come back. She's a bitch from hell anyway."

As Josie walks out of the bar, she yells to Venus Lily that she'll call her Thursday, and Venus nods with a smile. The men all turn to watch Josie go by, and as she eases out the door she's bombarded with the sound of catcalls and whistles. Then she hears the tyrannical bar-tender yelling for the men to shut the hell up, that Josie might be working for her starting next week, that she'd better never hear any-one make a dirty remark to her, and that if anyone even looks at Josie wrong they'll have hell to pay.

Walking down the bank to the main road, Josie stops and glances back toward the small bar isolated on top of the hill. Now I know one of the reasons I'm here, she thinks, and she wonders what lies in store for her at that particular desert watering hole, what mysteries will sneak through the crack in the door, what messages will dance across the counter in the cool dark world of Don Juan's.

Still deep in thought, Josie meanders along the road and finally turns onto the driveway that leads to the trailer. Passing Tarantula's house, she notices the old woman in the front yard watering a fig tree, her face almost hidden behind a huge straw hat.

"It's the only fruit tree I'll allow myself," Tarantula says without looking up. "Because of the waste. I hate goin to Tucson and seeing people spray water all over the place, it running out of their yards and onto sidewalks like it's not worth a thing. You don't see any green lawns on my property, do you?"

"No," Josie says, still unsure whether or not Tarantula is talking to herself. Anxious to return home and digest her excursion to Don Juan's, she starts to walk past her.

"That's because I won't have it," Tarantula says. "This place is a desert. It should look like one." Tarantula pushes her hat back on her head, revealing her brown weathered face.

Josie finds herself staring into the old woman's green eyes as though they are emerald planets from another galaxy. "So how did you get a name like Tarantula?"

Even though the sandy soil under the fig tree now has the color and texture of redeye gravy, Tarantula continues watering. "My name used to be Claire Jones," she says, "but when I was little I wandered away from our house one evening and fell into a gully. Got my foot wedged under a big rock and laid there till the next morning. I guess a lot of people were out looking for me, but they'd gone in the wrong direction. Anyway a whole bunch of tarantulas got curious about me and crawled all over my body the whole night. When my mother found me the next morning I told her what had happened, and she started calling me her little tarantula. I've gone by Tarantula ever since—Tarantula Jones until I married and Tarantula Garcia after."

"You must have been scared to death," Josie comments, wondering how much damage a night like that would do to a small child.

"Not really." Tarantula's eyes gleam with anticipation, almost as if she's waiting for a new creepy creature to scuttle across her body.

Josie changes the subject. "Guess what? I think I just got a job at Don Juan's Cocktails. Do you ever go there? It's miners that hang out there mostly, right?"

Tarantula grins. "Yeah, and, you know, just regular people, and then there's a few from that artists' colony."

"Artists' colony?"

"Yeah, there's an artists' colony outside of town. People come from everywhere to live in these little houses so they can paint and write and so on. At least they don't bother anyone. Sometimes they have art shows, and invite people in to see their paintings. Other times they have poetry readings if you're into that kind of thing. Sage is a pretty cultural town when you get right down to it."

"Well, I'll swear," Josie says. "I've always wanted to get to know artists. I figured I might find some down in Tucson. Never dreamed I'd find them in Sage."

"You want to come in for a while?" Tarantula asks. "It's about time for my soap."

Although Josie is thinking she should pass up the invitation, she impulsively says, "Sure."

Inside the dim spidery living room, Tarantula revs up the TV full blast. "Want a drink?"

"No thanks," Josie shouts over the roar.

As Tarantula pours herself a huge glass of tequila, Josie tries unsuccessfully to get interested in the soap. She stands and is about to go home when she suddenly remembers to ask about the only person she remembers from the old days in Sage. "Would you happen to have ever known a man named Dan Hawkins?"

Tarantula turns pale and squints her eyes. "Why are you asking about him?"

Josie is picking up some tension from Tarantula that she doesn't understand. "Dan used to come to our house a lot when I was a kid and lived here with my family."

"He's not around here anymore," Tarantula says abruptly. She grabs her head. "I'm getting one of my headaches—see you tomorrow." Leaving Josie standing there, she walks down the hall toward her bedroom.

"Wait a minute," Josie says. "Did you know him? Dan Hawkins?"

Tarantula wheels around, her green eyes shooting sparks. "I told you I've got a headache. I have to go to bed."

"It's real important that I find him," Josie says. The mood in the room has definitely changed, and Tarantula looks more haggard than before—the dark circles under her eyes are getting darker.

"Dan Hawkins is dead," the old woman shouts. "Are you satisfied? He is no longer among the living. Leave me alone."

Josie stands there a moment, so stunned she can hardly breathe. Then she walks out of the house. Dan Hawkins is dead, she thinks. He was the only person here who knew Cheyenne, and he's dead. An image of his tall lanky build flashes before her eyes. Until now she hadn't realized how much she'd been banking on seeing him. Deep down inside she'd thought they could get into interesting conversations about literature and art. She'd thought how proud he'd be of her when he discovered how extensively she'd been reading, and more importantly she'd hoped he would be able to tell her the whereabouts of Cheyenne.

Back in the trailer she slices some lemons and makes lemonade. As soon as her telephone is installed, she plans to start looking for her sister, calling hospitals in California. She wonders how Cheyenne is doing health-wise, but most of all she wonders why Tarantula Garcia reacted so strongly to her question about Dan Hawkins.

"I had to take a job in Tucson," Clarence says when he gets home that evening at six o'clock. "Couldn't find nothing any closer. I think I'll like it though."

"Who're you working for?" Josie asks, standing in front of the stove preparing supper.

"Monkey Wards," Clarence says. "I'm working for their service department, repairing TVs from eight in the morning till five-thirty in the evening. Prob'ly won't get home till almost six-thirty. That's kind of late to be getting home, but at least it's a job. They'll give us a ten percent discount on anything we buy. How about that?"

"Pretty good," Josie says, happy to see him so excited.

"Actually I started today," he says. "Already fixed one of their TVs. The only thing I hate is having to drive so far to work. Thirty-five miles is a long way, and it's hotter than hell down there. They're goin to have me doing the outside calls. Ain't too crazy about that."

"You'll get used to it."

"And," Clarence adds, "the other technicians are . . ." He looks at Josie and decides not to go on with his comment. "Never mind."

"Are what?" Josie asks.

"Two Mexicans and a black man. That's what," he says.

Josie grins. "Well, Clarence, just look on this as an opportunity to get to know all about people from different races and cultures."

"I already know about that, Josie. I was in Vietnam, remember? But in the army, people hung out with their own—the blacks with their own and the Mexicans with their own. 'Course there was Tommy. He was from Indiana. We used to sit around in the evenings and smoke pot. Tommy got blown into a million pieces right in front of me. He was the only black feller I ever got to know."

"You smoked pot? You were friends with a black man?" Josie is amazed. This is the first time Clarence has ever said one word about his experiences in Vietnam. The only evidence that he was even there is that he jumps at any sudden movement or sound and bolts upright in the middle of the night, breathing in short rapid gasps, his face broken out in a cold sweat.

"Did you like smoking pot?" Josie asks.

"It was something I did in the war. It ain't something I do now, and I don't want to talk about it anymore."

"Looks like you'd want to talk about your days in the war. Daddy always talks about being in World War Two. He seems to like to talk about it. How can you never talk about something that was such a big event in your life?" She's tried to get him to talk about Vietnam many times before, but all that results is an argument.

"I ain't your daddy. You don't want to hear about it anyway. You was prob'ly over here protesting with all them other fools."

"No, I wasn't."

"Yeah, but you agreed with them, didn't you?"

Josie remembers those lonely days when she was the only person she personally knew who was against the war. "Okay, I did, but I don't blame you for the stupid thing if that's what you mean."

Clarence glares at her. "You think it was stupid and still expect me to tell you about what happened over there? Well, it ain't none of your business. You don't deserve to know about it." He stomps off to the bedroom.

Josie stares at his closed door. Every time she tries to engage him in a conversation that gets into the reasons why they fight so much, he closes the door in her face. One thing is settled, she thinks. This is definitely not the time to tell him about my prospective barmaid job.

14

The next morning Clarence, still miffed from their altercation of the night before, eats his breakfast without saying a word. He has never been one to talk a lot, but when he's upset, silence booms from him like artillery fire. Josie sits there watching his Adam's apple bob up and down as he swallows his food, and she remembers that when she first fell in love with him, she had thought his quiet nature meant he was holding a secret deep inside that someday, if she were lucky enough, he might reveal. Now she wonders if maybe he just doesn't have anything to say. Even if he does, she knows for sure he doesn't want to say it to her.

When Clarence leaves for work, Josie washes the dishes with an ache in her stomach that won't go away. Finally she decides to get out of the house for a while, but when she stops by Tarantula's to ask directions to some local points of interest, the old woman refuses to open the door. "All I want is for you to tell me where that artists' colony is," Josie shouts, her hands pressed against the closed door. She knows Tarantula is inside because she can hear her moving around. "Are you mad at me?" she yells.

At last the old woman answers. "They don't like people out there poking around unless they're invited."

"I don't intend to poke around. I'm just taking a walk and thought I might go past it." Josie hears Tarantula step closer to the door. "I won't bother anyone."

"Oh, all right. It's out there in the direction of the junction, you know, where you turn to get on the road to Tucson."

"Thanks," Josie mutters. "I didn't mean to make you mad at me yesterday. I had no way of knowing Dan was dead. You must have been friends. I had no way of knowing that either."

"I'm not mad. Just go away and leave me alone."

Josie walks out to Sage and then heads in the direction of the junction. She looks around for what she imagines an artists' colony to be—people sitting in front of easels, or huddled together in passionate conversations, or singsonging poetry in strange lilting voices that place an unnatural emphasis on random words. Seeing and hearing nothing close to that, she decides to get off the road and explore.

Who knows? Maybe I'll even run into don Juan, she's thinking as she makes her way across rough desert terrain. It seems like a place don Juan would like to be, a place where he could let his dreams have full sway. She wanders around for a half hour or more, sniffing the air for a hint of the old sorcerer. She thinks she catches a whiff of him a couple of times, but he darts away like a pollen-carrying bee.

Finally Josie sits down on a rock, bows her head, and says a prayer to him. *"Please don't run away from me,"* she prays. *"Stay a while and talk. It's not that I want you to prove you exist. I already know that. What I want is for you to prove that I exist. I'm sure that a more able person would be having a lengthy conversation with you right now, but you've got to admit that I try to engage you. Doesn't trying count for something?"*

When she raises her head, she realizes that she is sitting atop a little hill that overlooks the artists' colony. A huddle of small white houses are barely visible through the scrub oaks that edge the hill. She sees a woman walk inside one of the houses, carrying a canvas and some paints, sees children playing in a front yard. *"Thanks, don Juan,"* Josie whispers. For an hour or more, she sits quietly looking down at the little houses. Every so often someone will step out on a porch or walk down the narrow street. She wants more than anything to go down there, introduce herself, and ask to see someone's work, but she's afraid she won't know what to say, that she'll just stand there with her mouth open, unable to speak.

That night when Clarence comes home, they eat supper in silence. Later they go to bed and lie together awkwardly like patients placed near each other in the ward of a hospital.

*   *   *

The telephone was hooked up yesterday evening, and Josie has been on the phone all morning, calling hospitals in San Francisco and Los Angeles since those are the two California cities she thinks her sister was more likely to have gone—San Francisco because of its bohemian reputation and Los Angeles because of its glitz. So far she has been unable to find any information on Ramona Clay. Either the hospitals won't give out information or they check through their medical records and come up empty-handed. Refusing to give up, she orders phone books from the two cities, figuring that when they arrive, she'll call every cardiologist listed.

Realizing she hasn't spoken to Brewster since their arrival in Arizona, she dials his number. "Hello, Daddy. How's it goin?"

"Well, it's about time," Brewster says. "I was beginning to think you fellers was lost or'd got in a wreck or something. Why didn't you call?"

"I wanted to wait till I got here, and then I had to get a phone installed."

"You just now got there? Lord, I could have gone across the country five times by now."

"Well, as you know Clarence ain't too speedy."

Brewster laughs.

Josie sighs. "I've been calling hospitals all morning, but I ain't had no luck in finding Cheyenne. I'm not giving up, though."

Brewster falls silent.

"How's your arthritis, Daddy?"

"What?"

"How do you feel?" Josie shouts.

"With my hands," Brewster says.

Josie cracks up. "Are you getting enough to eat?" She worries that he doesn't cook enough.

"Stuffing myself like a pig. Ida's coming to pick me up this evening. She's made chicken and dumplings and's taking me to her house for supper."

Josie begins telling him about Sage, about the old house they lived in, its state of disrepair, about the job Clarence got and the job she might have gotten.

"Well, looks like you fellers is doing all right," he tells her.

Josie pauses. "As soon as we get ahead a little, I'm sending for you, but right now . . ."

When they hang up, Brewster steps outside and begins walking toward the courthouse, hoping to chat with Ed Gibbs, to tell him about Josie's call and to ponder the state of the world. He won't tell him about Josie's search for Cheyenne, though. He's decided to keep that a secret, afraid if he tells anyone his long-lost daughter might still be alive, he'll jinx the whole thing. Of course she's alive, he thinks. How could I ever have thought different? He remembers when she was a child, sees her obstinate face, her troubling dark eyes. He loved her as much as any parent ever loved a child—he loved her dissatisfaction, her independence, the way she stood up to Dora.

He remembers that sometimes Cheyenne didn't seem exactly human, had so much energy you'd have thought she was running on electricity, was so full of life she shined like gold. He used to wonder if somehow she had been dropped down to them from outer space. She would have argued that point though. Cheyenne often behaved as if she were the only true human being and the rest of the population had been put on earth for no other reason than to try to please her. People followed her like puppy dogs. A person like Cheyenne always has a gang tagging behind, hoping some of the danger will rub off, Brewster thinks. Getting a crystal-clear image of her in his mind, he shakes his head in wonder that he somehow sired such a child.

When Brewster walks up the courthouse steps, he finds Ed Gibbs in an agitated state.

"The thing is," Ed says, as if he's been talking to Brewster all morning, "I ain't so sure why I didn't want to go to the war. Maybe I was just a coward."

Brewster sits down and looks askance at Ed. "I thought you said you got out of it because you don't like to shoot things."

"Maybe I don't like things to shoot me even more."

"What brought all this on?" Brewster asks.

"I don't know. Got the big eye last night and couldn't go to sleep. Had to think about something. Was you afraid when you was over there, Brewster?"

"Mostly I just did what I was told to do, not that I didn't believe in being there cause I did. It was the right thing. And sometimes I even had fun. Might sound odd to you, but you'd be surprised how much laughing takes place in a war. Still, I was scared, sometimes more so than other times."

"You're just saying that, I bet."

"No, I was afraid." Brewster looks down at the steps, remembering.

"How did you get over it? I mean, what was it like when you was afraid?"

"It was pretty bad." Brewster picks up a small rubber ball that is lodged in the hedge beside the steps. Bouncing it toward the street, he watches it roll and then disappear down a gutter. "I tried to tell Dora about it once, but it was too awful, I reckon. She stared at me like she thought I was making it up."

"Making what up?" Ed asks, all ears.

Brewster isn't so sure he wants to get into war tales today—bodies exploding, bloody arms landing here, shredded legs there—but the truth is he goes over those days in his mind regularly. "Prob'ly to some people it ain't that big a deal," he tells Ed. "Some peopl'd prob'ly say, 'So?'"

Ed blushes. "I bet I'd think it was pretty big since I ain't never been to a war."

"Well, okay," Brewster mutters, his mind drifting back through the years. "One of the worst times for me was outside a little village near Nancy, France."

"Where's Nancy, France?" Ed asks.

"Not too far from Germany," Brewster says, hoping Ed doesn't continue to interrupt him. "We'd split up, with squads taking different routes. It was morning and coldern all get out, but the sun was shining, and not hardly a drop of snow was on the ground. They was some icicles hanging in the trees beside the road, and the sun was hitting on them, making them all sparkly like diamonds. That's the first thing I remember of that day—the sun hitting them icicles."

"Does it snow a lot over there?"

"Most of the time. At least in the winter," Brewster says, then continues with his story. "We'd decided to get off the road and cross this field, sneak into town the back way, figuring the Germans was already there. Anyway it was when we was traipsing across that field that we started seeing the bodies. Looked like they'd been laying on the ground a week or more. They was all swoll up and stinking like nothing I've smelled since. All of a sudden I knowed we was goin to die too—all of us—right there in that field with the sun shining on them icicles. We'd get killed, and I couldn't help wondering if the dying would help anything as far as the war went." Brewster pauses. "Ah, you prob'ly don't want to hear this."

"Yes, I do," Ed says. "I like to know what I missed, to know if I could've stood up to it."

Brewster sighs. "Well, it's not pretty. It's rank as a old toilet." He takes himself back to that day in time, to the sun piercing the frozen air. "They was a line of trees edging the town, and I worried that the Germans was hiding in them with their guns cocked, ready to break out shooting any minute. All of a sudden it got so quiet I couldn't hear nothing but my own heart beating. I looked around at my buddy, Antonio Mancini from New Jersey, and thought, You're goin to be dead in a minute, Antonio. You'll never make it back to Newark. He smiled at me, and I smiled back, intending to warn him, but as it turned out I didn't have time. We were still smiling when it happened. Like a flash of lightening—they mowed us down flat."

"You got hit?"

"Yep, in my arm, but I was so scared I didn't hardly notice at first."

"What did you do?" Ed asks, breathing hard.

"I hit the dirt, crawled on my belly, and hid behind one of them swoll up bodies that had been laying there for a week. I tore off a piece of my shirt and bound it around the hole in my arm, trying to stop the bleeding. It slowed some but didn't stop right away." Brewster gazes straight at Ed. "That dead feller's body was bloated so big no one knowed I was behind it. Bullets would hit him right often, and he'd bounce up against me like a big old truck-tire inner tube. I laid behind him all during the shooting, which seemed like it lasted about twenty minutes, and I kept laying there a long time after the shooting stopped. My nose was buried in the hair on the back of his head, and he was stinking so bad I dry-heaved ever' few minutes. Even passed out once. It was the worst couple of hours I ever lived through. When I finally did raise up, it was almost noon and ever'one of the men with me—including Antonio—they was all dead."

"Lord have mercy," Ed says.

"I got up, stood over that body, and said, 'Thank ye, buddy. You saved my life even after you got killed.' Then I started out walking in the opposite direction of the town. Took me two days to finally run across the rest of my platoon."

"And you was scared all the time you was hid behind that body?"

"So scared I couldn't move. Sometimes I think I oughten of crawled up behind that feller. Maybe I ought to of just stood in that open field and died with Antonio Mancini."

"It was reflex, Brewster. You hit the dirt like people do when they get shot," Ed says.

Brewster stares at his feet and says, "Guess I just wonder about things sometimes, that's all—wonder how it was that I didn't have to have my legs cut off like my buddy George Wells did after our feet got froze in that foxhole, wonder why I didn't die with the rest of my squad that day in France. How did I come out of things scot-free?"

Ed grins. "You're one lucky son of a bitch, that's all. They say that if you dump a bag of sugar, they'll always be a few grains that stick to the side. You're one of them grains."

"A grain of sugar?"

"Yep."

Brewster eyes him suspiciously. "I don't know as I like being compared to sugar, Ed."

Ed blushes. "I didn't mean you was sweet, Brewster. I just meant you was lucky."

The two men sit there for hours talking about this and that. Brewster tells Ed about Josie and Clarence finally getting to Arizona, about Clarence's job, and about Josie's prospect of getting one. He lets him know about Ida's plans to fix him a supper of chicken and dumplings.

"Wish somebody'd fix me a big mess of that," Ed says. "I ain't had no chicken and dumplings in a long time."

Birds chirp in the mulberry tree on the courthouse lawn, women walk by on their way to the drygoods store to buy summer dresses. At two-thirty the elementary school lets out, and children run to the drugstore to gulp down Pepsis and eat potato chips. Their laughter bounces down the streets, ducks between buildings, shoots around traffic, and hovers over Brewster and Ed like the sunlight of a pretty spring day.

15

Josie pours herself another cup of coffee. She wishes Brewster was where she could look in on him every now and then, and she wonders how long it will be before she can actually send for him. She's pacing the floor when the telephone rings. It's Venus Lily Stamper asking her to come to work the next day.

"Lori won't be back," Venus says. "She's moved in with that man of hers. If you take the job, your hours will be from six-thirty in the morning to two o'clock in the afternoon, Monday through Friday. Three dollars an hour. I'll work with you till you catch on. What do you think?"

"Perfect," Josie says, realizing she should have told Clarence about the job before now.

She has a big supper ready when Clarence gets home that evening, all of his favorite dishes—soup beans cooked with ham hocks, fried potatoes, lettuce wilted with bacon grease, corn bread, and chocolate cake for dessert.

"What brought this on?" he asks, cramming his mouth full.

"Oh, nothing else to do."

Grinning, Clarence eats like someone breaking a diet.

Josie fiddles with her fork. "How's your work buddies?"

Clarence sighs. "Still trying to accuse me of being a racist? My work buddies are fine, if that's what you mean. They're all right."

"That's not what I mean, Clarence." Josie wonders if there is an easy way she can lead up to the fact that she has a job. Figuring there isn't one, she says, "Thought I might get a job."

Clarence glances up at her. "Really? Where?"

Josie picks at her food. "I don't know. Grocery store, bar, restaurant."

"Well, maybe, if that's what you want to do," Clarence says. "Grocery store or restaurant would be good. I don't know about a bar, though."

Josie sighs. "Actually I've already got a job. They want me to come tomorrow."

"Where?"

"It's uh . . ." Josie takes a large bite of potatoes. ". . . e . . . e . . . establishment."

"What kind of a establishment?" Clarence asks.

"You know, a place where people go."

"To do what?"

"Play games," she says, thinking of the pool tables. "And uh . . . talk and stuff. You know."

"No, I don't." An image of a shady motel flashes before Clarence's eyes, a place where women have sex for money. He sees Josie carrying clean towels to naked lowlifes in hot tubs, toting drinks to leering middle-aged men. Clarence remembers seeing a suspicious-looking place near Sage Junction called the Hot L Motel. He bets anything the Hot L has hot tubs.

"It's called Don Juan's," Josie says.

Clarence almost chokes on his beans. "Don Juan's?"

"Yeah, that's the name."

He stands up, now visualizing even stranger scenarios than before. "Is it some kind of weird Yaqui place? Is that what you mean?"

Josie stands up too. "No, Clarence. It's a bar. It has nothing to do with Yaquis, all right? It's just a little old bar that sits on top of a hill on the road to Rustle."

"You mean to tell me you'd work in a bar?" He grinds his teeth until they squeak.

"It's a job, ain't it?" Josie shouts. "Looks to me like we need the money."

Clarence plops back down to his chair. "We do need money, but not that bad. I don't want you working in no bar."

Josie wishes she could tell Clarence what the bar means to her, that it is a symbol for don Juan himself, that his spirit slides among the bar stools and darts around the beer bottles, that she knows instinctively she discovered the place for a reason yet to be revealed, but she realizes that he would simply block out her words if she told him something like that. He won't listen to deep-seated motivations of the psyche, so she always has to lie, giving him reasons that involve tangible things such as money, explanations that fit in with the puritan work ethic. "I've already checked out every other place in town," she tells him. "No one else needs to hire anyone. We could use the money, Clarence, and I'll just work there till we get on our feet. There's not a thing on earth wrong with them people in that bar. They're real nice, and Venus Lily Stamper and her sister Lily Venus— they're the ones who own it—are goin to pay me three dollars a hour plus tips. I don't see how I can pass that up, and what do you mean you won't have me working there? I'll work where I want."

Feeling as if he can't breathe, Clarence gets up and clamors outside. As Josie washes the dishes, he pees on the desert floor right in front of their trailer. How can she do me this way? he asks himself. Mom would kill me if she knew I was letting Josie work in a bar. And Pap, if he was still alive, would be embarrassed to look me in the eye.

Deep down he's still mad at Josie from the episode the other day when she nagged him to talk about his experiences in the war. Vietnam has been a sore subject between them throughout their marriage. It began with a letter he got from her while he was still there. He had seen his friend, Tommy, blown to bits just the day before, and he was so glad to get a letter from home, so happy at the prospect of reading the thoughts of someone who cared about the hell he was going through that his eyes were moist with emotion as he ripped open the envelope.

In the letter Josie said she'd give a million dollars to see him, that she loved him more than anything. She said she wished he hadn't gone to the war anyway, that she wished he'd burned his draft card and gone to Canada instead. She said the war was stupid and that the only thing it had done so far was get a lot of people killed for no reason. She said if anything happened to him, she intended to join up with the radicals and protest the war, protest the whole damned United States.

All Clarence could see when he read that letter was Tommy screaming as the sharp metal blasted through his body. *Radicals,* Clarence kept thinking. *She wants to join up with fuckin radicals.* A seed of distrust that verged on dislike settled in the pit of his stomach. He tried to overcome it because he loved Josie. He figured she was young and foolish and the fact that she was stateside, hearing nothing but news media propaganda, had twisted her view of the world. Besides, deep down, he knew she loved him.

Now, he isn't sure about anything because after years of trying to kill that nagging seed of distrust, it's still there. In fact, it has begun to grow and flourish. Even today, it's pushing itself out of the corner in his mind where he throws the things he doesn't want to face.

When Josie begins work at Don Juan's the next morning, it doesn't take her long to lose the scent of the old Yaqui sorcerer. She doesn't have time to contemplate the finer virtues of separate realities. Dozens of tramp miners, wild-eyed men with sweaty bodies and smoldering faces, whose graveyard shift knocked off at 6 A.M., are already waiting in the parking lot for the bar to open. They are men full of adrenaline and the need to talk loudly and antagonistically about what they've just been through for eight long grueling hours, about slackers who aren't holding up their end of the job, about whores who stole money from them down in Tucson last weekend, about the fast cars they bought that they wonder how they'll pay for once their services are no longer needed at the mine, about landlords who've thrown them out of their apartments, and about where the hell they'll go once this job runs out. Some say they're going to Alaska and disappear into the wilderness, others say they're going to California where they'll sit on the beach and let the cool sea breezes blow straight at them for the rest of their lives, but most say they'll go back to their homes in Alabama, or Louisiana, or Missouri, or Canada and await the phone call that will lead them to the next mine.

At first the men are a little awkward around the new bartender, eyeing Josie as if they're sizing up a shank of smoked ham, but Venus Lily puts them in a different frame of mind when she yells, "She's married, boys. Happily married. Get on with your business."

Josie is amazed at how quickly they obey Venus, with her frail body, pale face, and voice like God. It's almost as if she's their mother, one like Ma Barker. They receive every message she sends, and when two of the men don't obey her, when they keep yelling at each other about which of them won a drag race last Saturday night, Venus tells them to leave, and they walk out quietly with their heads hung low. Perhaps they mind her because she is the only bartender in town who will allow them to run up tabs, or conceivably they're afraid of what she might do to them, but most likely they just delight in the way Venus Lily Stamper handles herself.

By ten o'clock in the morning, the graveyard shift begins drifting out, heading for home and bed, and soon there are only five men left. Venus turns to Josie. "Well, whaddya think? It's like this every day."

"I feel like I've been in a whirlwind," Josie says. "But it's kind of exciting."

Just then a man in his sixties walks in, orders a beer, winks at Venus Lily, and gives her an all-knowing smile. "How're you doing this morning, Venus?"

"Fine," Venus says, "and yourself?"

"I'm doing fine too," he says, grinning bashfully. Then he whispers, "I'm surprised to find you working after last night. Thought you'd be too tired to come in."

"Why, Bobby Swanson, what on earth do you mean?" Venus says loudly.

The other men in the room start to laugh and poke each other in the ribs. "Here we go again," they mutter.

Bobby blushes. "After all that carrying on we did, I figured you'd sleep in."

"What carrying on?"

"You know."

"No, I don't. You must be talking about my sister."

Bobby rolls his eyes. "I reckon I know who I was with. No point in denying it."

"You're wrong, Bobby. I wouldn't go out with you if you were the last person on earth. And if you don't quit yammering about it, you can leave."

"Hey, Bobby," one of the men says, "don't you even know who you laid into last night? You'd better get a hold of yourself."

"Ah, shut up," Bobby says, swiveling on the bar stool until he's facing the opposite direction.

Venus winks at Josie. "He'll never know for sure either way."

"Was it you?" Josie whispers.

"You'll never know either," Venus says.

Josie nods toward the picture of the nearly naked woman, rising out of the clam shell. "Is that you?"

"Maybe. Then again, it might be my sister."

Josie laughs.

"It's time I taught you how to mix drinks," Venus says. "Most of my customers order beer or shots of tequila, but every now and then one will want a mixed drink." For two hours, Venus teaches Josie the craft of blending margaritas, bloody Marys, screwdrivers, Tom Collins's, martinis, and rum and cokes.

"I'm dying to meet Lily Venus," Josie says when the training is over. "I bet I can tell you two apart."

Grinning, Venus walks over to the jukebox, plays "Delta Dawn," and walks up and down the bar, hamming it up with the remaining men. Josie is fascinated by the way the customers' eyes shine with laughter in Venus's presence. "Did you ever know a Dan Hawkins?" she finally remembers to ask her.

A smile comes on Venus's face. "One of the best. Why?"

"Heard he was dead. What did he die of?"

Venus gasps and pours herself a drink of straight bourbon. "Well, that's the first I've heard of it. Who told you he was dead?"

"Tarantula."

"Shit, that old woman is crazier than a loon. Lies all the time over everything. Dan isn't dead that I know of. He moved to California.

Came in here all the time bragging that he was going. Left about two years ago." Venus taps Bobby Swanson on the shoulder. "Did you hear anything about Dan Hawkins dying? Tarantula told Josie he was dead."

Bobby wheels around to face Venus. "News to me."

Venus narrows her eyes and whispers to Josie, "Dan Hawkins worked for her. Did you know that? She took him in when he was still in high school, gave him a roof over his head."

"No," Josie says, her eyes widening.

"He stayed in that little trailer you're living in."

"What?" Josie's hair is standing on end. "He worked for her?" Her thoughts race back to the summer of Cheyenne's heart attack, to when they'd been digging up cholla cactuses for their mother. She can still hear Dan saying, *"Did you know this is private property? It belongs to the woman I work for . . ."* He was talking about Tarantula Garcia, Josie realizes. It all fits like a big puzzle. It's like everything is all mapped out, like there's certain people who are meant to be important to you in this life. She glances up at the ceiling and thinks she sees the glimmer of don Juan's smile.

"Probably the only way Tarantula can accept the fact that he left her is to say he died," Venus says. "She hasn't been right in the head since he went to California. Nobody knows for sure, but a lot of people think they had a little romance going on."

Josie stands there with her mouth open.

Venus grins. "I know. You're thinking how much older she is than him, but when Dan was here she still looked pretty young. She did most of her aging after he left."

"That's not what I'm thinking necessarily. I just want to know how you're so sure he's alive. He may have died after he left here."

Venus rolls her eyes. "Well, if he had, they'd have brought him back here to bury him. This is his home. No, that's just Tarantula talking. She makes up stories left and right. Gets worse with each passing day."

Just then Johnny Walker comes into the bar and says he heard that Mike Chandler, one of Venus's regular customers, got himself thrown into the Rustle jail. Venus grabs her purse and turns to Josie. "You'll have to take over a little sooner than we'd planned. I've got to go bail Mike out. That little Rustle jail ain't much bigger than a cracker box. No windows. Ain't got any kind of cooling either. A man will die if he stays in there long."

"Oh, yeah," Josie mutters. "Daddy wouldn't drink a drop the whole time we lived in Rustle, afraid he might get put in that jail." Still in shock from the Dan Hawkins revelations, her voice trails off to a whisper.

"I won't be gone long," Venus says, then she turns to Johnny. "Watch out for her. And help her out at the bar if it gets too busy."

As Venus Lily walks out the door, Josie keeps thinking, I'm living in Dan Hawkins's former home, sleeping in his bed. That might have been his English toffee and jalapeños that I found in the kitchen cabinets. What would make Tarantula say he's dead if he isn't? She is so lost in thought that she hardly notices her customers, doesn't hear Bobby Swanson order a beer.

Johnny steps around the bar and pours him a drink. "Don't worry. I'll take care of Bobby," he says. "Hey, none of us'll bite—at least not here and now. You'll have to get used to working the bar alone sometimes, cause Venus Lily is always going to Tucson or Rustle to bail someone out of jail. Venus can't stand the thought of anyone she knows being penned up. Her sister, Lily Venus, is the same way."

As Johnny tells Josie stories from the West Virginia hills, Venus's remarks about Tarantula and Dan Hawkins begin to fade from her mind. The sound of his voice reminds her of the green hills and trickling streams of home.

That afternoon the other twin, Lily Venus, bursts through the door with a gust of chatter, wearing an identical outfit to the one worn by her sister that morning. Everyone was right. The sisters look exactly alike. Lily Venus zips behind the bar and slings her purse underneath the counter. "Hi," she says to Josie in a voice as gruff as Venus Lily's. "Venus told me about you. Said you were from Kentucky."

"That's right," Josie says, ogling her. "I can't get over how much you fellers look alike."

Lily grins. "Well, I'm glad you showed up around here just at the time we needed help."

Bobby Swanson, who is pretty sloshed by now, interrupts their chat with, "Hello, Lily Venus. I'm surprised to see you. Thought you'd be too tired to come to work after last night."

"What're you talking about?" she asks.

"Last night down in Tucson. Don't you remember?"

"Remember what?"

"Shee-it," Bobby says, and throwing down the money for his beer, he stalks out.

Lily Venus looks at Josie and grins. "What's the matter with him, anyway?"

"I don't know," Josie says.

Lily eyes Josie carefully. "You look beat. Get on out of here and get some rest."

Bone tired, Josie exits the establishment and begins the thirty-minute walk home. She traipses along, dragging her heels, wondering what in the world is the truth about Dan Hawkins. When she gets to Tarantula's house, she bangs on the front door. "I have to know about Dan," she yells, but Tarantula doesn't come, doesn't acknowledge she's there.

16

The Arizona sun doesn't dilly-dally around. It pops up every morning like an unruly penis—headstrong, erect, and full of itself—bursts through bedroom windows with ruthless desire, and drums on sleepers' eyelids with a jarring beat, keeps drumming till they come to. Josie crawls out of bed and makes coffee, sends Clarence on his way to work. It's Friday, but she's home, having made an urgent request of Venus Lily to take the day off.

The San Francisco and Los Angeles phone books arrived yesterday, and this morning she begins calling doctors, taking on San Francisco first. By eleven o'clock she has called every cardiologist listed in the northern California city. Most of them won't give information over the phone, and the few who do agree to help her find no record of a patient with the name of Cheyenne or Ramona Clay.

Putting the phone down, Josie walks over to the window and watches the weeds being killed by the sun. The arid desert has caused her skin, hair, and eyes to become as dry as sand. Still she loves the land that surrounds her, the high desert with its red-tinted dirt and cool nights, the roughness of the terrain, the edginess of it, the sense of danger. She's already learned the names of some of the plants and trees—the ocotillo, manzanita, scrub oaks, and her favorite, the tall yucca with its flowering stalk.

Josie is fascinated by the men who frequent Don Juan's—Bobby Swanson with his search for the true identity of the twin he loves, and Johnny Walker, from Red Jacket, West Virginia, who comes to Don Juan's almost every day and chats with her for an hour or more. When she asks him how he can afford to spend so much time away from his ranch, he winks at her and explains that the men who work for him know their business. Sometimes he doesn't talk at all but stands rough and quiet by the bar, letting his fingers dawdle over her hands when he pays for his drinks. Even though she knows he's married—one day she overheard another customer ask him how his wife was doing—Josie has begun to dream of him at night. She imagines kissing his lips, running her fingers through his black hair and on down his muscular chest, knowing that in her dreams the lovemaking is probably better than it could ever be in real life.

Tarantula has hardly spoken a word to Josie since that very first inquiry regarding Dan Hawkins. Yesterday, the old woman was standing in front of her house, watering the fig tree, holding a water hose in one hand and a bottle of tequila in the other. Josie tried to get her to talk, but it was no use. Tarantula just stood there laughing a low spooky laugh, her upper lip puckered in a growl, the whites of her teeth showing. Then she sashayed into her house, leaving Josie alone with a pile of chill bumps and unanswered questions.

When Brewster moved his family back to Pick, Kentucky, in late August of '59, Cheyenne enrolled in the ninth grade at the new high school outside of town, while Josie, in the sixth grade, returned to the old elementary school, and it soon became evident that nothing would be the same as it had been before.

Josie was amazed at the change that took place in her sister practically overnight, and the most noticeable involved her appearance. Cutting her hair in layers, she rolled it with brush rollers and spent hours teasing and spraying it in front of the mirror. Plum-colored lipstick decorated her full lips that drooped in a perpetual sexy pout. Next came her eyes. She plucked and arched the brows, lined the eyes all around with black velvet eyebrow pencil, then blanketed the lashes with thick black mascara, squashing them with an eyelash curler until they curved high on her upper lids. She started shaving her legs and wearing straight tight skirts with a kick pleat in the back.

After the first week of the fall term, Cheyenne stopped riding the school bus and began hitching rides with an older friend, Sue White, who already had her driver's license. This meant that, unlike Josie, Cheyenne didn't have to be standing by the road at 6:30 in the morning to catch the bus; Sue didn't pick her up until 7:30. At night Cheyenne no longer listened to Jerry Lee Lewis. Instead she joined the Columbia Record Club and ordered albums that featured African conga drums, accompanied by eerie tribal chants. She was also crazy about island music, sprinkled with the fierce cries of unimaginable tropical birds.

On the other hand, Josie took to her room, spending hours reading book after book—*Green Mansions* and *Little Women* were her favorites. She read each of them seven times because she wanted to live in the worlds they offered and thought seven might be her lucky number. To have an unidentifiable language like *Green Mansion's* mystery woman who eludes her would-be lover by disappearing into dense jungles, or to be Alcott's Jo March, forever alive near Walden Pond in the post–Civil War days, was Josie's greatest desire. She even tried to persuade people to start calling her Jo, but no one would oblige. Undaunted, she memorized all of Jo's lines and would stand in front of the bedroom mirror and pretend she actually was Alcott's creation. Why can't I get in that book? she often wondered. *Get inside there.* Maybe if I concentrate hard enough I can. And she spent many an afternoon trying to block out the real world and become fiction.

"People around here are idiots," Cheyenne said late one night after she'd called Josie into her bedroom to listen to WLAC out of Nashville, Tennessee, a radio station that featured raw undiluted blues. "It's like peopl're dead, like they got married, had children, and died. Mommy and Daddy are dead too, you know." She whispered this under the plaintive moans and grunts of Muddy Waters and Bobby Blue Bland. "Well, that ain't goin to happen to me, and if you know what's good for you, you won't let it happen to you."

"Mommy and Daddy seem happy enough to me," Josie said, even though somewhere deep down she knew better.

"No they ain't. They get *okay* about once every two years, but the rest of the time they're pitiful. Ain't you ever seen Mommy standing on the porch just staring out toward the mountain with that blank look in her eye? Ain't you ever walked up to her when she was like that and asked her a question and she didn't even answer? Do you call that happy?"

"Well, Daddy usually acts like he's happy."

Cheyenne sighed. "He ain't got no better sense. What I'm talking about here is the way things are set up. It's all wrong. People stop living, Josie. They stop living way before they ought to. I'm not goin to get hooked in like that. I'm not goin to follow the crowd. I'm goin to do things different. You don't have to live the same way people have always lived. You can branch out. You can branch so far out people won't recognize you anymore. You won't even recognize yourself." Cheyenne's eyes shined with energy as she put on her album of African drums. "Listen to 'em, Josie. It's like they're calling us to come alive. Don't you feel it?"

In the dimly lit room glowing from a bedside lamp that was draped with a thick red towel, Cheyenne swayed back and forth, her shadow flickering on the wall behind her, and Josie really did feel it, felt the call of the wild African drums.

As the school year progressed, Cheyenne started coming home later and later in the evenings after school, and when she'd finally arrive, sometimes past dark and after the supper dishes had already been put away, she and Dora would get into great raging battles that lasted for an hour or more. They'd stand face to face yelling every name they could think of, as Brewster sank into the television with *The Rifleman* or *Bat Masterson*, and Josie went to her room, where she shoved pillows over her head in an attempt to block out the sound. Sometimes Dora would try to make in with her wayward daughter, but Cheyenne wouldn't give her the time of day, and then the silence would begin—days with neither of them speaking a word. Finally Cheyenne began sneaking out of the house at night. After everyone was in bed, Josie would fake a coughing spell as Cheyenne raised the window in her adjoining bedroom and jumped out into the night. Peering out the window as her sister walked to the road and slipped into a waiting car, Josie wondered how it was that Cheyenne had ended up with such energy. She wondered where her own was. All

Josie wanted to do was stand in front of a mirror and pretend to be the characters in a novel, to say their lines and hold her mouth the way she imagined they held theirs. Maybe I'm just like all the people Cheyenne hates, she thought. Maybe I died a while back.

As if to prove there was a small spark of life flickering behind her eyes, she stopped reading *Green Mansions* and *Little Women*, both of them being books her mother had suggested she read. Besides, Josie figured there was no such thing as a mysterious specimen of lost human perfection running wild in the jungle, and as for Marmy Smarmy March and her four young ladies—forget that transcendental shit. Forget trying to rise above the human race. She took out Dan Hawkins's reading list—that crumpled piece of yellow paper she'd stuffed into a box of mementos from Arizona, along with the turquoise stone, the fool's gold, and the broken purple-and-white geode. She started following Dan's suggestions and was soon reading the short stories of Edgar Allan Poe and the biographies of Lord Byron and Shelley with their free love and rebellious leanings. She lost herself in the bawdy world of Shakespeare and, memorizing the lines of his female heroines, she acted out their dramas on the stage of her small bedroom. Quoting Juliet, she often shouted, "So tedious is this day/As is the night before some festival/To an impatient child . . ." She read *Tropic of Capricorn* and *Tropic of Cancer*, especially the dirty parts—the dirtier the better. For Josie, the days slipped by uneventfully until well past Christmas and deep into the winter.

As it turned out, they didn't know Cheyenne was missing until she'd been gone two days. Cheyenne had asked Dora if she could spend the night with Sue White. Brewster had already gone to work, and Josie was on the school bus by the time Cheyenne got up that morning, drank some coffee, and walked out of the house toward the road. She always waited under a poplar tree to be picked up by Sue. It was cold that morning, and she'd bundled up in a heavy coat and tied a wool scarf around her head before walking outside. It was the last time Dora saw her. Brewster and Josie's last time was the night before when Cheyenne, in a great mood, had pulled out her old Jerry Lee Lewis records and insisted that Josie dance with her.

When Cheyenne didn't come home that first night, no one thought it unusual since she'd planned to stay with Sue, but when she didn't come home the next night, all hell broke loose. Dora called several teachers and found out that her daughter hadn't been to school for two days. The White family didn't have a telephone—Chester White had gotten rid of it when the local phone company billed him for a call he didn't make—so Dora, Brewster, and Josie piled into their '56 Ford and drove to their house.

"Well, she was *supposed* to stay all night with me," Sue said. "But when she wouldn't standing by that tree where I always pick her up, I just figured she was sick or something."

"Looks like you'd have come on to the house to find out why she wasn't there," Dora said, her lips tightening with anger and fear. "Didn't you have no more curiosity than that? She was supposed to stay with you that night. Didn't you wonder about it?"

Sue started to cry. "Cheyenne changes her mind a lot. I figured out a long time ago not to try and outguess her." Wiping her eyes, she stared at the kitchen table where the two families had gathered in the small house at the head of a hollow. "I just went on to school. Figured she'd changed her mind."

Dora took on a softer voice. "What about when she wasn't at school the second day? Didn't you think nothing was funny then?"

Sue sniffed and coughed. "By then I figured for sure she had the flu."

Dora tried for several hours to get more information from Sue, but she either didn't have it or wouldn't give it. In the ensuing days and weeks, sheriff's and police departments were called and a search was begun, but there wasn't a trace of Cheyenne, not a hair left behind.

"That goddamned White girl is lying," Dora blurted out one Sunday night, about a month after the disappearance. Hope of finding Cheyenne was beginning to fade, and Dora was fading with it. "Sue knows where Cheyenne is. That mealy-mouthed little shit-ass is a bald-faced liar."

Bonanza was coming on and Brewster was gearing up for his weekly trip to the Cartwright's Western spread, but he turned to

Dora, pleading, "Now, honey, you don't know that. Sue don't seem like a liar to me. We're just goin to have to wait. They'll find Cheyenne."

"You don't care," Dora screamed. "All you care about is your god-damned Westerns. I wish you had every Western that was ever made crammed up your hind end."

Barely contained anger glittered in Brewster's eyes. "You don't know everything, Dora. You don't know much of nothing."

Josie took all this in as she stood on the other side of the living room by the piano, idly picking out a tune while visions of Cheyenne drifted through her imagination—Cheyenne hopping freight trains all across the United States, sneaking aboard an ocean liner headed for the Tropics, hacking her way through the deep dark jungles of Africa. Josie smiled to think that Cheyenne had escaped, had shot herself straight into the heart of life.

"What are you smiling about?" Dora shouted, now standing in front of her. "You don't care either, do you? You don't care one little bit that your sister is out there somewhere prob'ly dead or dying. She could be starving to death right now, and here you stand, smiling. I guess you're happy about it, you hard-hearted cold fish. You spineless little turd. You don't have any feelings or a backbone either."

Dora often lost control when she was angry. Josie suspected she sometimes regretted the words that flew like knives from her mouth, but she also knew her mother wasn't one to apologize. Instead, if the mood struck her, you'd come home to find she'd fixed your favorite meal or that she'd bought you something—a pair of tennis shoes or a new birthstone ring. Josie studied her face, noticing how pale it was, and she suddenly felt that Dora wouldn't be much longer in this world. She didn't realize it until years later, but standing there look-ing closely at her, she could almost see the cancer budding in her breasts.

When the Los Angeles and San Francisco phone books turn up noth-ing, Josie begins to lose hope. Her worst fear is that Cheyenne's get-away all those years ago was clean and final, that like an experienced Indian warrior she had left nothing behind but false trails. She calls

Brewster to tell him the bad news. He doesn't have much to say, and they soon hang up. Pacing the floor, she listens to the weatherman on TV say it's 105 degrees in Tucson, which means that the temperature in Sage is in the high nineties. She stops in front of the swampcooler and lets the dank musty air sweep over her, then she rummages through her bookshelf, finds *A Separate Reality*, and begins to read.

17

Clarence bought Josie a car, paid five hundred dollars for a '72 Pinto with a bad carburetor and immediately set about repairing it. It's the only attention he has paid her lately. He goes to work, comes home, goes to work. Usually he doesn't notice she's around unless he's mad at her. Recently he has been mad because she made the phone calls to California. "It's a waste of time and money," he shouted when he found out. "We don't have money to burn."

"Listen to you. You sound like a parent. I bet that's one of Ida's sayings. Why don't you just say it doesn't *grow on trees,* and be done with it, Mr. Cliché," Josie shouted back.

She can't remember a time when they've gotten along any worse. Still she's grateful for the Pinto. It hums like a sewing machine, and she drives it to work today for the first time. Last week Venus Lily started allowing her to work the bar alone, and she's been opening the place every morning at six-thirty. Miners are usually standing at the door waiting for her, and sometimes she finds two or three guys inside sprawled on the floor, sleeping off the fun they had the night before. She is seldom afforded the luxury of a few moments of solitude before the onslaught of customers. Today the morning slips by like any other—the miners come and go, she pours drinks and takes away the empties. Josie begins to feel that she has fallen into a rut. Although the spiritual quality she has always associated with Sage is still alive and well, none of her expectations are coming true. The sorcerer, don Juan, is still elusive, and she doesn't know one thing more about Cheyenne or Dan Hawkins. Josie resolves that when her shift ends she'll make a beeline for Tarantula's house and quiz her until she breaks.

Wiping the counter, she notices Mike Chandler amble out the door. Then suddenly the bar is empty, and she's alone. She can't remember a time when there were no customers at all—no one laughing or arguing or plunking their glasses on the counter. Stillness emanates from the walls and creeps upon the dim room until there is only the sound of her jagged breath. She imagines the roof is gone and pictures how she would appear if someone happened to be spying on her from a plane flying overhead—they'd see a spooked, unsteady woman who looks as if she's losing her mind in the middle of a small desert bar. As Josie glances to the ceiling, sun gleams on disappearing wings; the roar of an engine fades to nothing.

"Jesus Christ, this is who I am," she whispers, as though the imagined plane had dropped a revelation, had not only shown her how she looked today, but how she would look thirty years from now. "Okay, if I'm not satisfied doing this for the rest of my life, what the hell do I want to do?" she asks herself.

Trying to remember situations that have made her happy, she recalls nothing but vague intangibles—the sound of water running over rocks, the particular shade of blue in a clear October sky. "I don't think they pay you for listening to water or watching the sky," she mutters. Finally it dawns on her that she has always enjoyed reciting lines from books and plays. Maybe I could be an actress, she thinks. Then she steps to the door and looks out at the dusty glare of midday Sage and grumbles, "Yeah, like there's theatres all over the place around here."

She wonders if her desire to take on fictional personalities comes from a need to be creative or from a dissatisfaction with who she really is. How can I be happy with who I am when I'm prob'ly not a real, dyed-in-the-wool person anyway? Josie thinks. What if I'm just a bunch of lines I've learned over the years, a monologue I started memorizing the minute I was born? Maybe fiction is as real as anything else. If there'd been a stick measuring my pain, it might have found that I was no more devastated by my mother's death than by reading the chapter where Beth dies in *Little Women*. Maybe the biggest difference was in how long the grief lasted. Book-pain usually ends pretty quick, but pain from losing a mother lasts for a while. What causes it to last longer? Possibly it's the sympathy you get. You're expected to be depressed—are rewarded for it with out-of-the-ordinary kindness and attention—and that's all the excuse you need. Yep, maybe the only difference between fiction and reality is that people feel sorry for you when you lose your mother, but they don't give a shit when you read a sad chapter.

Walking into the back room, she rubs her hands over the green felt of a pool table, racks the balls, grabs a stick, and she's poised for a shot when someone steps behind her.

"You're holding it wrong," a voice says.

Turning around, she finds Johnny Walker grinning like a possum. He puts his arms around her and positions the stick in her hands. Flustered, she almost falls face-forward on the table.

"Try it now," he says and steps back.

She aims the stick at the balls and manages to miss all of them.

"I can see I've got a course to teach," Johnny says.

Josie turns around and looks at him. "Don't you ever have to work on your ranch? I know you've got experienced people working for you, but looks like you'd have to be there more than you are. How on earth do you manage to make a living?"

Johnny chuckles. "I sure ain't never made one by working."

"How then?"

"I make mine by living."

"That pays your rent?"

Johnny grins. "You ask too many questions."

"If there's some easy way to make a living that I don't know about, I wish someone would tell me what it is."

"I thought women liked to work nowadays. It makes you independent, don't it?"

Josie puts her hands on her hips. "Do you call having to be in a place eight hours a day independent? Most of the time I like working here, but every now and then I'd like to be somewhere else. Looks like all I've done is trade jails, and I can't quit because I need the money."

Johnny shakes his head. "All I know is that I used to work in the mines everyday, but I wasn't living. Then I broke my back, and it was the best thing that ever happened to me. Got a settlement, bought my ranch, and now I make a little money off my cattle and orange trees—tend to my insides."

"I'd prob'ly never be lucky enough to break my back," Josie says. "Prob'ly what would happen to me is that I'd hurt it real bad, be in excruciating pain for the rest of my life, and no one would believe me."

Johnny steps toward her and rubs his fingers across her chin.

Josie burns from his touch. "You're married, ain't you? I bet you have kids."

"Two, but what have they got to do with it?"

"Seems like they ought to have something to do with it."

"They don't." He draws her close to him, rubs his hands through her hair.

"Don't you love your wife?" Josie asks. Her voice is shaking with emotion.

"I care about her just like you care about your husband."

Josie moves closer to him, and they kiss, grasping and clutching as if they're each other's last hope, but they're kept from going farther when Bobby Swanson stumbles through the front door, bitching and moaning about the price of gasoline. Josie steps away from Johnny, straightens her hair, and returns to the front room. "How's it goin, Bobby?" she asks.

"Them goddamned asshole oilmen. If I had a hold of one, I'd . . ."

Josie doesn't hear the rest of his tirade because she's watching Johnny step from the back room, tip his hat, and walk out the door. The rest of the day is a blur, and by the time her shift ends, she has forgotten her early morning resolve to drag some answers out of Tarantula. She's pulling into her driveway when she finally remembers. Jumping out of her car, she barges through the old woman's front door without knocking.

Tarantula is in the living room, leaning back in her chair, drinking tequila. "What do you want?" she snarls. She's wearing a sleeveless blouse, exposing wrinkled bony arms that look as dry as her face. Josie sits there thinking that all those years ago when Dan Hawkins came to visit, when he sat in Cheyenne's bedroom, reading poetry and raving about how one of these days he was going to Greenwich Village, he left them to go home to Tarantula. On the surface their affair seems like an odd alliance. Josie can't imagine the amount of gossip that must have traveled the streets of Sage concerning the strange pair. But who knows? she thinks. Maybe they had something the rest of us would have envied. Maybe there was something wild and spidery between them.

Almost as if reading her thoughts, Tarantula mutters, "Yeah, that's right."

Josie's skin crawls. "Tarantula, I know you don't want to talk about this, but I asked people down at the bar, and they say Dan Hawkins is alive. I want to know why you claim he's dead."

Tarantula smiles eerily. "Dan Hawkins? I've known him since he was a kid. I took him in when his mother died. He didn't have a place to stay, and I figured he'd be handy to have around. He seemed older than he was, and Dan was such a good-looking boy. Strong, had sense. Course he always had his girlfriends, and that was all right with me. But he had one or two that . . . one especially that I . . ." Tarantula pours herself some tequila and offers Josie a glass.

"Sure, I'll take one," Josie says, but she has no intention of drinking. She doesn't want to fog up her mind with tequila. "How did Dan die? Why is it that everyone else says he's alive?"

"Who says that?"

"People at the bar. Venus Lily for one."

Tarantula smiles and looks toward the tiny living room window as if remembering a happier time. "Well, if everyone says so, maybe he is. Yeah, I might have been wrong about that. Dan's alive. He'll be coming back any day now."

Josie tries to ignore the insanity in Tarantula's voice. "I don't know how to put this without it sounding nosy, but were you and Dan . . . ? I mean, did you . . . ? Was he your boyfriend?"

A laugh starts deep in Tarantula's throat, works its way to her mouth, and escapes. "My boyfriend? Yeah, I guess he was. Dan was my boyfriend."

Exasperated, Josie throws her hands up and shouts, "Damn it, Tarantula, I don't know whether to believe a word you say."

That night lying next to Clarence, Josie tosses and turns, unable to sleep for thinking about the touch of Johnny Walker's lips on hers, about what would happen if she followed her impulse all the way to his bed. She thinks about the weird way Tarantula reacted to her questions. That woman is spooky, Josie thinks. She may even be crazier than me.

Although she allows Josie to work the day shift alone, Venus Lily comes by sometimes just to see how things are going. This morning she arrives at ten o'clock and starts piddling around, sweeping the floor and wiping down tables. Josie usually enjoys Venus's company, but today she's so wrapped up in daydreams of Johnny—hoping he'll stop by when the bar thins out around noon—that she hardly knows Venus is there. When Josie looks at Johnny Walker from Red Jacket, West Virginia, she sees the whole exploration of the West, sees beardy-faced, dusty-eyed ramblers, men who first settled the Wild West of Kentucky and West Virginia, and when that no longer suited them, moved on to Indiana, Texas, and Oklahoma, and when those places got too full of people, tore out of them to Arizona and beyond. She sees all of this when she's facing him from behind the bar, mixing drinks, washing glasses, wiping the counter.

Suddenly Bobby Swanson bursts into the bar. "Hey, Venus Lily, I've got you this time."

"What're you yammering about?" Venus snarls as she sweeps.

"I gave you something to remember me by last night when you took that little cat nap."

Venus wheels around and looks at Bobby. Even though the weather outside is in the nineties, she's wearing a high turtleneck sweater. "We're goin to have to have you committed if you keep on imagining things, Bobby."

"I gave you a hickey, and you didn't even know it. Pull down that turtleneck, Venus, and let's have a look." He moves toward her.

"You come one step closer and I'll hit you over the head with this broom."

"Yeah, well, if you didn't have something to hide, you'd pull down that sweater neck."

"That's not it, Bobby. I just won't play into your crazy games. Now leave me alone."

As Bobby slumps down in his seat, Johnny Walker boisterously steps into the bar. He orders a beer and says, "Pretty blouse, Josie. Makes your eyes look green." He nudges Bobby. "It makes her eyes look green, don't it?"

Bobby doesn't even look up.

With the kiss from the day before still fresh in her mind, Josie smiles at Johnny, drops the towel she's holding, picks it up, and blushes.

Venus Lily, still sweeping the back room, suddenly yells, "Josie, come here a minute."

Josie leaves the bar and approaches her. "What is it?"

Venus squints her eyes. "I've noticed Johnny is flirting with you. He's a married man, and you're married too. Not that I'm such a goody-two-shoes, but I thought I'd point that out."

"I appreciate it," Josie says, and marches back to the bar, but now she can't meet his gaze because when she does she sees two long-faced, crying children and a grieving wife hiding behind his blue-green eyes. She sees Clarence, too, driving his Montgomery Ward van out in the blazing sun, working like a slave. And she sees herself as someone who wants to have her cake and eat it too. Married, she thinks. It ain't a pretty picture.

Venus hangs around the rest of the day, doing an inventory of supplies, but Josie tries to avoid her eyes. She feels like a kid whose mother caught her stealing candy. Later when Lily Venus comes in to take over her shift, Josie notices that she is wearing a turtleneck sweater, too. There they are, both twins, dressed identically. Poor Bobby Swanson, Josie thinks as she passes the barstool where he sits dejected and forlorn.

Stepping out into the bright sunlight, she turns to find Venus Lily following her out. "I want to talk to you," Venus says.

"What about?" Josie is still uncomfortable from Venus's earlier comment about Johnny Walker, a comment that seemed a lot like a reprimand. Venus may be right about things, Josie is thinking, but she doesn't have the right to advise me on my love life, especially after the way she treats Bobby.

"If I'd had a child, she'd probably be your age," Venus says.

Josie nods.

"Ain't you getting along with your man?"

"We're doing all right," Josie says. "It's just that . . ."

"What? He doesn't light your fire? Doesn't scratch you where you itch?"

Josie laughs. "Something like that. We don't like the same things. We can't talk—not really. We just go on day after day like . . . He never wants to do anything."

"Well, then leave him. Don't hang around where you're not happy. Don't waste time, Josie. The worst thing a person can do is waste time."

"But I care about him," Josie says. "At least I think I do. Deep down I've always suspected that none of us care about anyone but ourselves."

"Bullshit," Venus snaps. "All I know is that if you're not happy with Clarence then odds are he ain't satisfied either. Did you ever think he might be happier with someone else? He might be a different man."

Josie tries to picture Clarence with another woman, but it's impossible to imagine.

Venus stands there, her frail arms hanging limply, her eyes searching Josie's for explanations. "I don't mean to get in your business," she mutters. "You can do whatever you want."

Josie grabs hold of her hands and finds them rough as sandpaper—no doubt from washing so many shot glasses over the years. "Do you think anyone ever stays happily married for long?"

"I don't know," Venus says.

"Were you ever married?"

"Once."

"Why didn't you have children?"

"I tried to. It just didn't happen."

"I can't have them either," Josie says in a choked-up voice. "Ain't made right inside, I reckon. Prob'ly just as well." She doesn't know where the emotion is coming from. She's never been especially disturbed about her inability to have children. She wonders if it's just that she wants Venus to feel sorry for her and is using it as an excuse.

She starts to get into her car, but Venus stops her. "About once every two months, me and Lily close down the bar and relax. We deserve it after the long hours we keep. Anyway, this Sunday's our day to shut down. We usually fix a lot of food and just sit around the house, playing music. Sometimes we don't do anything—just stare at the walls. You're welcome to join us, and you can bring your husband if you want."

Josie smiles. "I'd love to. Don't worry about me, Venus. I'll be all right." Josie gets into her car and drives home.

Inside the trailer that evening, she lies on her bed, trying to remember what it was like when she was so in love with Clarence she couldn't think straight. When they were first married, she loved seeing him off to work in the mornings, dressed in his work clothes—his navy blue pants and light-blue shirt with the patch sewn above the pocket, identifying his business as CLARENCE TOLLIVER'S REPAIR. She even made up songs about him. One called "Blue-Eyed Man" went: *"You can pick me a dozen bluebonnets, sing me all your blues songs, and paint me nothing but blue skies. / Go ahead and try if you think you can, but you'll never make me leave my blue-eyed man."*

This memory seems like something that happened to someone else. Maybe people ain't meant to spend their whole lives together, she thinks. Again she tries to imagine Clarence with a different woman, a blonde with children, dogs, and cats, a woman who is partial to bird feeders, who loves to watch him work on his TVs.

18

It's Sunday morning, and Clarence and Josie haven't been out of bed long. Josie is preparing breakfast—putting bread in the toaster, dragging out her heavy cast-iron skillet, taking eggs and bacon from the refrigerator.

Clarence is sitting at the table, skimming the newspaper, when he happens on something he can hardly stand to read. It involves the Panama Canal and that little peanut-farmer-president, Jimmy Carter. Clarence can't bear the thought that American men died for that canal, and now some teary-eyed, bleeding-heart liberal wants to give it away.

Josie peers over Clarence's shoulder. "Don't you just love Jimmy? Did you know that they say he's the most intelligent president we've ever had? Yep, that's what they say, and I believe it. You know what else? He's kind. Just look at his eyes and that smile."

Clarence grits his teeth and tries to blank out Josie's words. He used to think that someday she would wise up and see the light, that she'd abandon her liberal notions, but now he doubts that will ever happen. Josie seems determined to disagree with everything he believes. If only Gerald Ford hadn't screwed things up and lost the election, Clarence thinks. If only he hadn't been such a klutz.

"Venus Lily invited us to her house for dinner. Do you want to go? It's at two o'clock this afternoon," Josie says as she plugs in her Mr. Coffee.

"Umm," Clarence mutters, still glaring at Jimmy Carter's picture. *Lordy mercy,* he thinks. Jimmy looks like that little man from *Mad Magazine.* What's his name? Alfred B. Newman? Alfred E. Newman?

Josie sighs and starts over. "Every now and then Venus Lily closes down Don Juan's and has a day of rest. Today's the day. She's invited us to her house for Sunday dinner."

"Really?" Clarence yawns and looks at the want ads to see if he can spot a job in the repair field that pays more than Montgomery Ward.

"So do you want to go?"

"Where?"

"To Venus's."

Clarence spots an ad for a technician at JC Penney. He circles it with a pen and keeps going.

Josie wheels around on him. "You're not listening to a word I say, are you?"

Annoyed, Clarence glares at her. "You asked me if I wanted to go, and I asked where?"

"Just forget it," Josie snaps and sets a plate of eggs on the table.

"Forget what?" Clarence asks.

Josie rolls her eyes and continues to cook.

"Tell me," Clarence says.

Josie doesn't answer as he sits there looking confused.

After breakfast, she washes the dishes while Clarence stretches out on the couch and turns on the TV with his new remote control. Later she sits at the table looking at the Arts and Entertainment section of the paper. She finds an advertisement for live theatre in Tucson and wonders what kind of credentials are required to act in local theatre. She wishes she had taken some of those college courses Clarence used to beg her to take.

Glancing up from the paper, she studies her husband as he lies on the couch intermittently dozing and staring listlessly at the TV. As usual he has adjusted the volume so low that it's barely audible to the human ear, and he has dimmed the brightness until visibility is almost zero. Josie can hardly make out the ominous shadows of actors as they pace fitfully across the dark screen. In the past when she has asked him why he adjusts the TV in such a peculiar way, he explains that keeping the volume low and the screen dim makes the set last longer. "Why do you want it to last longer if you can't see or hear it?" she often inquires, and Clarence usually smiles and shakes his head like a parent might shake his head when his child asks something cute but ridiculous.

Josie has come to the conclusion that Clarence's TV viewing is symptomatic of his overall view of life, which seems to be: *If You Act Like You're Dead, You'll Live Forever.* Becoming irritated just thinking about it, she gets up and indulges in a long relaxing bath, takes her time dressing and putting on makeup. Then she grabs her purse and starts to walk out the door.

"Where're you goin?" Clarence asks.

"If you'd been paying attention this morning, you'd know," she says and leaves him on the couch with his mouth dropped open in an odd mixture of a yawn and a look of surprise.

Venus Lily and Lily Venus live two miles past Don Juan's at the end of a dead-end road. When Josie gets there, she spots the two sisters sitting on the porch of their small adobe house. As she gets out of the car and walks toward them, they wave to her and smile. Once again, she can't help noticing how alike they are, dressed in their Levi's jeans and identical yellow plaid Western shirts with mother-of-pearl buttons, but Josie has formed a closer bond with Venus Lily than with Lily Venus, mainly because she doesn't see the other twin as often. Lily always arrives at work when Josie is getting ready to go home.

Pausing halfway up the porch steps, Josie says, "I know which of you is which."

Venus looks around at Lily and chuckles. "Really? How?"

"A person can see with more than their eyes, you know." The smell of frying chicken wafts out an open window. "Smells good," Josie says.

"Yeah, well, I'd better turn it before it burns," Lily says. She disappears inside the house.

"How is it that you can suddenly tell us apart? No one else can," Venus says.

Josie sits on the edge of the porch and dangles her legs off the side. "Shit, most of the people you fellers see on a daily basis are drunk. Naturally they can't tell you apart. You and Lily have eyes that are absolutely identical except for one thing. You look out of them in different ways."

"How's that?"

"For one thing, you know me better than Lily does. You look at me with more recognition. Actually, I figure if I can tell you apart, other people can too. They just say they don't because they get a kick out of playing your game."

"Bobby would love to tell us apart, but he can't."

Josie grins. "Bobby's . . . I mean, I love Bobby, but he's not one I'd pick to gather the finer details, you know? Besides he's always filled to the brim with Jim Beam."

A look of worry crosses Venus's face. "Don't tell anyone about what you think you've figured out. There's a reason me and Lily try to confuse people."

Josie eyes Venus, who is nervously picking a speck of lint from her shirt. "Well, I won't say anything. Who am I to say?"

Just then Lily steps to the door, tells them dinner is ready, and they go inside to eat. Lily, obviously proud of the fare, passes bowls of mashed potatoes, beans, and corn, and tells them to help themselves to the platter of chicken.

"This is just about the best I've ever had," Josie says, holding a drumstick.

"That's because I fried it, baked it, and fried it again," Lily says.

Venus beams with pride.

Josie notices that they even chew their food alike, that they hold their silverware the same way, and serve themselves identical helpings. She wonders how it would feel to have a duplicate of yourself sitting across the table, to not wonder how you appear to other people because you know exactly. After dinner, they go into the living room, and the two sisters play music for Josie—Lily on harp and Venus on flute. Josie is mesmerized by the ethereal sound.

"We used to play in clubs," Venus says.

"It was part of our strip act," Lily chimes in.

"Don't be telling her that. You talk too much," Venus says.

Lily ignores her. "We'd take turns rising out of a giant clam shell, dressed in nothing but ostrich feathers. I'd play the harp while Venus stripped, and she'd play the flute while I did."

"Well, why don't you just spill your guts?" Venus snaps.

"It was a real class act," Lily says to Josie.

"Sounds like it," Josie says, then casually adds, "So why do you want people to be confused about who you are?"

Lily looks at Venus, who is shaking her head no. "Can't tell you that," Lily says. "All I'll say is that it's something that happened a long time ago."

After a few more songs, Venus asks, "Why didn't you bring your husband, Josie? Didn't you invite him to come, too?"

"I asked him, but he didn't hear me."

Lily leans close to Josie and whispers conspiratorially, "Venus tells me you're flirting with Johnny. Don't blame you one bit."

"Shut up," Venus orders, glaring at her sister.

"Well, I'm just saying what I think. That wife of his is no good."

Josie perks her ears. "How do you mean?"

"I mean she's on drugs of some kind. Ain't got a lick of sense. Never even notices their two little ones. Johnny had to hire someone to take care of them while she just sits and stares into space. That's why he comes to the bar all the time. He can't stand to see her that way."

Josie wishes she hadn't asked.

"Yeah, well, he'll be in the same boat as her if he keeps drinking so much," Venus says.

Seeing that Josie is uncomfortable with the turn of the conversation, Venus and Lily start talking about all their other customers, telling her about people who are now dead or moved away. Often the sisters disagree about the facts: "He died back in '65," says Venus.

"No, it was '66," argues Lily. "Died of gangrene from a gum sore," Venus says. "No, it was cancer of the mouth," Lily counters.

Josie wonders how it would feel to have a sister with whom to argue the facts. "I've got a sister," she suddenly blurts out.

Venus narrows her eyes. "You do? Why didn't you ever tell me about her?"

"I've not seen her in a long time. She ran away from home. We didn't get along like you two. We fought all the time."

Venus and Lily shake their heads sadly.

Josie leaves an hour later and, driving away, she looks into her rearview mirror and sees the sisters sitting on the porch, apparently still bickering about one thing or another.

Although it's four o'clock in the evening, the sun is still bright in the sky and great white clouds are hanging low. A single black crow flies in front of her, causing her to wonder for a moment if the spirit of don Juan is trying to lead her to his lair. Driving past the bar, she spots Johnny Walker's truck parked in the otherwise empty parking lot. She slows, pulls alongside him, and stops the car. "Didn't you know we were closed today?" she asks.

He doesn't say anything. He's staring straight ahead toward the horizon. His hands are gripping the steering wheel, and his eyes are glazed, as if he's playing a scene over and over in his mind, a scene that always has the same ending no matter how it's played. Josie knows that look. She's worn it before.

Finally he turns to her. "Let's go for a ride."

She doesn't think twice. She gets out of her car and into his truck, and he turns on the engine and drives down the road leading to Rustle. At first the ride is silent except for "Riders on the Storm" by the Doors, which Johnny plays repeatedly. Josie looks out at the view in front of them, at the purple cast of the Galiuro Mountains that serve as a backdrop for Rustle. Standing almost in the center of the view is one flat-topped mountain that the locals call Old Tabletop. Josie remembers how much Dora used to love that mountain, how she used to say she'd like to be sitting right on top of it.

"God, the Galiuros are beautiful, ain't they?" Josie says to Johnny.

"Yeah," he says. "I can see them from my front porch. My ranch is about a mile up that road to the left."

"Really?" Josie mutters. She wishes he had kept quiet about where he lives with his wife.

Past Rustle, he turns on a narrow road leading toward the dry bed of the San Pedro River and stops near a small shack on the bank. They get out of the truck, and Johnny ushers her inside the small structure. With its one window shaded by an oak, the room is dark, and it takes Josie a few seconds to make the adjustment from the blinding sun outside. Along one wall sits a table covered with dusty odds and ends, and a small cot is pushed against the opposite wall, a floor fan positioned nearby.

Standing behind her, Johnny puts his hands on her shoulders and turns her around to face him. They stare into each other's eyes, exchanging information that is impossible to say with words. Clothes hit the floor—a shirt, a blouse, a bra. Shoes and boots get kicked to a corner, and jeans collapse at their feet. Josie and Johnny drop to the cot and fall on each other. They grope, moan, and clutch each other with rough glomming hands. Their fingernails dig into skin.

When they're finished, they lie quietly beside each other, staring at the ceiling as if they don't quite know what happened. Josie glances about the small dark room. "When we used to live here in the '50s, I almost got drowned in that river out there. It was a flash flood. Me and this little boy were playing right in the middle of that dry bed. All at once I looked up and saw something shiny coming straight at us fast and hard. The little boy saw it too. He said, 'Run for the bank as fast as you can. Don't stop to look at it. Just run.' We had no more than made it to the bank when the water roared past us like a wild animal on the rampage."

"Thank God for little boys," Johnny says.

Josie grins. "Whose house is this anyway?"

"Used to belong to a friend of mine. He died."

They begin touching and then make love again—this time more gently, kissing each other with hardly more than the looks in their eyes, holding each other with smiles. Later Josie lies her head on his chest as he smokes a cigarette. "What are we doing?" she asks.

"We're keeping ourselves alive," he says.

"This can't lead to nothing but trouble."

"I know."

Josie turns to the window that is draped in oak leaves. "We'd better go." Unspoken words hang in the air, words that tell them there's no future in this, no brightly colored perfect dream, that they'll never have anything together but what they just had.

A few minutes later they're on their way back to Sage.

When Josie gets home, Clarence hits her with "Where the hell have you been? I've been worried to death."

"I've been to Venus Lily's for Sunday dinner. She invited you to come too, but since you never listen to me, you missed out."

Clarence plops down on the couch. "Well, I wouldn't have went anyway."

"I know you wouldn't," Josie says. She turns on her heel, goes to the bedroom, closes her eyes, and sees nothing but the dark shack shaded by oaks on the banks of the San Pedro River.

19

It has been a week since their tête-à-tête at the San Pedro shack, and deep inside Josie and Johnny are howling for each other like lovesick hounds. It has been hard for them to hide their emotions from the gang at Don Juan's. Josie has dreamed about him every night. As a result of her emotional angst, she has been rereading all of Carlos Castaneda's books. She has also fallen into her old habit of performing in front of the mirror, acting out the parts of plays.

Tonight she dons a scarf about her head and holds forth as Emilia from *Othello*: "Let husbands know/Their wives have sense like them: they see, and smell,/And have their palates both for sweet and sour,/As husbands have."

Clarence stares at her as though he thinks she's losing ground. She hasn't resorted to these strange speeches since they left Pick.

Josie is aware that he is watching her. "And have we not affections, / Desires for sport, and frailty, as men have?"

"I don't know," Clarence says. "Do thou?" He rolls over in bed and goes to sleep.

At the bar the next day, Johnny slips Josie a note in which he asks her to meet him in the desert about a half mile behind her trailer. There's an old chimney out there, the only remnant of an abandoned house. He says he'd like them to have a midnight picnic by the chimney. "Meet me tonight at twelve o'clock," the note says. Josie catches his eye and nods an eager yes. He smiles, gives her a wink, then strolls out of Don Juan's like a cowboy who has just received pay after a long cattle drive.

* * *

Clarence used to visualize the day when he would retire with Josie to a huge house filled with the latest technological advances, a house where all the light switches had dimmers, where even the closets were electric so that in the fall of the year he'd flip a switch and their summer clothes would rise to a storage container in the ceiling while their winter clothes would conveniently descend. Now when he tries to see that house of the future, he can't get a clear focus. The fact is he isn't sure he wants their marriage to last until he retires. He doesn't know what to say to Josie anymore and doesn't have the energy to tell her how he feels.

Clarence hasn't told her much of anything, including the fact that he hates his job of repairing Montgomery Ward's TVs in customers' homes. It is somewhat surprising to him, but he's getting along with his coworkers, the two Mexicans and the one black man. They seem to him to be regular people with wives, mortgages, and jokes to tell, with talk of sports to bat around. It's not them but the work itself that Clarence hates. In Pick, it was Bernard who did outside calls, and Clarence always stayed in the shop. Here in Arizona, though, he has to do field work, and he hates going into strange people's homes. The other day he had to clean a microwave oven in which an old lady had exploded her Persian kitten, Fluffy. She'd been trying to dry the kitten's hair after giving him a bath. Clarence guessed she couldn't take the time to towel dry it, had to speed things up, had to be in a hurry like everyone else. Why did everyone have to be in such a hurry?

When the old lady heard the noise and realized what had happened, she couldn't bring herself to open the door to the appliance—she couldn't even go near it. What she did was call Montgomery Ward and tell them she needed a technician. Clarence couldn't get over the amount of blood that covered the interior. It took him an hour to get the microwave cleaned enough to take back to the shop. And all the while, the old lady just stood there moaning the cat's name, shaking like a sick joke. People were sad. They were the saddest sights on earth.

Clarence looks into his rearview mirror and finds that the small buggish car is still following him, and its horn beeps every few min-

utes. The irritating little Pacer has been on the tail of his Montgomery Ward's service van for quite a while, and every time he looks
into his rearview mirror, the driver gives him the finger and grimaces.
Clarence doesn't know what to do. If he pulls to the side of the road,
the man will follow suit—he will stop, get out, and beat the shit out
of Clarence. Clarence knows this with every fiber of his being. If he
drives back to the store, the bastard will follow him inside and beat
him to death in front of all his coworkers. It's as simple as that.

It all started a couple of hours ago. Clarence was driving south of
town toward his fourth service call of the day. He was minding his
own business, half in and out of daydreams that featured the hollow
he was raised in. He could picture perfectly the thick green hills of
early June, the mountain springs gurgling down the hillside, the
mayflowers all in bloom. He imagined himself still a boy, standing in
the creek down the hill from his house, his fishing pole held out in
front of him, the line dangling in water.

Every now and then he was shocked out of this reverie by the
sound of horns. The two-lane road he was driving on was narrow and
so packed with traffic that it was impossible for one car to pass
another. Clarence was moseying along at thirty-five miles an hour as
usual, and cars were backed up behind him for half a mile. Since he's
been in Arizona, Clarence has accrued quite a few points on his driver's license, all of them bestowed for driving so slow that he endan-
gers the safety of others. If he gets one more point, he'll lose the
privilege to drive.

Remembering this, Clarence speeded up from thirty-five miles an
hour to forty, but finally he couldn't stand it anymore. I'm a addict, he
thought. I want to go faster, but something won't let me. Quite suddenly he put his foot on the brake pedal, a little too hard as it turned
out, and almost came to a complete stop. Behind him, the small
Pacer slammed on its brakes too. In fact, the Pacer came within an
inch of ramming the van, but it didn't, and Clarence kept on trucking
down the road. Now there were no cars behind him because—
unknown to Clarence—several of them had crashed into each other,
and their drivers were exchanging insurance information. Finally he

noticed that the Pacer was behind him again. It has been on his tail ever since.

I'll run out of gas pretty soon, Clarence thinks, seeing that the gas gauge is headed toward the E. I'm goin to have to stop, but I'll wait till I get to a more crowded place where they'll be witnesses to what he's about to do. Ten minutes later Clarence pulls into a small shopping center, parks in front of a Smitty's grocery, gets out, and awaits his fate. The Pacer pulls right beside him and the driver gets out too.

The man who barrels up to Clarence shaking his fists is bald, red-faced, and weighs over two hundred pounds. "I just wanted to get a look at you," he shouts. "Have to see the man that caused a six-car pile-up and came away smelling like a rose."

Clarence's heart sinks. "Did anyone get hurt?"

"No, asshole," the man yells. "Thanks to you, we were all driving too slow to get hurt."

"What makes you say I caused them to wreck?" Clarence asks. With alarm, he notices the man is wearing brass knuckles. "I didn't cause nothing. I was just goin down the road."

The man's red face takes on a bluish hue, and he comes for Clarence head on, grabs him by the throat and starts choking. Then hitting Clarence with all his power in the jaw, he jumps into his car and speeds away.

"He'll get in another wreck if he keeps goin that fast," Clarence thinks as he lies on the pavement, staring after the Pacer. Then everything slips away and he finds himself back home in Kentucky. It's June and the garden behind Ida's house needs tending.

When Josie steps into her home that afternoon, the phone is already ringing. It's Clarence's boss saying Clarence is in the emergency room at a hospital in Tucson. "He got into a fight or something," his boss informs her. "I don't know exactly what happened yet. All I know is that his jaw has a two-inch cut, and it's deep. You'd better get down here."

A fight? Josie thinks, as she speeds down the road to Tucson. When she gets there, Clarence is under anesthesia and receiving his last stitch. When he comes to, a doctor tells them how to care for the wound and hands them a prescription to be filled. It is almost 8 P.M. by the time they get into Josie's Pinto and start driving home to Sage.

"Where's your car?" Josie asks Clarence as he slumps in the car seat.

"Ah ork," he replies. "It'll ee aw ight."

She has no idea what he just said.

They've been home an hour before the pain killers start to wear off and Clarence begins groaning and writhing in pain. When she gives him another pill, he begins to act more foolish than ever, waving his arms and bugging his eyes. He rises from the couch and turns on the stereo, drags Josie on to the floor, and makes her dance with him. Josie gives him a worried look, knowing he hates dancing. "Are you all right, Clarence?"

"Yeah, I aw ight," he says with a ridiculous grin.

And so the night progresses.

There's no way I can meet Johnny tonight, she's thinking. I can't even call to tell him I'm not coming. She paces the floor like a caged animal as Clarence lies on the bed, groaning. At midnight she goes to the window and looks out at the shadowy moonlit desert, knowing that Johnny is out there waiting but unable to do anything about it.

"I've got to get out of here," Clarence tries to say to Josie the next morning. His mouth is so sore he can barely form words. "Me and this place just don't jell," he says, but it sounds as though he's saying, "Ee a is ace us on ell."

Unable to understand one word, Josie shakes her head. Clarence's face is so swollen he doesn't resemble himself, and every time she looks at him she gets a pain in her own jaw. "Well, I have to go to work. Call me if you get worse or anything. There's some chicken soup in the refrigerator. All you have to do is heat it up."

She walks outside and jumps into her car. Pushing the gas pedal to the floor, she speeds toward the bar, hoping that by some miracle Johnny is already there. The frustration of being kept from meeting him in the desert has her biting her lower lip until it's almost bleeding. He prob'ly thinks I stood him up, she thinks, grimacing in agony as she drives to Don Juan's.

Josie is still thinking about Johnny when she steps into the bar and turns on the lights in preparation for the customers who are already lined up outside, but her thoughts of him soon disappear. Maybe it's because she's been rereading all the Castaneda books, but she receives a surprise visit from the old sorcerer himself. His presence is everywhere. He's so close she can almost feel his breath on her face. Even when she opens the bar door and the miners stampede in, all of them ordering drinks at the same time, she feels him. He's lighter than air, darting around the room like a bubble in a breeze.

Johnny doesn't come to the bar at all, and Josie is beside herself with worry. Oh, God, she thinks, he figures I don't care about him, that I've changed my mind about the whole thing. By ten o'clock the bar is thinning out with only Bobby Swanson and Mike Chandler sitting at tables in the back room, watching a soap opera, talking in low drudging voices about the characters on the show. Occasionally she glances in at them as she's cleaning the counter, washing and drying glasses.

"That'n right there," Mike says. "That's the new Margo. I heard the old one got on drugs in real life and couldn't work no more. But don't you think she's the spitting image of that wild girl that used to hang around Dan Hawkins? What was her name?"

Bobby Swanson points to the TV. "That? Shee-it," he grunts incredulously. "Well, I'm here to tell you that Margo—I don't care if she's new, old, or in between—don't hold a candle to Ramona."

Her heart pounding in her chest, Josie almost drops the glass she's drying. She walks around the counter and stands in the doorway to the back room, listening carefully to the men's voices which have suddenly become animated.

"I'd almost forgot about her," Mike says. "Uh, Bobby, do you remember that horse ride? Lord, God, buck-naked right through the middle of town. Said she was reenacting one of Lady Cadaver's greatest feats."

Bobby laughs. "Cadaver? Shit, you don't know a thing, Mike. It was Godiva, some woman that lived in England a long time ago. That's who she was trying to act like."

"Well, whatever it was, that was the wildest thing I ever saw in my life."

"I heard that," Bobby says. "Wonder whatever happened to her."

Josie walks up to the men. "Did you say Ramona? You knew someone named Ramona who used to hang around with Dan Hawkins?"

"Yeah, why? Did you know her too?"

"Maybe. I just wish I knew for sure where Dan was."

"I'd say he's in California," Bobby says. "It's where he told us he was going. That's where Ramona spent most of her time. She was here when he left, and I think they left together."

Josie glances up at the TV, where the soap actress who is playing Margo lies in a hospital bed crying out in pain. The girl does vaguely resemble Cheyenne, has a similar nose, the same high cheekbones and black hair. "You say Ramona looked like her?"

"A lot," Mike says.

"A little," grumbles Bobby. "Except Ramona was prettier. When she first came here (When was it? About '65?), she couldn't have been much more than nineteen or twenty. Made right in with Dan Hawkins first thing. She just up and left after about six months, stayed gone about a year then back she came again. It was like that the whole time—her taking off and coming back. Sometimes she'd bring old deadbeats with her, carnival people or hippie types, you know, long hair, guitars strapped across their backs. Dirty sons-of-bitches, if you ask me."

They're talking about Cheyenne, Josie thinks. It's her as sure as I'm alive. "It sounds like she might be someone I know. Do you know where in California she stayed?"

"You need to talk to that landlady of yours. Tarantula can tell you more than us. She knows all about Ramona and Dan. Probably knows more than she wants to know." He turns to Mike and grins. "We always heard she was a little jealous of them two."

Josie can barely wait until her shift comes to an end. As soon as it does, she jumps into the Pinto and drives down the hill from Don Juan's as if she's being chased by the law. Ten minutes later she's barreling up the drive to Tarantula's house.

She pounds on the door for five minutes and is about to give up when Tarantula staggers around the side of the house. "Don't break my door down. I was out back shoeing my horse."

"Shoeing your horse?" Josie says, bewildered. "You ain't got a horse. You've got two cows and a donkey. That's all the animals you have left."

Tarantula, who reeks from the smell of alcohol, says, "You wanta have a little drink with me?"

"Sure," Josie says. "I'm dying to."

A few minutes later they're sitting in the dim living room where their drinks leave rings of moisture on the cherrywood coffee table. "I know you don't want to talk about this," Josie says, "but something has come up, and you're goin to listen to me whether you like it or not."

Tarantula's green eyes glitter. "What're you talking about, Josie?"

"I have a sister that's been missing for a long time. You may have known her. Her real name was Cheyenne, but she went by Ramona."

Tarantula tries to stand up but falls back down on the couch. "Ramona is a whore."

Josie stares down at her glass. "Where is she?"

Wrapping her arms around her stomach, Tarantula rocks back and forth. "She killed him. She killed Dan. Shot him right between the eyes."

Josie's heart flipflops. "Cheyenne wouldn't do that. Why do you keep saying he's dead? Dan moved. He went to California, prob'ly with Cheyenne. Where is she? Do you know?"

Tarantula pulls off her straw hat and throws it on the table. "In hell, I hope." Here in the spidery living room, her sun-weathered face is as brown and scrubby as an old saddle, causing her green eyes to look as if they've been stuck on the wrong person. Josie is amazed at the pain emanating from her.

"I don't understand any of this. Tell me," Josie demands.

"She used to bring carnies over here. That's what kind of person she was—someone that would travel with carnies."

Josie stares down at the floor and forges ahead. "I have to know where she is. If you've got any idea, please tell me."

"I don't know about Ramona, but I know where Dan is. He's buried out there under the shade of that fig tree. I buried him myself."

"He is not," Josie shouts. "You're lying. If Cheyenne killed him and you hate her so much, why didn't you tell the police about it?"

Seemingly oblivious to Josie's question, Tarantula pours herself another drink. "Ramona used to go to San Diego a lot. I bet she's slept with every sailor in the entire naval fleet at one time or the other. The last time she left here, she was headed back to California. She slept with the hippies, you know. Used to bring them over here too. Ocean Beach, Ocean Beach. That's all she talked about."

Josie stands up and begins to pace, thinking how she would have never thought to look in San Diego. "How was she? I mean, how was her health? She had a bad heart. Did she have a doctor around here?"

"No, but she had one in San Diego. Used to talk about him all the time. Dr. Matthew Fierros. I'll never forget that name. He operated on her at least once that I know of—open heart surgery. I always had a feeling she was messing around with him too."

Josie takes out a pen and scribbles the doctor's name on a scrap of paper. "Was she all right, though?"

"I loved him, Josie. He was all I had. When he first came to live with me, I was in my forties, but I looked younger. He always had me to fall back on. Ramona treated him so bad, bringing her boyfriends over here, parading them around." Tarantula holds her head in her hands. "But I ended up with him. I'll always have him now."

Josie looks away from her, wondering if it is possible that she is telling the truth about the fig tree. "I'm sorry Cheyenne gave you so much trouble. There's times when she can be a lot of fun. Wish you could have seen that side of her."

"Oh, I've seen it. If it wasn't for that side, she'd never have got that kind of hold on Dan or me either. It's just that after she gets hold of you, she wrings you out like an old dishrag, her black eyes staring at you like . . ."

Josie sighs and looks down at the floor. "I'm goin home now," she says, "and I want you to promise me you won't go around telling any of your crazy stories."

"I'm not promising you anything," Tarantula says.

As Josie walks out the door she hears her still grumbling. "Fucked-up asshole, girl. Lying cheating sonofabitch." Out in the yard, Josie pauses by the fig tree while a cool desert breeze suddenly whips up from the south. In the tree a crow stares down at her, then glides off like a beautiful black omen. It sure is peaceful here, she thinks. It would be a good place to bury someone.

———————

20

Brewster wakes but continues to lie in bed, staring at the ceiling, dreading to get up and stretch his stiff legs into walking shape, dreading to even move, but wanting a cup of coffee worse than the dread. It's been raining for three days, and each drop stabs into his arthritic limbs like a steel tack. He rises, sits on the edge of the bed, and stares down at his knees, puffed up twice their size. "Damned mess," he growls and pops a Solganal from the pill bottle on the nightstand, gulps it down with a glass of water. Still dressed in nothing but his boxer shorts, he stands, winces with pain, and slowly moves toward the refrigerator. He pulls out a beer, gulps it down fast and hard, then steps over to the stove and puts on a pot of coffee. Well, let's see what kind of misery I can get through today, he thinks.

While he's waiting for the coffee, he takes a look out the window and notices it's stopped raining. He pops another beer, guzzles, and is finally starting to feel better, almost bearable, maybe. Another beer might do the trick, he thinks and quickly funnels another down the hatch. By now the coffee is done and he pours himself a cup, but he has to go to the bathroom to pee before he can taste the first sip. By the time he gets there, waits until the urine trickles out, and returns to the hydraulic hoist which serves as his kitchen counter, fifteen minutes have passed and his cup of coffee is cold. "Golden years, my ass," he mutters out loud. "People ought not to live past the age of thirty-five. I wish the Russians would drop that bomb and wipe out a few million old saggy-lipped, bony-butted people like me."

After coffee and toast, Brewster cleans himself up, figuring to go down to the courthouse for his daily conversation with Ed Gibbs before the midday humidity gets the upper hand.

"How are ye?" he asks Ed a few minutes later.

"Fair to middlin'," Ed replies.

"I'm glad somebody's doing all right," Brewster says.

"What's wrong?" Ed asks.

"Rheumatism. My limbs don't work no more. I used to sleep flat on my back with not a care in the world—both arms raised over my head and stretched out on the pillow. Now I can't sleep like that no more—can't raise even one arm all on its own. I have to take one hand to lift the other arm over my head. Always have to leave one arm free to do the positioning. It may not seem like much of a complaint to you, but it means a lot to me. Course you don't know what I'm talking about, with you just being sixty. Wait till you get in your seventies."

Ed chuckles. "Have you been to Ida's lately?"

"Whose?"

"You know. Ida Tolliver. What about having a woman come right to your house, pick you up, take you home with her, and fix you chicken and dumplings to boot?"

"What about it?"

Ed grins. "Looks like you've got yourself a girlfriend, that's all."

Brewster grunts. "You don't know what you're talking about, Ed. She's my in-law. I don't even like goin to her house. That friend of hers, old Viola Watson, is always there, blaring her eyes. What's wrong with that woman anyway?"

"Viola Watson from Racer Creek? She's that woman that don't talk. She talks to a few people, but I reckon she's real choosy. I heard she has a college degree. Her brother Ralph says she's a genius."

"How can they tell? She don't do nothing but stare straight ahead. What kind of college did she graduate from, anyway? One of them mail-order places?"

Ed laughs. "All I know for sure is that you've got two women chasing after you. Sounds pretty good to me."

"Well, you can have them," Brewster snaps. Maybe this little visit with Ed wouldn't such a good idea, he thinks. Sometimes the old fool pesters the shit out of me.

"Boy, you sure got a wild hair up your ass today," Ed says.

"I'm worried about Josie," Brewster grunts. "She said she'd call me every Sunday, but she's just called twice since she's been out there."

"Maybe she's real busy with her job and all."

"Maybe."

It is approaching noon, the sun is beating down on the street, still wet from the rain, and vapors rise, causing the air in front of them to shimmer. Brewster looks toward the end of town at what was once the old Palace Theatre, presently the Palace Bowl-a-Rama, remembering the smell of popcorn, the anticipation of COMING ATTRACTIONS. Now all Pick has in the theatre department is a drive-in. Who the hell goes to a drive-in besides teenagers wanting to diddle around? he wonders. And why is it that Westerns have gone out of style? He recalls gun battles, men walking toward each other on hot dusty streets to draw guns and die. These images cause him to think of the dream he had last night of some man breaking into his house. Brewster had dreamed he shot the intruder right in the belly. He always dreams of shooting some man in the belly, blood gurgling from the wound like water from a mountain spring.

His thoughts skip back to Belgium in the '40s. It was when he sneaked into a bombed-out church and found a sniper who for the past hour had been picking off American soldiers one by one. Brewster was easing along a wall, listening for movement, when he heard something drop with a clank to the floor. Turning, he saw the German soldier, the sniper no doubt, standing at the far end of the room. Without hesitating, Brewster fired, hit him right in the belly, and blood gurgled out of the wound, spreading over his shirt, soaking into the fabric like red dye. Later when Brewster walked over to get a better look, he noticed that the dying man was young, no more than eighteen, and resembled a cousin of his back home. Maybe he's kin to me somehow, Brewster thought as he watched the soldier take his last breath. "Shit," he muttered. "He'd of killed me if I hadn't got to him first."

Brewster leaned down and picked up a bronze-colored cross of Jesus that lay beside the boy. Glancing up at the wall, he saw the nail where it had hung, and he thought how if the cross hadn't fallen and made that clanking sound, he might never have spotted the boy.

Does that mean God was on my side that day? Brewster asks himself, ignoring Ed Gibbs, who is breathing heavily and sighing. Hell no. I'd say it was just blind luck, either that or God was playing games, having a laugh at us fellers. Wonder where that cross is now. Prob'ly thrown out in the trash. How can people be so careless with things that make the biggest difference in their lives? Deep in speculation, he thinks he hears Ed make some sort of comment.

"What did you say?" Brewster asks, still gazing toward the Palace Bowl-a-Rama.

Ed doesn't answer.

"Remember that old theatre in its heyday, Ed?" Brewster mutters. "People from all over the county would be packed in there on Saturday night. I used to go all the time."

Ed still doesn't answer.

When Brewster turns to look at him, his hair stands on end. Ed is slumped against the banister, his eyes wide open. *He looks dead, but that can't be. He was talking to me just a minute ago.* Brewster stares at Ed's chest, hoping to see movement—a sign of breath being taken in and out. There is none. His friend's eyes hold the same unfocused stare as the dead German soldier. They resemble Dora's eyes before he reached down to close the lids. Wait a minute, he thinks. This just can't have happened. Brewster glances out at the street where several people are walking past, unaware that they're filing past a dead man. *If they ain't noticed he's dead, then maybe he ain't,* Brewster thinks and, nudging Ed in the ribs, he whispers, "Ed, are you all right?"

Ed remains silent.

Brewster feels for a pulse, for a heartbeat, then holds his ear close to Ed's mouth, hoping to hear a faint breath. Nothing. He said something to me, Brewster remembers, but I was so busy with my own self-ish thoughts I didn't hear him good. He was prob'ly asking me to help him. He scoots away from Ed and studies his face closely. Yep, he's dead, he decides. That's all there is to it. How could anyone go like that? Just go with not much more than a word? How can people live their whole lives, struggling, fighting, whooping it up, and then fall dead right in the middle of a conversation?

Just then the sheriff's secretary, Colleen Henderson, comes out of the courthouse and springs toward the steps on her way to lunch. "Excuse me, Brewster. Could you scoot over some? If I don't get some food in me, I'll pass out," she says.

Moving out of her way, Brewster eases closer to Ed, and Colleen goes on down the steps and heads for her car. I dread the commotion, Brewster thinks. Everyone heaving and setting, running around like chickens with their heads cut off. Maybe I'll just give Ed a minute of peace before it begins, and Brewster sits there remembering the talks the two of them had, remembering complaints they made to each other, the laughs. A few minutes later when Sheriff Roy Barns comes out of the courthouse on his way to lunch also, Brewster stands up.

"Roy," he says. "Looks like we've got a situation here. Ed Gibbs is dead."

Roy bends over Ed and grabs his wrist. "Well, I'll be damned. What happened?"

"I don't know. Maybe he had a stroke or a heart attack. He went without hardly making a sound."

Roy heads back up the steps to call the ambulance.

"Hold it a minute, Roy," Brewster says and hurries to catch up to him. "Before all this starts, I want to ask you something. Do you know where Ed lived exactly?"

"On Starling Creek. Lived in a little trailer up there by old Judge Simpson's house."

"Thank ye," Brewster says. "I just never knew."

Roy turns and steps inside the courthouse to make his call.

*   *   *

Ed's death hit Brewster harder than he would have imagined. He wonders how his friend felt when he drew that last breath, if he ever got to know the full meaning of fear. Brewster has been in bed off and on for three days, wondering how he'll go when his time comes, if it'll be in the middle of a conversation. I doubt it, he thinks, looking around at the empty room. Not unless I'm talking to myself. He lies there and makes the world grow smaller and smaller until it's no bigger than the corner of the pillowcase his eyes are turned toward. It is then that the knock comes on the door.

Oh, God, just let whoever it is go away, he thinks. I don't want to see another old shriveled-up human face. I want to lay here with my pillow. That's all I want to do.

The knocking doesn't stop. In fact, the yelling begins.

"Uh, Brewster. Are you in there?"

It's a woman's voice. Sounds like Ida.

"*Brewwwsterrr.* I drove all the way down here, and I ain't leaving any time soon. Open up." She's been calling him on the phone since yesterday, yammering something about lasagna and linguini, trying to weasel an invite, but he would hardly talk to her and finally stopped answering the phone.

Brewster rubs his hands through his tangled hair, over the stubble of beard on his face as Ida's yells get louder. "Lordy mercy, she'll wake the dead," he grumbles and manages to roll himself into a sitting position. "All right, I'm coming. Just simmer down." After pulling on his britches, he stumbles to the door and opens it. Ida and Viola are both standing there, swinging a huge pot between them.

"I've got something good here," Ida says.

Viola does nothing but stare.

"What is it?" Brewster asks suspiciously.

"Chicken Cacciatore. It's even got some wine in it. How's that?"

"Well . . ."

"Ain't you goin to let us in? It's getting heavy."

Brewster steps aside as they brush past him and deposit the pot on the hydraulic hoist with a thud. "I've discovered Italian food," Ida says. "Let me tell you, Brewster, it's the best on earth. Do you smell that garlic, that basil, them tomatoes? Now, tell me that ain't the best stuff you ever smelled. I don't know what in the world's wrong with me that I didn't start cooking this sooner."

The smell of garlic already permeates the room. "It does smell strong. I'll say that."

Ida takes the lid off the pot, and a big smile spreads over her face. "Where's your plates? I'll get us some out."

"Over yonder in that dish-drainer by the sink."

"Get them, Viola," Ida orders and then glances at Brewster as if to say something. She takes a few steps toward him, acting as if there's a dirty spot on his chin that she's about to wipe off. "What's the matter with you?" she asks.

Brewster shuffles his feet uncomfortably. "What do you mean?"

Ida keeps coming toward him. "You look funny, bad. Like something that died about a week ago. What's wrong?"

"Nothing's wrong," Brewster says.

"He looks sick, don't he, Viola?"

Viola doesn't respond.

"Well, I ain't sick," Brewster says.

Ida glances around the room and spots the unmade bed. "Was you asleep when we come?"

"No, I was just laying down."

"What for? It's the middle of the day."

Brewster marches away from her and sits down at a stool by the hoist. "Are you goin to fix me a plate of that stuff or not? I'm starved to death."

"You know, Brewster, you oughten stay holed-up in here so much," Ida says when they begin the meal. "You oughta get out more. If a body starts laying in the bed all the time, they'll die."

"I used to get out all the time. Used to go down to the courthouse of the day and sit around with Ed Gibbs."

Ida nods sympathetically. "He died."

Viola twirls her fork in the linguini, wrapping it tightly around the prongs, then shoves it into her mouth.

"I was with him when it happened," he says.

Ida narrows her eyes into knowing slits. "All right, but you still oughten to lay around so much. You'll stiffen out like a old board."

Brewster glares at her. "And that'd be my business, wouldn't it?"

"That'd be a lot of people's business," Ida says.

Brewster blushes and continues eating. He is hungrier than he realized.

Later, they sit down to watch the afternoon soaps. Eventually, the two women leave, but not before Ida promises to bring him some fettucini with Alfredo sauce on the weekend. Brewster is stretched out on the couch with a full stomach and the knowledge that today was better than yesterday when he gets the call from Josie that sets a whole new chain of events into motion.

21

S he's in San Diego," Josie tells Brewster on the phone.
"Do you know her address?"
"No."
"Well, what're you goin to do?"

"I've got the name of Cheyenne's doctor. I'm goin to call him as soon as his office opens tomorrow. Maybe he'll know where she is. Other than that, I don't know what I'll do."

"What does Clarence think?"

"Ain't told him yet. He got in a little accident, had to have stitches in his face, and's passed out on pain pills."

Brewster sighs. He doesn't even want to ask. Finally he says, "Ed Gibbs died."

Josie's heart sinks. She'd always been comforted by the idea that Brewster at least had a friend to talk to. Now he's lost him. "I'm sure sorry about that."

"Died of a stroke all of a sudden."

Josie flinches, thinking how Brewster could go the same way and she would never see him again. She doesn't know what to say.

"Did you ever have fettucini with Alfredo sauce, Josie?"

Josie wonders if Brewster is losing his mind. "No."

"Well, I'm goin to have me some. Ida's bringing me a big pot next weekend. I just wish she wouldn't bring that old Viola with her when she comes. Viola ruins my appetite."

Josie brightens. "That's great that you're getting some good meals. Is Viola the woman that was at Ida's house that evening when we went over there for supper?"

"Yeah, but I don't want to even talk about her," Brewster says. "Just let me know if you find out anything else about Cheyenne."

When they hang up, he paces the floor, excited and a little afraid. Josie's making headway, he thinks. Looks like she actually might find her. If she does, I just hope they get along. He remembers how his daughters used to be when they were still at home. If Cheyenne was in the right mood, she could charm you—even if you were the most long-faced, sad-eyed person on record—into thinking you were God's gift to the human race, but when she turned against you, she could make you feel like a whole army of people were calling you every name they could think of. More often than not, it was Josie she turned against. He hates to admit it even now, but he has always thought that Cheyenne was in complete control of those mood swings. He suspects they were deliberately used in order to throw people off guard. Brewster sighs, hoping her attitude has softened over the years.

Josie is in the living room, daydreaming about Johnny Walker while Clarence sleeps in the bedroom. Today Johnny had come by the bar and said, "How's your husband? I heard he got hurt."

Josie smiled with relief. "I was wondering if you'd heard."

He sneaked her a wink and said, "Guess you're having to be a nursemaid."

"Pretty much."

When she handed him a drink, his fingers strolled over hers for half a minute. There were other customers in the bar, making it impossible for them to talk further, so he tipped his hat and left.

Coming out of her daydream, Josie tries to pinpoint her feelings for Johnny, to figure out if they will last beyond the present run of passion. Suddenly she knows that Clarence has wakened. She can always tell when he's awake because that's when a ball of restraint lodges itself in her stomach. It's as though Clarence in all his waking hours holds her back from something she should be doing, but she doesn't know what that something is. She walks into the bedroom and finds him groggy from pain medication, sitting on the edge of the bed, staring at the TV. There's a special on about a flood in Illinois. Houses are washing away, people's lives are being destroyed, and rescue workers are being heroic.

"Wook at dat," Clarence says in a barely understandable voice. He points to the TV where a rescue worker has climbed on top of a floating house to save a cat and her kittens. "Ain't dat somesing?"

"I can't see anything, Clarence. The screen is too dark. I wish I could see it. I would love to be able, just occasionally, to make out what's happening on TV."

Clarence rolls his eyes. "Dat 'eller is 'aving some cats," he says, holding his jaw and grimacing in pain.

"I'll take your word for it."

"He could be kill him'elf. He's wisking his wife," Clarence says heatedly.

"Yeah," Josie grunts. "But would he be risking his life if the cameras weren't rolling? If he was out there alone and no one was watching?"

"Sewer he ood," Clarence says. "I ood."

"I know you would, Clarence, but I bet ninety-five percent of the rest of the world wouldn't. They just do it because it makes them look like heroes, because it gets them on the six o'clock news, because reporters write articles about them, and the mayor gives them awards."

"Dat's a sorry-ass ay to wook at tings."

"I know, but unfortunately that's the sorry-assed way *tings* are."

She leaves him and goes back to the living room. She can't be around him for long. His stitched, swollen face gnaws at her constantly. Josie figures the angry motorist didn't hit Clarence because he was driving too slow. No, she figures the man smashed Clarence's jaw so he'd look pitiful and cause her to feel like shit.

At the bar the next morning, Josie calls Dr. Fierros's office only to find that he's on an extended vacation in Africa. "That's too bad," she tells the secretary. "This is Josie Clay Tolliver, and I really need to talk to him about my sister, Ramona."

"Ramona?" the secretary asks.

"Yeah, she's a former patient of his. I think he performed surgery on her."

"Ramona Clay?"

"Yes, do you know her?"

"Dr. Fierros has been looking for Ramona," the secretary says, excitedly. "Do you know where she is?"

Josie's heart plummets. "No, I was hoping he'd know where she is."

"We haven't seen her in over a year, but I'm sure she'll come back. She always does."

Josie's voice chokes up. "When will Dr. Fierros be there?"

"In about a month."

"Tell him I'll call him," Josie says and hangs up.

Well, that's that, she thinks, and pours herself a drink of Jim Beam. Who knows when she'll go back to San Diego. Even if she does show up, she'll prob'ly be gone again by the time I find out about it. Maybe the only hope I have of ever seeing her is to move there and wait till she returns, but I can't leave Sage now that me and Johnny are doing whatever we're doing.

The day goes by slowly, and Johnny doesn't show. Bobby Swanson sits at the bar looking morose as usual. Mike Chandler loiters in the back room playing a lone game of pool. At one point, Josie calls Clarence and asks how he's doing, but she can't understand a word he says. It will be another two weeks before the stitches come out. Finally her shift ends, and she steps out into the bright sunlight. She's unlocking her car when she spots Johnny's empty truck in the parking lot. Feeling someone staring at her, she wheels around and finds him standing behind her.

"Hello," he says. His blue-green eyes almost make her forget her name.

"Where were you today?" she asks him.

Johnny sighs. "The baby-sitter quit, and I had to find someone else to take care of the children."

"Oh," Josie says. She doesn't want to know the details of his life at home, to hear about his drugged wife, crying children, and the baby-sitters who quit.

Johnny takes her face in his hands and kisses her. "Let's go to the shack."

Josie smiles. "I'll have to make a call first, tell Clarence I'm goin shopping in Tucson or something. He's not been able to go back to work yet, won't be for a couple of weeks, and he worries if I'm five minutes late." She wonders if Johnny hates hearing about Clarence as much as she hates hearing about his wife.

A half an hour later, they're lying on the cot in the shack, staring into each other's eyes. "Sorry I couldn't meet you by the chimney that night. I kept standing at the window looking out in that direction, knowing you were there. It was almost more than I could take," Josie says.

Johnny kisses her on the nose, wraps a strand of her hair around his fingers. "Yeah, I stayed out there most of the night, thinking you weren't interested anymore. But that's all right. I found out what happened the next day. Lily called and told me."

They kiss long and hard and make love while outside the late afternoon sun is blazing on the horizon and a crow perched on an oak branch near the window squawks like a creature gone insane. After-wards, they lie close, holding each other. "I guess I'd better go," Josie says.

"Not yet. I want to take you somewhere else."

"Where?"

"It's a surprise. Just follow me when you get into your car. You'll like this place."

A few minutes later Josie follows him out of Rustle and through Sage. She follows him out to Sage Junction, where he turns onto a dirt road that seems to lead nowhere. About a mile later, he turns onto yet another narrow dirt road. Around the next bend they find themselves surrounded by a dozen small white houses. The artists' colony, Josie thinks. Johnny stops his truck near a huge barnlike structure and gets out. Josie pulls up behind him and rolls down her window. "This is the artists' colony, ain't it?"

Johnny walks up to her car. "Yes, it is. I thought maybe you'd want to hear some poetry. Well, are you goin to get out?"

Josie grins. "How did you know I'd like poetry?"

"I know more than you think I know," Johnny says.

Josie gets out of the car and follows him toward the barn. "Do you come out here often?"

"All the time. Some of my best friends live out here."

"Why didn't you tell me this before?"

"It didn't come up," Johnny says.

Inside the barn, paintings are hung on all the walls. A stage is positioned near the far end of the room, and in front of the stage are enough chairs to seat forty or fifty people. There are already about ten people sitting in the front row.

"Johnny," one of the men says in greeting, "I was beginning to think you'd given up on us. Where have you been?"

"Trying to keep out of trouble and failing," Johnny says.

The man laughs. "Who's this with you?"

"A friend of mine. Josie Tolliver to be exact. She likes poetry. Not that she has told me so. I can tell just by looking at her."

Blushing, Josie pulls Johnny over to a painting on the far wall. "Why did you bring me here?" she whispers. "News about us will be all over town by tomorrow."

Johnny grins. "These people are my friends. They know my situation."

"Well, you'd better be right. I'm not ready for Clarence to know about this yet."

Just then a man of about forty, dressed in bell-bottom jeans and a maroon T-shirt, steps onto the stage and yells, "WHITE-HOT, BLINDING-WHITE LIKE MY UNBORN BABY'S EYEBALLS, LIKE MY MOTHER'S BLEACHED PEPSODENT TEETH, LIKE MY FUTURE WIFE'S WEDDING DRESS, LIKE THE COTTAGE CHEESE OF MY LATEST RIPENING MALIGNANCY, LIKE MY VERY OWN FUNERAL SHROUD IS THIS BLANK PAGE OF UNWRITTEN WORDS THAT GROWS WHITER AS I BECOME MORE BLIND."

"That's Mick Balinski," Johnny whispers to Josie. "He's got writer's block."

When Mick sits down a pale woman wearing a long dress and a blank expression replaces him. Her graying hair hangs to her waist, and she looks like someone who has never known the joys of makeup. Speaking in the strange lilting voice Josie has heard on poetry records, her words describe butterflies and bees and Scottish heather, but Josie gets the feeling that's not what the poem is about. She wishes the woman would just spit out what she's trying to say, but it doesn't happen. The poet, her voice thick with emotion, goes on and on about bird nests and pine needles and the skittery cavorting of grasshoppers: "*the MUSIC of LEGS rubBING togeTHER,*" she sings.

An artist gets up and displays his latest painting, which he proudly proclaims to have been formed from the earth itself, from the desert floor, from mashed cactus flowers, from beaten-up Sage stones. Josie likes it. Later she asks him how much he's selling it for.

"It's not for sale," he grunts as if he thinks she should have known that.

Later Josie and Johnny go to Mick Balinski's studio and have a few drinks. "Have you ever figured out what's keeping you from writing?" Johnny asks him.

"Probably just laziness," Mick says soberly. "It's getting worse. I can't stand to even look at paper anymore. Pens give me indigestion." He puts on an album of Frank Zappa, who is singing about growing dental floss in Montana.

Josie eyes Mick carefully. "Have you ever been to that theatre in Tucson? You know, the live one? I think it's called the Childress. Is it any good?"

Mick smiles. "It's pretty good. Why?"

"No reason. I've just been wondering how hard it is to get into something like that—local theatre."

"Are you an actress?"

"No, but I've always liked to pretend to be characters in books."

Mick grins. "Well, then you're an actress."

They sit around, play music, and drink a few beers. Then Josie says, "I guess both of you fellers knew Dan Hawkins."

Johnny grins. "What is this with Dan Hawkins? You were asking about him down at the bar one day. Did you know him or something?"

"Yeah, back when I used to live here. He's the only one I remember from that time."

"Dan Hawkins was a talented sonofabitch," Mick Balinski chimes in. "Better writer than me. He would never read his stuff though, wouldn't try to get it published. Said life was the real art, that writing and painting were just stand-ins. I wouldn't doubt if he wasn't quoting that girlfriend of his, Ramona. She was always saying things like that."

Josie narrows her eyes. "You knew her?"

"Yeah," Mick says, with a grin on his face. "I knew her, but I think old Johnny here knew her better."

Josie feels as though someone just gave her a swift kick to the stomach, and suddenly she is suffocating from the hot summer air that occupies every nook and cranny of the small studio. The smiles on Johnny and Mick's faces are almost threatening now, and the two men seem to be taunting her with their ignorance of Ramona's true identity. Johnny knew her, she thinks with near disbelief. They prob'ly had a midnight rendezvous every night of the week. They may even have made love at the shack by the San Pedro. Hardly able to breathe, Josie mutters to Johnny, "You knew her too?"

He blushes and directs his response to Mick. "Hey, man, are you trying to get me into trouble?" Then he turns to Josie. "Yeah, I knew her too, but it was a long time ago. Why do you ask?"

"How *well* did you know her?" she asks, almost whispering now.

Johnny gives Mick a dirty look and sighs. "Not well at all. She was way too much, you know?"

Josie looks at him, knowing for a certainty now that Johnny was once Cheyenne's lover. She finishes off her beer, walks to the window, and looks out at the sun setting behind the Catalinas. "I'd better be getting back now, Johnny. Clarence will be worried."

As they walk out of the studio to the parking lot, Johnny drapes his long, comforting arm around Josie's waist, gives her a little pinch. "I thought maybe we could go straight from here to the place out in the desert. I hate to let you go tonight."

Josie stands by her car, grasping the door handle, staring into his eyes. He's everything she wants. He's a man for one thing, not some puny imitation, and he's blessed with the kind of smarts an education can't buy. She's thinking that if he hadn't gone out with Cheyenne, he'd be damned near perfect. "Fraid I can't," she says to him. "You see, I don't know how I feel yet about the fact that you fucked my sister."

Johnny steps back and looks at her as though she's lost her mind. "What are you talking about?"

"Ramona is my sister. I also don't know how I feel about the fact that you apparently go out with every woman you meet."

"Ramona was your sister? I don't believe it. You don't look nothing alike."

"That's what everyone says."

"Well, how was I supposed to know you were sisters?"

Josie opens the car door and sits down behind the wheel. "The point is that if you go out with every woman you meet, sooner or later you'll find out you've dated sisters."

Johnny leans his head through the car window. "I've not been out with that many women. I'd say about three since I've been married, and that's only because my wife may as well be dead. She never has a thing to do with me. She's lost to the world, so Valiumed-up she don't know her own name."

"Were you in love with her?"

"My wife? Yes, I was at one time."

"Not your wife. Ramona. Did you love her?"

Johnny turns his back as though he's going to walk off. "I thought I did for about five minutes."

"Well, that may have been five minutes too long," Josie says. She starts the engine and drives away before he has a chance to say anything else.

22

A few minutes later, she pulls into the driveway beside the trailer. The light in Clarence's bedroom is on, and she wonders if he's had anything to eat today. Dragging herself out of the car, she walks into her home like an old woman who has forgotten how it feels to have a man say her name in a soft whisper.

"Where er you?" Clarence asks. "I een acing the foor for hours."

Josie grabs him by the arm. "Did you ever have a crush on Cheyenne?" she shouts. "Did you ever kiss her in the hallway at school? Did you ever have a date with her?"

Clarence is dumbfounded. "What?"

"You heard me."

"You not aking sense."

"I'm just asking you if you ever went out with Cheyenne."

Clarence rolls his eyes. "No, foo, I idn't."

"Well, you're the only one," Josie says. "Yep, you're among the unlucky few."

Clarence holds his jaw and grimaces. "Would you fix me somesin ta eat? I'm hungry."

Josie goes into the kitchen and starts supper. As she dices vegetables for the soup, she tries to put the image of Cheyenne and Johnny out of her mind, but it's no use. She sees them necking in dark cars, breathing heavily in movie theatres, snuggling in dinky motel rooms.

"What's wong ith you?" Clarence asks.

"I found out where Cheyenne is."

"You did? Where?"

"San Diego."

"Weally?"

"Actually she's not there right now, but that's where she's been most of these years."

"Well, I'll be dam. How you fine out?"

Josie tells him what Bobby Swanson and Mike Chandler said in the bar, about some of the things Tarantula said, leaving out the story that Cheyenne killed Dan and that he's buried beneath the fig tree. She tells him about her call to Dr. Fierros's office, how interested the secretary was, what she said.

Clarence just keeps shaking his head.

Josie hands him a bowl of vegetable soup, and he eats slowly, then goes to bed. She continues to stay up though. Sitting on the couch in the dark, she tries to picture her sister clearly in her mind, but it's no use. Cheyenne remains shaded by darkness, knee-deep in mystery, lit only by a waning moon. Josie's memory of her is covered by a veil of promises and illusion. Like a phantom Cheyenne dances just beyond reach, seducing everyone that Josie cares for, leaving them with weak, corrupted hearts.

Josie goes to work as usual, but Johnny doesn't come into the bar all day. That's just as well, she thinks. I don't know what I'd say to him if he did. At home that evening, she washes the supper dishes, while Clarence lies on the couch watching his dark TV.

"Do you like it here in Sage?" she suddenly asks him.

"Yeah, I wove it," Clarence snarls.

"Is your job perfect and everything?"

"Yeah, specially the dwiving part and, a course, the human contac."

Josie sighs. Clarence's jaw is still swollen, and due to the resulting speech impediment, she is unable to tell whether he's being sincere or sarcastic. She's pretty sure he doesn't like Sage, but if for some weird reason he has developed a love for the place, she wouldn't know because they never say more to each other than a few casual words. "I just wondered, because I was thinking we could move on. I don't believe this is working out too good."

Hope rises in Clarence like a cheese soufflé. "You mean you wanna go back home?"

"No, I might want to move to San Diego."

"San Dago?" Clarence asks, disoriented.

"Forget it," Josie says. "Just forget the whole thing."

The next day Johnny comes into the bar and hands her a note requesting once more that she meet him at midnight by the chimney out in the desert. Josie nods that she will, and that night when Clarence has fallen to sleep, she sneaks out of the trailer to begin the half-mile walk. Lit only by the thin sliver of new moon, the desert is eerie and filled with shadows. She sees eyes peeping out at her from the manzanitas, hears tiny feet scampering across the sand. She can't imagine what she will say to Johnny.

Finally she's there, and he steps from behind the chimney.

"Glad you could make it," he says.

She stands there awkwardly folding her arms around her waist.

Johnny walks closer to her, touches her face. "It wasn't that big a thing between me and your sister, Josie. It was just fun, you know."

Josie backs away from him.

"It didn't mean anything. I've never cared about anyone the way I care about you."

"Sounds like a line," Josie growls. "Bet you say that to all the girls."

Johnny throws up his hands. "What girls? There ain't been that many. You want this to end, don't you? You don't want to be happy."

Josie wishes she could grab him around the neck and pretend that everything is all right, but she can't. "This thing with my sister—I . . ."

"I've told you it didn't mean anything."

"You don't understand. All my life I've not been Josie. I've been Cheyenne's sister. It's been, 'Oh, yeah, you're Cheyenne's sister. Boy, wasn't she something? There was never anyone like Cheyenne.' " Josie listens to her voice and doesn't like the sound of it. It sounds as if it belongs to a whining child instead of a grown woman. "Anyway, I can't be with a man that used to be hers, at least not until I've . . . I need to find her, Johnny. I need to talk to her."

Johnny takes her face in his hands and kisses her. Then he lets go and steps back. "I never kissed her that way."

Josie plops down on the ground. "I'm thinking of moving to San Diego. That seems to be her home base. Maybe after I've talked to her, I can come back."

Johnny sits down beside her, puts his arms around her shoulders. "It may be too late then, Josie. Things change. People change. You may not want me then."

Tears start to fall from her eyes. He tries to kiss her again, but she pushes him away. "I can't," she says, then jumps up and blindly runs home.

After work, Josie stops at the library and picks up some books on southern California. When she gets home, she says to Clarence, "I'm goin to move to San Diego so I can have a better chance of finding Cheyenne."

"Shee-it," Clarence says. The subject of Cheyenne is a sore one with him. He's still mad about the phone bill he had to pay after Josie made those calls to L.A. and San Francisco. He never liked Cheyenne anyway.

Seeing the disappointment hanging like a shroud on his face, Josie says, "I'm not asking you to go with me. I don't want to force you to do something you don't want to do. I've already ruined your life once. You can go on back to Kentucky, but I'm goin to San Diego. It's something I have to do. I'll need to wait until I save enough money, though."

"What makes you think Cheyenne will ever go back to San Diego?"

Josie sighs. She's grateful that Clarence's speech is almost back to normal. At least she can understand what he is saying. "Dr. Fierros's secretary said she always returns."

"So what if she does? She left you fellers, didn't she? Ain't called none of you once. Looks like you'd take the hint."

"I don't care if she left us," Josie yells. "I still have to find her. I have to . . ."

"To what?"

She trembles with mixed emotions. "I don't know. What difference does it make?"

"Well, I can't keep traipsing around the country with you. It's like you're on this big Cheyenne freeway and won't ever exit off."

"I'm not asking you to go. Really, Clarence, if you want to back home, I'll understand. I won't be mad or anything."

"I never thought I'd want to live in California." Clarence turns away from her and sighs. Since their move to Arizona, he has forgotten the slings and arrows of his last months in Pick. All he remembers are the color of mountains in summer, the smell of a good spring rain, the thrill of standing on a creek bank catching fish. He's thinking that maybe he will go back.

"I used to think about it," Josie says. "Outside of Sage, California was my second choice. I checked some books out of the library that tell about it. There's pictures and everything. It's a real pretty place. I'll say that much."

"Can I see the books?"

Josie hands one to Clarence. It is open to a page of photographs that show the Pacific Ocean, scenes that feature fishing boats with smiling men and women hauling in all manner of colorful ocean fish. The book covers the coastline too, white sandy beaches littered with beautiful women, their tanned bodies and beautiful faces turned up to a gently shining sun. Clarence studies the pictures closely. His eye is on one of the women in a photograph—her blond hair is the color of cornsilk, her blue eyes the color of sweet williams. His sore jaw sags downward, his mouth parts, and his eyes become fixed in a sexual trance.

During the night Josie wakes and finds the bedside lamp turned on and Clarence still studying the book with almost as much interest as if it were an electronics manual.

Two weeks pass and Johnny has not returned to the bar. Both Lily and Venus ask Josie if she knows the reason, but she plays dumb. She wishes she could call him and tell him everything is all right, but she can't envision kissing Johnny without feeling Cheyenne's lips on his, can't imagine looking into his eyes without seeing her wayward sister staring back at her.

Clarence's stitches were removed several days ago, and he has gone back to work. Every evening when he comes home, he keeps his nose in the California books until he falls to sleep. He's been thinking about what he should do. At first he was pretty sure he wanted to go back to Pick, but the more he thinks about it the more he's coming to the conclusion that it isn't the right thing for him. After all, he no longer owns the TV repair shop. What would he do for a living? Another thing to consider is the technical opportunities that California offers. From the books he's discovered that California is one of the main electronics centers in the United States. *I could prob'ly learn how to repair computers over there,* he thinks.

Finally one night after dinner Clarence says, "I've decided I'm goin to California with you."

Josie, who has been keeping mum about moving, studies him closely. His face is hard to read. He looks happy enough, but she suspects he's packing some hidden emotions. "Are you sure, Clarence?"

"Never been surer of anything," he says, grinning. "California's growing on me."

Josie turns on the faucet and begins running dishwater. "I don't know about us, though, Clarence. What's goin to happen to us? We don't seem to get along anymore."

He looks down at the floor. "I know, Josie. I'm not goin because of you. I'm goin for myself. But I'll have to give a two-week notice."

Josie has no idea what to say. She manages to smile, then turns back to the sink and begins washing dishes.

The next day when Venus Lily stops by the bar, Josie hits her with the news that she's leaving.

Venus stands there with her mouth open.

"I'm sorry to leave you with no one to help out," Josie says.

Venus scoots a shot glass back and forth on the counter, trying not to look upset. "I thought you kind of liked it around here."

Josie tells her what she's found out about Cheyenne, how Cheyenne changed her name to Ramona and used to date Dan Hawkins. She tells Venus that she has to find her.

"I knew Ramona," Venus mutters. "She used to come in here all the time. She could beat any man playing pool. Never seen anything like it."

"Yep, she's good at just about everything."

Venus grabs hold of Josie's hand. "You don't have to do this. You're looking for something that ain't there. Can't you see that?"

Josie glares at her. "If Lily was missing, wouldn't you want to find her?"

Venus pours herself a drink. "What has Cheyenne ever done for you?"

"What do you mean?"

"Did she ever save your life?"

"No," Josie snaps. "Did Lily save yours?"

"As a matter of fact she did." Venus steps into the back room, making sure no one is there, that the bar is empty. Returning, she takes another drink. "I told you I was married once, didn't I? That I tried to have a baby but it didn't work out? Lily was living with me and my husband, Robert, at the time. She didn't have no place else to go. Anyway when I was in the hospital having the baby, Robert forced himself on her, beat her up pretty bad in the process. To top things off, my baby died after the third day. When I got home and found out what happened, that Robert had raped Lily, something snapped in me. I shot him, Josie, shot him right in the heart. When the police came, I told them I'd killed him in self-defense; but they put me on trial for first degree murder, and I plead not guilty. When Lily was called as a witness, she testified that I hadn't killed him at all and swore up and down that she'd done it. Of course, I kept to my same old story, saying I'd killed him in self-defense, but the more I said it, the more Lily told them she was the one. The jury didn't know who or what to believe and found me not guilty. They never did bring Lily to trial. I guess they thought no jury would ever be able to decide which one of us did it. Anyway, that's what a real sister will do for you. She'll kill the sonofabitch that rapes you, or she'll risk her own life to keep you from going to prison or the chair. It seems to me that Cheyenne has never really been your sister, that all she's done for you is run as far away from you as she can get."

Reeling from Venus's story, Josie has forgotten her own problems. "Is that why you and Lily try to confuse people as to who's who?"

"Robert has a couple of brothers who know in their hearts it was me. Thing is they could never tell me and Lily apart, but if they was to track us down and find out for sure which one is which, they'd kill me in a minute."

Josie looks around at the cool dark walls of Don Juan's, at the rich mahogany bar, at the picture of one of the twins standing in front of the giant clam shell. She would never have thought that Venus and Lily carried such a tragic secret. She's beginning to think everybody has one. Taking hold of Venus's hand, she says, "I really appreciate you trusting me enough to tell me that. I promise I won't ever say a word to no one about it." Josie starts to shake with emotion. "God, I can't believe what people have to go through in this life."

Venus pours them both a drink. "Yeah, but did you get my point about what sisters should be to each other?"

Josie smiles. "Me and Cheyenne'll prob'ly never be like you and Lily. I guess I just want to find out who we are like. Anyway, I hate leaving you in the lurch. Hope you'll be able to find someone to take over for me."

"Someone always turns up."

"I'll be back to see you fellers from time to time. I'll call you too."

Venus grins. "Actually I'm kind of surprised you'd leave Johnny. I thought you had a thing for him. What ever happened between you two?"

"Nothing," Josie says. She gets a clear image of him, almost feels the touch of his hands on her skin. "Nothing really happened."

After Venus leaves, Josie is once again alone in the bar. Wishing don Juan would suddenly materialize, she walks around the room, trying to memorize the pool tables, the fireplace and bar, thinking how she'll miss the noise, fights, and laughter of the tramp miners, not to mention the gruff, dictatorial voices of Venus Lily Stamper and her sister, Lily Venus.

She thinks she sees the old sorcerer flit past the corner of her eye as she walks behind the counter and pours herself a drink. *Is that why you led me here?* she asks him. *To help me find Cheyenne? I thought you wanted people to abandon their families.*

He doesn't answer her, and she wonders momentarily if it's possible he has nothing to do with anything in her life. She wishes Johnny Walker would suddenly step through the door, but she knows he won't return to the bar until she leaves town.

Not long before they go, Josie says to Clarence, "Let's drive to town and get a good look at that old adobe mansion again."

"It ain't a mansion, Josie."

"It's a mansion to me," she says.

When they pull in front of the dilapidated house, Josie notices that the former tenants' vehicles are not parked in front of their old apartment and that there are no curtains on the windows. She gets out of the car and peeps inside. The apartment is empty except for a few pieces of battered furniture. Clarence gets out of the car too, and comes to stand beside Josie.

"I feel like I'm looking right into the past," Josie whispers.

She scans the walls of the living room, remembering where their old couch sat, which wall the TV was pushed up against. It's then that she sees the cross.

"As I live and breathe," Josie says, astounded.

"What?" Clarence mutters.

"It's Daddy's cross. Clarence, he brought it back from the war. I know it's the same one."

Clarence sighs. "What would it be doing here?"

"We must have forgot to take it down. It prob'ly ain't worth nothing, and whoever owns this place just left it hanging there all these years. Well, I'm goin to get it."

Clarence widens his eyes. "You can't do that, Josie. It'd be stealing."

"How can you steal something that's yours?"

"You don't know for sure it's yours."

"Yes, I do, goddamn it." She tries the front door, but it's locked.

Then she walks around to the back door, punches a piece of cardboard from one of the panes on the French doors, reaches inside, and opens the latch. Running into the apartment, she yanks down the cross and stuffs it into her shoulder bag while Clarence stands outside, yelling in a loud raspy whisper, "Josie, you'll get us arrested. Someone's prob'ly looking at us right now."

Josie steps into Cheyenne's old bedroom. There's just a cot in it now and a particleboard chest of drawers. But she remembers where Cheyenne's bed was. Josie can almost see the three of them—Dan Hawkins, Cheyenne, and herself—as they were then. Cheyenne is lying in bed, and Dan and Josie are sitting close to each other on the floor. Dan is reading *Howl* by Allen Ginsberg. Suddenly Cheyenne, her eyes shining like coals that are ready to burst into flames from the sheer energy of the poem, lets out an uncontrollable howl that deafens all of them. Dora runs into the room, yelling, "What in the world is goin on?" Her voice still echoes in the air.

Clarence yells, "If you don't come on, I'm goin to leave."

Josie walks slowly out of the room, out of the house, out of a summer that will never come again.

Thinking how happy and surprised he'll be to get it, Josie mails the cross to Brewster the next day. Then she calls Dr. Matthew Fierros's office and finds out that he's still on vacation. She hangs up the phone and paces back and forth, hating to wait another minute to grill the doctor about Cheyenne. Utterly frustrated, she walks out to Tarantula's house and stands by the fig tree, staring down at the damp sandy dirt, wondering what she'd find if she could see through it six feet deep.

Maybe I ought to get me a shovel and find out for sure, she's thinking, when suddenly Tarantula steps out of the house and comes to stand beside her. "You believe me, don't you?" the old woman mutters. "You know I'm telling the truth."

"Get away from me," Josie shouts. "We're leaving in a few days, and I can't wait till I won't have to look at your face anymore." As she runs back to the trailer, she's thinking she doesn't care to know what really happened to Dan Hawkins until Cheyenne has a chance to tell her side of the story.

Sitting at her tiny kitchen table she thinks how unbelievable it is that she and Clarence have been in Sage for only three months. They arrived in mid-April, and it is now July 15. So much has happened, it seems as though she has been here a lifetime. She looks out the window at the terrain, but it's fading from her sight. In her mind she's already gone.

A few days later Clarence and Josie pack their things, foregoing a U-Haul this time since they have two cars that will hold everything they own. As they're walking back and forth from the trailer to the cars, Clarence says, "Did you ever get out there to that artists' colony, Josie?"

Josie flinches. "No, why?"

"Judy down at Hudson's Grocery said she thought she saw you over there. I told her she must have been wrong."

"Well, she was wrong," Josie says, and remembering the night that Johnny took her there, tears come to her eyes. "I kind of regret I didn't, though."

Clarence sighs. "Just as well. Them people ain't no more than anyone else. All they do is fiddle around with paint and words. What good does that do anybody?"

Josie wishes Clarence's comments didn't bother her so much, but they do. She figures they'll always bother her. A couple of hours later they get into their cars and set out. They drive down from Sage, the Catalina Mountains leading them into Tucson, where they get on I-10 to Casa Grande then switch to I-8, heading straight for the Coast.

PART THREE

---

*Where Shadows Run
the Show*

23

They arrive in San Diego at midnight, check into a shabby motel on El Cajon Boulevard, and fall sound asleep. Josie is awakened the next morning by the sensation of something cold and moist brushing against her lips. Opening her eyes, she finds Clarence dangling a huge bunch of purple grapes over her face.

"*Grapes of Wrath,*" she shrieks, and starts to laugh.

"Grapes of what?"

"Wrath," Josie says. Foolishly, she supposed for a moment that he'd bought the grapes on her first day in California because he knew how much she loved Steinbeck's book. She used to read passages of it aloud to him when they were first married. Now, though, she can see he doesn't remember any of that, and it hits her that more than likely he never really listened when she read to him.

Clarence rolls his eyes. "Wish you'd make sense every now and then. They's a little grocery store about a block down the street. Figured you was as hungry as I am."

"Well, I am," Josie says, biting off a grape. She decides it doesn't matter that he wasn't thinking of Steinbeck when he bought the grapes. She chooses to believe that his bringing them to her is a good omen anyway. Clarence has done this often in the past—unwittingly brought her things that are meaningful to her. "They've got so much taste," she says. "I never had grapes this good."

"And big too," Clarence says, stuffing several into his mouth. "We've got to get out and find us a place to live. It looks busy here, Josie, like they's plenty goin on. I bet I won't have any trouble finding a job." He draws a newspaper out of a grocery bag and starts looking through ads for apartments and houses.

"I want to see the ocean first," Josie says.

Clarence grunts and says, "Look at this house: *'two bedroom, one bath, furnished, with canyon view—three-ninety-five a month.'* That's pretty high rent, but I'd rather live in a house than a apartment. I can't stand people being jammed right on top of me. Besides, looks like everything out here is high. You'll sure have to get a job. Hell, we'll both prob'ly have to work night and day."

"Are we goin to stop by the ocean first?" Josie asks.

"No, goddamn it. We don't have time," Clarence snarls. He circles several ads and locates the houses on a city map. "Will you please get some clothes on so we can go?" he yells.

So much for good omens, Josie thinks. She knows he's stressed out, but she doesn't see why they can't make one little side trip to the beach before spending a hot frustrating day looking for a place to rent. Doesn't he have a puny little trace of adventure lurking somewhere in his soul? She spits a grape into the trash can and gets dressed.

"Stay behind me," Clarence orders after they check out of the motel. "We'll have to travel two freeways just to get to that first place. If I exit, you exit. Got it?"

"Got it," Josie mutters.

Not long after they get back on I-8, she sees a sign that says BEACHES, so when Clarence begins signaling to turn at the next exit, Josie pulls alongside him in the parallel lane and shakes her head vigorously. "No!" she yells as she points straight ahead toward the sign.

Clarence turns white in the face. He's yelling something that Josie can't hear, his shoulders hunched over the steering wheel, both hands gripping down as though he's choking it to death. He rolls down his window and shouts, "Get the hell behind me, Josie. We don't have time to go to the beach right now."

Still unable to hear what Clarence is shouting, Josie shakes her head, no. "I'm goin," she yells. "You can follow me if you want to, but by hell, I'm goin."

Clarence blows his horn, and Josie blows hers. Then Clarence turns and looks toward the ramp where he needs to exit, and for a moment Josie is afraid he'll turn off on it, that he'll go looking for the house he circled in the paper, and they'll become lost from each other forever. She discovers that part of her wishes it would happen, that she'd get separated from Clarence, become lost in the city of San Diego, and be forced to figure out how to make it on her own. At the last minute Clarence pulls out of the right-hand lane and follows behind her, his face fixed in a blank look that indicates he's stepped out of his body because if he remained inside it he might seriously injure someone.

A few minutes later Josie is standing on Ocean Beach, her mouth dropped open in wonder at the waves rolling toward her. Their roar permeates her body and mind, blocking out the surrounding noise—the laughter of children digging holes in the sand, the yelping of teenagers playing volleyball and flying kites. She imagines she's standing on some craggy shore in England, fog rolling toward her like the waves. "Roll on, thou deep and dark blue Ocean—roll! / Ten thousand fleets sweep over thee in vain . . ." Josie whispers, reciting from Byron's famous poem. She can almost see the poet standing by the sea, shouting his poem to the wind, his arms outstretched, his dark cloak whipping in the breeze.

I could stand here forever, she's thinking, when Clarence steps behind her. "I've just about had it with you," he says.

She turns around. "Look at it, Clarence. It's so big and blue and shiny. See that ship on the horizon?"

Clarence grabs her arm. "We don't have time for this. We've got to find a place to live today. Do you hear me? We've both got to find jobs tomorrow. We don't have time to stand around looking at the ocean. What's to see? It's just a great big hole of water. I've seen water all my life."

Josie is vaguely surprised by the tears that fill her eyes and blur the sea in front of her. She feels as if Clarence has turned the Pacific Ocean into a giant underwater business complex, and she realizes that as far as he is concerned, living in San Diego will be no different than living in any large city, that he'll go to work and come home . . . go to work and come home . . . go to work and come home . . . forever.

"Okay," she says. "Let's go find a house and move into the damn thing."

As they walk back to the parking lot, Clarence pulls the map out of his hip pocket. "Here, if you'd just take the time, I'd like to show you where we're goin to be looking for houses." He points to the communities of Mira Mesa, Kearny Mesa, Allied Gardens, and Clairemont. "That cashier at the grocery store this morning told me the best place to live was anywhere north of I-8, said that it's when you get below I-8 that you get into trouble."

"What did he mean by that?" Josie asks Clarence, eyeing him accusingly.

"I don't know. Maybe he just meant it's nicer north of 8."

"And what makes it nicer, Clarence? Is it because there's no blacks up there? No Mexicans? Is that it?"

Clarence narrows his eyes. "Don't start, Josie. He just meant it was a better place to settle—not rundown and slummy. I don't know what he meant. I'm sick and tired of you accusing me of being a racist every time something like this comes up. What do you want me to do? Go running up and down the street yelling to the top of my lungs that I'm not prejudiced?"

"I just want you to be honest, Clarence. I want you to tell me what you really think. That's all I want. You never tell me what you think. I don't know you from Adam."

"And what about you, Josie? What do you really think? You ain't never even been around a black person."

Josie steps back and glares. "Well, maybe that's because we always live in places that are north of I-8."

"Just get in the goddamned car, Josie, and let's go find the fuckin house."

"All right, asshole. You lead. I'll follow."

The place they finally move into is a small, partially furnished house, painted white and trimmed in dark green, sitting at the back end of a cul-de-sac on the edge of Tecolote Canyon in the slightly north-of-I-8 community of Clairemont. It has two bedrooms, one bath, a small kitchen, and a combination living room/dining area. An olive green sculpted carpet dating from the pre-shag period covers all the rooms and has a pungent odor of cat spray just underneath the dinette set. That odor is the only flaw Josie can find, and she figures she can get the smell out if she scrubs hard enough. Even if she can't get rid of the smell, the house is worth it since from the backyard it offers a view that takes in a large part of Tecolote Canyon and a corner of Mission Bay, where sailboats bob on the water day and night. That first evening Josie plops herself down in a lawn chair on the covered patio behind the house, looks out at the sailboats, and says, "I must have died and gone to heaven."

"Well, heaven's got a price," Clarence says. "I ain't been here one whole day, and I've spent almost a thousand dollars after getting some groceries, buying some interview clothes, and paying the first and last month's rent."

While seagulls fly overhead and hawks swoop and glide over the canyon, Josie stretches out on the warm grass and lets a balmy breeze sweep over her. "The price may have been worth it," she says.

The next day they both go looking for jobs. Clarence is lucky, finding a job at JC Penney right away. The pay is higher than in Tucson, and best of all he doesn't have to make outside calls. He can work to his heart's content in the service department at the store.

Josie doesn't have as much luck. She searches all the open bars in the beach areas, starting out in Ocean Beach and going on to Mission Beach and Pacific Beach. She can't find a bartending job anywhere. Finally she returns to Ocean Beach, walks out on the pier, where two old men have their lines dropped into the choppy waves. With salt-water misting her face, she sits down on the wind-scarred boards, lets her feet dangle over the side, and sinks into the drone of the men's voices, the white noise of the ocean, the rhythm of the beach.

Later she walks north following the edge of the waves that continuously wash across the wet sand. Teenagers throw Frisbees over her

head, and sandpipers run around the lapping tide so fast their feet
and legs are blurred by speed. A mother sits in the damp sand helping
her two small girls build sand castles. The mother is tall with long
tanned legs, and she reminds Josie of Dora, the way she's talking to
her children so intently.

Sometimes Dora would guide Josie and Cheyenne up the mountains that surrounded their house and teach them the names of all
the plants and trees. She showed them where the mountain mint
grew. Standing in the cool shadows of trees, Dora would pick a sprig
of mint and hand Josie and Cheyenne the dark green heart-shaped
leaves. "Here," she'd say, "it tastes like Spearmint gum. Your grandpa
used to make tea out of it. It's so good." Her voice was as cool as the
mountain itself, and at those moments Josie thought that if the earth
had a mother, she must be exactly like Dora. Dora also introduced
them to a plant she called *sheep sour,* and the girls would stuff clumps
of it into their mouths. To them, it tasted like unsweetened Kool-Aid
powder—so sour their mouths would draw shut and saliva would
surge over their tongues in small insistent rapids. Sometimes Dora
led the girls into caves, where they would hunker on gray powdery
floors and call for doodlebugs to come out of their houses and play. If
the words were chanted exactly right, and if at the end of the chanting, Dora, Josie, and Cheyenne turned around three times while
remaining in a crouched position, little swirling holes would appear
in the gray dust and doodlebugs would poke out their heads.

Those were the days of fairy tales, the days that made the bad
times appear dim in comparison. Josie tries to remember the words of
the doodlebug chant. "Doodlebug, doodlebug," she mutters, "Doodlebug, doodlebug . . . Doodlebug, doodlebug, your house is on fire."

When Josie gets home that evening, Clarence is already there.

"Did you find a job?" he asks her.

"No, but I spent hours in Ocean Beach."

"You need to get a trade," Clarence tells her, "so you won't have to
work in a bar."

"Yeah," Josie growls, "I guess a trade is the answer to everything.

Forget the ocean. Forget sunsets, caves, and doodlebugs. Forget everything that makes life worth living and get a trade. What kind of trade?"

Ignoring her sarcasm, Clarence says, "Learn to type. Become a secretary. I hear some of the colleges around here are pretty cheap. You've got to take a few typing classes so you can find work."

"I'd rather be a bartender," Josie says. Then she looks at him and knows he has a point. "Okay, okay, I'll check it out." Besides, she's been thinking more and more about taking some drama classes and figures this is the perfect opportunity.

But the next day, she finds she isn't in the mood to enroll in college, and she lies in a lawn chair until noon, staring out at the corner of Mission Bay, lost in daydreams, becoming the hawk soaring high over Tecolote Canyon, then turning into a seagull, feeding on yesterday's scraps. When she thinks of Don Juan's Cocktails, the twins, and Bobby Swanson, a feeling of sadness sweeps over her, and she wonders if she'll ever see them again. She can't allow herself to think of Johnny—the pain is too deep.

The whole thing with Tarantula, including the story about the fig tree, seems like a weird dream that never really happened. Sometimes Josie wishes she could tell Clarence about Tarantula's story, but she knows she can't. Clarence would call the police in a minute, she thinks. He'd have that spot dug up, and I can't let anyone do that until I ask Cheyenne what really happened. A memory of her sister tying her to a tree and threatening to burn her alive flashes before Josie's eyes. Could she actually kill someone? Torture, maybe, but kill? I doubt it. Looking out at the corner of Mission Bay, she realizes she needs to call Cheyenne's doctor again to see if he's back from his vacation.

"He's back," the secretary says excitedly when Josie calls, "and he's anxious to see you. When can you come?"

"Be right there," Josie says.

A half hour later she steps into Matthew Fierros's office and finds him standing behind his desk writing something on a small notepad he's holding in his hands. Since his secretary had told her that he was anxiously awaiting their meeting, Josie had expected him to greet her with enthusiasm. So far, he hasn't glanced up. She wonders if he always fakes coolness when he's anxious or excited. She examines him closely. Because of his short stature and dark complexion, she thinks he looks like Al Pacino might look when he gets a little older, and she figures that if Cheyenne were physically attracted to him she can understand why. Sitting down in a soft leather chair, she crosses her legs and looks around the room at the diplomas and awards that line the walls.

"I'd hoped she was here in San Diego."

"I haven't seen her in nearly a year and a half." Dr. Fierros pauses for a moment, his eyes moving slowly across her face. "There isn't much of a family resemblance."

"I know."

The doctor sits down in the leather chair and taps his pencil on the desk. "When did you see her last?"

"Nineteen-sixty. Guess that'd be seventeen years now." Josie tells him the whole story, tells him how she found out his name, how she tracked him down, tells him how much she wants to find Cheyenne. "Did she ever mention us, her family?"

"Not really. She just said she was from Appalachia. I worry that she isn't taking care of herself," he says. "She needs to be on medication, and I don't know if she's seeing another doctor. She hates doctors generally."

"Have you been looking for her?" Josie asks.

"I hired a private detective."

Josie blinks. "That seems to be goin above and beyond the call of duty."

Dr. Fierros walks to the window and peeps out of the blinds, his back turned to Josie. "We were involved. I knew it was a mistake, but . . . You talk like her. Did you know that? Your voices are the same—the same accent, the same tone."

Josie stares at the back of his head. His wavy gray-black hair is long and laps over the edge of his collar. She wonders if his involvement with Cheyenne was a game on his part. Was he merely curious about the living habits of the poor.

"I operated on her twice," he says. "She was doing fine. We were both doing fine, and then her phone was disconnected, her apartment was vacant, and she was gone."

"How did she pay for that apartment? I mean, what did she do for a living?"

"She was a bartender."

Josie lurches forward in her chair. "You're joking. I was a bartender too. Ain't that something? We were doing the same thing."

Dr. Fierros sighs. "She just didn't show up one day, and that was that. She didn't have close friends except a couple of carnival people who came around sometimes. They don't live here, though. They just bum around. I hate to worry you even more, but there are times I think something might have happened to her."

"No," Josie says. "She's all right. I feel it, you know? She just disappeared again—that's all. She always disappears. Like I told you, she had a whole other life goin on in Sage, Arizona. She's prob'ly somewhere else right now, living it up. She might still be right here. Do you think she could be?"

Dr. Fierros sighs. "I guess it's possible that she could sink into a world just out of sight of this one. Yes, she could be here."

Josie fidgets in her seat. "You'll prob'ly think I'm being silly, but you've seen her since I have. What kind of music did she like? What kind of books? Movies? What was she like?"

Dr. Fierros smiles and sits back down. "She's crazy about Dylan and the Stones. I took her to see the Stones once. We drove up to L.A." He drifts off in a memory.

"I like those same people," Josie says. "What kind of books?"

"I'm not as sure about that."

"How about movies?"

"We didn't go to many, but I remember she really liked *The Last Picture Show.*"

"I loved that movie," Josie says, remembering how she'd begged Clarence to go to Hazard with her to see it, and when he'd refused, how she'd gone alone.

Dr. Fierros's phone begins to buzz, and he picks up the receiver. "Be right there," he says. "I wish I could talk to you longer, but I have to see a patient." He hands Josie a card that includes his home number. "If you find her, if you find out anything, please give me a call. Even if you just want to talk . . ."

Josie stands. "Thanks. I'll let you know if anything turns up."

Later when she returns to the small house in Clairemont, she sits in the backyard remembering how Dr. Fierros said he was worried that something had happened to Cheyenne, and she tries to imagine her sister being dead, gone for all time. "No, she's alive," Josie whispers. "Cheyenne is like a bird, flitting from one place to another. She'll never get caught. How would it feel to be like that, to have no worries, to drift on a balmy breeze, to light down every so often and dramatically affect people's lives, then fly off with no regrets?"

Josie looks up and takes in the beauty around her. The light of day in San Diego is the most beautiful she's seen in any of the places she's been. There is a glow in the air that looks as if the sunlight is being reflected off something shiny and otherworldly and then filtered through a gold silk screen. She walks over to the huge bougainvillea plant that droops over the fence in the backyard, blindingly beautiful with its magenta bloom. It seems to her that she's been thrown inside an enchanted bubble, where all imperfections have been eliminated. Remembering an old saying about the difference between gold and glitter, she touches one of the bougainvillea petals, wondering if it's real.

24

Josie wakes the next morning feeling that she is not quite connected to her body. Clarence has already gone to work, and the emptiness of the small house in San Diego echoes all around her. She feels as if she might drift upward and start spinning in the air. The prospect is exhilarating but frightening because there's always the possibility that when a person leaves her body she won't be able to come back. One morning in Pick she had drifted out of herself for a moment, had become lighter than air, a shiny ball of oxygen and light. She had soared out of the house and rose past the treetops almost to the clouds. Then she had swooped down and hovered over the creek, where she stayed for a while, staring at her shimmering reflection in the water. If only we weren't trapped by our bodies, Josie thinks. If only we could come and go as we pleased. She lies there trying to overcome her fear, trying to break out, to escape, but it doesn't happen.

I know I should prob'ly leave Clarence right now, but I can't, she thinks. Before leaving him, I need to get a job like everyone else. *But I don't want to become like everyone else,* she screams silently. Suddenly she has a burning need to hear Venus's voice, to talk to a person who knows exactly who she is. With shaky hands, she picks up the phone and dials Venus's number.

"Hello," Josie says. "It's me. How's it goin?"

"Josie?" Venus grunts in her raspy voice. "Well, I'll be damned. You actually called. I didn't think you would. Thought you'd forget all about us."

Josie laughs. "No way. Have you found anyone to replace me?"

"Yeah, we hired the girl that worked down at Hudson's Grocery."

"Is she working out okay?"

"Pretty good—not as good as you, though. Everybody keeps asking about you."

Josie grins, happy to be talking to Venus again. "I wish I was still over there," she says. "This place is real pretty, but it don't hardly seem real." She pauses, almost afraid to ask the question she most wants to ask. Finally she comes out with it. "Do you see Johnny much these days?"

Venus sighs. "No. His wife's sick. She's been in the hospital. No one knows exactly why, but rumor has it she overdosed. It's not the first time she's done that, you know."

Josie doesn't say anything.

"She's done it twice before."

"Why?" Josie asks. "What's wrong with her?"

"Screwed up. She had a sister that went crazy as a loon. Maybe it runs in the family."

Josie thinks of Cheyenne and Dora and herself. "Yeah," she says, "maybe it does. Well, I guess I'd better not run up too high a phone bill. I'll talk to you later."

"Wait," Venus says. "I just wanted to say that, well, any time you get dissatisfied with that place, you can come back here and have your job back."

Josie grins. "Thanks, Venus." She hangs up and sags down in the chair, closes her eyes, and sees Johnny the way he looked when he stood across from her at the bar. Surrounded by thick black lashes, those blue-green eyes twinkled at her like lights shining through fog. As he talked, his black hair kept falling over his brow, and his voice was so deep that it seemed to roll out of him like low thunder. She wishes she hadn't overreacted when she found out he'd been with Cheyenne. All he had done was go out with a woman everybody wanted. He didn't know she was my sister, Josie thinks. He didn't even date her that long. God, I wish I hadn't come over here. I wish I was back in Sage with the ocotillos and manzanitas, with the ghosts of Indians and the spirits of old cowboys.

*   *   *

Absent the bricks and ivy of Eastern colleges, El Camino College looks more like a high school than an institution of higher learning. So much for atmosphere, Josie thinks as she steps inside the pastel-plastered main structure and picks up a college catalogue.

Back home, she scans through it looking for the classes Clarence wants her to take. Under business administration in all its boring practicality, she finds them, takes note of class schedules, and moves on in search of the drama section. Almost all her life Josie has pretended to be fictional characters. I ought to be able to do it in front of people, she thinks as she breaks into a cold sweat. She circles the classes she intends to take: business English, typing, and accounting for Clarence's sake, and introduction to drama and beginning acting for her own. She decides not to tell Clarence about the drama classes right away, figuring he'll have a shit-fit when she does.

"Looks like you finally did something that makes sense," he says when Josie tells him about her trip to El Camino and shows him the catalogue. He plans to take some computer classes himself when he feels more secure with his new job, when he has learned every inch of it and is getting bored.

"Knew you'd like it, but in the meantime, reckon I ought to keep looking for work? Can we make it without me getting a job right now?"

"Don't worry about it," Clarence says. "We can make it. Bernard just sent me a back payment. I reckon that old repair shop has started doing great." Clarence looks down at the floor. "I've got a little surprise. Just something I picked up on the street. It's out in the car."

"What is it?" Josie asks.

"A dog. Just wait till you see it, Josie. It's the prettiest little dog in the world."

Josie smiles. "It might suffocate. Don't you know better than to leave it in the car?"

A few minutes later Clarence returns with the dog, a buff-and-white spotted cocker spaniel, an aging male with a dirty coat, who appears to be critically malnourished. "Ain't it pretty?" Clarence asks.

He is the ugliest dog she's ever seen. "Yeah," she says, "it's a real doll." She reaches out to pick up the animal, but he growls. Taking him anyway, she begins petting his head while he squirms to get away. "This poor little feller looks like it's starved to death. I bet it's been lost for weeks." She looks for ID tags, but there are none. "Do you guess someone abandoned it?"

"Maybe it run off."

"Did you get it any food? We don't have any food for it."

Clarence takes the dog back from her. "Yeah, I got it some of the most expensive dog food made. This little feller ain't going to have nothing but the best."

"What're we goin to name it?" Josie asks.

"I've already named it Butter," Clarence says. "I got it some toys, too. It has to play." Clarence goes back out to his car and brings in the loot.

A few minutes later Butter is gobbling down the best food Clarence could find like there's no tomorrow. "If it keeps eating like that, it'll gain its weight back in no time," Josie says.

When the dog has eaten his belly full, Clarence surprises Josie by saying, "Let's go take it for a walk on the beach."

They drive down to Dog Beach, a section of Ocean Beach where it is legal for pet owners to allow their dogs to run unleashed. Butter tries to frolic in the sand but manages to bang one foot into the other and fall flat on his face.

Josie grins. "I've never seen such a klutz."

"Maybe I ought to of named it Gerald Ford," Clarence remarks.

They look at each other and laugh.

Later they buy foot-long hotdogs from a nearby stand and sit on the edge of the pier. Josie has only eaten half of hers when Butter snaps it from her hands and gulps it down—onions, relish, and all.

"I've never seen a dog eat onions, Clarence," Josie says.

"Me neither. Looks like we got a original."

When they return home, they lie on the couch and manage to make love while Butter reclines at their feet snorting and grunting.

When the lovemaking is over, Josie stays for a moment in Clarence's arms, wondering if there is still an outside chance they can make it. He has such a good heart. Who else would have picked up Butter? Most people would have left a mangy dog like that to die on the street.

"Clarence?" Josie mutters. "I'm sorry I'm always nagging you."

"Ah, you don't nag . . . much."

"Yeah, I do. I'm always nagging you to talk about the war, and I accuse you of being a racist when I know you're really not."

"What's got into you?"

"Nothing. I just want you to know that I don't think you're a bad person."

Sound asleep, Butter begins snoring loudly.

Josie stares curiously at the dog. "Jesus, the windows are rattling."

Clarence smiles. "It can do anything it wants to. You just leave it alone."

Josie goes into the bedroom and looks at the college catalogue again. She wonders what they'll study in introduction to drama. Will they read the plays of Shakespeare, some of which she almost knows by heart? Will they read Lillian Hellman and Tennessee Williams? She opens a box of books, drags out a copy of Hellman's plays, and begins rereading *Toys in the Attic*. From the next room comes the sound of Butter eating again, and she hears the dog doing something else—biting himself? Licking himself? She can't tell which. Then she hears Clarence say, "That's all right, little feller. You'll be just fine."

Josie gets up and slips down the tiny hallway and looks in at them. Clarence is sitting on the couch, staring at the TV, and Butter is lying close beside him, his head on Clarence's knee, drooling white foam on his new master's pants. Josie gets an eerie feeling that she has seen them sitting like that a thousand times before.

25

Brewster sits on the edge of his bed, staring at a letter he's already read three times. Putting it down, he gets on the phone. "Ida? How'd you like to drive me to Louisville?"

"What for?"

"Some of the Kentucky boys that was in World War Two are having a reunion this weekend. It's the division I was in. I got a letter from the man that's organizing it. I've been invited, and we're welcome to bring guests. I thought you and Viola might want to go with me." He hates to invite Viola, but he figures Ida will be more likely to agree to the venture if he does.

Ida turns red in the face, her heart beating fast. "You mean for me to drive you?"

"Yeah."

Ida has never driven on a freeway, and the thought of going all the way to Louisville is the most frightening idea that's ever come her way. "I'd like to, Brewster, but I've got so much to do. I've been canning beans all week."

Brewster's heart sinks. If Ida won't go, he'll have to go on the bus alone—not a pleasant prospect. "I guess I'll have to go by myself then," he says.

Ida can't stand to hear him sound despondent. "Do you know anyone that'll be there?"

"Might know a few. There was two other boys from Kentucky right in my platoon. They called us the three briarhoppers. One was from Bowling Green and the other was from around Louisville. I don't know if either one'll be there. That'un from Louisville got his feet and most of his legs froze off. I figure he's prob'ly dead by now."

"I'll have to think about it," Ida says, but she doesn't have the heart to turn Brewster down. The next day she calls him and says she'll be glad to take him, that she and Viola are looking forward to it. "But why do you have to leave so early? They ain't no point in taking off at five in the morning."

"What if we have a flat and have to walk somewhere to get it fixed?" Brewster says. "The way you drive, you'll prob'ly get us lost. We need to have time to spare."

"I've never got lost in my life," Ida snaps, "and if you don't hush up about it, you can find you another driver."

They grumble at each other for several more minutes and hang up.

Three o'clock Saturday morning, Brewster gets dressed and fixes himself some breakfast—eggs, bacon, and toast. He takes the bronze-colored cross of Jesus, the one that Josie found in the old house, out of his suitcase, polishes it till it shines, and puts it back. Sitting on the couch to wait, he falls asleep and is soon visited by a dream regarding the upcoming night's reunion. He sees Antonio Mancini from Newark, who is still smiling even though there's a bullet hole between his eyes. Standing to Antonio's left with a grin on its face is the bloated body from the frozen field near Nancy, France. To Antonio's right is the German sniper from the church library in Belgium, blood still gurgling from his stomach. The three shadowy ghosts from Brewster's past are hovering near the entrance to the hotel, motioning for him to enter. When he wakes, he is moaning and groaning so loudly he can hardly hear the pounding on the door.

"Brewster? Are you all right? What is goin on?"

"Nothing's goin on, goddamn it," he yells back. "I'll be right there."

Opening the door, he finds Ida, staring at him with a concerned expression. "I was just having a dream," he mutters, "and I don't want to talk about it." He glances out to her car and sees Viola slouched in the back seat, her big round face glowing like a moon. I don't know if I can take this, he thinks, but he gets his suitcase, turns out the light, and goes.

A half hour later they're sailing past the outskirts of Manchester, heading toward London and beyond. Brewster is sitting in the front seat beside Ida. He's gazing out the window, trying to keep his mind off the fact that Viola is sitting directly behind him staring at the back of his head. She'll prob'ly burn a hole straight through me by the time I can ever get out of this car, he thinks. As usual she hasn't said a word. Ida has told Brewster that Viola talks to her when no one else is around. Brewster finds that hard to believe. All he's ever heard her do is smack her lips while eating. It occurs to him that she isn't real, that maybe she's a big inflatable doll that people like to keep around. Yep, he thinks, they just blow her up and place her here and there—stick her on the couch, stand her in a corner, or set her at the kitchen table—wherever they want her to be, and the only two things she was designed to do is stare and eat.

Brewster turns to look at Ida, who is driving and griping at the same time.

"A dream that tears at a person like that ought to be told," she's saying.

Brewster sighs. "It's not worth telling. The main thing a person needs to learn in life is when to talk and when not to."

"Ain't that the truth," Ida says. "Remember old Arthur and Laurie Griffith? They showed up at our house all the time. Stayed for a week sometimes, and they both stunk like rotten onions. They'd just sit at the kitchen table yammering night and day about every old thing in the world. Every time we seen them coming we knowed we'd had it."

Brewster glances around at Viola. Her eyes are fixed right on him—big, round, and empty like a cow's eyes. "Course sometimes people don't talk enough," he says to Ida.

"Well, I'll have to admit you usually don't have a problem talking, Brewster."

"I know it, but you've got other friends that keep pretty closed-mouthed."

Ida glares at him then turns around to Viola. "Is everything all right back there?"

Viola doesn't blink an eye.

They go on like that for two hours, talking and driving. Just north of Lexington, Ida is forced to get on the freeway, and she's as frightened with the reality of it as she has been with the dread. "Is that the ramp you reckon I get on?" she screams when the exit to I-64 comes up.

"Looks like it," Brewster yells back. "It says Louisville, don't it?" He knows if he were driving he'd be almost as nervous as Ida. It's been years since he's driven anywhere substantial.

Ida takes the ramp at sixty miles an hour, her tires screaming like banshees. "What do I do now?" she yells. "This lane is running out."

"Get in the other one," Brewster yells.

"Oh, Lord, we'll get killed." Flipping her turn signal, she squeezes into the other lane.

"You're doing just fine," Brewster tells her.

After they've been driving for another half hour, Ida turns to Brewster and says, "You didn't think I could drive on a freeway, did you? Well, you was wrong, Buster. They ain't nothing I can't do."

The traffic increases when they enter the outskirts of Louisville. The highway widens to three lanes, and exits shoot out in all directions. "What road do I get on now?" Ida screams.

"That'n right there," Brewster yells. "No, not that one! That one—264 West. It goes straight to the hotel."

Ida nearly sideswipes a semi as she careens onto the 264 exit.

"You're doing just fine," Brewster says again, wondering if they'll ever get back home.

At the hotel, Brewster, Ida, and Viola exit the car like war victims and stagger into a coffee shop in the lobby. "Let's just sit here a while till we get our bearings," Brewster says, shaking all over. Although he announces to everyone within earshot that he'd prefer a good stiff drink, he orders the women and himself Danish pastries and coffee.

They eat in silence until Brewster says, "I never thought we'd live to tell about this day. Course it ain't over yet."

"You're pushing your luck, Brewster," Ida says. "Maybe you'd like for us to go on home and leave you here."

After catching their breaths, they leave the coffee shop and return to the lobby. Ida stares up at a crystal chandelier. "I didn't notice before, but this place is pretty fancy," she whispers.

At the end of the lobby, they see a door on which a banner is posted welcoming the Kentucky veterans. "That's it, I reckon," Brewster says, feeling like a relic from a time gone by.

When they check into their room—a double with two king-size beds—Brewster flops down on one bed, and Ida and Viola on the other. They fall into silence, then sleep. A couple of hours later, Brewster wakes to find Ida shaking his shoulder.

"What're you goin to wear tonight?" she's shouting at him.

"It's there in my bag," Brewster grunts.

"Law' have mercy," Ida says when she drags his outfit from the suitcase. "You can't wear this old thing. We're goin to have to buy you something."

"Shee-it," Brewster grunts again.

"Get out of that bed," Ida shouts. "You need some new britches and a shirt. Why, them people will be spruced up tonight. You have to dress when you go to events like this."

"Will you shut up?" Brewster groans. He turns over and puts the pillow over his head.

Ida grabs his arm and drags him out of bed. A little later they're all standing in a Kmart, where Ida and Viola are sizing him up for new duds—an olive green leisure suit with flared pants legs and a long square-tailed jacket with wide lapels and stitched front pockets. The shirt they've chosen is white with wide olive green stripes.

"I wouldn't wear that to a dog fight," Brewster scoffs.

Ida narrows her eyes. "Why, this is what people are wearing, Brewster. If you had any sense of style, you'd know that. Now, we ain't goin no place with you if you wear them dirty Levi's and that twenty-year-old flannel shirt. You'll wear these new clothes or you can find another way back home."

Brewster sighs with disgust. "If I've learned one thing from all this, it's don't ever step out of the house with a woman that's got the keys."

When they walk into the banquet hall that night, the band is playing "Moonlight Serenade." Brewster stands there a minute, memories pouring over him like driving rain. "I've never seen so many old people together in one place in my life," he grunts.

"Ah, shut up," Ida snaps.

The first person Brewster recognizes is Price Gibson, from Bowling Green, one of the three briarhoppers from yesteryear. "Uh, Price," Brewster yells, "remember me?"

Price looks at him with a puzzled expression. "I . . . uh . . ."

"You don't remember me, do you?" Brewster says. "Well, I can see why. I don't look a thing like I used to. It's me, Brewster Clay. Do you remember now?"

Price's face breaks into a smile. "Brewster Clay? By God, I reckon I'd know you anywhere." Price takes on a more serious look. "Guess who else is here," he says and points to an old man in a wheelchair. "It's George Wells. He got his feet froze clean off right about the same time yours froze, as I recall. You fellers was in the same hospital room, wouldn't you?"

"Yeah," Brewster mutters. He nods toward Ida and Viola. "Price, this here is Ida Tolliver and Viola Watson. Wish you'd keep them company while I say hello to George."

"Be glad to," Price mutters, leading the women to a table. On a small stage a band is playing "I'll See You in My Dreams." Price takes a closer look at Ida, who is wearing a powder blue dress that sets off the pale blue of her eyes. "Would you care to dance?" he asks.

"I'd love to," Ida says, batting her lashes.

While Viola settles in at the table and Ida begins a night-long dance with Price Gibson, Brewster approaches George Wells, who is sitting apart from the crowd in his wheelchair. He's wearing a leisure suit not unlike Brewster's except that it's rust-colored. Brewster glances furtively at George's feet, hoping against hope that he'll find shoes, and he does. George is prob'ly wearing some of them artificial legs, he thinks.

He's still gazing at the shoes when he hears George say, "They didn't grow back, Brewster, if that's what you're thinking."

"How're you doing, George?" Brewster asks between nervous coughs.

"Fine, as you can see. Got a new suit out of the deal anyway. See you got one too." The two reunited soldiers look at each other and laugh.

Just then the man who organized the event gets up to make a speech. "Let's get out of here," George says. "I don't want to hear all that handkerchief-swiping stuff. There's a little balcony behind that door if you'll be so kind as to wheel me out."

As Brewster wheels George to the balcony, he is hit by the memory of that night in the foxhole. It was twenty below zero, and they were trapped. If they'd stuck their heads out, their heads would have been shot off. They knew their feet were freezing, but there wasn't much they could do except kick them back and forth, rub them, and pray the blood would keep flowing.

From the balcony they look out on the city lights of Louisville. "Do you still live around here?" Brewster asks.

"Not far. Down in E-Town." George lights a cigarette. "I guess you have a family."

"Two girls. My wife died a long time ago."

"I got married once too. Married the woman who customized my prosthetics. It didn't last long, though." George looks up at the sky so intently he appears to be counting the stars. "Do you ever think about it, Brewster, that night in the foxhole?"

Brewster grunts. "Sometimes."

George takes a long puff on his cigarette and throws it off the balcony to the shrubbery below. "I've thought many a time about trying to find you. The only reason I came to this thing is that I thought you might show up."

Brewster starts to say something, but George stops him. "Let me talk first. I hate that I acted so bad when we were in the hospital. It was like I blamed you for the fact I lost my legs. It's just that I couldn't understand it. Both of us were stuck in the same foxhole, wearing identical shoes and socks on the same cold night for the same amount of time. We came away with legs froze black as stove pipes, but yours healed and mine had to be amputated."

Brewster grins. "If it makes you feel any better, my feet and legs hurt all the time from poor circulation caused by that frostbite."

"Sorry to hear it," George says.

They look at each other and smile awkwardly. "Reckon that feller in there has stopped telling his sob stories?" Brewster asks.

"If we're lucky," George says.

Back inside, the band is playing "Stardust." Brewster wheels George to the table where Viola is sitting alone. "Where's Ida?" he asks Viola.

Viola doesn't answer, but she points to the far end of the dance floor where Ida is still dancing with Price Gibson, her head resting snugly on his shoulder.

"Looks like she's keeping herself busy," Brewster mutters, then he turns to George. "This here is Viola Watson, George. She's a . . . well, I guess she's a friend. Don't get insulted if she don't talk to you. I ain't never heard her say a word to no one."

The rest of the night passes slowly. George and Brewster rehash more of their war days, while Ida and Price Gibson dance to almost every song. A few times the two dancers return to the table looking flushed and excited, hanging onto each other's every word. At one point Brewster glances over at Viola and thinks he sees a tear running down her cheek, but on second thought he decides it's probably sweat.

The next day as they're driving home, Brewster and Ida hardly speak a word. Ida appears to be in a daze, as if her mind is somewhere else on someone else. Brewster is preoccupied too. He reaches into his bag, drags out the cross from the Belgium church, and holds it in his hands. More than anything he's glad he got to see George Wells again, to know that George has lived a long life in spite of what happened to him. Brewster glances at Ida and wonders if that smile on her face has anything to do with Price Gibson. Price was always lucky when it came to women.

26

Butter has gained five pounds, and he lives for Clarence. All he does is lie in a corner and lick himself until Clarence comes home from work in the evenings. The dog won't have anything to do with Josie no matter how hard she tries to make friends with him. Every time she walks past him, he growls, bares his teeth, and barks, or he'll just lie there and give her the evil eye. When Clarence is home, Butter snuggles in his lap and stares up at him, blissfully.

Lately, the dog has been sleeping with them, too, and he snores the whole night. When he isn't snoring, he's breathing heavily and biting his own feet until they bleed. Not only does Butter bite himself, he drools constantly. White foamy froth comes out of his mouth and gets on the sheets, and on Josie and Clarence's feet and legs. But worse than all the rest, he stinks. His face smells like a toilet because he's always nosing in his own rear end. Butter's snoring, grunting, biting, licking, and drooling together with Clarence's own ticking sounds are just about to get the best of Josie. She wakes up every morning with darker circles than the night before.

Finally she takes Butter to a vet, who diagnoses the dog as having out-of-control allergies for which he prescribes medication that is supposed to stop him from scratching himself. Later, Josie will learn that it doesn't work. He also tells her that Butter has a deformed nasal membrane that will cost six hundred dollars to repair, but Clarence says that even if they had six hundred dollars to spend, he would never use it to pay someone to cut on Butter's face.

"Then why does it have to sleep with us?" Josie shouts at Clarence. "I'm not getting any sleep. My school starts pretty soon. I need my rest."

Clarence strokes the dog's head. "I don't have the heart to put it out."

"Fine," Josie says. "Guess I'll find somewhere else to sleep." There is no bed in their second bedroom, so Josie takes a pillow from Clarence and Butter's bed, spreads a sheet on the living room couch, and lies alone for the first time in years. I've been passed over for a dog, she thinks. I've never known anyone that this has ever happened to. Remind me not to call home about it. Remind me not to tell Daddy or Ida.

Even though she has known for months that their marriage appears to be drawing to a close, sleeping in a different room brings the reality of it a degree closer. She begins to remember how things were before she married—how she belonged to no one but herself, how she didn't have to take anyone else into consideration before doing something. Right now, I could sit up all night, she thinks. I could walk outside and lay down in the yard, and Clarence would never know it. He wouldn't raise up and say, "Where're you goin this time of night?" because he wouldn't know when I got up. She begins to wonder how life will be if she leaves him, how it will feel to live alone.

Clarence has just left for work, and Josie is drinking coffee, turning the radio dial from one station to another, trying to find something dark and strange and thought-provoking, but all she can find are songs by the Beach Boys or the Doobie Brothers. Turning off the radio, she tries to conjure an image or two of don Juan, but he's nowhere around. Don Juan prob'ly doesn't have a taste for southern California, she reasons. She looks out the window at the gray sky and wishes it would go ahead and rain. "Put up or shut up," she mutters. "Fuckin place." She feels as though there is nothing in San Diego for her. Cheyenne has dropped out of sight. There's no Johnny to make her feel alive. No music, no don Juan, no rain, no Cheyenne, and no Johnny. There is no one but Clarence, who grows more distant each day, and Butter, who is glaring at her from the opposite side of the room.

This is what she's thinking when the telephone rings. It's Dr. Fierros. "I got a postcard from Ramona," he says.

Josie's heart does a flip-flop.

Dr. Fierros continues. "She says she's been in Austin, Texas, that Jerry Jeff Walker, Guy Clark, and Townes Van Zandt are the best musicians on earth, that she might come back here soon, but that she's traveling right now, hitting the road, and doesn't know where she's going."

At the mention of the three Texas musicians, Josie finds herself becoming angry. It's clear to her that she and Cheyenne have a lot in common, even Jerry Jeff, Guy, and Townes. Why hasn't she ever tried to seek me out, to find out who *I* am? Josie wonders.

In spite of herself, she asks, "Is that all she said?"

"That's all."

"Are you in your office? Do you have the card with you?"

"Yes."

"I'll be right over."

"Wait. Meet me for lunch in Old Town. One o'clock at the Casa de Bandini?"

"Be there," Josie says.

An hour later, she finds Matthew Fierros sitting in the restaurant's courtyard. Wearing a gray, perfectly tailored suit, he looks as though he's dressed to go to a convention. "Had you rather go inside?" he asks her.

Josie looks up at the gray cloudy sky. "No, it's fine," she says and sits down in one of the wrought-iron chairs. "Where's Cheyenne's card?"

Dr. Fierros hands it to her. On the card is a picture of a cowboy. He's sitting on a black horse, looking out toward a range of purple mountains with the sun sinking slowly behind them. Sagebrush rolls at the horse's feet, an armadillo waddles nearby. On the cowboy's face is a look of complete sadness until one studies more closely and sees the roguishness in his eyes. "Perfect," Josie says. She turns over the card and stares at Cheyenne's handwriting—the widely looped Es and Ls, the boxy Ms and Ns. It's the first time she's seen her hand-writing in years.

"You can keep it if you like," the doctor says.

A waiter comes by and takes their orders, brings them huge glasses of margaritas. All the while Josie holds onto the card as if it's a rare oyster that carries poison in its pearl. "Tell me something, Dr. Fierros. Are you sure Cheyenne never said anything about us, about, you know, her family?"

The doctor turns his head to the side and sighs. Finally he answers her question with one of his own. "Do you ever get angry about the fact that she has never contacted you?"

Josie looks out at the mariachi who thankfully are storming a table at the far end of the courtyard. It will take them a while to get to theirs. "I've always thought something major would happen if I ever saw her again, that all my questions would be answered. Pretty stu-pid, right?" Josie shrugs. "Life goes on. I'll be goin to college pretty soon, and I intend to take some acting classes. I never thought I'd turn out to be someone who feels like they have to do something, but I guess that's how I feel right now."

"There's nothing wrong with doing something." Dr. Fierros smiles and takes a drink. "You sound so much alike. It's amazing. Your voices are identical."

"Yeah," Josie says, becoming irritated. "You told me that same thing the last time I saw you. Anyway, Cheyenne prob'ly couldn't answer my questions. I'm the one who has to do that."

Dr. Fierros nods sympathetically, which irritates Josie even more. "You're right," he says.

The waiter brings them large tortilla shells filled with salsa, spicy meat, and melted cheese and topped with sour cream and guacamole. They glance around at the half-empty courtyard and eat in silence. Then out of the blue, Dr. Fierros says, "You have beautiful eyes."

Josie looks at him distrustfully.

"Would you like to go to a movie with me some night?" He smiles at her invitingly. "I've wanted to call you since that first day you came into my office."

Josie is astounded. M E N. They'll go from one sister to another. No problem. No skin off their noses. No big deal. "No, I wouldn't," she says. "Besides, I'm married." Since leaving Sage, she has been biting her nails to the quick, and her fingers are so mangled-looking that she's been trying to keep them hidden as much as possible. Now she raises her left hand from her lap and lays it on the table so that her ring finger is in full view.

Dr. Fierros looks down at her hand and turns red with embarrassment. Josie glares with disgust at his red face and squeamish eyes. Now she can't imagine why Cheyenne was ever attracted to him, to this doctor in his little gray suit. "But the fact that I'm married ain't the only reason I won't go out with you," she says.

The doctor flinches and his face turns a deeper red than before. Obviously he hadn't expected to be insulted. "If it's because of your sister, I wouldn't be so loyal. She did talk about her family, you know. She said she was so bored with all of you that she thought she'd die before she could get away."

Suddenly the mariachi dressed in shiny red vests, black velvet pants, and colorfully beaded sombreros are standing at their table, joyously singing in harmony, perkily strumming their guitars. "Oh, is that really what she said, or did you just make that up on the spot?" Josie asks.

The doctor chuckles as the mariachi sing their unusually light-hearted version of "Maleguéña Salerosa." "Why do you keep looking for her, Josie?" he asks.

"I know what you're doing," Josie yells at him over the music. "You just want to find out if we're the same in bed. Is that it, Dr. Fierros?"

The mariachi don't seem to notice that Josie and the doctor are arguing. Either that or they're getting the thrill of their lives out of playing over them. Glancing angrily at the most jovial of them, Josie takes a few bites of her salad.

"That's not it," Dr. Fierros shouts, veins popping out on his face. "I had thought you weren't like Cheyenne at all. I'd thought you were more sensible, more . . . Obviously, I was wrong."

There are several words that seem designed to send Josie into a rage and *sensible* is one of them. She hates everything about it—its spelling, its definition, its usage, and most of all the people it describes. "Sensible?" she screams. "You think I'm sensible? I guess you think I'm *courteous,* too." She shoves a bowl of salsa over the edge of the table, and it dumps into the doctor's lap.

The mariachi begin playing "South of the Border."

"Are you crazy or something?" Dr. Fierros yells.

"Just be sure to tell me if you ever hear from her again," she says and stands up to go.

The mariachi smile exuberantly, their feet tapping like woodpeckers, their eyes sparkling like stars on a clear spring night. Josie puts the postcard in her purse and leaves.

At home, she wonders if she'll keep meeting men who have a history with Cheyenne, if she'll always be their second choice. Deep down she knows that what the doctor said is true—that Cheyenne left because she thought her parents and sister were much too boring to be around. She *doesn't care,* Josie thinks. How did she get that way? There was no deep emotional wound to ruin her forever. Maybe it was just a decision she made one day. She might have been jumping rope or wading in the creek when the idea first came to her, and from that time on the only meaningful thing in her life was her own gratification. Or maybe it wasn't an idea she needed to develop. Maybe she was born that way. Cheyenne could turn into a different person, take up a different view of life in a minute, and maybe nothing's wrong with that. But why did she always have to turn into such a asshole?

Josie sits still, doesn't move a muscle as the sadness sets in. The most dismal realization is that, in some corner of her thoughts, she's been banking on Cheyenne to teach her how to break out of the trap she's in. Why can't I do that by myself? Josie thinks. She glances at Butter, whom she sees as a symbol of civilization gone awry. Butter, who with his allergies and other afflictions, needs constant attention, who couldn't survive on his own if his life depended on it.

"All we do is bitch and moan from our safe little ruts," she says to the dog. "We love bitching, don't we?" Butter looks at her as if he understands exactly what she's saying, and Josie begins to feel a strange affinity with the animal, a reluctant sympathy for his plight. "I still need to find Cheyenne," she says to him, "even if all I do when I find her is tell her to go to hell."

Butter takes a deep breath and lets it out irritably. Then he farts and lumbers over to the window to keep an eye out for Clarence.

Josie decides to call Brewster.

"She's not here, Daddy," she says, trying to disguise the anger in her voice. "She sent her doctor a postcard saying she might come back though."

"Cheyenne will either turn up or she won't. We can't make it happen," he says.

Already, the sound of Brewster's voice has put her in a better mood. "We've got two bedrooms, Daddy. I know you'd like it here—it's so pretty. Are you ready to come out? This place is only half furnished, but that's no sweat. I can get you a bed tomorrow."

Brewster sighs. "I'll have to think about it a little more."

Josie's heart sinks. "I thought you wanted to come. That's what we planned."

"I know we did, and I will come, but I just can't tear out of here right now. I have to think about it, get things ready. By the way, thanks for sending the cross. I can't believe you found it. What do you think it means? Do you think it's a sign I ought to get religion?"

"No, that's too obvious. The trouble with signs is that no one ever knows what the hell they mean." Just then Butter staggers toward her and flops down on the floor. "Daddy, I almost forgot to tell you that we've got this dog. It's the awfullest-looking thing you've ever seen. It's supposed to be a cocker spaniel, but it looks like a big walrus."

Brewster starts to tell Josie about his recent trip to Louisville, but he hasn't digested it yet, doesn't know what to say. When their conversation ends, he walks over to the refrigerator and gets himself a beer. He could tell from the sound of her voice that she was upset—maybe from something Cheyenne said in the postcard or from what the doctor told her. He hopes his daughters' old fights haven't resumed before they've even found each other. It occurs to him that Cheyenne is now in her early thirties, the same age as Dora when he married her. They were alike in more ways than one, but Dora's anger came from sadness. He doesn't know where Cheyenne's comes from.

He remembers how Dora looked back when they were first married. She wasn't a beautiful woman. Her nose was a little too long and her eyes too wide-set for her to be what you'd call a great beauty, but she was tall, had those long legs and wild curly hair, and there was a sense of excitement about her. It was like a fire was smoldering just beneath the surface that might explode any minute. Sometimes her temper got the best of her—that was for sure, Brewster thinks. She was so mad that half the time she couldn't say a word to anyone.

He recalls a day when Josie was four or five. He was still sitting at the table after supper. Cheyenne and Josie were playing on the porch, and Dora was washing the dishes and looking out the window over the sink, staring at the mountain that rose behind their house. All at once Josie, so excited she was squealing, came running into the kitchen to ask her a question. It was one of those big questions children sometimes ask. Josie tugged at Dora's skirt. "Is the sky like a ceiling, Mommy? If you touched it, would it feel like a ceiling?"

Dora didn't speak, didn't acknowledge her at all.

"Mommy," Josie whined. "Is it? Is the sky like a ceiling?"

Dora kept standing there washing plates, dipping them in the rinse water and stacking them in the drainer as she stared stoically out at the mountain.

"Tell me, Mommy." Josie was beginning to cry.

Brewster stood up from the table. "Answer the child's question, Dora."

Dora didn't acknowledge him either, didn't change her expression, didn't blink an eye.

Crying harder now, Josie began stomping her feet. "Tell me," she cried.

Brewster bent over Josie. "The sky is . . ."

"I don't want you to tell me," she screamed. "I want Mommy to tell me."

Once again Brewster tried to answer Josie's question, but she ran to her room and began crying herself to sleep. Dora let the dishwater out of the sink and went outside, brushed past Cheyenne and walked up the road.

Cheyenne stepped inside. "Why does she do that? What's wrong with her?"

"If your mommy's not in the mood to talk, she won't, and that's that," Brewster said.

The next evening when they were all seated at the supper table, Dora looked straight at Josie and said, "The sky is exactly like the ceiling, Josie, and we're trapped here underneath it. If you touched it, it would feel just like our ceiling."

"Oh," Josie said and asked for some Jell-O.

Cheyenne glared at Dora. "That ain't true, Mommy, and you know it." Then she turned to Josie. "It ain't true, Josie. The sky is like air. You can fly through it forever."

Josie stared down at her plate. "Can I go play now?"

"Yes," Dora said. "You can go play now."

Brewster figures there was something inside Dora that often got the upper hand, that wouldn't allow her to show emotion other than the sadness and anger in her eyes. He remembers the effect she had on people when she walked into a room—it was instant respect. She never had much to say in a crowd, but when she did speak, everyone would shut up and listen. He'd always thought that if there had been a disaster and people needed someone to lead them to safety, they'd have picked Dora out of a hundred other choices. Even though she often seemed dissatisfied with the children and with him too (either Cheyenne was too wild or Josie was too tame or he was too middle-of-the-road), Brewster recalls the way she read books aloud to them almost every night, the way she catered to Josie and Cheyenne, told them they were the most special people on earth. Actually, she went a little overboard on that track, telling them, "There's us, and then there's the other people, the little citizens, the dull-heads. Always keep that in mind, children." Sometimes he worried that she had lumped him in with the dull-heads, that he wasn't really part of the circle she'd built with the children.

Lately, he has been thinking a lot about Dora. He's been thinking about her because of Ida. From the beginning of summer, Ida had been coming by with a pot of some new Italian meal, but since he introduced her to Price Gibson on their trip to Louisville, she only calls him once or twice a week. Price drove down to visit her last weekend and took her to a dance club in Hazard. "And to think I've been putting up with that old Viola Watson," Brewster growls to himself. "I wouldn't have let her darken my door if her and Ida wouldn't friends." Actually Brewster was and still is a little afraid of Viola. He figures it's at least possible that someday she might get it into her head to grab hold of an ax and hack someone to death.

It's not so much that he has romantic feelings for Ida. He simply enjoyed their talks. All summer they rambled on about the old days, about square dances, corn shuckings, bean stringings, and molasses stir-offs. They talked about how times have changed, about how Pick has grown and keeps on growing. They compared the clothes they used to wear to school, flour-sack dresses and knee pants. They reminisced about the one-room schoolhouses, remembering little stories they used to read in their primers, the games they played on the playground.

Brewster sits on the edge of his bed and wonders if maybe he should visit Josie and Clarence after all.

27

Yesterday Josie went to El Camino College and registered for the fall semester. Then she went to the college bookstore and bought her books. The accounting, typing, and business English texts required for her practical classes—her Clarence classes—looked about as dull as she expected, but the drama books kept her skimming through them for hours.

In Beginning Acting she'll be performing a scene from a play by the second week. What particular play remains a mystery and won't be known until the class meets. The required books for her intro to drama class include plays by Tennessee Williams, Arthur Miller, and Samuel Beckett. She's already read most of their plays, but last night she started reading them again.

Josie has been sleeping alone on the couch for two weeks, and Clarence is annoying her more than usual. He's begun complaining about her cooking, about the way she wears her hair, about things he never used to complain about. She wonders what is wrong with him. She is so distracted by gloomy thoughts that the phone rings three times before she hears it.

"Hello," Johnny says when she picks up the receiver. "Are you still happy over there?"

"Johnny?" Josie gasps.

"How's the tan progressing?" he asks, and Josie can just see the teasing smirk on his face.

She rolls her eyes. "Shut up."

"Met any movie stars lately?"

"I'm goin to hang up if you don't stop."

"Sorry. It's just that I hate California cause it gets to look at you everyday and I don't."

"How's your wife?" Josie asks. "I heard she's been in the hospital."

Johnny sighs. "She was, but she's out now. I don't know where she is. She took off for parts unknown."

Josie is stunned. "Did she take the kids?"

"No, she left them with me. Took off a couple of weeks ago. Don't have any idea where she went. So, do you like San Diego?"

Josie pauses, wondering what he's really asking. "Haven't been here long enough to tell," she says, "but I guess you could say that if Sage and San Diego were folksy rock singers, Sage would be Bob Dylan and San Diego would be James Taylor, least that's the way it seems to me."

"Have you found Ramona?"

Josie flinches at the mention of her sister. "No."

"Why don't you come back then?"

She takes the receiver away from her ear and stares at it as though she's holding a living thing. Finally she speaks into it: "We just barely got over here, Johnny. I can't come back now. Clarence acts like he loves San Diego. He's always talking about how he loves his job, about the great people he works with. He says he believes he can promote into a pretty high-paying position over here. He would never agree to move back to Sage right now."

"Well, why don't you come back by yourself?"

Josie sighs. "I wish I could, but I can't. I've enrolled in school. It's hard to explain this, but I'm goin to have to start doing something with myself. In a couple of years I'll be thirty years old, and I don't have a clue as to why I'm on this earth. I need to find out."

"Can't you find that out over here?"

Josie throws her hands up, exasperated. "I can't leave right now. Cheyenne's doctor got a postcard from her. She might turn up any day."

Johnny is silent for a moment. "So you won't come back then?"

"For once in my life, I need to stay put until I figure things out."

He pauses, and Josie tries to visualize how he looks on the other end of the line.

"I need you to be here, Josie," he finally says.

She wants to tell him she needs him too, but she can't because she needs a lot of things and doesn't know which thing she needs most. Holding on to the receiver, she doesn't say a word.

"Well, don't come back then," he growls and hangs up the phone.

Josie hangs up too, sits down in the middle of the floor, and grabs her head. Tears roll out of her eyes, and she begins to moan so loudly that Butter rouses from sleep and looks at her as if he thinks she's gone insane. She isn't certain how she feels about Johnny. All she knows is that she felt alive when she was around him and that she doesn't feel that way anymore. Hours pass and she still sits there, staring at the sculpted designs in the carpet.

Clarence is late getting home from work that evening. He has decided to stop at the local health food store. One of the secretaries at the service shop at JCPenney's has been eyeing the bologna sandwiches he has for lunch every day and has begun telling him about the wonders of vitamins, telling him about health food, too. She says the best place to grocery shop in San Diego is at GreenTree Grocers, that the food is organically grown, and that if he wants to prevent a future heart attack, he'd better start changing his eating habits. Sally Waterford, who keeps a blood pressure device with her at all times, took Clarence's blood pressure on his break this morning and told him it was high—one hundred and forty over ninety-two. "You need to get that down to one hundred and ten over seventy," she told him. "If you don't, you're asking for trouble." Her warning is of great concern for Clarence, since his family has a history of heart disease. His own father died suddenly of a stroke.

He walks into the store and starts buying. He buys vitamins A, B, C, and E, buys minerals and herbs, too, buys zinc, fish oil, magnesium, garlic pills, and beta-carotene. Then he goes up and down the aisle buying organically grown vegetables, wheat germ, carrot juice, lentils, black beans, oats, raw sunflower seeds, banana chips, decaf coffee, and fig bars for desert. Sally told him that he needs to exercise more, and that the best way to do it is to leave his car at home and bicycle to work. "That way you'll not only get yourself into good physical condition, you'll cut down on exhaust fumes. You'll be saving the environment, Clarence. Think about it."

As far as Clarence is concerned, Sally Waterford knows everything. She reminds him of his mother, Ida, the way she gets so excited over her interests. Sally told him that one of these times she'd bring him a miracle mushroom that would stave off all manner of disease. She said it was a mushroom you had to cultivate yourself, that if you put it in a jar of tea and let it set for a week, it would grow another mushroom just underneath the original one. She said that after seven days you were supposed to take both mushrooms out of the jar and then drink the tea, just a half glass every morning until it was gone, and that you could just keep making the tea from the new mushrooms you'd grown. She said it was an ancient Chinese custom that prolonged life. Clarence can't wait to try it.

Sally is two years older than Josie, but there is a world of difference between them. Originally from Wisconsin, Sally has common sense, a lot of it. She is a hard worker too, types ninety words a minute. The other workers in the office, the clerks and technicians, get a little irritated at her because she tries to tell them what to eat and which vitamins to take, but Clarence never gets irritated. He figures if you know what is best for people, why shouldn't you tell them? She's pretty too, neat as a pin, not tousled and half put-together like Josie. Her clothes are never wrinkled, her shoes are always shiny, and her hose never has a run. She has red hair, blue eyes, the prettiest fair skin he's ever seen, and she doesn't seem to daydream either. He has not once noticed her staring vacantly into space. Why can't Josie be more like Sally? Clarence wonders as he drives home from the store.

When he bursts into the house and deposits his groceries on the kitchen table, Josie saunters into the room and glares at the healthy loot and then at him. "So where's the food?" she inquires. "Since when did you start grocery shopping anyway? I thought you said that particular activity was women's work."

"I've changed my mind," he says.

Eyeing the bean sprouts, Josie becomes increasingly annoyed. The thought that Clarence, of all people, seems in the process of becoming a health nut is more than she can take at the moment. "What is this shit? Bird food? Monkey snacks? This looks like something you'd throw to animals at the zoo. And what the hell is this decaf coffee crap? I'm not drinking that, Clarence. Why on earth would anyone want to drink coffee if it doesn't have caffeine in it? If you intend to stop drinking coffee, by God, stop drinking it. Don't substitute some fake coffee shit."

"I'm just trying to make us healthy, Josie." He's got that Clarence-look on his face, the one that says she ought to be more *sensible.*

Josie can't take it. "If you were to *ever* have sex again, wouldn't you want it to be real?" she asks him. "You wouldn't want to have some kind of decaf sex, would you? Some kind of almost-real-but-missing-the-climax sex. It's the same thing, Clarence. This is goin to turn you into something fake. You'll look like Clarence but you won't be him. You'll be Decaf-Clarence."

Clarence rolls his eyes. "What are you *really* mad about, Josie? This ain't it."

"Yes, it is. And do you know what makes me even madder? It's when someone says, 'This ain't what you're really mad about.' " She grabs the coffee and bean sprouts. "Why is it so hard to believe that I would be mad about this? This coffee and these bean sprouts are exactly why I'm mad. There's nothing deep, dark, or psychological goin on with me, but there's something very deep, dark, and psychological goin on with you. Anyone who always wants to believe there's a hidden reason why a person gets mad has a problem. People like you are needy. You need more to be happening than there really is."

"You're overreacting, Josie."

Josie glares at his calm, sober face. He's right, she thinks. I am overreacting, but that's all he's right about. Everything else about him is wrong. "*Overreacting?*" she shouts. "That sounds like a word someone would use if they were having a problem in their *relationship.* We're not in a fucking relationship. We're just plain old-fashioned

married. Married people don't overreact. They fight like sons of
bitches."

Josie stomps outside, plops on the grass in the backyard, and with
great care begins picking bougainvillea petals that have fallen to the
ground. Although the grocery situation is truthfully what threw her
into a tizzy, she is well aware that there are other elements at work.
Her weird encounter with Dr. Fierros, the depressing call from
Johnny, her confused feelings for Cheyenne, and the new Clarence
with his healthy cuisine have joined forces and are marching straight
for her with their swords drawn.

She often daydreams that some night she'll jump into her Pinto
and drive to the far North. Beside her in the car seat she'll have a bottle of Old Bushmills and a portable cassette player. She'll fly through
the eerie night, sipping Irish whisky and playing "Dead Flowers" by
the Stones over and over again. Her car will speed toward the tip-
end of Alaska, through blizzards and all manner of inclement
weather. Forget the warm easy climes of the South. Josie longs for bitter winter wind, cutting ice, and frozen snow that will bite into her
skin. She'll drive until the car won't go anymore. Then she'll ditch
the car and continue walking north through knee-high snow until
she can walk no longer. Finally, lying down in the soft white seductive
bed, she'll turn up the volume of her cassette player and blast the
Rolling Stones until she dies.

"Don Juan," she whispers, suddenly thinking of the old sorcerer,
"do you still hear me?"

28

Josie struggled through her Clarence classes during the morning hours, all the while cursing the fact that people are forced to get trades, that they have to limit and stifle themselves just to exist. Why do I have to go to college, where people are busily training themselves to spend the rest of their lives in boring jobs? How did this world get itself into such a state?

But that was her day classes. Now it is night, and she is sitting in her beginning acting class waiting for her teacher, Mr. Fletcher Wayne, to show up.

Last night she told Clarence about her decision to take drama. "What do you want to take drama for?" he asked. "Are you planning on becoming a movie star?"

"Yes, asshole, that's my plan," she responded.

About thirty-five other students, ranging in age from eighteen to fifty, are waiting too, staring up at the closed curtains of the stage in front of them, becoming more antsy with each passing minute. Josie has never been this nervous in her life.

"Where is he?" asks a fiftyish woman, sitting beside her.

"Who knows?" gripes a bitter-looking young lady in her twenties. Seated directly behind them, she leans down and whispers, "From what I hear, he's always late. Someone told me he has a drinking problem. I just wish I could have gotten Mr. Jorge, but his class was full."

"A drinking problem?" the fiftyish woman asks. "I wouldn't have taken this class if I'd known."

"I've heard he keeps a fifth of Jack Daniel's locked in his desk drawer," the bitter-looking young lady says.

Josie sits quietly listening to the snip-snap of the voices around her, but all of the chattering ceases when Fletcher Wayne steps into the room. He appears to be about thirty-five, tall and skinny, wearing jeans, a hand-embroidered tunic, leather sandals, and a semi-matching leather hat that droops here and there around his face. His beard is brown, curly, and shaggy, and his eyes are so dark brown they're almost black. He enters the room like a king entering his kingdom, like a god. People shut up.

Jumping onto the stage, he drops his satchel of books and sits on the stage floor, allowing his feet and legs to swing over the edge. He looks out at the faces of his new students as if they're berries ripe for the picking. "Okay," he says boisterously. "Let's see what kind of actors you are. I want to know what I'm dealing with. You there. You in the pink." He points to the bitter-looking young woman who only a few minutes before had been making her complaints about him known. "Get up and talk. I don't care what you say. Just say it right."

"What do you mean?" she asks. "I'm not prepared."

"Who the hell is?" Fletcher shouts.

"But I don't know what to do."

"Recite the Pledge of Allegiance. Sing 'Mary Had a Little Lamb.' I don't care what you do as long as I'm impressed. Go ahead."

The young woman stands and hurriedly recites a Pepsi commercial, and when she is finished, Fletcher stares at her blankly and shouts, "Next."

And so it proceeds down the rows, each student standing, quoting some innocuous poem or song or line from a play, then sitting down while Fletcher remains blatantly unimpressed. Josie is petrified. She has no idea what she'll do when it's her turn. At first she's thinking about something from Lillian Hellman, but she's afraid Lillian isn't good enough for Mr. Wayne. Finally she decides to do a passage from

Richard III, specifically Queen Margaret's farewell to Queen Elizabeth, hoping against hope that Shakespeare will satisfy the hard-to-please Mr. Wayne.

Only two more people and it's my turn, she's thinking, as her stomach balls into knots and her heart nearly beats out of her chest. She can no longer take a deep breath because her air passages are closed off at some point just below her collarbone. These people are prob'ly only interested in modern, experimental playwrights, she reasons. They'll think I'm pretentious, that I'm a stuffy, nerdy idiot who is trying to impress them by reciting Shakespeare. Josie is trying frantically to think of something else, to draw another monologue from her blank mind, when Fletcher Wayne suddenly points at her and shouts, "You!"

She stands, and in a rickety voice, mutters, "This is from *Richard III*, act four, scene four. It's Queen Margaret's farewell to Queen Elizabeth." Josie hears a pencil drop, someone cough, someone else sigh. She begins spitting out the words in an unnaturally hoarse, cracked, almost cartoonish voice: "I call'd thee then vain flourish of my fortune; / I call'd thee then poor shadow, painted queen, / The presentation of but what I was. . . ."

Josie pauses because she can no longer breathe—there is no air left in her, and there is no Brewster to make her feel better, no Clarence to lead her away before things get worse. She is totally alone for the first time in her life. Glancing at the other students, she suspects they are filled with dread that she will do something unspeakably embarrassing like start to whimper, suck her thumb, and go irretrievably insane. Suddenly Dora's voice is shouting in her ear. "To hell with them, Josie. They're just a bunch of dull-headed little citizens who don't know whether to shit or go blind. Can't you see that we're better than them? God, I've raised a sheep, a weak, watery little wimp. Fuck them, Josie."

"No," Josie shouts silently, "fuck you, Dora. You're the one who needs to get laid. Stick to your own business. This is mine." As Josie's angry eyes travel over the students, they glance nervously away from her, but she notices that Fletcher Wayne is encouraging her with his dark brown eyes. No, she thinks, and looks away from him. I don't want you to help me.

She focuses on a portable blackboard that is positioned near the edge of the stage. Imagining it is one of the bedroom mirrors into which she's spoken the lines of books and plays all her life, she begins to see herself as Queen Margaret preparing to bid farewell. She has no idea how much time has lapsed since she stopped speaking. It could be five seconds or five minutes. Either way, she resumes Margaret's farewell, and with each word her voice grows stronger. By the time she gets to the questions part of the speech, Josie is no longer a student at El Camino College. She has become Queen Margaret. "Where is thy husband now? Where be thy brothers? / Where be thy two sons? Wherein dost thou joy? / Who sues, and kneels, and says 'God save the Queen'? / Where be the bending peers that flattered thee? / Where be the thronging troops that followed thee? / Decline all this, and see what now thou art. . . ."

In some separate part of her consciousness, she is aware that most of the students are listening now, that they are strangely transfixed by her performance. "Now thy proud neck bears half my burthen'd yoke, / From which even here I slip my weary head, / And leave the burthen of it all on thee. / Farewell, York's wife, and queen of sad mischance, / These English woes shall make me smile in France."

After uttering that last line, it takes her a few seconds to return to herself. When she does, she looks around at the students. At first they stare at her silently, then to her amazement, some of them break into applause. Smiling slightly, she sits down and glances shyly at Mr. Wayne.

"Interesting choice," he says. "I've never heard that particular speech done in a Southern accent, but that's okay. Was it a device, or are you from the South?"

"I'm from eastern Kentucky," Josie says, blushing while everyone stares at her as if she's a member of a primitive species they never thought they'd see in person.

"Well done," Fletcher says. "I'm impressed." Then he turns to the class. "Well, let's get on with it. I want you to split into groups—any-where from two to four—and prepare a scene for next week. You will choose your scene from any play by one of the writers on my list. A lot of you took this class because you thought it would be easy. You were wrong. Right now there's thirty-five of us, but in a few weeks we'll be down to half that size. By the end of the semester we will in fact be a small, cozy, intimate little family."

He passes out a list of playwrights, and Josie picks for a partner Mary Bingham, the same fiftyish woman who had earlier seemed concerned about Fletcher Wayne's drinking habits. She suggests to Mary that they do a scene from *Toys in the Attic*, and they agree to meet on the weekend for rehearsals.

Filing out of the class, a few of the students stop by Josie's seat to tell her what a great job they think she did. Josie isn't quite sure if they're telling her this because they feel sorry for her or if they really mean it, but she finally decides to believe the latter. She is just getting ready to walk out the door when Fletcher Wayne taps her on the shoulder.

"You may not realize this, but once you allowed yourself to get into the scene, your performance was pretty amazing. What training have you had?"

"None," Josie says.

"I mean what colleges have you attended?"

"This is the first one."

"How did you come to know that part so well, then?"

"I read a lot," she says.

He smiles and walks away, and Josie hurries out to her car.

When she gets home, Clarence and Butter are already in bed. She feels like running into the bedroom and shaking Clarence awake to tell him about Queen Margaret's farewell. She wants to tell him how amazing it is that she actually did it, how performing makes her feel alive, but Josie realizes that he'd just roll over and start ticking, that he wouldn't be in the least interested. She gets her pillow and sheets and spreads them on the couch, lies in the dark living room, staring at the familiar shapes—the TV, the chair, the stereo—but tonight they seem alien to her, like they might be something out of Castaneda's strangest dream.

29

"There's all kinds of gnats and fruit flies and stuff swarming around your tea," Josie yells to Clarence, who is sitting in the living room tending to Butter, wrapping the dog's foot with gauze bandages, then covering the whole thing with an old gym sock in a futile attempt to keep him from gnawing his foot off.

Josie swats at the flies and gingerly lifts the cheesecloth that covers the jar. The sight underneath almost makes her puke. The fleshy mushroom, which had the dimension of a medium-sized cookie when Clarence dropped it into the tea six days ago, is now the size of a rather large pancake. White moldy-looking froth is stuck to it all the way around.

"Clarence, this stuff right here will kill you. It's a hotbed for germs. I hope you know that," she yells to him again.

Clarence appears in the doorway. "Put that cheesecloth back on the jar, and leave it alone." He yanks the cloth from her hands and restores it to its original position, then returns to the living room and continues doctoring Butter.

Josie puts a pan of bread into the oven, stirs a pot of beans, and thinks about her present situation. She and Clarence haven't had sex in over a month, and he shows no sign of missing it. In the past, even when they weren't getting along, they eventually made their way back to sex, but now it seems out of the question.

Maybe he's masturbating, Josie thinks. That would be okay. God knows I do, but what if he's engaging in something else? Possibilities dart through her mind and hang upside down like bats in a cave. Most of the scenarios she imagines are absurd. She knows this in saner moments, but sometimes when she's lying alone at night, they take hold.

She considers the possibility that Clarence has somehow turned gay. Can people do that? she wonders. Not according to the gays she's seen on Phil Donahue. A more worrisome possibility is that Clarence and Butter are . . . well, that they're somehow . . . The thought is almost too horrible to consider, yet there is no escaping the fact that night after night the sound of sucking, squishing, licking, and ticking emanates from their bedroom. No, that can't be, Josie tells herself. Those noises are the result of Butter's fascination with his own hind end, of his vampire-like appetite for his foot, of Clarence's mysterious predilection for making ticking sounds during REM. Sometimes, though, Josie finds herself staring at them suspiciously, especially when Butter is lying in his lap, licking his pants' leg, staring up at him with a love that cannot be denied.

God, what a sorry person I am, Josie thinks. It's been years since me and Clarence were truly in love, and now I begrudge him getting some affection from a dog. I have to make something nasty out of it, don't I? What low self-esteem I must have to be jealous of a little dog, a cocker spaniel, for Christ's sake.

The third possibility is even stranger than the Butter theory. Sometimes in her loneliest moments, Josie imagines that Clarence is having an affair, that he has at last found a woman who likes to watch him repair televisions. With the thought never entering her mind to wonder where he is when she's at school, she figures Clarence can't be having an affair since he's always home.

Either way, it's over, Josie thinks. There's nothing left of us but a great big pile of dog hair. Lying on the couch that night, she finds it impossible to sleep for thinking about lost love. Mostly she thinks about Johnny Walker, how great it was that day in the shack by the

San Pedro River. She can almost feel his lips pressing against hers, can almost see his eyes staring down at her. I shouldn't have brushed him off when he called me, she thinks. I should have told him I'd go back to Sage as soon as I could. When she finally falls to sleep, she dreams she's still tending bar at Don Juan's and Johnny is leaning against the counter holding her hand.

The next morning she calls Venus and asks her for Johnny's phone number.

"I can give it to you," Venus says, "but it won't do you any good. He's back in West Virginia."

Josie's heart drops. "He didn't move, did he?"

"He said he was going on a vacation but said if it suited him good enough he might stay."

"What about his ranch?" she asks, panicking. She's always thought that she would see him again. "He can't just walk off and leave it, can he?"

"His hired hands are taking care of it till he decides what to do. How's the weather over there?"

"Oh, it's warm and sunny, about seventy-five degrees, just another perfect day in paradise."

Venus keeps chatting, saying something about Tarantula having turned into a complete drunk, saying people are finding her asleep by the road early in the mornings. She relates all the latest news from Sage, but Josie barely hears her. All she can think about is that Johnny has gone back to West Virginia, that he's probably lost to her forever.

Fletcher Wayne always makes a grand entrance into the classes he teaches. Sometimes just before he walks through the door, Josie hears him talking conspiratorially to ill-defined people of whom she never gets a satisfactory glimpse, young men and women who always seem to lurk in the shadows outside the auditorium just prior to his arrival. He'll say something to them like, "See you in *Tee-kwana* later. One o'clock, right?" Then with a faint smell of pot trailing behind him, he'll come strolling in as if he has a multitude of irons in the fire.

Josie has been feeling a little uncomfortable around Mr. Wayne. Recently she overheard a couple of students grumbling that he's paying her special attention. It's true. The previous time the class met, he spent twenty minutes picking apart her scene, telling the class what she'd done right, what she'd done wrong, explaining ways in which she could improve. Tonight she and Mary Bingham are doing one of Josie's favorites, *A Streetcar Named Desire*. Josie is playing Stella, and Mary has the more difficult role of Blanche. They get through it without a hitch, and when they're finished, Fletcher says, "Okay, switch roles."

"But I don't know the Stella part," Mary complains.

"Just read it." He hands Mary a script. "Do you know the Blanche part, Josie?"

"Yes."

"Thought so. Go ahead."

They begin the scene where Blanche is having a long tirade, calling Stanley an animal. Fletcher yells for them to stop. "I want you to do the part in some new way, Josie. You need to stretch or you'll fall into a rut."

Josie embarks on the needed transformation, but she stops when Kim Petry, whom she'd dubbed "the bitter-looking young woman" during their first class meeting, begins shouting.

"Wait a minute," Kim shouts. "Are you going to spend the whole class on Josie again? What about the rest of us? I'm supposed to do my scene tonight."

Josie looks at Fletcher, awaiting what she is sure will be a nasty reply. Having smelled alcohol on him earlier, she knows he's been drinking.

"What scene are you doing?" Fletcher yells at Kim. "Another Pepsi commercial?"

"That's it," Kim shouts. "I'm making a complaint to the administration, and if anyone else wants to join me, I'll be talking to them tomorrow." She jumps from her seat and storms out the door. Three other students follow her.

"Continue, Josie," Fletcher says. "Go forward with the scene."

Unable to say a word, Josie stares at him unsteadily. "Maybe we should . . ."

Fletcher throws down his copy of *Streetcar*. "You're right, of course. Maybe we should call it quits for the night. That's right. Everyone go home. We'll try it again next week, and please feel free to make your complaints. Complain to Mommy, Daddy, the Pope. Complain to whoever the hell you want."

People glance at each other uneasily, gather their books, and file out as if they're leaving the scene of a crime. Even Mary, who is on stage with Josie, steps down and walks out morosely. Josie can't bring herself to leave and just sits there, staring at her shoes until she becomes aware that Fletcher is standing in front of her. "Wanta go have coffee or something?" he asks her. "I'd like to talk to you."

Josie's heart is beating fast. "I don't know," she says, glancing up at him.

"There's a twenty-four-hour coffee shop on Hotel Circle Road that I like to go to sometimes."

She follows him out the door, and a few moments later they're sitting at a booth in the crowded coffee shop, staring down at their cups. The walls around them are white, and the floors are hardwood with a light oak stain. A frond from a potted palm butts against Josie's shoulder, and a giant hanging fern swings over her head. Filling their cups with coffee, a waitress, wearing a green-and-white polyester uniform, sets several plastic containers of half-and-half on the table, then walks away.

"Normally I hate this kind of place," Fletcher says, "but somehow this one works for me. Remember the old coffeehouses back in the sixties?"

"Actually I was never in one."

"They were great—blues singers, folk singers, people reading poetry. I don't know what kind of age we're in now, but I don't like it."

Josie stares into Fletcher's eyes, trying to see what they have seen. "Do you go to Tijuana a lot? I overhear you sometimes telling people that you'll meet them down there." She eyes his army-green T-shirt, no doubt left over from the days when wearing army-greens purchased at surplus stores somehow meant you were against the war.

"Yeah, Tijuana's okay. Actually, all of Mexico is okay. Wish I lived there. I hate this fuckin town, that school."

"Will you get into trouble if Kim makes a complaint?"

"Who knows? I don't care." Fletcher finishes his cup of coffee and signals the waitress for some more. "I guess I am guilty of paying you special attention, but do you know how long it's been since I've had a student in either of my classes who has talent? Do you know how sick I am of trying to teach buffed-up jocks and cheerleader prom queens how to act? They don't want to learn anything about acting. They want to go to Hollywood and become movie stars overnight. And then of course there are those who just take the class because they think it's an easy A."

Fiddling with the plastic half-and-halfs, Josie says, "But ain't you supposed to teach them anyway?"

Fletcher smiles at her. "I love the way you say *ain't*, the way you talk like that and yet come off sounding like a somewhat Southern yet totally convincing Shakespearean queen. It's such a refreshing contradiction."

Josie blushes. "I need to get rid of this accent, don't I?"

Fletcher grins. "You need to learn other accents, but keep your Southern one. I insist."

Josie laughs. "I couldn't get rid of it if I tried." She likes the way his brown eyes smile. "I'm worried about this Kim thing. Maybe you ought to, you know, give . . . uh . . ."

Fletcher sighs. "Yeah, I know. Guess I'll have to cool it. Damn, I hate teaching. I've been thinking about chucking the whole thing and going to New York. You know, just go there and stick with it until I either nab a part or starve to death."

Feeling stupid for not having realized until now that he isn't only a teacher but an actor too, Josie asks, "Are you acting right now? In any of the local theatres?"

"No." He waves his hand off to the side as if shooing away a bad memory. "It's a long story." Suddenly he perks up as if he has thought of something important. "You know, I used to give acting lessons on the side, concentrating specifically on Shakespeare. I'd put an ad in the paper, get about three or four students, and we'd meet at my apartment. It gave me some extra pocket change and allowed me to at least give *those* students my full attention. Would you be interested in something like that?"

"I'd love it," Josie says, her heart beating a mile a minute. Acting is the only thing she has right now. It's why she gets up in the morning.

"Okay then, it's settled. I'll let you know when I'm ready."

They leave the coffee shop and walk together through the poorly lit parking lot. "Well," he says, looking down at her as she unlocks her car door, "this was, ah . . . this was . . . I enjoyed the talk. See you in class tomorrow night."

They keep standing there, and he takes hold of her hand, rubs his fingers over hers, then suddenly lets go of them. He stares down at her wedding band. "Funny, I never noticed that ring before. Guess I've been too busy staring at your eyes."

Josie remembers when people didn't have to see her ring to know she was married. Her marital status flashed on her face like a neon sign. Now she has been mistaken for a single woman twice in just a little over a month. She looks at Fletcher and blushes. "Well, I uh . . ."

"You're married."

"Yep."

"Happily?"

"Nope."

He smiles. "See you tomorrow."

Clarence and Butter are in bed by the time Josie gets home. She lies on the couch and tries to watch Johnny Carson, but she can't concentrate. Instead, she thinks about her dying marriage to Clarence and marvels that her feelings for Johnny Walker are still alive in spite of the fact that he is apparently out of her life for good. She remembers how Fletcher Wayne smiled at her outside the twenty-four-hour coffee shop, and she tries to ignore the way he treats his class, the way he parades his own sullen brand of insolence like a two-year-old carrying a worn-out blanket.

30

Butter is now so obese that Clarence can't get him to go for walks anymore. They'll start out, go down the driveway and onto the sidewalk, but that's as far as Butter will go. While his jowls flop and spew drool, the rotund dog lies down and lets out heavy sighs of disgust. No matter how hard Clarence tugs on the leash, he refuses to budge. He won't even hop up on the couch anymore—Clarence has to lift him.

On days when Josie doesn't have school and is alone at the house, the dog doesn't follow her from room to room—he precedes her. She'll be walking down the narrow hallway, and he'll make sure he's right in front of her, moving slowly as a turtle, blocking her way with his large grotesque body. He'll take a step, then look back at her to make sure she's still behind him. She'll nudge his rear and he'll take another step, then look back at her again, scowling. When she tries to step over him, she often trips and pitches headlong to the floor. It's only then that Butter smiles, or appears to.

She often dreams of locking him in a closet, stacked to the ceiling with food—steaks, hamburger, chicken, turkey, and pork—mountains of it, and letting him eat until . . . She wonders if things would have been different if Clarence hadn't named him Butter, if the name itself has made the dog who he is. Still there's something about him that fascinates her. His sad, angry eyes tear into her heart. Like an old tragic king from one of Shakespeare's plays, he frets and anguishes and eats himself, licks the blood from the self-inflicted wound on his foot. He looks at her as if she should know what to do, as if she could help him if she tried. Josie can't get away from the fact that she cares about the dog in spite of herself.

Today she returns him to the vet, who prescribes a collar that fits around his head like a trumpet, a contraption that promises to stop him from gnawing himself. When she puts the thing on him, he begins to howl in the most grievous agony she's ever heard, butting into furniture, banging into walls, and he doesn't stop until Clarence comes home from work.

"What the hell have you got on him?" Clarence shouts. He yanks off the collar and throws it in the trash.

"The vet says it needs to wear it, that it's the only way to stop Butter from biting itself."

"That vet's a asshole. Anyone with any sense wouldn't make a dog wear something like that." He picks Butter up and carries him into the living room, mumbling, "Don't worry, old feller. I won't let them do that to you again."

Josie follows them. "You think you're taking good care of Butter, but you're killing it."

"Butter ain't a *it*," Clarence says. "He's a *he*."

Josie rolls her eyes. "Oh, really? You used to say *it*."

"Well, I don't anymore."

"Does it make a difference? Did you care any less about Butter when you called it *it*?"

"No, but maybe I've got more respect for him now."

Seeing this as another example of Clarence being seduced by cockamamie notions, Josie flares like a torch. "You need to stop practicing everything you hear preached. Be a little choosy."

Clarence shakes his finger in her face. "Butter ain't a thing. When you call him *it*, you just show your ignorance."

"You wanta talk ignorance?" she asks. "Fine. *He* is a okay word used to show a person is male. Male is good. I like male, but that's all *he's* used for. *He* and *she*, for that matter, are trapped by gender, limited in scope."

"I don't want to hear your stupid theories," Clarence shouts.

"*It*, on the other hand, covers all emotions—like *it*, love *it*, hate *it*, fuck *it*. I get chills just thinking about *it*. Amazingly, *it* covers all philosophical, creative, and scientific thought."

"Will you shut up?"

"*It* stands for all living creatures, including human beings and dogs, because, as you know, human beings and dogs are living *things*. It's mysterious too. I often dream of getting right down to the core of *it*. Possibly *it's* the secret of life. *It* may even be . . . oh my God . . . GOD!"

Clarence flops on the couch and puts a pillow over his head.

Butter foams at the mouth.

Josie stands there for a moment looking down at her husband's skinny frame, and suddenly she is sorry for her outburst. Clarence, who was always thin, has lost ten pounds since taking up health food. At first she tried to prepare his vegetarian meals, but they seldom turned out to his liking. Sometimes she would sneak a little chicken broth into the rice so she could stand to eat it also, but Clarence always caught on and turned it away. The only thing she can cook that he will eat is a pot of soup beans, minus the ham hocks, of course. Since she refuses to cook beans every night, she often lets Clarence fend for himself, figuring if he gets hungry enough he'll learn how to cook. Right now, though, he subsists mainly on fruit, nuts, and raw cabbage.

It occurs to her that he might actually die, and the guilt is eating her alive, knowing that if it weren't for her, he would still be in Pick, working in his TV repair shop, happy as a lark. It's my fault that his business went bad, she thinks. It's because of me that we moved away, that he's gone on this weird diet, that he's feeding Butter to the grave, that he's crazy as a bess bug. She plops down on the floor at Clarence's feet. Butter glances around at her as if to say, "See what you've caused?" Josie reaches out to pet the dog, but he snarls and bites her hand. Then he looks up at her mournfully and starts to squeak and whimper as though he's sorry he did it.

She stares down at the teeth marks on her palm, at the dark bead of blood rising. "It's all right, Butter," she whispers. "I'm all right."

"He don't want to be around you right now," Clarence says.

"I know," Josie says, "but I have to talk to you, Clarence."

Clarence sighs and turns his head toward the window.

"I want to know what's wrong with you," Josie says.

"Nothing's wrong. I just don't want to talk. I've been working all day, and I'm tired."

"You've changed. You don't eat anymore. You just come home and sit down on the couch with Butter and watch TV." Tears have filled her eyes. She wipes them. "I'm sorry if I've made you like this."

Clarence still won't look at her. "I don't know what the hell you're talking about. As usual, you've been sitting around thinking about things too much."

"You never look at me anymore," Josie says. "Can't you stand to meet my eyes?"

He suddenly turns and glares at her. "There, are you satisfied? I don't want to look at your big, round, scary gray eyes. They look crazy."

"You think I'm crazy?" Josie shouts.

"Yes, I do."

"Well, I think *you're* crazy. How's that?" Josie throws up her hands and heads off to the empty bedroom to lie on the floor and stare out the window at the California quail that gather daily in their back-yard. Catching a glimpse of her reflection in the window, she can't help noticing how much she resembles her mother. She even has the same look in her eyes, the same anger and sadness. They say you turn into your mother, she thinks. Maybe I already have.

Josie was just eleven when Dora died, and it's been a long time since she has recalled the details. Now she finds herself going back to that pretty summer day when Brewster and Dora came home with the news.

They'd made a few stops after leaving the doctor's office, and when they stepped inside the house, Dora was carrying a bag from the drygoods store. In it were three new gowns, all of them nylon and lacy—a mint green, an aqua blue, and a peach—that she took out and held up to the light from the window. "Pretty, ain't they?" she remarked to Josie, who was sprawled on the couch watching TV.

"Yeah," Josie said, not yet knowing their significance.

When Dora walked upstairs to her bedroom, carrying the gowns, Brewster nudged Josie. "Let's go for a drive. I have to tell you something."

Josie could see by his expression that something was in the works. She thought for an instant that maybe her father and mother were getting a divorce. It wasn't as though the word *divorce* hadn't been bandied about from time to time. Still, trying to pretend that nothing was out of the ordinary, she followed Brewster to the car and stifled the part of herself that wanted to ask questions, removed the part that was afraid to breathe, leaving little of herself but numbness.

They had just gone a couple of miles when he told her about the cancer. "Can't be operated on. It's spread all over her," he said. His eyes were fixed on the winding road in front of them, his hands gripping the steering wheel.

Josie said nothing, didn't make a single comment or ask one question. Rather, she turned her head and stared out the side window as they whizzed by the river and mountains. Near the small houses beside the road, people were working in gardens, and children were playing in front yards. She hated them for acting as though nothing was wrong, as if this was a day like any other. She wondered how she and Brewster would get along without Dora around to make them see things as they really were, without Dora, who always said what she thought whether it hurt anyone or not. How could they possibly live without her wisecracks and laughter, without her telling them how they ought to think and act? Closing her eyes, Josie focused on trying to become a stone that nothing, not even her mother's death, could chip away or break.

As the days progressed and Dora took to her bed, Josie tried to make her room as pleasant as possible. She arranged the sheets and pillows just so, drew back the curtains so a clean breeze constantly blew across her bed. She cut fresh flowers daily and put them in a vase on her nightstand. She sat by her bed and asked her if she would like to be read to. Josie determined that if her mother was going to die, her death would be beautiful. Her face would grow tragically pale and mysterious. Her tresses would cascade in stunning waves on the plumped-up pillow, and when she drew her final breath, birds would fly into the room and sing while the heavens opened and angels descended to carry her off.

Every day Dora lay there and watched as Josie fussed around the room, straightening dresser scarves, cutting rose stems. Finally she said, "You don't have to work so hard to make it nice, Josie. This ain't a game. I'm not a character in some old movie or in one of the books you're always reading. I'm not Beth in *Little Women*. I'm not Cathy in *Wuthering Heights*. It's just me, and I'm dying. This is real."

Josie stopped dead in her tracks. She felt as if she'd been struck in the stomach with a sledgehammer. Suddenly she saw herself as a shallow ridiculous person who couldn't face the facts, someone who hid the truth behind room decor. She sank down in a chair by Dora's bed. "I was just trying to . . ." She stared at the floor, unable to speak another word.

Dora reached out and took her hand. "Look at me, Josie."

Josie lowered her head even further. "I can't . . ."

"Yes, you can. Look at me."

Slowly Josie raised her head and saw Dora as she really was. Her hair had been cut short—there were no cascading tresses. Dark circles drooped beneath her eyes, and her cheeks were gray and sunken. Although her stomach was so swollen that she looked pregnant, the rest of her body was almost skeletal.

"I appreciate what you've been doing," Dora said. "But this thing is goin to get worse. You've never seen anyone die. It can be ugly. There'll come a time when you can't make everything nice, and I don't want you to feel like it's your fault. I just need to tell you that while I've still got my wits."

Josie started sniffling, trying to hold back the tears.

"Come here," Dora whispered.

Josie got out of the chair and lay down beside her, rested her head on Dora's shoulder. Not having lain beside her mother since she was seven years old, she felt awkward until Dora draped an arm around her and gently stroked her hair. Josie began to relax, felt comforted. They didn't say anything more, just lay quietly, while outside bees buzzed around a rosebush near the window and a car tore down the road at high speed, its tires peeling rubber as it took the curve. There were no explanations of past wrongs or rights, no apologies spoken. It was just Josie and Dora, lying together, while a quiet truth passed between them.

Now, Josie walks down the hallway and peeps into the living room at Clarence. She resolves then and there that the fighting will stop and that neither of them will have to die in order to be set free.

Clarence has been seeing Sally Waterford for the past two weeks. It all started when he stopped by her house one evening to repair her ancient stereo. All the while he was working, she hunkered beside him, asking questions about what he was doing. She was really interested, not just pretending to be, the way Josie always did. Later she invited him to stay for dinner, and not being in a particular hurry to get home since it was one of Josie's school nights, he accepted. She fixed the most nutritional supper he ever ate—baked eggplant, long-grain rice, steamed vegetables, a garden salad, and fruit cocktail for desert.

It felt so good to be sitting there, eating healthy food, listening to Sally talk, her red hair swept to one side, her pale skin glowing in the dim light. He was struck by the alert, rational look in her eyes, by the way she waved her finger in the air while accentuating certain words. Sally was raised on a dairy farm near Milwaukee and has worked hard every day of her life. Unlike Josie, who doesn't seem to give a damn whether she has any money or not, Sally knows its value. "We're going to have to do something about it, Clarence," Sally told him that night. She was talking about the tax system, how unfair it was. "These taxes are eating us alive."

"That's right," Clarence said, amazed at how informed she was. He was pretty sure that Josie didn't even know people had to pay taxes, let alone be worried that the rates were too high.

After the meal they kept sitting at the table, drinking tea, while she pointed out the new countertop she'd insisted the landlord install, but it was when Sally was showing him her needlepoint—little pictures she'd stitched somehow, put into frames, and hung on the walls—that the first kiss occurred. They were sidling down the narrow hallway of her apartment, checking out the framed owls, ducks, and bears when he accidentally brushed his arm against her breasts. He turned to her, intending to apologize, when suddenly she grabbed hold of him with both hands and planted a big kiss squarely on his mouth.

At first he was taken aback, but seconds later he was kissing her just as hard as she was kissing him. They staggered down the hall to her bedroom and made love for several hours.

Feeling badly about deceiving Josie, he can hardly stand to look at her anymore. The minute he walks into the house, he gets depressed. His affair with Sally goes against everything he ever believed was right, but he can't help wishing it was her that he was married to, that they could have healthy dinners together every evening, and that later he could sit around watching TV while she stitched her little animals. All Clarence can do when he comes home is lie on the couch with Butter and feed him until his belly is full as a tick's, making sure that at least the dog has everything he wants, even if what he wants is bad for him.

31

For the past week the administration has been sending spies to check on Fletcher's classes. As a result, he has improved his attitude toward the other students. Even so, Josie feels uncomfortable around him, and she's been ignoring his smiles and knowing glances at every turn. She doesn't know if she'll ever get involved with another man, but she's committed to the drama class. If not for her own self-imposed rehearsals—standing in front of the mirror and learning the lines to every play they cover in class—Josie might sink into a depression so deep she would never get out.

Sitting at the kitchen table, she is jarred out of her thoughts by a ringing telephone. When she answers it, she is surprised to hear Dr. Fierros's voice on the other end of the line.

"Hello, Josie. I've heard from your sister."

"Is she coming back? By the way, I'm sorry I dumped that salsa in your lap. I was in a pretty bad mood."

"She's already back," Dr. Fierros says, ignoring her apology. "She asked me to call you."

"She's here?" Josie stops breathing, then gasps, "She's here in San Diego? Where?"

"She's camping at the San Luis Rey Indian Reservation."

"She's living with Indians?" Josie smiles. It's what she'd expect Cheyenne to do.

"Not exactly. The campground is open to the public. She wants you to meet her there at ten o'clock. You don't have much time."

Josie can't say a word. Her air is closed off in much the same way as when she recited Margaret's farewell the first night of Fletcher's class.

"Grab a pen and paper, and I'll give you directions," Dr. Fierros says.

Trembling, Josie writes them down. "But what do I do when I get there?"

"Just drive to the lower grounds and park at the first empty campsite. She'll find you."

Josie's thoughts are whirling out of control as she hurriedly gets dressed and jumps into her Pinto. She clips the written directions to the visor and begins the forty-five-minute drive to the reservation. Taking long deep breaths, she tries to calm down, but it's no use. This is the moment she's been waiting for since the day Cheyenne disappeared. She doesn't have any idea what to say to her, not a clue as to what to expect. She wishes she had been able to talk to Dr. Fierros longer, to have asked him some questions, but there was no time.

As she drives down the interstate, it occurs to her that Cheyenne doesn't know their mother is dead, that she'll have to tell her. But what will she tell her? She has no idea what she'll say to her about anything. Turning into the entrance of the campground, she looks around for other campers but sees none. An old Indian man dressed in a T-shirt and jeans comes down the steps of a small structure that looks as though it might be a store and motions for her to come to a stop. "There's only day camping this time of year," he says. His long white hair reaches almost to his waist, and the skin around his eyes is wrinkled in deep grooves, suggesting that he might have spent most of his life laughing at the world. "You'll have to leave by seven o'clock this evening."

"Fine," Josie says. "Just point me toward the lower campground." She quickly pays him, and he returns to the steps and sits down. As she drives past the small building, she notices that the blinds on the windows are drawn, and she sees a sign above the closed door that says the campground is closed from October 1 through February 1. It is now November 5. She thinks about going back to ask the man why he's allowing her to camp, but she decides he most likely changed the schedule after the sign was already painted. Continuing on, she finds a nice spot to park near the river bank.

There are no campers in view, no one anywhere, and she gets an eerie feeling that she's the only person in the entire campground. Getting out of the car, she sits on a rock, and listens to the roar of the San Luis Rey River as it rushes over the huge boulders in its path. She keeps her eyes peeled on the narrow dirt road that leads deeper into the grounds, hoping to see Cheyenne step into view, but she sees no one. Feeling as though she's being stared at, Josie glances in every direction and spots several large crows in the sparsely leafed branches of a nearby oak, sitting silently, almost as if they're keeping watch. She starts singing "Blue Moon of Kentucky" as loudly as she can. Between refrains, she hears a twig snap and, turning quickly, thinks she sees the old Indian man step behind a tree. Josie realizes that at this point she's probably imagining things, but moments later his shadowy image still hasn't left her mind. She is on the verge of driving home when she hears the voice behind her.

"Josie?"

She turns around, and there stands Cheyenne. She's tall and skinny, wearing a pair of jeans, a flimsy top of purple gauze, silver earrings and turquoise beads. Her long black hair is tied back in a pony tail and drooped over one of her shoulders. She hasn't changed much in the face, but her black eyes have a hard edgy look, as if they belong to someone who spends a lot of time on the open road.

A smile spreads on Josie's face, and at that moment she doesn't remember the fights, the name-calling, or the shoulder-hitting. "Cheyenne?" she says and starts to step toward her, to put her arms around her, but Cheyenne makes the first move.

Taking hold of Josie's arm, she says, "Let's walk a while. I want to show you something."

"I'm glad I finally found you," Josie says, giggling as they go, struggling to get a full-on view of Cheyenne's face. "I just can't believe this." She slaps one of her hands against her leg as if to stress the matter.

Cheyenne doesn't say anything in reply, but she smiles.

They're on a small muddy path, an obstacle course of rocks, roots, and fallen tree branches, that runs parallel with the river. "Where're we goin?" Josie asks.

"Just up here where I'm camping," Cheyenne says. "It's a pretty place. You'll like it."

All Josie wants to do is sit down somewhere, regardless of the surrounding scenery, and catch up on what's been happening in their lives, but she continues to walk alongside her. Soon they come to a place where the path ends, and there's the choice of either wading into the river, which appears to be waist-deep, or inching around a huge bald-faced boulder that juts from the hillside into the water.

"Take your pick," Cheyenne says, "but I'm goin around the rock. I don't want to get wet right now."

Josie studies her choices. "Can't we just sit here a minute? I'd like to talk to you. It's been a long time."

Cheyenne starts around the rock. "Come on," she says.

Josie rolls her eyes, and plunging into the water, she growls, "May as well get wet now because if I went around that rock I'd fall into the river anyway." Her teeth chattering like rattlesnake buttons, she wades to dry ground, where Cheyenne is already standing dry as a bone and laughing. Josie has no idea whether the laughter is good-natured or mean-spirited. Even staring directly into her sister's eyes, it's impossible to glean anything from them. Cheyenne turns her back and keeps going forward.

Soaked and ice-cold, Josie feels like a seven-year-old again. She follows her sister down a narrow path that soon opens into a meadow dotted with tiny yellow and blue flowers. The river has also widened at this point, and several small islets stand midway across. The view before her looks like one of those watercolor scenes painted in a children's storybook. "Beautiful," Josie mutters. Cheyenne nods and smiles.

Passing under an overhanging tree branch, Josie feels a sudden chill that frightens her. It is almost as if someone reached out from a grave and touched her. "Did you feel that?" she asks Cheyenne. "It got cold all of a sudden."

Cheyenne eyes her carefully. "I wondered if you'd notice anything.

This is where the spirits start talking to you." She continues walking forward.

Josie just stands there. "What spirits? How much farther do we have to go?" she asks.

"Not far."

As Josie catches up to her, the trail ends again, this time at the foot of a sheer rock wall. "Don't tell me we're goin to scale this," Josie says.

"It's easier than it looks," Cheyenne says. "All we have to do is slip inside that crevice. There's footholds all the way up."

Josie glares at her. "Damn it, can't we just sit down and talk? I'm not a mountain climber."

Cheyenne slips inside the crevice. "Come on, Josie. You can do it."

Josie follows her into the crevice and finds that Cheyenne was right. The climb up is easy, and on the other side is one of the most beautiful sights she has seen in California. It isn't a grand arena with magnificent vistas. Rather, it's the simplicity of what lies before her that is so beautiful. The river roars over a small waterfall, where hummingbirds hover to drink from stray flecks of flying water. Underneath the falls, the water pools into a deep blue-green hole that looks perfect for swimming. A huge rock at the edge of the river looks as though it were designed for bathers to climb and warm themselves in the sun. Off to the side of the path is a wooded area where tall leafy trees stand like giant beings who have gathered for a midday conversation and are gesturing lackadaisically with their long graceful arms.

Josie notices a small camp set up directly in their midst. "Is that your place?" she asks, pointing to the trees.

"Yep," Cheyenne says. "Pretty, ain't it? Do you want a beer?"

"Yeah," Josie says as she climbs to the top of the rock and lies down.

Cheyenne sprints to her campsite, returns with a couple of Buds, and sits down beside her. "It's way better here than back there where all the weekend tourists go. There ain't many of them ever make it down this far." Cheyenne stops talking and stares off into the distance, silent as the rock she's sitting on. It would be easy to think she isn't human at all, but a rare mushroom that sprouted from the rock after an unexpected rain.

Josie sips her beer and tries to refrain from asking a million questions all at once. "You seem to know this place pretty good. Do you stay here a lot?"

"It reminds me of Kentucky."

"It's a little like it, I guess," Josie says. She wants to add that she's surprised Cheyenne ever comes here if it reminds her of home, but she holds her tongue. "How's your health, Cheyenne?"

"Fine."

"Well, you look good. Hardly changed at all."

Cheyenne glances around at Josie. "You sure have. I can't get over how much you look like her . . . like Mommy."

"That's what they tell me," Josie says. "Apparently I look like her and you act like her. Least you and her used to act pretty much the same. I don't know how you are now."

"Yeah, well, I never understood that comparison. Could you see her living out like this?"

Josie realizes this would be a good time to broach the subject of Dora's death, but she decides to put it off a little longer. "Actually, I could. I don't think she was completely happy being married, having children. She might have loved this kind of life."

Cheyenne chuckles. "Maybe you're right. But then I don't think happiness is what people ought to be after necessarily. They oughta soak in everything—happiness, right along with sadness, craziness, cruelty, discomfort, and everything else. People who go around seeking happiness and fun without the rest are pretty one-dimensional, pretty boring, if you ask me."

Josie laughs. "Well, I must be just about the most multidimensional person alive then, because misery is my middle name."

Cheyenne lies back on the rock and looks up at the clouds. "How are they anyway, Mommy and Daddy?"

Josie doesn't answer her right away, and there is a long enough pause before her response that Cheyenne looks around at her quizzically. In a rushed voice Josie says, "Daddy's doing fine."

"Really?" Cheyenne leans toward her as if wanting more.

"He's got his problems, you know, his arthritis, but overall he's doing fine."

Cheyenne smiles. "Still the same old Brewster?"

"You got it." Afraid that Cheyenne will ask about Dora next, she changes the subject. "Seems odd that you and Dr. Fierros hooked up. He's silk suits, science, and imported wine. You're gauze, beer, and rock climbing. How did that romance start?"

Cheyenne chuckles. "Beats me."

"Yeah, well, I don't like him," Josie says.

"Why? Did he try to get in your pants?"

"As a matter of fact he did."

Cheyenne laughs. "He told me you were married. Who to?"

"Clarence Tolliver."

"Oh, God," Cheyenne gasps. She rises to a sitting position, wraps her arms around her knees, laughs hysterically. "You've got to be joking. Clarence? He was in my class. Do you have children?"

Josie glares at her. "No, we don't, and why are you laughing? What's wrong with Clarence?"

"Nothing. I mean, it's just that he don't know what to do with himself. And you, well, I just don't know how you make it together, that's all."

Josie sits up. "You're wrong about Clarence. He knows exactly what to do with himself. He had his life all mapped out until I changed it for him, and now he's mapping it out again. He always knows what to do. As for me, you don't know who I am anymore. You remember a child. I've changed."

Cheyenne smiles. "So what are you doing with yourself?"

"I'm goin to school, for one thing, and me and Clarence are prob'ly goin to get a divorce."

The two sisters look at each other and break out laughing. Then Josie says, "Okay, okay, we're not exactly the match of the century. So what're you doing with yourself?"

"As usual I'm trying not to get caught," Cheyenne says.

"By who?"

"No one in particular . . . everyone."

"So you're saying you're prey? Just sort of in general?"

Cheyenne turns to Josie, her eyes suddenly revealing a deep sadness. "Yeah, that's exactly what I'm saying." She drinks the last of her beer and walks over to the tent, returning with a portable tape player and a small cooler. "Ready for anothern?"

Josie nods, and Cheyenne drops in a cassette and starts singing along with the music, "*I'm going home with the armadillo . . .*" Drinking another beer down fast, Josie begins to harmonize with Cheyenne, while in the trees crows banter back and forth like doo-wop singers. When the song ends Josie says, "Hey, we're pretty good."

"Yeah," Cheyenne grunts. "Didn't know you could sing like that."

Josie contemplates the fact that if Cheyenne hadn't run away, they could have been basking in the sun and singing all these years. "Why do you say you're prey, Cheyenne?"

Cheyenne lies back on the rock. "Cause that's what I am. I don't fit, you know. I should have been born a few hundred years ago. I want the whole world to be like it is here right now, but it ain't. I want to live off nuts and berries, to hunt and cavort among the trees and rocks." She looks toward the river and stretches out both her arms. "I could sit and stare at a dragonfly's wings all day. There's no way I could be like you. Can't marry and go to school. Those're not my dreams. I'm prey, Josie. I get chased further every day." She lowers her arms and stares sadly down at the rock. "Look at me. I'm living at the far end of a campground in off-season. Nothing's wild anymore. There ain't hardly anyplace left for me to go."

At that moment, Josie can hardly bear to look at Cheyenne. Her sister seems so fragile, so endangered that she's afraid she might disappear before her eyes. "You like it here, though, don't you?" she asks her.

"Yeah, I like this place," Cheyenne says. She turns over on her stomach, props up on her elbows, and traces a depression in the rock with her fingers. "I always knew you'd be just fine. Knew the minute you were born that you'd fit right into this world."

Josie catches the bitterness in her voice. "Well, I've never seen myself as fitting in."

Cheyenne laughs a small sardonic laugh. "You see both sides, that's all. I guess growing up around me ruined things for you. If I hadn't been your sister, you might have been just like everyone else. You'd have had a normal life. As it is, you're torn between my way and theirs."

Insulted, Josie blurts out, "I didn't need you around to make me different, Cheyenne. I'm perfectly capable of being abnormal all by myself. And why didn't you write or call once during all those years? We thought you were dead. Didn't you know we'd think that?"

Looking bored, Cheyenne sighs, turns her head away, and says nothing.

"They said you must have been kidnapped," Josie says, "but I knew you'd gone on your own. I even understood why. Mommy kept trying to keep you under control, and you got tired of being told what to do. I always thought your bad heart might have had something to do with it too. Maybe you thought you didn't have much longer to live and wanted to cram in as much as possible. I understand all that, but what I don't understand is why you didn't let us know you were okay." Josie shakes her head. "You were just fifteen when you left, so I figured if everything was goin okay, you wouldn't call till you were eighteen. You'd be of age and no one could make you come home if you didn't want to, but your eighteenth birthday came and went. That's when I started thinking like everyone else—that you were dead. I guess that's what you wanted us to think."

Cheyenne smiles. "You know me better than I thought you did."

"No, I don't. How could you leave at fifteen and never look back? No one treated you that bad."

Cheyenne sighs. "Why does a grape taste like a grape instead of a orange? I can't tell you why I'm the way I am. Look, Josie, we can talk about this later. Right now the sun is shining, we've got a lot more music to play, and if we don't start drinking this beer, it'll get warm. Let it rest for a while, okay?" She grabs her guitar and begins singing "Paddy West."

Although Josie is still unsatisfied, she reluctantly joins in, and the rest of the afternoon passes slowly. From time to time the thought crosses her mind that she's missing her day classes and that if she stays much longer she'll miss her evening drama class. Occasionally, she thinks she should bring up the subject of Dan Hawkins, but she decides against it. The idea that Cheyenne could have killed an old friend always seemed doubtful, but now it seems ludicrous.

Later, Cheyenne builds a campfire and fries the fish she'd caught before Josie's arrival. It isn't until they're sitting around the fire after the meal that the subject of Dora comes up.

"You never told me about Mommy," Cheyenne says. "Is she still hard-assed as ever?"

"She's dead," Josie says, not knowing how else to say it.

A look of shock crosses Cheyenne's face, then anger. "You wouldn't be telling me that to see how I'd react, would you?"

"She died of cancer. You left home in January and she died in June."

Cheyenne glares at her. "I guess you blame me, don't you?"

"Last I heard, running away from home won't cause cancer."

Cheyenne walks back out to the rock by the river and sits down. Josie stays by the fire and watches her digest the news, sees waves of memories wash over her. Cheyenne's face contorts into a mask of agony, and she clinches her hands into fists as though she's trying to hold all the pain inside her, to keep even a drop from escaping. Finally she returns to her place by the fire and sits there silently, her face swollen from crying.

"Do you want me to tell you about it?" Josie asks.

"Yeah," she mutters.

"She was strong as usual," Josie tells her. "Didn't even take the morphine they offered. Said she'd rather be in pain than in a daze, that she didn't want to die without knowing it. Actually, her mind didn't stay sound anyway. It was the pain, I reckon. Got so one minute she'd make sense, and the next she wouldn't."

"Did she ever ask for me?" Cheyenne asks.

"Well, no, not until that last week, but by then . . . She got it in her head that we were still little, thought you were six and I was two. She kept asking to see us. They paraded me in a few times, but she didn't know who I was. That last day, though, she knew everyone. I almost think she was happy when she died. After they'd closed her eyes and laid her out, they finally let me into the room. There was a smile frozen on her face. Do you know what her last words were? 'I see the prettiest little stars.' That's what they told me she said."

Cheyenne sits there for a moment, silently mouthing Dora's last words. Then she shakes her head and says, "Leave it to Mommy to give a account of the very last thing she saw. Pretty. I mean, the words she said. I'd prob'ly say something like *fuck*." She chuckles. "So you wouldn't in there with her then? When she actually died?"

"No, I was upstairs reading a movie magazine, drooling over an eight-by-ten photograph of Michael Landon. Yep, I was fantasizing about 'Little Joe' as Mommy took her last breath."

"Jesus Christ, Josie. Michael *Maudlin* Landon?"

"I'm afraid so." They look at each other and break into laughter. "I was eleven," Josie sputters between laughs. "Give me a break."

Dusk is beginning to settle among the treetops, to drift down around them like fog. "That Indian man said I had to out of here by seven o'clock," Josie says. "What time is it?"

"I never know what time it is." Cheyenne drags out another six-pack of Bud. "You don't have to be anywhere, do you? Choose my side just this once, Josie. Break the rules."

Josie opens another beer while Cheyenne plays a haunting melody on the harmonica. Darkness is moving in now, and the wind picks up, whistling through the trees, blowing gusts of fog that look like ghost shadows creeping across the ground. She remembers what Cheyenne said earlier, *"This is where the spirits start talking to you."* Looking around at the eerie trees and river, she half expects the earth to split open and swallow them. Anything is possible tonight, she thinks as she closes her eyes, concentrating on Cheyenne's music. When she opens them again, the old Indian man is sitting beside her, smiling. "I thought I told you to leave by seven," he says.

Josie jumps straight up. "God, you scared me half to death. I didn't hear you come. I'm afraid I lost track of time."

The old Indian crinkles his eyes and laughs. Cheyenne puts down her harmonica. "This is Jasper," she says. "He moves around like a cat. No one ever hears him. We don't have to leave at seven. He's just kidding."

Jasper laughs to himself.

Josie cautiously sits again and takes another sip of beer. "I didn't mean to jump like that," she mutters. She stares unabashedly at Jasper and notices the strength in his aging but wiry frame, is stuck by the way his hair gleams like silver in the firelight.

When she looks away from him to the flames, he taps his fingers on her shoulder. "Why are you so afraid?" he asks her.

The touch of his fingers feel like small tentacles of wind. "I don't know," she says, her voice trembling. "I've just been feeling spooked." She glances at Cheyenne and laughs nervously. "This is the first time I've seen my sister in years. Guess I'm thrown off kilter."

"Did you ever consider that maybe things *are* off kilter?" Jasper starts laughing boisterously, causing Josie to smile in spite of herself. She eyes him carefully, and an idea starts gnawing at her that he might not be Jasper at all, that this old man might be the sorcerer of her dreams. "You wouldn't happen to know a guy called Castaneda, would you?" she asks him. "Do people ever refer to you as don Juan?"

Now it's Cheyenne who laughs. "Wow, you must be freaked out. You mean don Juan from the Castaneda books?"

"Okay, forget it," Josie snaps. She stands and walks away from the campfire to the trees.

Jasper follows her, once again tapping her on the shoulder. Josie jumps. "Are you trying to scare me to death?" she asks.

"I just want to show you something," he says. "Look closely at these trees. Check out the whorls in the bark. Remind you of anything?"

Josie stares at the spot he's pointing to. "I bet you carved it, though. Just to scare innocent campers. Am I right? So they'll have a story to tell when they go home."

Jasper takes a flashlight out of his pocket and shines it directly on the spot. "That's not carved, Josie. It's just the bark, the way it grew."

Chills creep up Josie's spine as she realizes Jasper is right. The faces were formed naturally in the bark, their eyes on the verge of tears, their mouths open in perpetual screams.

"All of these trees have faces," Jasper says. "They're the souls of the Indians who once lived here. The eyes are sad because they knew their children and their children's children wouldn't lead the free life they did. They're screaming for the loss. This is special ground you're standing on."

Josie looks from the trees to Jasper and sees tears in his eyes. She runs back to where Cheyenne is still playing music, remembering how the minute she first saw the trees she thought they looked like people. Unable to deal with the overload, she lies down, curls up by the fire and closes her eyes, thinking she'll wait until tomorrow to ask Cheyenne more questions. Out of the blue, it occurs to her that Clarence doesn't know where she is. She finally drifts to sleep listening to the music and watching Jasper sit by the fire. Sometime during the night, she wakes—or perhaps she only dreams she wakes—to find Cheyenne tucking some cover around her.

The next morning Josie is wakened by the cawing of crows. She throws off the blanket that Cheyenne covered her with during the night, sits up, and looks around. The campsite is empty. The tent is gone, the beer cans, fish bones, and bread crumbs have been picked up, and Cheyenne is nowhere in sight. The only remnant from the day before is the burned-out campfire. Josie sits there for a while, rubbing her eyes, unable to believe what she's seeing. She really isn't sure if the previous day's events actually occurred. Maybe I'm finally losing my mind, she thinks. Maybe I drove out here on my own, hiked to this particular site, sat down, and imagined the whole thing. Then she remembers the trees and decides to have a look in broad daylight. Amazingly the faces are still there, their sad eyes almost crying, their screams forever echoing their loss.

Josie goes down to the river and throws water on her face, pulls back her tangled hair, drapes Cheyenne's blanket across her shoulders, and starts hiking back to where she parked the day before.

Soaked from wading the river, she finds her car intact and Jasper leaning against her bumper smiling.

"Oooohwee," he says, when she approaches him. "Cheyenne told me about that don Juan guy you thought I was. Man, I'm not that weird yet."

"Where is she?" Josie asks.

"Gone like a little bird. Flown away."

"Who are you anyway?" Josie growls. "I know you don't work for this campground."

Jasper laughs, takes off running, and disappears into the trees.

Josie gets into her car and begins the drive home. The whole time with Cheyenne was like a dream, and she hates the fact that it was she who did most of the talking, telling Cheyenne about her marriage to Clarence, about Dora's death. She doesn't know much more about her sister than she did before. What she did find out is that Cheyenne doesn't think she fits into the world as it is, that she claims to have been born into the wrong time period, that she wants all the world to be like the campsite on the banks of the San Luis Rey River. Josie glances at Cheyenne's blanket lying on the car seat and wonders if she'll ever see her again.

32

D addy, I saw her," Josie says when she calls Brewster.

"Cheyenne?"

"Yeah, can you believe it? I met her at a campground, an Indian campground. Liked to scared Clarence to death, though. He didn't know where I was, and I stayed out there all night."

"How's her health? Is she with you now? Can I talk to her?"

Josie opens the drapes and stares out the window. An uneasy feeling has begun gnawing at her that the whole day at the campground with her sister was a sham, that Cheyenne was just playing a poor-me-stuck-in-this-ugly-modern-world routine. "She seemed just fine, but I'm afraid she's gone again. Just dropped out of sight. I called Dr. Fierros, and he doesn't know where she is either. I've got a feeling, though, that she's not far away."

"Well, if you fellers are around a telephone the next time she comes around, I'd appreciate it if you'd call." Brewster pauses for a second and says, "How's everything else?"

"Out of whack. For one thing our dog, Butter, keeps getting bigger while Clarence gets skinnier. He's on some kind of strange diet. I don't know what I'm goin to do with either one."

Brewster widens his eyes. "Why, Clarence was already skinny as a rail."

"Rides to work on a bicycle, too. Can you beat that? He's stopped driving."

"I'd say that's a plus," Brewster says.

Josie laughs. "I'd prob'ly lose my mind with worry if I wasn't taking these acting classes. They say I'm pretty good at it. I may audition for a part at a theatre in town."

"You're acting? Do you plan to do a Western?"

"No, not yet, Daddy." She wonders if he thinks it's that easy to land a part in a movie. "Have you thought anymore about coming out?"

"Yeah, I'm thinking about it."

After chatting a few minutes about nothing in particular, they hang up, and Josie plops on the couch, still thinking about Cheyenne, exhausted from it, but unable to stop.

"Just a hundred dollars," Josie is saying to Clarence. It's morning, and they're sitting at the kitchen table, where the cat spray still wafts up at them from the carpet. Josie drinks coffee and eats toast while Clarence drinks herbal tea and chews on a banana chip.

Last night as she was leaving class, Fletcher Wayne touched her arm and informed her that his outside class in Shakespeare will start next Saturday. His fingers felt like fire on her skin. The truth is, Josie can no longer ignore Fletcher's attraction to her, and she's beginning to respond to his smiles.

Josie eyes Clarence closely. "Five Saturdays of intensive training for a hundred dollars. I think that's a pretty good deal."

"How many other people are taking it?" Clarence asks. He's afraid her teacher is some weirdo who's getting her into his apartment for the purpose of raping her and then beating her to a pulp.

"There's three others. A man and two women."

Clarence sighs. "Okay. If that's what you want." He feels so guilty about his growing feelings for Sally that he can't bring himself to deny Josie anything.

When Clarence leaves for work, Josie walks out to the front yard. It's the first week in December, but the temperature is in the high sixties. By the time the fog burns off at nine o'clock, it will be even warmer. Across the cul-de-sac several elementary-age kids walk out of their houses on their way to school with little packs strapped across their backs, carrying brightly colored cartoon lunch boxes. She sits down on the grass and stares up at the still-gray sky. Almost every day, she calls Dr. Fierros to ask if he's heard from Cheyenne, and he always says he hasn't. Josie is beginning to suspect he's lying.

Even so, she's tired of thinking about it and is beginning to visualize herself never giving Cheyenne another thought. After all she has other worries, namely Clarence. Lately they've been avoiding each other as much as possible, and when they do find themselves in the same room, they speak politely, nod, and smile. Having finally gotten her typing speed up to sixty words a minute, Josie figures she's almost ready to look for a job. Still, the fact remains that she doesn't want to be a secretary. She wants to be a bartender. Maybe I ought to just leave here, go back to Arizona, and get a job in Sage, she thinks. Returning to the house, she calls Venus to see if there is still a chance of getting her old job back.

"God, I'm glad you called," Venus says. "So much has happened."

"What?" Josie says, hoping she's going to tell her that Johnny has come back.

"Tarantula Garcia died. Stroke, I guess. They found her laying under a tree in her front yard, dead."

Josie doesn't have to ask if it was the fig tree; she knows. Since her visit with Cheyenne she has managed to convince herself that Tarantula was lying about Dan being buried under the tree. Now, once again, she isn't so sure.

"We hoped Dan might have heard about it somehow and shown up for the funeral, but he didn't come," Venus says.

I hope it's not because he's six feet under, Josie is thinking. She wonders what was going through Tarantula's mind as she lay down on that red soil and died.

"And on a lighter note," Venus is saying, "Lily Venus and Bobby Swanson ran off and got married."

"You're kidding," Josie says. "I thought you fellers were afraid to let people know who was who."

"Well, Lily started pining over him. I don't know, I just figured it was time we gave up on it. Tired of living scared, I guess."

"That's great," Josie says. She can just see the smile on Bobby's face when he finally found out the true identity of the woman he loves. "You know what? I'm tired of living scared, too, which brings me to one of the questions I wanted to ask. Has Johnny come back yet?"

Venus sighs. "No, honey, he's still in West Virginia. Ain't sold his land yet, though. As long as he's got his ranch out here, he might come back."

What if I let the only one go? Josie thinks. The only man I'll ever feel this way about. "Yeah, well, a person prob'ly ought not to bank on it," she says.

Venus chatters on about other Sage news, and the conversation finally ends without Josie ever asking about a job.

33

Brewster walks over to the refrigerator and takes out a beer. These last few weeks, he has been thinking more seriously about going out to Josie's. His renewed interest is due largely to disillusionment with the situation at hand. Price Gibson has started coming down to see Ida every other weekend, and Ida is getting cockier by the minute, behaving as though Brewster is a slow-witted child who can't take care of himself. She has even suggested he move into her house, says his makeshift apartment is too cold, that he'll freeze to death this winter.

At the first sign of fall, Ida bought herself a new furnace that blows hot air into every room through vents in the floor, and that's all she talks about. She says it's the best furnace ever made and claims she doesn't know how she lived until she got it. "Your old stove don't put out enough heat to keep a mouse alive," she tells him each time she calls.

Every Sunday she attempts to drag him out to her car and force him to spend the afternoon at her house. "So you can get warm," she says. He won't go on the Sundays that Price is there, though. He can't stand to see the two old fools sitting on the couch, necking like teenagers. He even hates to go to her house on the Sundays when Price isn't visiting because naturally Viola Watson is there, sitting in a corner of the living room, her arms folded tenaciously around her ample waist. Although Viola looks to be in her fifties, Brewster has since learned that she's sixty-five. He guesses people don't wrinkle when they sit around all the time like a knot on a log. When he gripes to Ida about Viola's constant presence, she tells him that Viola's house is colder than his and that she comes over to get warm too.

Finally Brewster calls Ida and says, "Don't bother trying to drag me to your house next Sunday cause I'm not goin."

"Fine," Ida says. "Be that way."

When Sunday comes, Brewster is at home, enjoying the peace, sitting in his favorite chair, playing the guitar, straining to remember the words to "Little Stream of Whiskey." He can't get his arthritic fingers to work right, but every time he plucks the wrong string, he pretends it didn't happen, lets his mind sail right over the blunders. He's singing loud, his shaky voice missing every other note, when the door opens and Viola Watson steps inside without knocking.

"Howdy, Viola," Brewster says, a little startled.

Viola doesn't say a word.

"Is Ida with you?"

Viola sits down in the wing-back chair and stares at Brewster.

He gets up, opens the front door, and looks out. He doesn't see Ida's car parked anywhere, but he sees an old '52 Ford truck parked on the side of the street. "Is that your truck?" he asks. He realizes that asking Viola a question is pointless, knows that it makes more sense to talk to a dog or cat or even a plant than try to carry on a conversation with her. At least a dog'll wag his tail, a cat will meow, a plant will droop. Viola never reacts at all. What in the world does she want?

He eases over to the grease rack, picks up the phone, and dials Ida's number. "Hello," he whispers. "Guess what? Viola's here."

"She is?"

"Why don't you come down here too? I don't know what to do with her," Brewster whispers, hoping Viola doesn't hear him.

"I can't," Ida says. "I've got to finish this afghan. I'm making a special one for Mossie Stubblefield. I promised her last week I'd have it done today, and I'm way behind."

"Why did Viola come?" Brewster whispers.

"Beats me," Ida says.

"Shit," he says and hangs up.

He goes back to the couch and sits down. Viola stares straight at him. She doesn't smile, doesn't frown, doesn't change her expression in the least.

Fine, Brewster thinks. Well, I'm just goin to act like she ain't around. He turns on the TV and starts watching.

Viola keeps looking at him, her eyes boring like moles into his face. Unable to concentrate any longer, he turns off the TV. I'll fix her, he thinks, and picking up the guitar, he commences playing and singing loudly. When that doesn't get a rise out of her, he starts singing vulgar songs he learned when he was in the army, figuring the bad words will send her packing. Since he only remembers two or three army songs, he begins replacing the verses to regular songs with coarse words he makes up on the spot. He changes the words of "A Tisket, A Tasket," to "*A twitchet, a twatchet. If it itches, let me scratch it.*"

Viola doesn't blink.

Growing even nastier, he changes "The Streets of Laredo" to "*As I passed out on the tits of Lorraina, as I passed out on Lorraina today . . .*"

Even Brewster is embarrassed by that one, but Viola isn't fazed.

He puts his guitar down and drums his fingers on the arm of the couch. Finally he stares back at her. Viola's face looks like a moon pie, and her blue eyes are round as golf balls. Her nose resembles a small piece of blown-up bubble gum on which someone has painted two black dots, trying to pass them off as nostrils. Brewster would bet his life that her nose doesn't come with a membrane, that if you touched her nose, it would sink in. Sagging at the corners, her lips make her look as though she's slightly pissed off about something. She always wears her gray hair drawn into a tidy bun. He wonders how long her hair would be if she let it down. He can't get over how smooth her skin is—not a wrinkle on it.

All the time he's staring at her, she stares back with never a hint of what is going through her mind. Finally he's had enough. "Well, I'm goin to bed now," he tells her. "When you get ready to leave, just go."

Brewster gets up and staggers over to his bed and lies down. Of course he can't go to sleep. Who could? He turns on his side with his face to the wall and lies there for five minutes without moving a muscle, breathing heavily as if he's gone to the world, hoping against hope she'll think he's asleep and go home.

It doesn't happen.

In order to blot out his present situation, he tries to think of other things. He thinks about Josie and Clarence, knowing they have marriage problems even though Josie doesn't do much more than hint at them. He worries about Cheyenne's hobo way of life. Josie said Cheyenne had been living in a campground in the off-season. Sounds pretty dangerous, Brewster thinks. Why, someone could come along and slit her throat. They's all kinds of old weirdos in California.

Still in the middle of a dire scenario, he feels a hand touch his shoulder. With a start, he looks up, and there stands Viola. She's bending over him with an intense look in her eyes.

"What is it?" he gasps.

She lifts her dress and pulls it over her head.

"My God," Brewster squeaks, unable to avoid gaping at the large breasts swinging toward him. He scoots as far as he can to the other side of the bed. "Get away from me. Go home!"

Viola smiles.

Oh my God, Brewster thinks, she's moving her face muscles.

Viola crawls into the bed and puts her huge arm around him. He tries to sit up but finds he can't move. Turning his face to the wall again, he thinks, If she gets on top of me, I'll smother to death. Finally he braves up enough to turn around and look at her. Viola's eyes are twinkling like Christmas lights, and she's still got that smile on her face.

"Viola," Brewster manages to say, "get a hold of yourself. You ain't in your right mind."

"They ain't nothing wrong with my mind," Viola says, plain as day.

Brewster almost blacks out when she speaks. "You *said* something?"

"That's right," Viola says. Her voice is deep and throaty.

Brewster's mind darts back to when Ida told him that Viola talked to her when no one else was around. He'd never believed it for a minute. He'd thought Ida was just saying that to make Viola seem more normal. "How come you never talked till now?" he asks her.

"I have to make sure I like someone before I waste words on them," Viola says. "I talk to Ida all the time."

"But to no one else?"

"I don't like hardly anyone else. Least I didn't till you come along," Viola says, winking.

Brewster ignores the wink, pretends it didn't happen. "Damn, Viola, that's goin a little overboard, ain't it? To just not talk?"

"I like goin overboard," Viola says. Then she takes hold of Brewster's head and draws it toward her, kisses him on the mouth before he knows what's happening.

This is it, he thinks as she kisses. This woman's goin to fold herself around me, and I'll never be found. When I yell for help, my voice will sound so weak and far away that even if people hear me, they'll think they're dreaming. No one will come to save me, and I'll die.

Brewster hasn't been kissed in a long time, and he begins to realize that Viola's lips are soft as rose petals. He's surprised to find himself enjoying the feel of her mouth on his. He's even more surprised when he starts kissing her back. His arthritis begins to melt like ice cream left sitting on a warm stove. How many years has she been saving that kiss? he wonders. Am I the first man she's ever kissed?

He pulls off his shirt, and they both get into the swing of things. Viola heaves as he hoes. Thirty minutes later, they're both lying in bed, panting like old dogs on a hot summer day. Brewster is almost afraid to look at her, afraid she isn't there, that he dreamed the whole thing. If I did dream it, I'm goin to check myself into a hospital, he thinks. Then he turns around and looks. She's there.

"What're you staring at?" Viola asks.

Brewster shakes his head. "What would Ida think if she knew about what just happened?"

"Ida already knows I like you."

"She does?" This is too much, Brewster thinks. He is so drained from all that's happened that he involuntarily closes his eyes. Exhausted too, Viola pulls the blanket over their tired bodies, and they drift off to sleep.

34

Saturday finally arrives, and Josie stands in front of the mirror, putting on makeup, getting ready for Fletcher's outside Shakespeare class which starts at four o'clock. She's nervous about meeting the other three students, imagining they are much more adept than she. They're prob'ly just doing this to brush up, she thinks.

Looking at her own face in the mirror, she rolls her eyes and shakes her head, realizing it's time she stopped lying to herself. She's not just putting on makeup out of nervousness about meeting the other students. She wants to look pretty when she sees Fletcher Wayne. Josie sneaks through the living room and eases past the couch where Butter is curled beside Clarence, watching him while he sleeps. Quietly picking up her purse and keys, she tiptoes out the door.

Fletcher lives in a garden apartment complex on Adams Avenue in the community of North Park. Josie likes North Park. There is a sense of small-town there that reminds her of home. People wave when they pass each other on the streets, which are lined with neighborhood markets, auto repair shops, and hardware stores. On either side of Fletcher, groups of young college-age kids room together. Their TVs and stereos are constantly blasting. As soon as Josie and the other three students arrive, Fletcher steps outside and yells, "Hey, turn down that lousy Bee Gee shit."

Strangely, the kids oblige. Josie figures Fletcher must have had run-ins with them before and has them bluffed. Finally the session gets under way. One of the women students used to perform Shakespeare when she was younger, but she hasn't acted in ten years. The other is younger than Josie and has only performed in high school. The male student has done a few used-car commercials, but now he wants to do something more serious.

Fletcher starts them out with scenes from *King Lear*. Josie is Cordelia. The other two women are Goneril and Regan. The man has several roles, the fool, Edgar, Kent, and Gloucester, and Fletcher plays the old man himself, Lear. It is the first time Josie has really seen him act, and she is overwhelmed by his talent. In act 4, scene 7, they do the scene where Cordelia and Lear are reunited. Josie is so swept away by the magic and emotion that she can hardly bring herself back down, and she's shocked when Fletcher announces the session is over.

The other students, who seem impressed by her performance, leave quickly, but Josie lingers, fiddling with the notes she took. Sometimes she worries that Fletcher has just been telling her she's talented because he's attracted to her. She wants to ask him if he thinks there's a chance she'll ever act on a real stage, but most of all she wants to feel the warmth she felt when his fingers brushed against her the other night after class.

"You were great tonight," Fletcher says. "Would you like me to help you with your accent?"

"Sure," Josie says.

"Actually, let's not waste our time on that right now. I'll loan you some of my tapes. They're pretty good. I'm sure you'll catch on in no time."

"Thanks," Josie says. "Well, I guess I'd better go."

"Why?"

"You prob'ly have plans."

"Not really," Fletcher says. "I was going to go out for a bite to eat and then come back here and listen to some jazz all alone. Contrary to popular belief, I'm actually a lonely guy, a shut-in almost. What kind of food do you like?"

"Anything but health food," Josie says.

"How about Japanese?"

"Sounds good." Josie has never eaten Japanese food, doesn't have any idea if she'll like it, but she's game for anything. A few minutes later they're sitting in a small Japanese restaurant on Fifth Avenue, eating sashimi, drinking saki.

"What did you talk me into ordering? Is this stuff cooked?" Josie asks.

"It's marinated."

"That's all? Lord, it'll kill us, won't it?"

Fletcher takes a huge bite and smacks his lips. "You don't like it?"

"I prefer my fish cooked," Josie says.

"So how's the marriage going?" he asks, pointing to her wedding band.

"It's been fizzling out for a long time now. Nobody's fault. It's just the way it is."

"Why haven't you left him?"

Josie stares down at the sashimi, takes another drink of saki. "I'm still in the process of learning a few things."

Fletcher grins. "Let's go back to my apartment and listen to some jazz."

His dark brown eyes shoot out little fingers of heat that fumble all over her. She knows that if she goes back to his apartment something is bound to happen between them, but at this particular moment that's exactly what she wants. "If I do, I'll need to call Clarence. Tell him I'll be late, so he won't worry."

"That's fine," Fletcher says. "Ready?"

Josie stands, suddenly realizing that the saki has done a number on her. She can hardly get her bearings, can barely walk. They decide to leave her car in the parking lot, and Fletcher drives her back to the apartment. As soon as they get inside, she calls Clarence. There is no answer.

"What did he say?" Fletcher asks when she puts down the phone.

"Nothing. He didn't answer," Josie says, bewildered.

"Maybe he didn't hear the ring."

"He always hears everything. Every little noise, he jumps like he's been shot. The war did that for him."

"Maybe he's gone out somewhere," Fletcher says.

"He never goes out, but maybe he's in the backyard for some reason. I'll call him back in a few minutes." Josie walks over to Fletcher's bookshelf and spots *A Separate Reality* by Carlos Castaneda. "I don't believe this," she says. "You like Carlos Castaneda?"

"Yeah. Pretty interesting."

"Do you believe the dreaming stuff?"

"I don't believe anything," Fletcher says.

"I used to read all the time," Josie says, ignoring his cynicism. "Especially the Castaneda books. Don't have time for it now, though."

She checks out his stereo and album collection. "Oh, God, you've got Dave Van Ronk. This is amazing. I've never met anyone who knows he exists."

Fletcher sings a verse of "Candy Man" and asks her if she'd like some wine.

"Maybe just a little."

He pours her a drink and puts on Thelonious Monk. They both sit on the couch and prop their feet on the coffee table while jazz slithers around them like a snake in the grass. Then as if someone yelled *start*, they turn their heads toward each other and kiss long, hard, and naturally as though they've been intimate for years. "Well, it's about time," Fletcher mutters, when they come up for air.

Josie smiles.

She kicks off her shoes and Fletcher kicks off his. They stretch out on the couch, their noses almost touching, and stare into each other's eyes. Doing nothing more than lying close, they get lost in the current running between them, are almost paralyzed by anticipation. Finally they resume kissing, touching, holding.

"I've got to call Clarence again," Josie says, forcing herself off the couch. She picks up the phone and dials her home number. There's still no answer. "I'm afraid something's wrong."

"Don't worry about it. He's probably just out."

"But I told you, he never goes out. How can I explain to him that I'm goin to be late if he's not answering the phone?"

"Do you want to go home?"

"No." She knows she should go, but the fact is she loved the way Fletcher's mouth felt on hers just moments ago, the heat she felt lying so close beside him. In addition to the saki and wine, the varying beats from the jazz and from the rock music that is once again spilling from the adjoining apartments bombards Josie's senses, and she becomes removed from inhibition, unleashed, set adrift in discombobulated rhythm. "I want you to make love to me," she says.

Fletcher crosses the room, lifts her in his arms, and carries her to his small dark bedroom, where they kiss, hold each other, and have sex that is as slow and slurred as an amiable drunk reminiscing with a stranger in a bar.

Later, Fletcher sits with his back against the wall, while Josie lies facing him, her feet propped on his shoulders. In that position they talk about their pasts, about their mothers, fathers, siblings, their grandparents. Fletcher tells her how it felt to grow up in Seattle, Washington, about his father who went insane and his mother who lives alone. Josie tells him about Dora and Brewster, about Cheyenne and Sage. She even tells him about the fig tree.

"That old woman fed you a line," he says.

"I hope so," Josie says. "Maybe someday I'll get myself a shovel and find out." She looks at the clock on the wall. It's twelve o'clock. "Think I'll call Clarence again." She goes into the living room and dials the number. There is still no answer.

She opens Fletcher's bedroom door and says, "He still isn't answering. Something's wrong. You'd better take me back to my car. I've got to go home."

Clarence was only pretending to be asleep when Josie left for class this afternoon. As soon as she was safely away, he poured Butter a bowl of food and took off for Sally Waterford's apartment. They made love and wallowed around in bed for several hours. Finally he remembered to look at his watch. "I'd better get home," he told Sally. "Josie's class is over."

"Why don't you phone home and tell her you're at work, that they called you to come in for a special project?" Sally's red hair was tousled, her mouth pouty, and her eyes drooped around the edges, making her look too sexy for words. "Besides," Sally said, "I want to show you my stock portfolio. I'd like your opinion."

"You've invested in stocks?" Clarence was impressed beyond belief.

"Sure. Haven't you?"

Clarence called home, but Josie hadn't returned. "They've prob'ly got caught up in their class and don't know when to quit," he said.

Clarence and Sally lost themselves in a deep conversation about Ginnie Maes, money markets, and blue-chip stocks. Clarence called home again. Josie still wasn't there. "They're prob'ly sitting around talking about what a good job they did in class," he told Sally. "They do that, you know—brag on themselves all the time. Josie sure does anyway. She's always talking about how everyone applauds when she does a scene, how good they say she is. If them people was really any good, looks like they'd be in movies where they could make some money. Josie almost acts like she's too good to go to Hollywood, criticizes every movie I like. I sort of like Burt Reynolds in a movie. Josie hates him. Well, let them brag on themselves. I don't care."

"Won't she be suspicious when she goes home and you're not there?" Sally asked.

"Let her be," Clarence said, feeling more brazen with each passing minute. "I'm tired of all this sneaking around anyway."

Sally prepared him a scrumptious vegetarian meal. They drank sparkling cider and watched TV for a while, then they went back to bed. In a few minutes Clarence was as erect as a soldier playing taps. He reached for a condom and started putting it on.

"Do you have to wear that thing?" Sally asked him. "It's not like I'm going to get pregnant. I'm on the pill."

All the time he'd been seeing Sally, he had worn condoms. It was something they'd pounded into his head when he was in the army. "If you're goin to screw around, wear rubbers," they'd told the soldiers. Clarence looked at Sally, realizing how stupid he'd been, that she was about as far from a whore as a person could get.

"No," he said, "I reckon I don't have to wear it."

After making love two more times, Clarence snuggled beside her, loving the softness of her skin, the way it smelled like talcum powder. He dozed for a while, then woke with a start, guilt seizing hold of him like a Saturday-night wrestler. What have I done? he thought. Josie's probably home by now, and I'm not. What will I tell her? I don't have a excuse. Clarence looked at the clock; it was twelve-thirty. Bolting upright, he said to Sally, "I've got to get home."

Now Clarence drives toward his house like someone dying to go to the bathroom, focused only on getting there and nothing else. He wonders if Josie would believe him if he told her he was unexpectedly called to work and that when he was driving home he had a flat tire and had to walk three miles to a find a open garage with a mechanic on duty who could fix it, it being Saturday night? Then he remembers that he has a spare tire, and that Josie knows he can fix a flat. Maybe I could tell her I was driving home, picked up a hitchhiker, a scroungy-looking bum, who tried to rob me, but that I managed to take the gun away from him, made a citizen's arrest, and was held up at the police station telling them my story until now. That might work, Clarence thinks. Shit, no. She'd never believe I picked up anyone. I'm screwed. That's all there is to it.

He's about to turn into the little neighborhood where they live when he looks into his rearview mirror and sees her. Josie is about a half block behind him. He recognizes her Pinto since its right headlight is a little cockeyed. What in the hell is she doing out this late? he thinks. It must be close to one o'clock. That's a little late for people to be sitting around bragging on themselves. Maybe they's something else goin on. Oh, God, I wonder if she's seen me too. Clarence guns his engine and zips around the street corner toward home.

Someone must have stolen it, Josie thinks when she sees Clarence's car in front of her going sixty miles an hour. That can't be him. He'd never go that fast. But then the headlights of an approaching car light up the driver's side, exposing the shape of Clarence's head. Josie hits her brakes, pulls to the side of the street, and parks.

He must be out looking for me, she guesses. He prob'ly thinks I've been in a wreck. No doubt he's been out since seven o'clock this evening searching for accidents, checking hospitals and morgues. I can't believe I stayed out this long. Well, I ain't goin to lie about it. If he asks me where I was, I'll just tell him. May as well let it end now. She starts the engine and drives slowly to her house. Clarence's car is parked in the driveway. The lights in the house are off.

She unlocks the front door and steps inside, expecting Clarence to come charging at her any minute, accusing her of everything under the sun. It doesn't happen. She turns on the lamp in the living room and listens for his footsteps. She doesn't hear a sound. Tiptoeing down the hallway, she peeps into the bedroom. Clarence and Butter are lying side by side, seemingly gone to the world. Bewildered, Josie returns to the living room. I wonder if I just imagined seeing him out there. She slips outside and puts her hand on the hood of Clarence's car. It's still hot to the touch. No, I was right the first time, she thinks. Well, if this ain't the damnedest thing.

She goes back into the house and sits on the couch, trying to figure out why Clarence isn't yelling at her. Ah, fuck it, she finally decides, then lies down and goes to sleep.

The next day is Sunday, and when Clarence and Josie finally get up that morning, they eye each other suspiciously. At breakfast they eat slowly, stealing furtive glances, each wondering if or when the explosion will occur.

"How did your class go last night?" Clarence finally asks her.

"Good," Josie says. She stares into her coffee as if she just spotted a fly floating face up.

"You were a little late, weren't you?"

"A little." Josie takes a big bite of toast. Here it comes, she thinks. He's goin to start yelling any minute.

"I was so tired last night, I went to bed about eight o'clock," Clarence says. "Didn't hear you come in."

"Really?" Josie says, trying to keep a poker face. "I must have got home about eight-thirty." Why is he lying like this? she wonders. Why is he letting me off the hook?

"I was dead asleep by then," Clarence says, looking at her strangely.

"You were?"

"I thought your class got out at six-thirty. Why were you late?" Clarence asks, casually.

"Oh, we were just sitting around talking about the scene we'd been working on."

"Yeah," Clarence says. "I see how that could happen. Well, hope you had a good time."

Later, Clarence tells Josie he's decided to watch Sunday football. He knows Josie won't stay in the same room where a football game is playing. That way he won't have to look at her.

"But I thought you hated football, Clarence."

"Not really. I sort of like it."

Josie goes into their empty second bedroom and recalls the love-making from the night before, remembering the feel of Fletcher Wayne inside her.

Clarence stares at the TV, but he may as well be staring at the wall. Josie was right. He hates football. I know why I'm lying about last night, he thinks, but why is she lying? Where was she anyway? Finally he walks outside and pees on the bougainvillea.

35

J osie is washing clothes, but her mind is on other things. Becoming increasingly sure that Dr. Fierros is lying when he says he doesn't know her sister's whereabouts, Josie is thinking of marching into his office for a confrontation, and when she finds out where Cheyenne is, she's thinking of telling her exactly where to shove her disappearing act. Josie throws Clarence's shirts into the washer, picks up a pair of his pants, and turns the pockets inside out. It's then that the evidence falls to the floor—the two packages of rubbers, or condoms, or whatever is the latest term that people use to nicen them up. She prefers to call them rubbers. One package is empty, the other unopened.

"Well, that's just fine, Clarence," she says, while the washer and dryer hum and slosh. "At least you're fuckin somebody."

But she feels betrayed.

Now, why would I feel this way? she wonders. Especially since I had an affair with Johnny Walker and am having one with Fletcher. Still the sick feeling won't go away. She tries to imagine Clarence lying in bed with another woman, and she wonders what they talk about, wonders if he ticks when he dozes after sex. Does she look the opposite from me? What kind of personality does she have? Why am I reacting this way? I should be happy he's seeing someone. Am I such a selfish shit-ass that I think it's perfectly all right for me to have a good time but that it's not okay for Clarence?

That evening when he gets home, Josie has a huge vegetarian

meal waiting for him. Earlier she scoured her cookbook for ideas and came up with something truly edible—cold spaghetti salad that is meatless but tasty, stir-fried vegetables, black beans, and a mixture of fresh pineapple and strawberries for desert.

Clarence is amazed. "What did you do this for?" he asks.

"I'm tired of seeing you starve to death." Josie eyes him closely, trying to get used to the idea that there might be a woman somewhere right now who is falling in love with him. It's the strangest concept.

"Well, this is good," Clarence says.

She feels uncomfortable sitting there with him, watching him eat his meal. Clarence, whom she has known since she was a child, may as well be an alien from outer space. "Let's go to a movie," Josie says. She doesn't know why she says it. The words just come out of her mouth.

"I'm pretty tired," Clarence says, "You can go, though, if you want to."

Josie watches him chew. If Clarence were like most men, finding a couple of condoms in his pocket wouldn't necessarily mean he's having a serious affair, but with Clarence that is exactly what it means. She imagines that when they divorce and he marries this other woman, his life will be perfect. He'll have a nice house somewhere far to the north of I-8. His wife will keep it neat and tidy even though she works full-time at a well-paying job. They'll probably have children who make high grades, have paper routes, become Boy Scouts and Girl Scouts. They'll go on perfectly planned vacations every year and have vegetarian Thanksgivings. At Christmas they won't have a real tree; they'll buy an artificial one because they don't like the idea of cutting down living things, not seeing the irony in the fact that Christmas trees are grown on farms and harvested like the many heads of lettuce they eat.

"Well, glad you enjoyed the meal," Josie says. It's over, she's thinking. My marriage to Clarence really is over. The finality of the realization strikes an odd mixture of terror and elation in her heart. "Think I'll go for a walk."

* * *

"Next Monday is finals," Josie tells Clarence, lying. Actually she is already finished with her finals at El Camino and is pretty sure she passed with flying colors. "My acting teacher ain't giving us a test. We have to do a scene that counts as our final. I'm planning to spend all day tomorrow with Mary Bingham so we can rehearse. Actually I may as well just stay at her house tomorrow night. We won't get done until late, and I'll be too tired to drive home. I prob'ly won't get back here until late Sunday morning."

"That's fine," Clarence says, trying to hide his excitement. A whole night with Sally. It will be the first time he's stayed the entire night with her.

Josie pours herself another cup of coffee. Of course she has no intentions of staying with Mary. She's spending the night with Fletcher, and the thought of it makes her quiver all over.

Brewster is standing by the sink, coughing and turning blue. A couple of weeks ago he got a flu that won't let him go, and that in addition to the sex with Viola has him so muddled he can hardly function. He needs time to mull things over—a lot of time. Viola comes over every day now and wears him out. He knows he wouldn't have took sick if not for her shenanigans. Ida and Price are beside themselves with glee. They break out laughing with sheer joy every time they see him and Viola together. "When are you goin to marry her?" Ida asks him every time she calls.

"Just because you and Price are getting married is no sign I'm about to," he retorts. Ida and Price are planning to get married in the spring, but Ida hasn't had enough nerve to tell Clarence. She's afraid he'll be against it.

Brewster has to admit that he and Viola have had some good times, but there's got to be more to life than fun, he thinks. I'll prob'ly be tired of her in another week. He has decided to accept Josie's invitation to visit. Thank God her and Clarence live all the way in California, he thinks as he reaches for a handkerchief to blow his nose.

He figures the California sun will dry up his flu in no time, and the trip will put some distance between him and Viola Watson, give him time to think.

Stumbling over to his chifforobe, he opens the door and stares at his three pairs of faded Levi's and four flannel shirts. He opens a drawer and inspects his socks and underwear, which are all either permanently stained or threadbare. He checks out his medicine drawer to see if he has enough Solganal on hand. He does. At least he won't have to visit that shitty clinic before he leaves. Staring into the mirror on the bathroom door, he studies his sunken cheeks, his red splotchy nose, his forehead with its blue veins that crisscross like highways on an aging roadmap. "Well, old man," he says, "are ye about ready to travel?"

Early the next Saturday morning, Brewster opens his suitcase for the third time since he got up. Viola, Ida, and Price will be arriving at nine o'clock to drive him to Louisville to catch the plane. He checks to make sure he packed his medicine, his toothbrush, and his razor. He fumbles around in his coat pocket for the airline ticket. Yep, it's still there.

When his three escorts finally show up, Ida takes one look at him and says, "You're a fool for traveling the shape you're in. You ought to be curled up in bed." She turns to Viola. "Viola, why are you letting him go?"

"Because he wants to," Viola says, blushing. "He needs to visit his daughter, don't you, Brewster?"

Brewster grins. What else can he do but grin?

When they finally pile into the car, Ida drives and Price sits beside her in the front, while Viola squeezes up close to Brewster in the back. They've just gone past the outskirts of Pick when Viola, blushing profusely, reaches out and tweaks Brewster's cheek, lowers her hand to rub his knee, and leans her head on his shoulder. *What am I goin to do with this big woman?* Brewster is thinking. *Maybe when I'm in San Diego I'll figure it out.*

In the front seat, Ida is still griping at Brewster for heading out of town with the flu. "I can't believe you're setting out somewhere this sick," she says, "and to think you didn't let them know you was coming. They might of needed time to get things ready for ye. I wouldn't blame them if they got madder than wet hens."

"Well, don't you go calling them now," Brewster says. "I want this to be a surprise."

"Maybe they don't like surprises. I sure don't."

"You'd better not tell them, Ida," Brewster growls.

"Okay, okay. But if it was me . . ." Ida goes on like that for a hundred miles.

When they finally get to the airport in Louisville, they step into a delicatessen for coffee. Ida, Price, and Viola sit around with Brewster for about an hour. Then Viola gives him a big kiss full on the lips, and they leave. "I'll see you in a month or two," he says as they walk away from the booth. Viola turns around and blows him another kiss.

Brewster continues to sit there, drinking coffee, blowing his nose and coughing. He's got a long wait. The plane doesn't take off until 7 P.M. his time, arriving in San Diego at 10 P.M. Pacific.

While Brewster is flying over Nevada, Clarence and Sally are sitting on her couch watching TV and necking, and Josie is with Fletcher in his apartment, drinking wine, eating French bread and Brie cheese.

"I want you to show the fuckers, Josie," Fletcher says. "I want you to be the best there is. I want this whole town to be knocking at your door. Just promise me that when you make it big, you won't forget your old teacher."

"When was the last time you acted?" she asks him.

He takes a drink of wine. "Let's don't talk about me. Let's talk about you." He finishes the glass and pours it full again.

"Why did you stop?" Josie asks.

"Got tired of starving." Fletcher gets up and puts on David Bowie's *Low* album. "I went to New York when I was in my twenties, thinking I'd land a part by the end of the first week. It didn't happen. I went back to Seattle, got a few parts in local theatre, even went to Holly-wood and worked as a waiter. Nothing ever happened. Then I came down here and auditioned for the Old Globe, began to get parts. It went okay for a while, but then I started having these run-ins. It's all so political, Josie. Like everything else, it's politics. I finally just chucked it and began teaching. Acting is shit."

"I thought you told me once that you were thinking of goin to New York to make a stab at it again."

Fletcher grins. "Hey, don't start getting preachy, okay? Would you like to hear some down-and-dirty blues?"

"Yeah," Josie says. "Put some on."

"No, I mean in person. Blind Jimmy Deacon is playing in Ocean Beach in this little hole-in-the-wall called Mojo's. The man is great."

"Well, let's go, then."

While Brewster is landing at Lindbergh Field, Josie and Fletcher are driving toward Ocean Beach. Outside a storm is in process. Josie has never seen it rain this hard since she's been in San Diego. Even with the windshield wipers turned on high, Fletcher can hardly see how to drive.

Brewster steps out of the airport into the pouring rain, catches the first taxi he sees, and gives the driver the address of Clarence and Josie's house. It costs twenty dollars to get there, leaving him with only forty dollars to see him through his visit. As the taxi pulls away, Brewster walks slowly and painfully up the driveway, pulling his cap farther down, the rain pounding like fists against his tired body.

Thought Josie said it never rained much out here, he says to him-self. What in the world does she call this?

Noticing that there are no lights on in the house, he figures they are already in bed. "Well, I'll just have to wake them up," he grumbles as he knocks on the door. No one comes. He knocks louder, and still no one comes. He tries to open the door himself. It is locked. Walking through the front yard, he finds what looks like a bedroom window. He taps loudly against the glass. Nothing. He goes back to the front door, finds a buzzer, and presses his finger against it for at least five minutes. Bells chime loudly all through the house, rousing no one. If he weren't too tired to raise his arm, he would scratch his head.

Either they've died in their sleep or they're gone, Brewster thinks before he loses his breath coughing. When he finally gets his breath back, he re-inspects the driveway, noticing that Clarence's Nova isn't there. Could it be in the garage? He tries to open the garage door. It won't budge. His feet and legs are killing him after being cramped in the plane for six hours. Well, if this ain't a sight, he thinks. Then he notices a little gate to one side of the house. Unlatching it, he steps into the backyard, finds the covered patio, and makes a beeline for shelter.

He drops his suitcase, falls to a lawn chair, and sits there for a minute catching his breath and collecting his thoughts. If they've gone out somewhere, they'll be back some time tonight, he reasons. But what if they're on vacation? Lordy mercy, Ida was right. I ought to of told them I was coming.

"I never dreamed I'd freeze to death in San Diego," he grumbles as he gets up again and tries to open the garage's back door. Naturally, it is locked. Walking the length of the house, he discovers one window that isn't covered with curtains. It is the second bedroom that Josie still hasn't gotten around to furnishing. Peering inside, he sees the dog she told him about. It is growling at him with the most hateful expression he's ever seen.

Josie is right, he thinks. It does look like a walrus. Still, they wouldn't go on vacation and leave their dog alone. They're just out, he decides, and begins to feel a whole lot better.

With the cold rain beating against his face, he returns to the patio, drags his flannel shirts out of the suitcase, dons them, then puts his jacket on over them. He also puts on a second pair of Levi's. Already beginning to feel warmer, he lies down in the lawn chair and falls to sleep.

Sally is showing Clarence how to do needlepoint as Josie and Fletcher step out of the rain into Mojo's. The place is packed with college kids from UCSD, State, and El Camino College, most of whom seem to know Fletcher. "Hey, man, why aren't you in *Tee-kwana?*" one young man shouts as he pats Fletcher on the back. A young girl, wearing a pair of cutoffs that are so short her buttocks are clearly visible, comes gyrating toward him, grabs him around the neck, and kisses him on the mouth. "Fletcher, honey, where you been?" she coos. Then she slithers away like a garden-variety snake.

"Maybe she didn't see me standing here," Josie says to him.

"Don't worry about it. It's nothing."

As Blind Jimmy Deacon appears on stage and begins wailing the blues, Fletcher orders bourbon—one shot glass after another, and when he starts chitchatting with a blonde who is standing to his right, it hits Josie that she isn't the first student with whom Fletcher Wayne has become entangled. *Duh,* she thinks, and starts ordering shots of tequila that cut through the smoke in the bar, making the dim room glitter and shine. At one point she turns to say something to Fletcher, but he isn't there, and he stays gone for at least half an hour. Oh, well, she thinks, and gets into a deep conversation about overpopulation with the boy standing behind her. Blues pounds against the night like the drowning rain.

Clarence and Sally are making love for the third time when Mojo's closes at two o'clock in the morning. Josie and Fletcher are obliterated with alcohol. "How're we goin to get home?" Josie sputters.

"Don't worry about it," Fletcher grunts. "Nothing bad ever happens to drunks."

"Yeah, right," Josie says.

They take turns driving home. Fletcher has a go at it until the rain and double vision become too pronounced; then Josie takes over. Finally they get back to his apartment and fall into a heap on the couch. "We're goin to have our first fight tomorrow," Josie mutters and passes out.

Now it's four o'clock in the morning, and it has been raining all night. Clarence is ticking away in Sally Waterford's apartment, and Josie is still sprawled on Fletcher's couch sound asleep. Outside the temperature has dropped to the thirties, making it the coldest spell San Diego has had in a long time. With the wind whipping out of Tecolote Canyon straight at him, Brewster is still asleep in the lawn chair, but in his dreams he's at Ida's house where her furnace blasts hot air at him from all sides. Viola is sitting in the corner blowing kisses, while Ida yells from the kitchen that supper is ready. "We're having stuffed tortellini," she yells.

36

Clarence wakes at 6 A.M. and keeps lying in bed for a moment, gazing at Sally, who is still asleep. He thinks she looks like a goddess, the way she's resting so regal and unruffled. Since they got so little sleep last night, he figures she'll probably stay in bed half the day. Although he hates to leave her, he knows he has to make it back to the house before Josie gets there. Without waking Sally, he jerks on his pants and takes off.

The rain is still pouring down, and it takes him longer than usual to get home, but finally he pulls into his driveway and goes inside the house. Butter is waiting for him, chomping at the bit for something to eat. Clarence fills his bowl with pure beef and watches him gobble it down. Then he brushes Butter's hair and teeth and fills the food bowl again. Clarence loves to watch Butter eat.

When the dog has finally had his fill, he starts wobbling around the house barking, going to the front door, the back door, the windows, howling.

"What the matter with you?" Clarence says. "Simmer down and come over here to me."

Reluctantly the dog stops and lumbers over to the couch. Clarence lifts him up and places him on one of the cushions, and they both lie there quietly and doze off.

"Must be nice," Josie says to Fletcher, "having all those starry-eyed young girls thinking you're some kind of guru of the theatre, the King of Drama, a wise, all-knowing sage, a Mr. Coolest-Man-on-Earth.

How many of them have you slept with? What number am I? Number one thousand?"

"What are you talking about?" Fletcher asks. They just rolled off the couch a moment ago and are standing like zombies by the refrigerator, drinking glasses of tomato juice.

"I'm talking about all those girls last night who were shaking their butts at you."

"Oh, them," Fletcher mutters. "Must have missed it. Don't remember a thing."

"That's convenient," Josie says. "Guess you blacked out, right?"

"Must have."

"You took off with that blonde, didn't you? You were standing there talking to her, and then suddenly you were both gone. What did you do? Screw her in the parking lot? Did you do it in your car, the one you drove me home in?"

Fletcher stares at Josie with a look of bewilderment. "I swear to you I didn't. I don't remember a thing."

"Sure you don't," Josie says. "It's too bad you don't remember some of your best times. Do you remember screwing me? Or did you forget that too?"

"Of course I remember. Josie, you're mistaken about what happened last night. I remember talking to the girl, but that's all. There was nothing else to it. She took one of my classes last year. She's got a boyfriend, and they're planning to get married. I swear."

"Well, where were you, then? For half an hour?"

"I don't know. I was probably just walking around talking to people."

"I didn't see you," Josie says.

"It was too crowded in there to see two feet in front of you."

Josie glares at him. "Either way, I've got to go home."

"Are you sure?"

"Yes, I'm sure."

"Wish you'd stick around," he says. "We could spend all day in bed."

"Can't," Josie says, managing a half smile.

Driving home, she notices the rain has turned back into the lazy drizzle that occurs most often in San Diego, a drizzle that mists gently against the windshield. The events of the previous night are still paramount in her mind, and she's thinking she should call off the whole thing with Fletcher. When she arrives home, Clarence and Butter are still lying on the couch asleep. Clarence prob'ly just got home too, she thinks. She goes into the kitchen and is putting on a pot of coffee when Butter wobbles in and starts nuzzling against her legs.

"What is it, Butter?"

Butter snorts.

"Do you want some breakfast?" She pours some food into his bowl, and Butter scarfs it down. Then he lumbers over to the kitchen door that leads to the garage and starts to bark.

"Is something out there?" she asks, opening the door. "Have we got a mouse?"

Butter waddles into the garage and begins sniffing at the back door that leads to the patio. Josie opens it and looks out. The rain has completely stopped now, the sun has come out, and the air smells so clean and crisp it almost hurts to breathe. She glances around the patio and sees Brewster lying in the chair, looking pale, sweaty, and swollen twice his size. His cap, having fallen off during the night, is lying on the cement, and his suitcase is close by, open and almost empty.

"What on earth?" Josie screams and runs over to him. She can see now that he isn't swollen but wearing numerous outfits of clothes.

"Daddy, get up!" she screams, as she tries to shake him awake.

Brewster opens his eyes and grins.

Josie starts to cry. "You scared me to death. Let's get you in the house."

She tries to pull him up, but he's dead weight. "Come on now. We've got to go in the house where it's warm." She looks at his sweaty face and lays her hand on his forehead. "Lord, you're on fire."

She runs back into the house and drags Clarence off the couch.

"What in the hell is wrong with you?" Clarence mutters, half asleep.

"You've got to help me get Daddy in here," she says. "He's out there on the patio froze to death."

Fully awake now, Clarence runs outside and stands over the lawn chair, staring in disbelief.

Brewster looks up at him and smiles. He tries to say something, but can't. It takes all his effort just to take a breath.

Clarence pulls him up, puts one of Brewster's arms around his shoulder and the other around Josie's. They drag him into the house and lay him on the couch. Josie spreads blankets over him and puts on a pot of chicken soup. "We'll have you running around like a teenager before the day is out," she mutters to herself as she stirs the pot.

Brewster sees them walking back and forth, but they look blurry as though he's viewing them through dirty water. He feels like fainting, and his heart is beating a mile a minute from working so hard to keep him breathing. He wishes he could just go to sleep.

When Clarence hunkers by him and tries to get him to drink some water, Brewster shakes his head, no. Josie hunts through the medicine cabinet until she finds the thermometer. She sticks it into Brewster's mouth, tells him to keep his lips closed, and waits. His temperature is 104 degrees, and his rattling breath is more shallow than ever.

"We've got to get him to a hospital," she tells Clarence, crying. "He's not getting any air." They stand there a minute staring at each other, then lift Brewster up, drag him to the car, and go.

Later at Sharp Memorial Hospital, a doctor tells them that Brewster has pneumonia.

"Will he be all right?" Josie asks.

"I can't promise you that," the doctor says. "I will say, though, that he's getting the best care possible. He strikes me as a pretty stubborn man. That will help."

Josie smiles between her tears. "He's stubborn all right."

The doctor leaves, and they sit beside Brewster's bed, watching him sleep. "Let's get some coffee," Clarence says. "He don't even know we're here." He leads her to the cafeteria, where they sit down at a table. "I'll get us something to eat. Be right back." When he returns, he's carrying two hamburgers and two orders of French fries.

Josie stares at him. "Have you gone off your diet?"

Clarence blushes. "I got a craving for meat."

After the meal, they drink Cokes and coffee and glance at each other nervously. "Someday real soon we're goin to have to talk about the reason neither one of us was home," Josie says. "But let's not talk about it right now."

"What do you mean?" Clarence asks.

Josie sighs. "Why don't you just admit we need to talk?"

Clarence turns away from her as though he just heard someone behind him call his name, but Josie knows nothing is back there but his own inability to face their problems.

"Well?" she says.

"Just let me know when you're ready," Clarence mutters.

When they return to Brewster's room, he's still lying there with his eyes closed. Josie keeps trying to talk to him, but all he can muster is a slight smile. He looks so pale, so small and fragile. She takes hold of his hand and squeezes, unable to imagine a world without Brewster Clay, and if there could be such a world, she's not sure she wants to be part of it. Looking up at Clarence, she says, "This is my fault. If I'd come home last night, he wouldn't be in this shape."

Clarence lays his hand on her shoulder. "Don't do that, Josie. Don't get caught up in blaming yourself. All you need to be thinking about is Brewster getting well." He starts pacing the floor. "There's no point in us both being here," he finally says. "Think I'll call a cab and go home, leave you with the car. When you get tired, I can relieve you. We can take turns."

Josie nods.

When he is gone, she sits in the chair by Brewster's bed and watches him breathe. Every so often he moans or tries to turn over, but not once does he seem fully conscious or acknowledge she's there. *Cheyenne ought to be here*, she keeps saying to herself. *If she came, the surprise alone would prob'ly jar him out of sickness*. Josie closes her eyes and visualizes Brewster when he was younger and stronger, and she keeps that image in her mind until she finally dozes off.

When Clarence returns to the hospital the next day, it is already past noon. "Don't you have some finals today?" he asks Josie the minute he comes into the room.

Josie blushes. "Actually, that's one of the things we need to talk about. I'm already done with the semester." She grabs Clarence's arm. "There's something I've got to do. I've been sitting here thinking about it all night and half the day. Stay in here with Daddy a minute." She goes out to the nurses' station and says to one of the nurses, "Call Dr. Matthew Fierros and tell him to come."

"Is he one of your father's doctors?"

"Just tell him to get over here, that Josie Tolliver needs him to be here right now." Josie goes back to the room and waits with Clarence. "I think Dr. Fierros knows where Cheyenne is," she tells Clarence. "Just wait with me cause when he gets here, I'm goin to make him take me to her. I'm goin to drag her butt here."

A few minutes later, a nurse informs Josie that Dr. Fierros is engaged in surgery and can't come until that evening. So it isn't until nearly six o'clock that Josie finally confronts him in the hall outside Brewster's room.

"You know where Cheyenne is," she says, narrowing her eyes. "Don't bother denying it. Daddy is in that room, and he might be close to drawing his last breath. Take me to her right now. If you don't, I swear to God I don't know what kind of fit I'll throw."

Dr. Fierros sighs, remembering the salsa Josie dumped on his new gray suit in front of at least a dozen people at Casa de Bandini, and she did it for practically no reason. He can't fathom the kind of scene she might create under these circumstances. "Okay," he says, "but I don't know if she'll be able to come."

"Why not?"

"She's been on a drinking binge. She does that sometimes. But I threw out all the liquor this morning, so maybe . . ."

"If she's drunk, we'll sober her up."

"Yes, but you don't know how . . ." He stands there staring at Josie for a moment, then says, "Okay, okay, let's go."

Josie pokes her head into Brewster's room and says to Clarence, "Stay here until I get back. I won't be long."

A few minutes later she's in Dr. Fierros's small red sports car speeding toward La Jolla. "So she's been with you this whole time. Thanks for letting me know."

"She wouldn't agree for me to tell you," he says.

They turn into an upscale residential neighborhood, and several minutes later they pull into the driveway of a white Spanish-style home with a red tile roof. The garage door rolls up automatically, and they drive inside. "She's going to kill me for this," he says. "She didn't want you to know where she was."

The minute they enter the house, they are hit by a volley of loud music. "Sounds as if she's managed to buy some more booze," Dr. Fierros says.

In the living room, they find Cheyenne sitting on the floor, seemingly engrossed in the glass she's drinking from. Looking up at Josie, a sardonic smile spreads across her face. "Well, look what the cat drug in," she says in a slurred voice. "It appears I've been caught again. I'm always getting chased, found out. How did you do it, Josie? No doubt you had help from the good doctor. Are you happy now? Why don't you try living your own life sometime?"

Josie stands there, thinking how different Cheyenne is now than she was on that day in the campground. It's a 180-degree switch in personality, the same switch that often occurred during their childhood. "Daddy came out here," she says, "and he's sick. In the hospital. I thought if he could see you, he might get better. He's got pneumonia."

A tinge of fear shows in Cheyenne's eyes—but then she grins and says, "My being there wouldn't help him one way or the other. Everybody dies. The only thing you can depend on is that when it happens, you'll die alone. Go back to your dull little world, Josie. Play nursemaid to your heart's content. Just keep me out of it."

Now Josie sees nothing in Cheyenne's eyes, no feeling at all, unless a needless smirk of defiance counts as emotion. It's as if she'd told her the time of day instead of telling her that Brewster has pneumonia. "You always act like nothing matters to you, but when I told you about Mommy dying, you . . ."

Cheyenne's smirk grows in intensity. "I was putting on a show that day, trying to win you over so you'd stop asking me boring questions about why I never once called home in seventeen years. By the way, I didn't call because I didn't want to hear your mealy-mouthed little voice." She studies Josie's face closely, as if hoping to find tears forming in her eyes. "I hope you're not goin to start boo-hooing."

Josie realizes in that moment that the awe she has felt for her sister since they were children is vanishing completely—going, going, gone—like the tail end of a behind-schedule train. "Maybe your little crying jag at the campground was a lie," she says to her, "but then again, maybe it was the truth and what you're saying today is a lie. That's what you like, right? You like to keep people unsure of how you feel. It's the way you put the hooks in. Kept me hooked for years, but you know what? I'm done with it. You prob'ly think you're a good actor, but you're not. Acting and lying ain't the same thing. A good actor feels the part she's playing, becomes the character. You're just a shitty-assed liar." Josie turns to Dr. Fierros, who is leaning against the wall with his head lowered. "Would you take me back to the hospital?"

He nods.

She looks again at Cheyenne. "You are a pretty sad sight, but you ain't worth crying over."

Cheyenne shrugs and pours herself another drink.

On the ride back, Josie doesn't say a word. She wishes she'd never left Brewster's side. She wonders how long she's been gone. An hour? A lot can happen in an hour.

As they pull into the parking lot, Dr. Fierros turns to her and says, "Cheyenne has problems too. She needs to have more surgery, but she refuses. She'll die if she doesn't . . ."

Josie barely comprehends what he's saying. He drops her in front of the lobby entrance, says, "I hope things work out," and drives away.

When she enters the hospital room, Clarence is pacing the floor. "God, I'm glad you come back. He ain't doing too good, Josie. He's . . . Is Cheyenne here?"

"No," Josie whispers, and afraid Brewster might be able to hear her, she says, "She wasn't there. She'd already left."

Brewster watches them through the shadowy slits between his eyelashes. He tries to smile but his mouth won't move, tries to open his eyes to no avail. I can't die yet, he's thinking. I didn't even get to visit with Josie, and I was hoping to see Cheyenne again. Hell, I don't even know how I feel about Viola yet. Wonder where I'll go if I die. Will Dora be there? Wonder if she's still sad. He remembers the smile on her face just before she died, how she'd looked toward the ceiling and said, "I see the prettiest little stars." Them stars must of made her happy, he thinks. Suddenly Ed Gibbs pops into his mind. Reckon he'll be there? I know one thing, he thinks. If the afterlife has a courthouse, Ed'll be sitting on the front steps.

Josie walks over to the bed, leans down, and kisses Brewster on the cheek.

Wanting to tell her she'll be fine no matter what happens, Brewster strains with all his might to form the words, but he can't. He manages to open his eyes and tries passing words to her with a look.

"Daddy?" Josie says. She turns to Clarence. "Something's happening. Run and get the nurse in here right now."

Seconds later several nurses and a doctor rush into the room, wheeling a machine, and force Clarence and Josie out into the hall, where they hold on to each other and pace back and forth in front of Brewster's room. Fifteen minutes later, a doctor steps out and says, "He's back, but it will be touch and go for the next few days."

That night Josie and Clarence sit in chairs by Brewster's bed and watch him sleep. Traveling back through the years, Josie remembers when Brewster taught her how to fish on the riverbank outside of Pick, recalls the songs he sang to her on his old guitar—"South of the Border" and "Filipino Baby," among countless others, but mostly she thinks about the smile that always spreads across his face when she walks through the door.

Josie glances around at Clarence. "Glad you're here," she whispers.

"You ought to try to get some sleep." He drapes his arm around her shoulder, and they sit like that throughout the night.

37

For the next five days Brewster teeters between life and death, and Josie has been spending her nights sleeping in a chair by his bed and her days sitting in the same chair, dozing and reading books. Clarence brings her changes of clothes, and she showers in the bathroom in Brewster's room. This morning she drove to a bookstore and bought a copy of Castaneda's latest book, *The Second Ring of Power.* Now pulling her chair close by Brewster's bed, she begins to read and soon discovers that apparently when don Juan jumped into the abyss at the end of *Tales of Power,* he ceased to exist in the ordinary world. This is not something she wanted to learn. She'd thought he would jump back out of the abyss. Glaring at the book, Josie closes it, not wanting to read about don Juan's disciples. She's only interested in the old man right now, wants him to be alive.

She looks over at Brewster, lying so still in bed, breathing with difficulty, the tube of oxygen hooked in his nostrils, and realizes she needs a break. Craving coffee, she goes down to the cafeteria and drinks several cups. When she returns half an hour later, a couple of nurses are hovering over her father's bed.

"What is it?" Josie asks, panicking.

"He's awake," one of the nurses says. "He's been asking for you and for someone named Viola."

Josie runs to his bed and stares into his tired black eyes. "Daddy, how do you feel?"

"With my hands," Brewster says, grinning.

Laughing, she wants to throw her arms around him, but she's

afraid of crushing his fragile frame. The rest of the day he falls in and out of sleep, but a slight tinge of color begins spreading on his ashen face, and Josie finally breathes a sigh of relief.

That night she goes home for the first time since Brewster has been in the hospital and finds that in her absence Clarence bought furniture for the empty bedroom. She stretches out on the new bed and falls into a deeper sleep than she's had in a week. The next morning Clarence has already gone to work when Josie wakes. She keeps lying in bed, too tired to move, and doesn't stumble into the kitchen until eleven o'clock. She's having her first cup of coffee when Fletcher calls.

"Where have you been?" he asks.

"How did you get my number?"

"Mary Bingham gave it to me. Why haven't you been answering your phone? Why did you miss the Shakespeare class this week?"

Josie tells him about Brewster.

"Sorry about your dad, but do you think you could meet me for lunch? I really need to talk to you."

"Fraid I can't. I'll be leaving for the hospital in a few minutes." She'd rather not deal with Fletcher right now. When she pictures him in her mind, she doesn't see anything but trouble, a tired whiny sort of trouble.

"I could meet you in the hospital cafeteria," he persists. "How about twelve-thirty?"

"Fine," she says, noticing a desperate tinge to his voice. She's afraid if she doesn't agree to the lunch, he'll make an unannounced visit to Brewster's room.

When Josie drives to the hospital, she goes directly to the cafeteria. Fletcher is already there, sitting at a table for two. She buys a cup of coffee and joins him.

"What did you want to talk to me about?" she asks as she sits opposite him.

His dark brown eyes stare deeply into hers. "What's wrong, Josie? You act as if nothing ever happened between us."

"Maybe nothing did. I get the feeling I'm not a special case, that you've been pretty close to a lot of your students."

"That's not true."

"Either way, I don't want to argue about it right now."

Fletcher's eyes twinkle with excitement. "Good, because I don't want to argue either. Actually, I've got a proposition for you. The Nelson Theatre is auditioning for a production of *The Children's Hour*. They've already cast Martha, but Karen is still up for grabs. You'd be perfect in that role. The audition is tomorrow. Rehearsals will begin in a couple of weeks."

Josie looks at him strangely. "I'm not ready for something like that. Besides, I can't be in a play right now. When Daddy gets out of the hospital, he'll be staying at my house till he's completely well. I'll be taking care of him."

"Can't you audition anyway? It would be good experience."

Josie glares at him. "What would be the point? I actually might get the part, and then I'd have to turn it down."

Fletcher stirs his coffee with a swizzle stick, looks down at the table. "Can't you at least audition as a personal favor to me?"

Josie stares at him suspiciously. "Why?"

Fletcher strokes his beard and looks away from her. "It's that asshole in the drama department at State, Ron Beasley. We were having a few drinks the other night and . . . He thinks his prize student has it in the bag. I just want to prove him wrong. Actually, I made a bet with him that you'd get the part."

"A bet?"

Fletcher blushes slightly. "Why not? I know you'll get it. Once the part is yours, just tell the director that your father has become ill and you have to take care of him. There'll be no harm done. They'll simply give the part to the other girl, but at least I will have won the bet."

Josie feels something akin to pity for him as she stands up and says, "I have to go."

Fletcher jumps up and grabs her arm. "Don't leave me in the lurch, Josie, not after all I've done for you."

"I'm not so sure you did that much," she says, but even as she's saying it, she knows he gave her encouragement when she needed it most. "Did you ever consider that I might *not* get the part?" she says. "How would you feel if I caused you to lose your bet?"

"That won't happen."

"I'll have to think about this," she says. Leaving him there, she walks to the elevator. I should have told him to go to hell, she's thinking on the ride to the third floor.

When she enters Brewster's room, he's lying there awake and smiling. They talk for a couple of hours. He tells her how frustrating it was when he arrived at her house and no one was home, tells her about peeping through a window and seeing her ugly dog. He has no recollection of the next morning when she found him on the patio. He talks about Viola and says his close call with death has made him realize what's really important. He can't wait to get back to her, he says to Josie. "I still ain't too old to cut the mustard."

Amazed at his resilience, she beams with pride. She wants to tell him about everything that has happened to her since she left Pick, but she figures it can wait. When Brewster finally tires of talking and falls asleep, she sits there thinking about the favor Fletcher asked of her. Maybe I ought to do it, she thinks. At least it would show me whether or not I can be competitive, and Fletcher's right about one thing: If I win and have to turn it down, no real harm will be done. They'll just give the part to the runner-up. After going back and forth on the decision several times, she finally calls him and says she'll go through with it.

Fletcher accompanies Josie to the audition and stands just inside the door, assessing her every move as she walks onto the stage. Before she begins the monologue, she glances over at him, noting his barely disguised panic, his threatening smile. Josie is shaking with fear until she begins speaking and turns into someone else.

Later, Fletcher tells her he's sure she got the part, but that evening the theatre calls her to say they haven't made a decision and that she is to return for another audition the next day. "I'm surprised I even got a callback," she tells Fletcher on the phone.

"I am too. I thought they'd give you the part immediately. The other girl can't act. All she can do is rely on tricks and overdone facial expressions."

The next day, Fletcher in tow, Josie returns for the second audition and clinches the deal. When she walks on stage, electricity fills the air around her. After she speaks the last word of the monologue, she glances at the director and is sure the part is hers. Later, he merely confirms what she already knows.

"Let's celebrate," Fletcher says as they're walking out of the theatre. "Go for a drink."

Josie doesn't think it's a good idea. She can tell he's already been drinking, that he has probably been drinking since he got up this morning. Still, she's so overcome by her success that she really does want to celebrate. "I ought to get back to the hospital. I feel like I've been neglecting Daddy. And I need to call the director and tell him I can't do the play. This little deal will prob'ly give me a bad name around here. I prob'ly won't ever be able to land a part again."

"Not when you tell him your dad is ill and that you have to take care of him. Come on, let's just have one drink to celebrate and then you can go."

With mixed feelings, Josie agrees, and they end up at a small bar on Fourth Street, taking a booth at the far end of the room. Fletcher sits there for a moment, staring into her eyes.

"What?" she asks. "You're making me nervous."

"Usually people make mistakes during their first audition. You didn't," he says.

"Yes, I did. I left out a word or two, and didn't do some of the lines the way I'd planned. My blocking was off a few times." Josie feels uncomfortable with Fletcher's compliments. Although they seem sincere, there is a slight edge to them that suggests he's accusing her of something. It's almost as if he's saying, "You're good, goddamn it. You're so fucking good you make me sick."

"I know that monologue word for word," he says, "and I didn't see you do anything that wasn't right on."

"Thanks," Josie says. She wishes she was anyplace but here.

The waitress brings them their margaritas. Fletcher downs his and orders another one in addition to a shot on the side. Josie is still working on her first. She starts listening to the music on the jukebox. An old Beatles' song is playing. She glances at the other people in the bar. The customers are mostly men who appear slightly down on their luck, who look bored or depressed or both.

"Wanta dance?" Fletcher asks.

"There's no dance floor."

"Doesn't matter. We can dance right here." He points to the floor beside the booth.

Josie can tell that Fletcher's last drink has almost pushed him over the edge, but she figures one final dance won't hurt anything. She knows it will be their last because what remains of the feeling she has for him is slipping like smoke through her fingers.

They stand and start swaying to "The Long and Winding Road." When the song ends, they sit down and Fletcher orders another shot of tequila. All at once he stands and shouts to the other customers, "I want you to all have a drink on me. I'm celebrating the amazing success of the woman with me. You'll be hearing about her pretty soon. She's the best damn actress in San Diego. Josie, stand up and take a bow." Now there is more than just a tinge of anger showing in his voice. "Looks like the little lady's shy today," Fletcher shouts, "but she isn't shy when she's on stage. No sir, she's quite the ham, comes right out of herself. She's the supreme thespian, better than Redgrave, slicker than Fonda, even outdoes Geraldine *Fucking* Page."

The somber men in the bar stare straight through him, as if he isn't there, as if they're staring through a street bum who is asking them for money.

Fletcher orders yet another shot.

"I'm leaving," Josie says.

"Don't go yet. We have to celebrate."

"You celebrate," Josie says, standing. "I'm goin to the hospital."

"You're not mad, are you?" he asks as she walks away.

At a pay phone near the restroom, she calls the director and tells him she won't be able to take the part after all. Then she walks past Fletcher's booth and steps outside.

He follows her. "Where do you think you're going?"

"As far as I can get from you. Just don't bother calling me anymore."

He grabs her arm. "You learn what you can from me and leave, is that it? Who do you think got you that audition?"

Josie sighs. "All I know is that I don't want to be around you anymore."

"Fine," he shouts, throwing up his arms. Then he disappears into the darkness of the bar.

Over the next few days, Fletcher calls Josie several times, but she keeps telling him the same thing, that she won't see him again, and the calls taper off and finally become nonexistent. He's prob'ly got himself another fresh young pupil, Josie thinks, someone else who will hang on his every word. Glad it's not me anymore. When she remembers that she was actually the director's first choice in the audition, she's amazed at her luck and begins to realize that luck wasn't the only ingredient, that she must have been pretty good to boot.

The hospital finally releases Brewster, and he returns to Josie's house to begin the recuperation process. She stays close by him, feeds him chicken soup, and they talk about the old days. Sometimes she drags out her guitar, and they sing songs. Once in a while he asks her about Cheyenne. Josie tells him she doesn't know anything about her.

One day he says, "I think more happened between you and your sister than you're saying. I don't like being left in the dark, and when you get old and sick, you'll know how I feel."

Josie blinks. "I didn't mean to . . ."

Brewster brushes his hands aside. "I know you didn't. But I wish for once you'd tell me what's goin on. Dora never would tell me anything either. Seems like half the time I didn't have a inkling what was goin on in my own house."

"Okay. We had a falling out. Are you happy now?"

"No, but at least I know the truth. Why did you fall out?"

"Does it really matter what set it off this time? You know we hardly ever got along."

Brewster sighs. "Used to be that even when the two of you fell out, you still tagged around after her like she was the ring-tailed leader."

"Well, I guess you could say she's not my hero anymore."

Brewster grins. "That's prob'ly for the best. The thing is, sometimes people pay more attention to their heroes than they do to theirselves."

"You're right about that," she says.

Viola calls several times a week, and when Brewster talks to her, he's as giddy as a teenager. Josie loves hearing him sound so hopeful and alive. When he's well enough to get out of the house, she takes him to the beach, and they fish off the pier.

As they stare out at the ocean, Josie says, "Look at it, Daddy. It's just sitting there, begging to be crossed."

Brewster smiles. "Well, if you ever decide to cross a ocean, I hope it's the Atlantic and that you stop by Torquay, England. Real pretty little town. We stayed there a while before we was shipped over to Normandy for that big invasion."

Josie tells him she'll check it out if she ever gets to England.

Brewster chuckles. "Speaking of traveling, I'm about ready to head back to old KY."

"Are you sure you're up to it?"

"Can't wait to get back to that big woman."

On the day of his departure, it's Josie who drives him to the airport. They ride in silence until Brewster says, "Do you ever miss Kentucky?"

"All the time, but looks like I've got started down a different road."

"So when're you and Clarence goin to split up?"

Josie glances around at him and smiles, amazed at how much he knows without being told. "Pretty soon. Just make sure you tell Ida that me and Clarence still care about each other. I don't want her to think we're all bitter."

When Brewster gets on the plane, Josie stands at the window, watching as it carries him back to Viola and the new life he's creating for himself. She wonders if she'll ever be as cocksure as Brewster, as confident of who she is and where she wants to be.

38

Josie and Clarence don't talk about the night that Brewster arrived in San Diego until he has gone back to Kentucky.

"Clarence, I've made us some tea," Josie says one morning. "I think it's time we talked."

Clarence, who is pouring Butter's food, glances up at her as if he's been called to active duty. He puts away the bag of dog food and sits with her on the couch.

As he drinks his tea and Butter sits in a corner snorting, Josie says, "I didn't really stay with Mary Bingham the night that Daddy came out here. I was with my teacher, Fletcher Wayne. It's not a very interesting story, just one of those teacher/student flings. Anyway, that's where I was. Where were you?"

Clarence looks down at his cup, squirming from the discomfort of the subject at hand. "What do you mean, flings? You don't like him anymore?"

Josie sighs. "Not really." She can tell he wishes she was head-over-heels in love with somebody so he'd be off the hook. She decides to let him off. "He's not the only man I've gone out with. I had a little fling with someone in Sage, too."

Clarence glares at her accusingly. "Who? That Johnny guy?"

Josie's mouth drops open. "How did you know about him?" Just the sound of Johnny Walker's name causes her temperature to rise and her breath to come in short gasps.

"I didn't know, but you sure used to talk about him a lot."

"I talked about him?"

"Yeah, almost every night. You'd say things like, 'Johnny came by the bar today and he said, 'blah, blah, blah,' and you'd get all giggly and stuff."

Josie smiles. "I can't believe I did that."

"Well, you did."

"Must have been stupid. Anyway, where were you that night, Clarence?"

He blushes and looks away. "I was just out, you know."

"No, I don't know. Tell me."

"I was with this woman, Sally. We're just friends."

"Friends?"

"Yeah. She worries me to death. Drives me crazy."

Josie smiles. "That's what you used to say about me when we first started goin out. Said I worried you to death, that I drove you crazy."

Clarence turns red as a beet. "You still do. Anyway, I don't see any point in talking about this. There's nothing to say."

"Yes there is. I just want you to know that I'm going to start looking for work tomorrow. As soon as I get a job and save enough money, I'll get out and find a apartment."

"You don't have to do that," he says. "I can give you the money to rent a apartment."

"I don't want to do it that way. I'd rather do this all on my own. I know it means that we have to stay together a while longer, but I don't see how a month or two more can hurt."

The next day Josie gets up early, goes to an employment agency, and lands herself a job. She'll be starting next week, working for the Econo-Health Insurance Company, entering insurance claims into a computer. Clarence is ecstatic, bowled over by the pay and benefits she'll receive. Josie isn't half as excited. Although she realizes she has no chance of really living until she gets out on her own, she worries that she may be sinking into a worse trap—the trap of going to work, coming home, and going to work again.

The Econo-Health Insurance Company's offices take up three floors of the wood-and-glass building in Mission Valley where Josie works. Her particular department is located on the second floor. Holding nothing but a cathode-ray tube, a CRT, her desk is one of three that are positioned in a pinwheel around a ceiling-to-floor pole that contains electrical outlets. For eight hours each day, she mindlessly enters insurance claims into the computer, and after her first week of employment there, she's already bored to death.

In '78, the dress code is casual at Econo-Health. A person can wear just about anything she wants to wear. Josie and a few of the other women in their late twenties wear jeans, T-shirts, and sandals, but most of the younger women, who are either fresh out of high school or dropouts from college, dress as if they're going to a dance club. They wear heels, black hose, and silky dresses, and they're constantly talking about the discos they went to the night before. Their faces have so much makeup you could scrape it off with a knife. They dream about buying luxury cars and landing boyfriends with money. They talk about going to night school and taking classes in computer programming. Computers are the future, they say.

"I used to dream of hitchhiking across the United States," Josie complains one day to a couple of the women who, like her, are approaching the age of thirty. "My heroes were hobos and old men who sang the blues. What's wrong with people? Looks like I came to California ten years too late. I should have moved out here in the sixties."

The jeans-clad women shake their heads and sigh. "Yeah, it was great back then," one says. "We used to make candles and sell them for nickels and dimes at the Ocean Beach pier. We hitchhiked to San Francisco all the time, camping out along the way. Everyone was always giving you pot. Never had to buy any . . . And the music. . . . I hate this goddamned disco crap."

"I came out here from Illinois with my boyfriend, Bobby," the other woman says. "He had a brother who lived in Linda Vista. We rolled up in our dilapidated Volkswagen van and just sat there staring at the house his brother lived in. It was painted with abstract designs in pink and turquoise blue. There were dozens of sunflowers six or seven feet tall growing in the yard. All at once this girl stepped out of the house. She had strawberry blond hair that hung in ringlets down to her waist, and she was wearing a granny dress. Remember granny dresses? She came wading through those sunflowers to greet us, bees and butterflies swirling around her. It was like something out of a fairy tale. She turned out to be Bobby's brother's girlfriend, and her name was—get this—Jenny Weed. Bobby's brother is a marketing special- ist now, and I don't know for sure where Jenny is. She left town about five years ago. The last we heard she was meandering up the coast toward Eugene, Oregon."

"Yeah, well, maybe I ought to take off somewhere," Josie says. Then she and the two women turn back to their cathode-ray tubes and resume entering insurance claims.

Josie has now been at Econo-Health for almost two months and has enough money saved to start looking for an apartment. Lately Clarence has been spending an increasing number of evenings with Sally, and sometimes he doesn't come home at all. This evening when Josie returns home, paycheck in hand, Clarence isn't there. Sagging to the couch, she kicks off her shoes and stares at the walls. Hearing the shuffle of feet, she looks down the hall and sees Butter come wobbling into the room. He stands in front of her looking pitiful until she finally reaches down and lifts him up to her lap. She's stroking the dog's head when she gets the call from Dr. Fierros.

"Cheyenne's gone again," he says.

Since Brewster's illness, Josie has managed, for the most part, to put Cheyenne out of her mind. Now here she is again. "Figures," Josie says, rolling her eyes. "Don't tell me you're surprised."

"She left a couple of days ago without saying good-bye. I just want to say that if you ever see her again, if she gets in contact with you, try to get her to go to a doctor." His voice breaks. "She's dying, Josie."

It hits her for the first time that what Dr. Fierros has told her about Cheyenne's condition isn't a weird dream, that it's real. "Why won't she let anyone operate on her?"

"She says she's spent too much time in hospitals, that she won't step inside an operating room again."

Josie doesn't know what to say.

"Try to find her, Josie."

"Sorry, can't do that."

"Don't give up on her."

Josie is suddenly aware of how deeply the doctor cares for Cheyenne. She figures he must love her immensely to put up with her erratic entrances and exits. "I appreciate what you're trying to do," she tells him, "but I don't intend to look for her anymore."

She hangs up the phone and paces back and forth, thinking that Cheyenne may be a asshole but at least she does whatever the hell she wants. "That's more than I can say for myself," Josie mutters.

She remembers the day of the callback audition, looking across the booth at Fletcher in that little bar on Fourth Street, remembers the anger in his eyes, anger that was put there because he wasn't doing the thing he most wanted to do—act. She sees herself moving into an apartment and working the rest of her life at Econo-Health, never remarrying, not even dating, never auditioning for another part in a play, never having anything but thousands of long dry days stretching endlessly before her. I've got to do something, she thinks. It hits her that she has no ties, that there's nothing to stop her from doing whatever comes to mind. The first thing that comes to mind is Sage, Arizona.

Maybe I could stop down in Tucson and audition at that little theatre, she thinks. Maybe I could get my old job back at Don Juan's. She tries to conjure a picture of Bobby Swanson and Lily Venus being married, but it's hard to see. Then Venus Lily pops into her mind, causing a smile to sprout on her face. She sees Matt Chandler playing pool in the back room, sees Johnny Walker tip his hat as he walks through the front door. She wonders what Sage will be like without him, if she'll still like the town as much.

The next day, she withdraws her savings, returns home, strolls into her bedroom, and starts packing. She's almost finished when Clarence walks into the house.

He hears her in the bedroom and peeps in. "Hey, what're you doing? Did you find a apartment or something?"

"No." She closes the lid of her suitcase. "I'm goin back to Sage, Clarence."

He looks bewildered. "Sage? What do you want to go there for? When did you decide this?"

"Last night."

Josie can see Clarence's cheek muscles move around and around as he starts grinding his teeth. "Well, you can't go. How's that? I ain't about to let you. You don't even have a job over there, don't have a place to live. Think about all the great benefits you've got at Econo-Health, the vacation time, the pay. They ain't no way you can leave that."

"Yes, there is," Josie says. "I'll find a job and a apartment. No big deal. Everything is goin great for you over here, Clarence. You love your job. Got your dog, your girlfriend. I don't have a thing. I'm goin back to the place where I was happy."

Clarence scoffs. "I thought you got dissatisfied over there. It was your idea to leave."

"I did get dissatisfied from time to time but not half as dissatisfied as I've been here. When I finish packing, I'm leaving. Maybe I'll come back next weekend to pick up the rest of my things. Actually it might take a couple of trips."

Clarence stomps off down the hall. After Josie has finished carrying the last of her essentials to the car, she meanders out to the back-yard and stares at the boats on Mission Bay. Feeling something wet brush against her ankles, she looks down and finds Butter standing at her feet, panting. "Hello, there. Did you come to say good-bye?"

Butter snorts.

She looks back at the bay. "This is such a pretty place, Butter. I don't think I've ever seen anything to compare with it. Maybe I don't fit into pretty places, though. Maybe I need something a little uncouth, a little raw, a little wild and unsettled."

Staring at her while she talks, Butter huffs and puffs as if commiserating.

Clarence steps out of the garage and stands beside her as she looks out at the water. "Great view, ain't it? Don't see how you could leave it. I'll be worried to death about you."

She reaches down to pet Butter, who stands quietly and lets her stroke his head. He doesn't try to bite her hand, doesn't even snort. "Take care of this old dog, Clarence," Josie says.

"I will."

"Well, I'd better be goin. See you." Josie starts walking away.

Clarence grabs her arm, then looks away, embarrassed. "See you later," he says.

Josie walks through the garage and out to the driveway, jumps into her car, and drives off.

39

Midway between San Diego and Yuma, evening shadows fall on distant mountains, giving them the purple cast that is advertised in countless songs about the West. Josie is on a stretch of road where there is nothing—no houses, no service stations, no sign of civilization other than carloads of people whizzing by almost as though they're running for their lives. People drive across such landscapes in a hurry because how would it feel if their cars broke down and they found themselves stranded in a dark desert at night with only the moon to guide them, with hardly a sound other than the yipping of coyotes dancing around a fresh kill? Don Juan territory, Josie thinks, where shadows run the show, a place of sunsets and sage, of crows and coyotes, of sorcerers and strange dreams. *God, I'm glad I'm back.*

She is so excited by her circumstance—to be finally driving toward something other than work or home—that she can hardly sit behind the wheel. She takes a bottle of Old Bushmills out of a bag beside her and takes a token sip. Then she turns on her cassette player, remembering how she used to dream of escaping to the North with its biting wind, snow, and ice, its deadly seduction. She begins listening to the Stones, all the while thinking how different her present reality is from that old dream. Now that her escape is actually at hand, she's driving toward one of the hottest states in the country, a place where she may finally begin to live.

It is one o'clock in the morning when she begins to see the lights of Tucson. She checks into the first motel she sees, but finding it impossible to sleep, she paces the floor, thinking about where she's been and where she might be going. At dawn she lies down and sleeps until the afternoon.

When she wakes, she gets dressed and finds the Childress Theatre, the one she used to read about in the Tucson paper. She marches inside and asks the manager when they're auditioning next. He tells her they're in the process of casting a play right now—*Look Back in Anger,* to be exact—and that she can come tomorrow morning at nine o'clock for an audition.

"One of my favorites," she says, smiling.

Back at the motel, she chooses a monologue and stands in front of the mirror practicing the rest of the evening and half the night. The next day she performs like someone on fire, but when the audition is over, she returns to her room, tormented by doubts and insecurities. To make matters worse, the director doesn't call her with the news until late that afternoon.

"Rehearsals start next week," he says when he calls. "Be there."

After a few incoherent exclamations, she hangs up and walks over to the mirror. "I guess this is what can happen when you try," she whispers to her reflection. For several moments, she strolls around the room, smiling as if she's been told an inside joke. Then she calls Brewster.

"Daddy, you'll never believe what I've done."

Brewster grins. "What?"

"I've left Clarence, and I'm sitting in a hotel in Tucson right this minute. Not only that, but I'm goin to be in a play."

"Sounds like you've been busy."

"Can't talk long. I'm goin to Sage. That's where I'll be living. How's Viola?"

"Fine. Actually she's here right now. We've been playing gin rummy." He reaches out and tweaks Viola's nose. Viola giggles.

"That's great," Josie says.

After telling him good-bye, she takes a shower and gets dressed, checks out of the motel, and drives toward Sage. Arriving in town just as the sun is setting, she parks by the old adobe mansion and stares out toward the horizon. The sky is blood red as the sun gradually descends beyond her view. It's the first week in March, and there's a chill in the air. She has never been in Sage this early in the spring. It occurs to her that last year at this time, she was still in Pick, dealing with the effects of the ad she'd put in the paper. Josie pulls her sweater a little closer to her chin, waits until the evening shadows take over, then she starts driving toward Don Juan's.

As she goes up the narrow road to the bar, she is hit with a flood of memories of Johnny Walker. She brings to mind that first day when he sneaked up behind her as she was playing pool, remembers the shack by the San Pedro. She looks around the parking lot, hoping that through some weird twist of fate she'll spot his truck, but it isn't there. She gets out of her car and walks up to the scarred and battered door. From inside she hears loud talking and laughter, hears Venus Lily's gruff dictatorial voice. When she steps through the door, the first thing she notices is the change in clientele. She doesn't see a single tramp miner, and from their appearance Josie would guess the new customers to be members of the artists' colony.

When Venus Lily spots Josie, she runs from behind the bar and grabs her around the neck. "Look who's here!" she yells. The customers turn around, but the only one who recognizes Josie is Mick Balinski, whom she had met the night Johnny took her to the colony.

He grins at her and waves.

"Where is everybody?" Josie asks. "I don't see hardly anyone I know."

"Didn't I tell you, honey? That job ran out a while ago. The tramp miners are long gone." Venus grabs hold of Josie again. "Well, don't stand here all night. Have a seat," she says, and pulls her over to a barstool.

Someone yells for a beer and Venus hurries down to the other end of the bar. Josie looks around at the dark walls and smoky atmosphere of Don Juan's. Funny, she's thinking, you leave a place for eight months and just about everyone disappears. It's as if certain people are meant to be in a group at certain times, and it takes the whole bunch to hold things together—one person leaves and it all falls apart. "Where's Bobby Swanson?" she asks Venus when she returns.

"Since him and Lily got married, neither one of them show up around here much."

"Did they move out of town?"

"No, they still live here. They just don't come around. Lily's turned into a homemaker from hell. Sits around reading *Better Homes and Gardens* all the time, and Bobby's just about stopped drinking."

Venus goes back to her bartending duties, and Josie gets into a conversation with an artist who says she doesn't paint anything but yuccas. She says she doesn't need to paint anything else, that everything worth painting can be found in the yucca plant. Josie is fascinated by that concept—that you can explore the world, maybe even the universe, in just one thing. Maybe that's what Ida is doing while she crochets all those afghans, she thinks.

Later, as Mick Balinski is walking out of the bar, he stops by and taps Josie on the shoulder. "Heard from Johnny lately?" he asks.

Josie manages a smile. "Nope. Have you?"

"Not a word since he left." Mick leans in closer to her. "He told me why you broke up. I would never have brought Ramona's name up if I'd known. It really wasn't that serious between them. I had no idea you were sisters."

"No one did," Josie says. "It ain't your fault we broke up. Look, I don't want to talk about it right now, okay?"

Mick looks as if he wants to tell her something else but thinks better of it. "Well, don't be a stranger. Feel free to come out to some of our shows." He grins and walks away.

It isn't until the bar clears out at midnight that Josie and Venus start talking in earnest.

"Are you visiting or have you moved back?" Venus asks.

"I reckon I've moved back," Josie says. "I'm acting now. Got a part in a theatre in Tucson."

Venus's eyes grow as big as golf balls. "Really? My God, an actress?"

"Don't guess you need any help now that most of the miners have gone," Josie says.

"Actually, I don't. I'm just running two shifts now. Don't open up weekdays until about noon, weekends at ten in the morning. Judy's still working for me. You said you knew her, right? Used to work at Hudson's? You can probably find something else. You could get a job in Tucson for sure—work there and live here." She narrows her eyes. "So you've left Clarence for good?"

"Yeah," Josie says. She pauses, then adds, "Don't guess Johnny has come back yet."

"Nope," Venus says, "but the last time I talked to him he said he really missed his ranch. I've got a feeling he'll be back." Suddenly Venus grabs her head. "Oh, Lord, I almost forgot to tell you. She's here. Your sister is in Sage right now."

Josie slowly sits her glass on the bar. "She's what?"

"Showed up a few days ago. She's staying out there in the artists' colony. She's stopped by the bar a couple of times. I'm surprised she didn't come tonight."

Josie rolls her eyes, feeling as if someone just told her she had to sit in on three consecutive accounting classes. "How long's she staying?"

Venus grins. "Honey, all I can tell you is that she's here."

Josie takes another drink. "Fuck."

Venus narrows her eyes. "I thought you'd be happy she was here."

Josie glares at her. "Well, I'm not."

"I take it you finally caught up with her and it didn't go too well."

"You could say that." Josie thinks for a minute and says, "Who cares? It's not my problem she's here. Maybe it's her problem."

Venus lights a cigarette, pours Josie another glass of beer. "Where're you staying tonight?"

Josie looks around, hoping to get a whiff of don Juan or at least his ghost, but neither seems to be around. "I thought maybe I'd get a room down at the Hot L."

Venus grins. "Not if I have anything to say about it. You can stay with me. That little house is awfully big and empty now that Lily's gone. You can stay in her room tonight. Actually you can stay there as long as you want."

Josie smiles. "Thanks, Venus. I'm sure glad you didn't take off like one of those tramp miners. It's good to know that at least something hasn't changed."

Venus closes the bar, and they walk to their cars. Josie stops for a moment to take in a deep breath. The air is crisp and cool enough that when you exhale, little puffs of mist escape into the night. She looks out past the bar in the direction of Venus's house and feels as if she has come home. "Are you sure you don't mind me staying at your house tonight?"

"Wouldn't hear of nothing else," Venus says. She touches Josie's shoulder. "Do you want me to call Johnny and tell him you're here? It might speed him up a little in coming back."

Josie sighs. "No. I don't want him to come back because of me. If we were to see each other again, things might not be the same, and I don't want to feel obligated. Not that I won't be happy if he shows up on his own."

Venus nods, and both women look off into the darkness as a lone coyote begins howling at the moon.

"God, this place is something," Josie says.

40

Venus is up cooking breakfast, perking coffee, but Josie doesn't budge. She's still in bed, thinking about all the things she needs to do. She needs go to Tucson and find a job, for one thing, and she knows that any *sensible* person would look for an apartment down there, so they wouldn't have to drive the thirty-five miles to Sage after a long day of working and a night of acting in a play. I'm not sensible, though, Josie thinks, and she peeps out the window at the rugged high-desert terrain.

Gradually, she decides she isn't going to do anything today except lounge around, or maybe—if the mood strikes her—go for a drive. She gets up, takes a shower, and joins Venus for breakfast. After the meal, Venus leaves for work, and Josie finds herself alone in the small house with nothing to do but think about the events of the past year, a year in which nothing much happened except that her whole life changed.

Although she hopes she doesn't have to be around Cheyenne every day, she realizes it wouldn't be the end of the world if they accidentally ran into each other. She no longer holds a lot of anger—she just feels that her sister belongs to a part of her life that is over. The only thing that still nags at Josie is the fig tree. Is Dan Hawkins buried there? She has asked herself that question a thousand times, and, although there have been moments when she's thought the opposite, she's pretty sure that Cheyenne didn't kill him. Cheyenne has no use for the dead, Josie thinks. She wants people to be alive so she can mess with their minds.

Still a small sliver of doubt remains. The fact that Tarantula lay under that same tree and died adds to Josie's uncertainty. After mulling things over for most of the day, she decides to find out for herself. She rummages around Venus's tool shed, comes up with a shovel, then throwing it into the back seat of her car, sets out for Tarantula's house. On the way, she stops by Hudson's grocery for some Cokes, water, and beer, and it's while she's in the store that it occurs to her that Tarantula's property may have changed hands, that some of the old woman's relations might be living there. She decides to quiz the new cashier.

"I'm not sure, but I think her house is still empty. They've been trying to find a living relative, but as far as I know they haven't had any luck," the cashier says.

It's late afternoon when Josie pulls into Tarantula's driveway, gets out of the car, walks up to the door, and knocks. No one answers. She turns the knob and finds the place locked, peeps into the windows and sees no one. She walks out to the trailer behind the house. It looks exactly as it did the day she and Clarence left.

Josie goes back to the car and takes out the shovel and a couple of Cokes, walks over to the fig tree, and starts digging. After going past the top layer of sandy soil, she hits earth so hard and crusty it feels like a bed of rock. "Jesus Christ," she mutters, "I can't dig through that." She sags to the ground and pops open a Coke. For an hour she sits there thinking about a multitude of things, most of them featuring Johnny Walker. She wonders why she dreams about him almost every night. *Is it because the thing between us was just beginning? If we had gone on a little longer, would I have realized it was a mistake?* She looks around at the growing dusk and decides that in a little while she'll walk out to that old chimney in the desert. She wants to see it again by moonlight. She's even thinking that tomorrow she might go down to the shack near the San Pedro, that she might retrace the whole affair.

Suddenly she feels someone standing behind her and turns to find Cheyenne.

"I've been looking for you," Cheyenne says.

"How did you know I was here?" Josie asks. Mostly what she feels is irritation that her daydream has been interrupted.

"The clerk at Hudson's told me you were asking about this place." Cheyenne glances at the Coke. "Can I have one?"

"I don't know that we have anything more to say to each other."

"Sure we do. I was drunk the last time we talked. I don't remember what we said."

"We said we weren't goin to talk anymore."

Cheyenne pulls off her backpack, sits down Indian-style, and pops open a Coke. "That ain't what we said. You're lying. I didn't think you liked liars."

Josie grins. "Well, maybe I was wrong. Lying's kinda fun."

"You acted like my lying was a pretty bad thing."

"Yeah, but you don't lie for fun. You lie in order to confuse and control people, the way you control Dr. Fierros, like you controlled me when we were kids."

"You don't know that for sure."

"You're right. I don't, which of course is my point."

Cheyenne rolls her eyes. "How's Daddy these days?"

"Fine."

"I guess you took care of him till he got completely well."

"Yeah, I did, and I don't regret it for a minute, because, as you know, I'm good, kind, and well-behaved . . . and, yes, pretty damned near perfect. Pleased with myself too. Don't leave that out. Real pleased with myself."

Cheyenne sighs. "I prob'ly didn't mean all the things I said that night at Matthew's house."

Instead of responding, Josie keeps looking from the disappearing sun to the full moon.

"So why're you sitting out here with a shovel, Josie?"

"Tarantula told me you killed Dan Hawkins and that she buried him under this fig tree. I came out here to dig him up, but the ground is hard. Too much work."

Cheyenne laughs. "Gave up, didn't you? Well, I guess that prob'ly means you don't think I'm guilty."

"I don't, but I do wonder why Tarantula lied about it. I also wonder why she laid down here under this particular tree to die."

Cheyenne sighs. "Who knows what was goin through her mind? Maybe this was the first place they ever fucked. Maybe she figured— God, I can't believe I'm saying this—that their love was buried here or something. All I know is that Dan is in New York, where he always wanted to go. I call him pretty regular. Want me to call him right now? Come on, let's go up to the store and call him from the phone booth."

Josie waves away the suggestion.

Cheyenne rummages around in her backpack and, holding a flashlight, writes a phone number on a piece of paper. "You just wish I'd leave, don't you?"

Josie shrugs. "I don't care one way or the other."

"Yeah, well, that's the way it happens all the time. People give up on me, and I turn up like a bad penny. The party's over, and I show up blowing whistles and waving flags." She hands the paper to Josie and says, "Here. It's Dan's number. Call him sometime."

They sit for a moment in silence, the full moon shining on their faces.

"Dr. Fierros told me you're dying," Josie says. "Said they want to operate on you, but you won't let them."

"Shit," Cheyenne yells. Her arms begin flailing around as if they're trying to find someone to hit. "That goddamned Matthew. It's none of his business to of told you that."

"Well, I guess it is your choice."

"You got that right." Cheyenne looks at her squarely. "The whole thing—the way I live, how long, where—it's all my choice."

Josie stuffs the paper with Dan's phone number into her jeans' pocket, thinking maybe she'll call him sometime but not in order to find out if he's alive. She knows he is.

"I'm leaving tomorrow," Cheyenne says out of the blue. "Heading north. I've always wanted to see Alaska."

Stunned, Josie wonders if she somehow sneaked into her mind and stole that old dream. "That's where *I* used to want to go," she mutters. "Dreamed about it all the time. Driving to the far North, Old Bushmills, the Stones." It dawns on her that Cheyenne is probably going north for the same reason she once dreamed of going—to die.

"You used to want to move there too?" Cheyenne asks incredulously. "Damn, this is a sign. I know you won't believe this, but I came out here to ask you to go with me. Will you?"

Josie shakes her head. "Don't want to any more. Used to, but that was when I was real attracted to tragedy. Besides, I've got this acting job. It's a lot of fun."

"You're acting? Where?"

"At a theatre in Tucson. It's what I've always wanted to do. I'm good at it."

"Why didn't you tell me?" Cheyenne's eyes flash with anger.

"Didn't think to," she says, surprised by her reaction. "You don't tell me everything, do you?"

Cheyenne turns her head away. "I could sure use the company."

"Oh, I doubt you'll be alone for long." Josie suspects that Cheyenne's whole life is spent making friends, staying with them until she's bored, then leaving them and starting the process over again.

Shrugging, Cheyenne stands as if to go. "You know something? You're the only person I ever wished I was more like."

Josie almost starts to laugh, but then she notices the serious expression on Cheyenne's face. Maybe she's convinced herself she means it, Josie thinks, but more than likely she's trying to charm me into goin with her to Alaska for no other reason than to see if she can. "Shucks, you wouldn't be bullshitting me, would you?"

Cheyenne flinches just long enough to cause a normal person to think her previous compliment was sincere, but Josie believes she flinched because the charm didn't work. A smirk soon spreads on Cheyenne's face, and she says, "Maybe. Yeah, I prob'ly am."

"That's what I thought," Josie says.

Cheyenne starts to walk away.

"Do you need a ride somewhere?"

"No, it's a nice night." Cheyenne takes another step, then turns and says, "Sage is a pretty good place. Glad you moved back here."

From the light of the full moon, Josie sees her smiling, and that's how she'll always try to think of her—she'll try to remember the smile on Cheyenne's face as she walked away.

41

Josie has been working as a waitress in Tucson at one of those restaurants where businessmen entertain their clients for lunch, but it's at night that she really comes alive.

The Childress, a small theatre in the basement of an old hotel, only seats forty people, but tension among the actors runs as high as if they're playing to a roomful of New York critics. When Josie stands offstage waiting for her cue, she feels as if she might cease to breathe, turn blue, and die, but when she steps on stage, it's as if someone switched on a light.

She has even begun to feel that way in her day-to-day life. Not that everything is perfect, she thinks. My imagination gets up on the wrong side of the bed sometimes. But that's all right. I don't want perfection. Don't want to have everything figured out. People who think they've got all the answers have scary little smiles that make my stomach queasy.

Last week the director informed her he'd received a grant to form a traveling Shakespeare company that will perform in small cities and towns throughout the Southwest. "It will be a three-month tour," he said, and asked if she'd like to be part of it. She said yes immediately. Her bosses at the restaurant told her they'd try to hold a position for her but couldn't guarantee it. Josie isn't worried, though, figuring she can always get a job as a waitress.

Tonight was the last performance of *Look Back in Anger,* and after the cast party, she drives toward Sage, bone-tired. The last night of a play is a celebration, but it's also a sad good-bye to an old friend. It's two o'clock in the morning when she finally gets home. Usually when she walks into the house, she glances into Venus's bedroom just to make sure she's still there, to assure herself that her friend is still breathing, that she hasn't died or gone to West Virginia or Alaska. Tonight when Josie checks on her, Venus mutters, "Clarence called and said for you to call him back no matter how late you got in."

Josie runs to the phone and dials his number. "What is it?" she asks, her voice growing louder with each word. "Is anything wrong?"

He's been trying to contact her for the past week, but no one is ever there when he calls. Groggy from sleep, he mumbles, "I just wanted to tell you something, but you're never home."

Josie takes a deep breath and tries to settle down. "What's up?" she asks.

Clarence reaches out to Sally, who is sleeping soundly beside him, and runs his fingers through her hair. "Why ain't you come for the rest of your things?"

"I've not had time, Clarence. Prob'ly won't be over for a while longer. I'm getting ready to go on tour with a Shakespeare company. How do you like that? Pretty good, ain't it?"

"Yeah," Clarence says. Then he hems and haws as though he wants to say something else but doesn't know how.

"What is it, Clarence? How's that old dog doing?"

"Butter's all right. I just wanted to . . . Sally's pregnant."

Josie smiles, knowing how much Clarence always wanted to be a father. "You know what, Clarence? I used to feel guilty about causing you to leave Pick, but looks like it was the best thing that ever happened to you. If we'd stayed there, you'd never have met Sally, we would have both been miserable, and you would never have had a child."

Clarence is embarrassed by what he's about to say. Stuttering, he says, "Anyway, because Sally's pregnant and everything, we're thinking we ought to get married."

A smidgen of jealousy runs over Josie, but she shoos it away. "Guess me and you'll have to get a divorce first, won't we?"

"I reckon so," Clarence mutters.

"Well, just send the papers any time, and I'll sign them. I'll be here about two more weeks before I go on tour. If you can't get it done by then, just mail them to me wherever I'm at. I'll send you my schedule."

Josie goes to bed and lies there staring out the window at the moonlight, thinking about the number of people who have gotten married or are on the verge. Lily and Bobby are happy as turtledoves, and Brewster called last week to say Ida and Price Gibson had tied the knot. Said he might get married himself to Viola Watson. Now Clarence and Sally are taking the plunge. Will it never end? she wonders. Actually, she's happy that both she and Clarence have found brand-new lives, but she has to admit to a little sadness that their past is gone forever.

Venus gets up and peeps into her room. "Are you all right, Josie?"

"Yeah. Clarence is getting married."

Venus stands there quietly for a moment, then says, "Well, you try to get some sleep now. Think I'll get up tomorrow and fix us a breakfast like you've never had before."

Josie smiles. "I'm all right, Venus. Go on back to bed."

The night before Josie leaves on tour, Venus throws a small party, inviting Lily and Bobby Swanson for dinner. Although Josie has seen them several times since her return to Sage, she is still amazed at the change that has taken place in both of them. Lily sits around giggling like a schoolgirl, and Bobby Swanson's whole appearance has changed. He dresses neat as a pin and looks as if he's grown a few inches taller.

After dinner the four of them play music and sing, and even after Lily and Bobby say their good-byes and go home, Josie and Venus still continue to play the guitar and harp. When the phone rings an hour later, they think it's Lily calling with something else to say.

Picking up the receiver, Venus promptly slaps her hands on her knees. "Where're you at?"

Josie sits there, idly listening to the one-sided conversation.

"When?" Venus is saying. "Next week?"

Josie strums the guitar and looks out the window at the night.

"No kidding," Venus says. "You got one? You should have done that a long time ago."

Josie sees a star shoot toward the horizon and disappear.

"Guess I'll have to break out that bottle of Johnnie Walker I've been saving," Venus says. "It'll be waiting for you."

Josie's mouth drops open as Venus hangs up the phone. "Who was that?" she asks.

"Johnny is coming back next week. He's got himself a divorce. How do you like that?"

Josie tries to act nonchalant but it's no use. "Does he know I'm here?"

"No, you told me not to tell him, and I didn't."

Josie sighs. "Actually I won't be here when he comes. I'll be on tour."

"Yeah, but you'll be back at the end of summer, won't you?"

Josie props the guitar in the corner. "Guess we'll have to wait and see what happens, that's all."

When Venus goes to bed, Josie walks out to the desert and sits down on a rock. As her eyes adjust to the shadowy manzanitas and scattered boulders around her, she thinks she sees the ghost of don Juan shining in a breeze that dances in a nearby oak. She imagines he's shaking his head and rolling his eyes, more than a little disgusted at her refound enthusiasm for the world. "Sorry, don Juan," she tells him silently. "Maybe someday I can fly with you to other realms, but for now I'm kinda hooked on this one. You say nothing matters. A lot of people have come to that same conclusion. Most see it as a bad thing, but you look on the positive side. I like your version better. Anyway, after figuring out that nothing matters, they decide that nothing is real either, that we're all actors in our everyday lives. You call your performances 'controlled folly.' Shakespeare said, 'All the world's a stage . . .' I could go on and on."

She's reminded of the play she's in at the present, the one that tells the story of her return to Sage, of her upcoming tour of the Southwest. "I'm so deep into this role that it really has begun to matter, and I like the way that feels," she tells don Juan. "I still know that behind it all nothing matters, but I figure there'll be plenty of time to explore that reality when I'm dead or dying. Till then I plan to keep auditioning for plays." As she says the last word, she thinks she sees him drift out of the tree, no doubt on his way to other worlds.

Looking up, she discovers a sky jam-packed with a million stars sparkling like diamonds on black velvet. It's quiet in the desert this time of night. Josie can't hear anything but an owl hooting somewhere in the distance. Drifting past her, a faint scent of sage stirs a childhood memory that quickly fades and is lost—something about eating a lemon dusted with salt, then chasing it with a bag of sunflower seeds while listening to a song on the radio—"*Honeycomb, won't you be my baby, Honeycomb, be my . . .*" She sees a fleeting vision of herself tearing out of the house, the screen door banging behind her as she runs with abandon down a red-dirt road.

That's how I am right now, she thinks. I don't know where I'm headed, but I'm out of the house and running, and the wind feels good on my face.